DESIGNING DESIRE

Tressie knew what she was doing when she joined Reed Dannon in bed. Or at least she thought she did. The handsome stranger was nearly recovered from the wounds that had brought him half dead to her lonely sod hut on the Plains. Soon he would be moving on—alone. Unless . . .

She moaned as his callused finger explored a nipple. His continuous touch sent tendrils of fire crawling over her flesh, and set her heart to pounding. She tried to remind herself why she was doing this, but her body continued to betray her.

"Whatever we do, it's just from our needs," Reed said down in his throat. "That's all, you understand? It don't mean anything, Tressie."

"Oh yes, yes, it does mean something," Tressie whispered back. She leaned forward, then delicately kissed the firm slant of his whiskered jaw. "Take me with you, please."

She knew she had won when he spanned her tiny waist with both hands and murmured, "Tressie," then turned his head so that their mouths locked. And now she was lost, lost in the raw power of his passion, no longer knowing who was seducing whom . . . no longer caring.

GOLDSPUN PROMISES

ANNOUNCING THE
TOPAZ FREQUENT READERS CLUB
COMMEMORATING TOPAZ'S
1 YEAR ANNIVERSARY!

THE MORE YOU BUY, THE MORE YOU GET

Redeem coupons found here and in the back of all new Topaz titles for FREE Topaz gifts:

Send in:

 2 coupons for a free TOPAZ novel (choose from the list below);
- ☐ **THE KISSING BANDIT**, Margaret Brownley
- ☐ **BY LOVE UNVEILED**, Deborah Martin
- ☐ **TOUCH THE DAWN**, Chelley Kitzmiller
- ☐ **WILD EMBRACE**, Cassie Edwards

 4 coupons for an "I Love the Topaz Man" on-board sign

 6 coupons for a TOPAZ compact mirror

 8 coupons for a Topaz Man T-shirt

Just fill out this certificate and send with original sales receipts to:

TOPAZ FREQUENT READERS CLUB-1ST ANNIVERSARY
Penguin USA • Mass Market Promotion; Dept. H.U.G.
375 Hudson St., NY, NY 10014

Name_____

Address_____

City_____State_____Zip_____

Offer expires 5/31/1995

This certificate must accompany your request. No duplicates accepted. Void where prohibited, taxed or restricted. Allow 4-6 weeks for receipt of merchandise. Offer good only in U.S., its territories, and Canada.

GOLDSPUN PROMISES

by

Elizabeth Gregg

A TOPAZ BOOK

TOPAZ
Published by the Penguin Group
Penguin Books USA Inc., 375 Hudson Street,
New York, New York 10014, U.S.A.
Penguin Books Ltd, 27 Wrights Lane,
London W8 5TZ, England
Penguin Books Australia Ltd, Ringwood,
Victoria, Australia
Penguin Books Canada Ltd, 10 Alcorn Avenue,
Toronto, Ontario, Canada M4V 3B2
Penguin Books (N.Z.) Ltd, 182-190 Wairau Road,
Auckland 10, New Zealand

Penguin Books Ltd, Registered Offices:
Harmondsworth, Middlesex, England

First published by Topaz,
an imprint of Dutton Signet,
a division of Penguin Books USA Inc.

First Printing, October, 1994
10 9 8 7 6 5 4 3 2 1

To my husband,
Don,
with love

A special thanks to Dusty Richards
and Lisa Wingate, and the gang
at Northwest Arkansas Writers' Workshop.
Without your help it would never have happened.

One

Tressie smoothed the mound of the double grave with the back of a shovel. Lifting her face, she squinted into a burning southwest wind that licked at the tears and sweat on her cheeks. Weary with grief and exhausted from chopping at the hard earth, she sagged against the wooden handle and gazed at the small plot of disturbed soil.

Almost immediately anger overpowered grief, for she found it somehow easier to manage. The unspoken fury she felt could be shouted at the endless white-hot sky, and she did just that, damning her father with long, anguished howls.

The eternal land swallowed her cries and fell silent. Across the arid and flat prairie, shades of dull brown spread like death as far as she could see in any direction.

Tressie folded both hands over her overalls, tilting her determined chin downward so that a curl of auburn hair brushed her cheek. Wide green eyes wet with grief, she moved her lips in silence, hoping for a prayer to comfort the shattered remnants of her soul. But none came. Hope withered and dried as the months passed with no word from her father.

After a long while she plodded back toward the soddy, dragging the shovel along behind. A stiff wind boosted her reluctant steps, snapping the coarse overalls against her legs. Carried on that wind came the distinct whicker of a horse. She stopped for a moment to scan the prairie, leaning on the shovel and shading her eyes against the brutal sun. She saw nothing but endless, wavering heat waves and burned grasses.

Oh, how she hated this terrible place. How she wished for someone, anyone, to come and take her away. There it was again; a soft blowing snort. This time she was certain there was a horse nearby.

Facing south, she spotted the lone rider. Man and horse appeared in the distance as if spewed from the earth itself. A familiar trick of the heat-scorched prairie, but a sight that never failed to startle her.

Still shading her eyes with one hand, Tressie studied the wavering image, afraid it was only another mirage. If real, who would it be? And where was he bound? Her heart pounded. Was this simply a foolish prospector short of food and water? After the gold strikes, men had poured across the plains like scatterings of lost cattle, some passing on by, others stopping to water at the well in the yard. At first she had been frightened by the strangers, but soon realized that they had but one thing on their minds. GOLD. GOLD. GOLD. It was like a wild disease with them, and one Papa soon caught. Surely there wouldn't be enough of the precious ore to go around.

Once assured that the horse and rider headed straight for her were not a figment of her imagination, Tressie whirled and ran for the house. At the unprotected doorway she tossed down the shovel and scurried inside. From the gloomy corner she lifted a long, heavy Kentucky rifle. Just in case this traveler had more than gold on his mind, she thumbed the hammer to half cock and fingered a percussion cap from the fireplace mantel. She had fired the gun off two days ago and reloaded it, just as Papa had taught her to do.

"Keep the powder dry and keep her loaded all but for the cap," he'd warned.

With steady fingers Tressie placed the cap on the nipple and waited.

Outside, the rhythmic thud of the horse's hooves ceased. Tressie held her breath and didn't move, but nothing happened. She peered from the open doorway. The dusty rear haunches and tail of a bony sorrel protruded from around the corner. Except for a flick of the matted tail, nothing stirred.

What was he doing hiding out back there? And why didn't he climb down or hail the house?

She crept a few steps into the sunny yard and hefted the gun barrel to aim at something but the ground. "What do you want?" The question came out like a squawk and she tried to work saliva down her dry throat.

No answer. She took a few more steps, the clumsy shoes scuffing up puffs of dust. The wind blew heavy with the odor of horse and sweat, and something she couldn't identify: a brackish, overpowering stench that made her remember the smell in the house before she had removed the birthing bed and burned it.

Inching past the corner of the house, she made out a figure slumped forward in the saddle, not moving. Tressie halted and swallowed harshly. It was blood she smelled. Too much blood. Maybe death, too, lurking just around that corner. Terror took her heart in its fist and she gasped for air past a gagging nausea. Despite all her heartache and loneliness, Tressie did not want to face death. Not some stranger's, and certainly not her own. Weariness washed over her and she staggered against the hardened sod bricks of the cabin.

A prayer came to her then, as it wouldn't earlier over the grave. It was only a simple plea for help, and she offered the words up with little hope they would be heard. She asked for just enough strength to see her through one more hardship. Goodness knows, there'd been plenty of those in her seventeen years.

Gasping in a breath, she spread her long legs and lifted the heavy barrel to sight on the rumpled shirt of the stranger. "Stay right where you are." The steadiness of the tone amazed her.

"I don't think I have much choice," came a feeble reply. The voice, though cracked by weariness, held an edge of determination. "I could use a hand here. I'd surely hate to fall off this horse, but I reckon it's about to happen."

Expelling a breath of relief, Tressie leaned the gun against the house. There wasn't enough punch left in this fellow to hurt a rabbit, let alone her. Though she was a strapping young woman, the man almost knocked her to her knees when he slid from the saddle into the support of her arms. For a while Tressie thought they wouldn't make it inside. A couple of times she had to stop and rest, and he wasn't doing a whole lot to help her, either. He did drag one leg after the other, but for the most part she supported his weight. He groaned with each step. With her head tucked under his arm, the gamy smell of his body nearly overpowered her. He must have been on the trail a long time without benefit of a good washing.

The corn-shuck bed in one corner of the single room appeared miles away, but Tressie got him there. Letting the limp body sprawl where it fell, Tressie ignored his pitiful moans. Exhausted, she collapsed into the rocking chair between the fireplace and the bed. It was Mama's chair and the only one they had managed to bring with them from Missouri. Resting there was the nearest she could come to the solace of her dear dead mother's arms.

It didn't take long for the aroma of cooking food to revive her. She remembered the pot of soup she'd set on the fire early that morning before Mama's birthing pains had grown so intense that all Tressie could do was tend her. She hadn't had a bite to eat since. With scarcely enough energy to crawl, Tressie made her way to the soup pot and ladled out a bowlful. She sat on the floor and drank the thin broth, relishing the few chunks of potato, cabbage, and squash.

"I wonder if I could have a sip of that?" the man on the bed said weakly.

Tressie filled the bowl again and reached it up to him. He managed to raise his head and grasp the bowl in one hand, but then was unable to put it to his lips. Lowering his mouth, he tried to lap at the soup like a dog. Tressie came to her knees and shakily tipped the rim to his mouth so he could drink. Broth dribbled down his darkly stubbled chin, but he managed to swallow some.

"We're a fine pair," she said. "Can't hardly tell which one is the worse off for our troubles."

He noisily sucked up the last drop and let out a feeble sigh before his head lolled back onto the bed. From the rhythm of his breathing he had either fallen asleep or was unconscious. Tressie could do nothing for him until she got some rest, and that was all there was to that. Dried blood caked one side of his shirt. He would either have to lie there and die in poor Mama's clean bed or hold out until Tressie awoke.

Before giving in to her own weariness, Tressie fetched the rifle from outside. Removing the percussion cap, she eased the hammer down and stood the precious weapon back in its place. Every muscle in her body quivered, begging for rest. At last she succumbed, stretching out on a pallet on the earthen floor, where she immediately fell asleep.

A narrow slant of morning sun crept through the window to lie warmly on Tressie's cheek. Having settled deeply into an exhausted slumber, she awoke with no memory of the man on the bed. Fear gripped her when she caught sight of him and remembered. He could have recovered enough to have had his way with her while she lay nearly unconscious on the floor. She immediately dismissed the thought as tomfoolery, considering his condition. A touch to his brow told her he had not died overnight, though he was burning with fever. Probably from the wound in his shoulder.

For a moment she left her hand lying there to study his features. Gaunt as he was, there was a savage grace about the shape of him. High cheekbones brushed by long dark lashes, prominent nose, a good sturdy brow. The hair, though dusty with travel, was long and black as a raven's wing. Washed, it would reflect the blue-purple shimmer of true ebony. Some Indian blood there.

He stirred and she jerked her hand away, afraid he
would awaken and find her staring. But he only shifted an
arm so that it lay across his chest. Though grimy, his nails
were trimmed, the fingers long and callused. She found
herself glad he hadn't died during the night.

Taking up the water bucket, Tressie went outdoors into
the pearlescent dawn. A breeze freshened into gusts,
whipping up spirals of dust devils that settled in a fine grit
on her skin. At the well she stripped out of the stiff overalls and bathed from a bucket of cold water, using a bar
of yucca-root soap to lather her short hair. The morning
sun would dry it quickly, bringing out the red highlights
she had once been so proud of. She remembered Papa's
anger when she had chopped the waist-long tresses off
during the backbreaking labor of that first summer they
had spent on the hot, windy plains. Never mind the only
water they had was hauled several miles in wooden barrels, he still wanted to keep his long-haired, winsome little
girl. Papa had always been unrealistic in his expectations
of everything life had to offer.

After the family had been there awhile, a drifter had
helped them dig the well in return for food from their
summer garden. Though everyone had been grateful, the
man's tales of gold strikes in Oregon Territory had been
what finally convinced Papa to abandon the farm and re-
new his quest for easy fortune, this time alone. The gold
camps were no place for the burden of a family, he explained to his tearful wife and daughter.

Papa. Oh, Papa, just see what you did.

A tear slid from one eye and Tressie slung it away with
an angry swipe.

She drew another bucket of water and poured it over

her head. The icy embrace drove away the last remnants of sleep, and she turned into the wind and closed her eyes.

The loss of her mother and the boy-child who had slipped from Mama's womb without uttering even one feeble cry overpowered her. Her heart swelled into a huge aching knot. She wanted to go home. Desperately missed the green Missouri hills and the thick forests and hidden streams. How she hated this unbroken, wind-tossed land.

What nonsense. If she were to survive, there was no time for grief or such useless longings. Just as well to put the yesterdays behind her; they were over and done with. Everyone was gone: Mama and the young'un in their grave, Papa off and wandering, gone to seek his fortune. Dead, for all she knew. But best not admit yet to such a possibility. For if he was still alive, she would find him one day. And she would look him right in the eye and tell him how much she hated him for leaving Mama to die. Going off and leaving the ones who loved him, for what? Tales of gold.

Tressie stood tall and pressed both hands into the small of her back, stretching, gazing out across the flat prairie. Out there somewhere Papa wandered. And she, left here alone, forever on her own, totally dependent upon herself for what happened to the rest of her life. The man inside, if he lived, might help get her out of this predicament. It was certainly childish to go on believing in Papa's return, for that wasn't going to happen. The admission surprisingly strengthened her resolve.

Wiping water from her eyes, Tressie caught sight of the horse the man had rode in on. The bony creature lay on the ground, feet stuck stiffly out to one side. The poor thing had fallen down dead during the night and she hadn't even heard it. She would have to get the saddle off and see what she could do about dragging the dead animal away from the soddy. Sure as anything, with this heat, the smell would soon attract hordes of flies and fill the cabin with a poisonous stench. A chunk of the meat would add taste to her normal fare of thin soup.

Squaring her bare shoulders, Tressie drew another bucket of water, stepped over the pile of dirty clothes, and walked naked to the soddy. She spared no further thought for the dead sorrel. There was only so much a body could handle at one time, and Tressie figured she'd about reached her limit.

All caught up in newfound considerations of her aloneness, she had yet to wonder about the condition of the man lying in the bed over in the darkened corner. He would either live or die, and she would do all she could for him. That was that. She stepped inside and nearly dropped the bucket when he shouted out:

"All dead. All. God help us. I can't go on . . . I can't."

Tressie recovered quickly. He was raving out of his head, probably didn't even know she was there. Who had shot him, and from who or what was he running? A half-breed Indian on the run could mean just about anything from a simple farm raid for food to a massacre. Perhaps he'd been involved in a robbery or killing and was purely an outlaw. The possibilities were endless, and she would find out as soon as he was coherent. Heaven knew, she had no desire to shelter a killer.

The one dress Tressie could still call more than a rag was dreadfully threadbare, and Mama's were much too small. She lifted it off a hook in the corner and wiggled her supple young body into the thin garment. Lean of shank, she'd look like a boy, were it not for her high, firm breasts. Once she might have taken more note of their maturation over the past year or so. Now it didn't really matter much. That the dress was stretched a bit too tight across the chest when she slipped it on barely caught her notice.

She had a patient to care for. He still slept, but made puckery faces when she pulled the blood-stiffened shirt away to look at his shoulder. The wound wasn't as bad as she'd expected. The bullet appeared to have passed through the muscle without hitting the bone. There'd been no bleeding overnight, but it did need a good cleaning, both front and back.

She cut away the rest of the shirt and drew in a ragged breath. He was skin and bones, his ribs standing out so you could count them. Most likely he had passed out from hunger as much as from the bullet wound. Poor creature. She smoothed a shag of damp hair back away from one cheek, felt the heat of his fever. Dear God, would he die? The thought brought unbidden tears. There had been enough death in this little cabin for a while. She feared it might only end when she herself died.

Tressie took the time to build a fire and heat plenty of water. The man needed a bath as badly as he needed anything, and she intended to give him one as soon as she cleaned and bound the wound. Granny always swore you couldn't even get over a runny nose if you weren't clean, and Tressie clung to that principle.

Steam from the water clouded her vision as she lathered a rag and washed the bluish wound, so perfectly round in the front where the ball had entered, gaping and ugly at the back where it had come out. She tried not to hurt him, but he groaned constantly until she finished. When at last the shoulder was bound in the remnants of one of her worn-out petticoats, the pitiful moaning ceased. He never once opened his eyes, even when she undressed him and scoured the dirt from his painfully thin body. Hand supporting the knee of one long leg, she washed the grimy skin and tried not to notice that he was a man.

Tressie was, after all, old enough to think of a man of her own, but the rawboned frontier life had presented no possibilities. Romance existed only in rare dreams that came only when she wasn't so exhausted she fell into a stupor at bedtime.

After completing the man's bath, she tucked a quilt around his shivering frame and lay a dampened cloth on his forehead. His fever had gone down some.

In the remainder of boiling water still in the pot on the coals, Tressie stirred up cornmeal mush. She was dipping the thick stuff into a bowl when he spoke in a dried and grating tone that startled her in its abruptness. "I thought you were a vision and I had died."

Tressie stood and took him the steaming bowl. "Well, I'm not and you didn't. Sorry, this is all I have. It's weevily, but filling."

He grabbed at the bowl, almost dumped its contents. She rescued it and offered the first spoonful, ashamed when he sucked air and rolled the steaming mush around in his mouth before swallowing.

"It's too hot," she said by way of apology, and began to blow on each bite before giving it to him. He gulped down mouthful after mouthful, pursing his lips for the next offering before she had it cooled.

His acute hunger embarrassed Tressie, and so she began to chatter as she fed him. "If we were back on the farm in Missouri, there would be milk and sweet cream butter from the cow and molasses sorghum for sweetnin' and flour for bread.

"Instead of this wearisome dry heat, there'd be damp cool mornings and long, lazy afternoons when a body could shell peas or snap beans or shuck corn out under the shade of a big old hickory and not even notice it was summer."

He concentrated on the movements of her mouth but didn't miss a beat in the feeding.

Caught up in her reminiscences, Tressie could almost forget the dilemma facing her and this stranger, and take his measure. His eyes, dark as bottomless caves, held a sadness that plucked at her. His long black hair shimmered with shades of blue since she'd washed it. The dark stubble of whiskers covering his square jaw looked more like he hadn't shaved in a while than like he might ordinarily wear a beard. She couldn't guess his age, though she thought him several years older than herself. Somewhere between twenty-five and thirty.

She continued to jabber and feed him, deliberately slowing down the process to keep him from getting sick. "I just have to make do because the cow died last winter, the sorghum run out before that, and Papa took our only horse when he went off in search of his fortune, so we couldn't ride in for supplies if there was any money, which there isn't." She bit at her lip. Telling that small lie was just in case he was a thief and might get ideas when his strength came back. Mama's few hoarded coins were well hidden.

"After the Preemption Act made squatting legal, Papa couldn't wait to leave Missouri and come out here. He talked about land that stretched as far as the eye could see, and how farming it would be so much easier than digging around in that rocky old Ozark soil." She snorted. "Wasn't even a year before he decided that was too tedious as well. And besides, there was talk about a strike at Grasshopper Creek, and so off he went. Couldn't talk of anything but the town of Bannack, Oregon, and gold those last few months before he left."

She sensed him watching her and looked up from under long lashes, suspending the last spoonful in midair. "My name's Tressie Majors, what's yours?"

He begged for the bite with his soft dark gaze and she gave it, then scraped noisily all around the bowl for every last morsel. He licked some off the corner of his mouth and darted a quick glance toward the pot on the fire.

She held the empty bowl a moment, challenged him, "I said, my name's Tressie Majors, what's yours?"

"Bannon. Reed Bannon. And I thank you, ma'am, for—" He broke off and lifted the thin coverlet. "Who in thunderation stole my clothes?" With that he pulled the quilt tight up under his chin and turned the brightest red Tressie had ever seen a man turn.

She felt a grin coming on and let it happen. There hadn't been a whole lot to laugh at lately, and it felt kind of good. "Would you like another bowl of mush, Mr. Bannon? There's plenty," she said as if he weren't laying there nearly stark naked. As if it were an ordinary day and there weren't a dead horse in the yard. As if she hadn't just buried Mama and that newborn babe out there on the prairie. As if she weren't a young defenseless woman all alone with a stranger in this place with no human habitation for fifty miles or more.

Tressie at last had someone to talk to. A man who blushed, and was near starved and who called her ma'am. Her mind echoed that he might be a killer, and she sobered somewhat.

She fetched him another bowl of mush and at the offer of the first bite asked, "Who shot you, Mr. Bannon?"

He raised thick brows, lips tightening and nostrils flaring like he smelled something bad. But he didn't answer right away, just chewed and swallowed slowly.

She waited awhile, sitting there holding up the empty spoon. Then she cut him a hard look so he'd know that this time she meant business. "I need to know if someone is going to ride up on us in the middle of the night, finish the job they started on you, and then do God knows what to me. I need to know that if you're going to remain under my roof, Reed Bannon."

"And if they are, will you kick me out? Not even let me have the rest of that?" He gestured and she gave him another bite. He swallowed it down and went on, "Maybe mount me on that poor old wore-out horse and send me on my way. You don't appear to be that kind of woman, if you'll excuse my saying so, ma'am."

At the mention of his horse, Tressie looked away. Should she tell him it was dead? She gritted her teeth. "Just tell me about that." She pointed the spoon at his bandaged shoulder.

He sighed with a weariness that made her almost ashamed she had asked. "That old horse out there?"

She gulped and nodded. Had he guessed?

"I stole him from a Union soldier in St. Louis and the no-good so and so shot me for my troubles. Hell, they had a whole corral of the beasts and I was afoot with a long way to go."

Tressie gaped at the man. "You just walked up and took a horse that belonged to the United States Army?"

"Union, I said Union. Not United States. Price's blue-bellies massacred us at Pea Ridge, and us that could walk away wasn't feeling too kindly toward those boys, you can bet. I didn't mind a little payback, seeing as how I liked to starved just getting to St. Louis."

"You were a butternut?"

"Butternut hell. I was in McCulloch's army. Me and thousands of other Indians fought there. We didn't turn our back on our kind, like some did." He aimed the accusation directly at Tressie. Folks from Missouri, she knew, were not looked too kindly upon by southerners.

She hurried to get away from that aspect of the conversation but continued to feed him. "But you're not wearing a uniform. Are you still in the . . . in the Rebel Army?"

Reed squirmed. "Look, I'm tired. I'd rather just finish that off and go to sleep, if you don't mind. We can hash this out later, when I'm feeling more up to defending myself against a little mite of a thing who hasn't the slightest idea of what war is all about."

"I know what they call a man who runs away from battle," she snapped. "But you go ahead and sleep now, if you've a mind to. As long as I know some owlhoot isn't going to sneak up on us in the night to get his vengeance against you. I would think that Union soldiers have a little more to do than chase one ratty deserter halfway across the plains."

He reared off the pillow, then grimaced with pain, clutching at the shoulder.

Immediately Tressie felt contrite. She shouldn't have pushed him so far when he was so sorely wounded. The wisest move would be to wait till he got better to finish this argument.

Besides, there were other, more pressing things to worry about. She had no idea what might happen tomorrow or the next day, but for right now things were looking up. Despite the story he told—and she wondered if all the truth had come out—his troubles could be handled in their own time.

What was important was that he looked like he might live. And though they had no transportation and only the tiny amount of money she had hidden away, as soon as Reed Bannon had recovered enough, she would get him to take her to Grasshopper Creek and the gold camps in search of Papa. He had to know what horrible thing he had done. He had to pay somehow for killing Mama and the tiny boy-child.

Two

After the brief recovery, Tressie's visitor lapsed into deep slumber. For a long while she tarried beside the bed, watching the rise and fall of his chest, gazing at the long dark lashes that lay on his gaunt cheeks. She was still enough of a child to let her imagination produce the most fabulous of fantasies about being carried away by a man like this. Oh, granted, he would be better nourished, perhaps more muscular, but with the same glorious golden skin and jet-black hair, the sad dark eyes, the mysterious past of this stranger.

Shaking off such nonsense, Tressie fetched the Kentucky rifle and possible bag and lit out in pursuit of the long-eared jackrabbit of the plains. Food was what this man needed most, now that his wound had been seen to. He must grow strong if he was to take her out of this place, set her in the direction of her runaway coward of a father.

Thoughts like that brought tears to Tressie's eyes, even as she stalked her prey.

When she was little, Papa would play with her, toss her high in the air, rub at her tummy with his soft beard and growl until she crowed with delight. And Mama loved him so, her hazel eyes following his movements around the place. Sometimes Tressie would catch her paused at her work, standing stock-still and gazing with adoration at Papa as he went about his own chores. And at night, in the small cabin, she would pretend sleep while they whispered and rustled around on the shuck bed. By then Tressie was a young lady, and so Papa was content to tousle her red hair in passing and call her his sweet daughter. He never ceased to tell her how much she resembled her beautiful mother.

Plodding along, Tressie had let her thoughts overpower her need to be alert. The jack bounded from a clump of grass off to her right, catching her unawares. She hastily threw up the gun, drew bead, and fired, missing the dodging critter and chunking up dust in his fleeing shadow.

"Durn, durn," Tressie muttered, and stopped to reload the rifle, chiding herself to pay more attention. The empty cavity in her belly did likewise, and the spirit of the man who could well be her salvation appeared to scold her for having failed.

It was nearly an hour later, and several miles northwest of the cabin, before she scared up another rabbit. This time she didn't miss.

She carried the limp, scrawny beast by the hind legs, his long ears trailing in the grass. Perspiration trickled from under her arms and down the middle of her back and the rifle grew heavy by the time she arrived back home. The horse carcass begged for attention, but first she drew some water, put it on to boil, and cleaned the rabbit. Once the stew was simmering over the fire, Tressie turned her thoughts to the poor dead animal outside. It would be a fearsome job hacking it up in small enough pieces to drag off from the cabin, but it was something that had to be done.

Just thinking about it made her nauseous, but with stoic determination she got out Papa's ax and laid it on the hearth.

Over on the corn-husk bed, Reed Bannon groaned and murmured scarcely intelligible words. She went to him, laid the back of one hand on his forehead. Feverish. Pray God he didn't get infection in the wound and go and die on her despite her care. Then she'd have two critters to haul away. This one would have to be buried as well.

Tressie shook her head with determination. One thing at a time, girl. Papa always said that, didn't he? Fine one to hold up as an example; still, the words rang true. Concentrate. Get the horse taken care of while the stew cooked.

Bannon wet his dry lips and smacked. She went to the bucket and dipped out a cup of cold water. He couldn't seem to drink from the tin rim, so she moistened a clean cloth and touched it to the pitifully cracked mouth. He made a soft sound down in his throat and sucked at the rag; his Adam's apple bobbed as he swallowed and he blindly followed the cloth when she moved it away.

When she brought him more water, the backs of her fingers touched the stubble of his cheek. Her eyes filled. She didn't even know this man, but she had to save him in order to survive. Watching his helplessness, the need became more than just that. She didn't want him to die, for it would cause her great sorrow.

The fire crackled and popped and Bannon uttered soft little sounds down in his throat. Mesmerized, Tressie laboriously fed him water until he fell back into a restless slumber.

During the remainder of that day and far into the night she fed him from the pot of rabbit stew as many times as he would take even a spoonful of the savory liquid. In between she took care of the horrendous task of removing the horse, limb by limb. She hacked off a portion of one shank and added pieces of the meat to the stew pot that also contained a portion of dried-up vegetables from the root cellar.

In starlit darkness, she finally bathed naked beside the well and went inside to fall into an exhausted slumber on her pallet beside the fire. All night she tended the flames so the stew would continue to cook. It could be another day before the horsemeat was tender enough to eat, but its sweet flavor would add richness to the gamy taste of jackrabbit.

By morning the gray cast had faded from Reed Bannon's skin and the raging fever was down. He looked hearty in a way he hadn't before, and she rejoiced. He would live.

She waited until several days later, the first evening he rose from the sickbed to eat at the table, to hit him with her proposition. His reaction annoyed and surprised her, considering what she had done for him. But that really wasn't fair, either. He had no idea how close he had come to dying, and certainly had no notion of what her lot had been. It was no use blaming him for the harshness of existence on the prairie.

"You want me to what?" he demanded between mouthfuls of horsemeat stew.

The glow of the kerosene lamp threw shadows across

the sharp planes of his face, making him look fearsomely savage.

Undaunted, she repeated her request. "Take me to the gold camps. Help me find my father."

"Do you have any notion what you're asking?" Reed said, drinking noisily from the bowl. "This stuff's almost good. Could I have more?"

"What do you mean, almost? You don't need to go complaining about the fixings." Tressie ladled his bowl full again. She didn't tell him that a chunk of his horse flavored the soup, but instead kept at her demands. "I'm a good shot. I wouldn't be any trouble. You've ate my soup and slept in my bed and took to my waiting on you." She felt her face flush remembering how she'd daydreamed about this man as if he were a knight in shining armor, come to rescue her from her wicked and evil stepmother.

His terse words put an end to her ramblings. "And I'm grateful." He eyed her over the rim of the bowl he'd lifted to his mouth, black eyes reflecting flashes of orange from the glowing coals of the fire. He was a devilishly attractive man, she couldn't deny that, but he had a way of provoking her.

She tightened her lips to prevent losing her temper altogether. "But not grateful enough to help me, is that right?"

How dare he deny her this? She had brought him back from death's bidding when she could have let him die. It would have been easier. Yet she was glad she had saved him despite the extra work his being here caused. Not the least had been getting rid of that awful dead horse, chopping its body up with the ax so she could drag the chunks of carcass far away from the cabin before it began to rot and draw vermin. It had been a horrendous job and ended in making her sick.

And what did he say when he found out? Just "Poor damned animal. I should have took better care."

Reed made short work of the horsemeat stew, steadfastly refusing to discuss her request any more. He unfolded his long and lanky frame, dressed now in the spare shirt and pants from his saddlebags. Only a few days of eating at her table and he looked less like a skeleton clothed in loose skin. He glanced at her but said nothing. Unlike most men around a young woman, he seemed not to notice that she was female except for expecting her to cook and clean and fetch for him. So far he hadn't talked about himself or why he had been riding across the plains, wounded and half starved.

Stepping out into the yard, Reed swung his arms in cautious circles, still favoring the right one. Even before leaving his bed, he had begun to exercise the wounded shoulder, and Tressie enjoyed watching when he wasn't aware of her presence. Taking such pleasure in the sight of a man made her feel just the least bit shameful. What would he think if he knew?

Cleaning the supper dishes in water heated in the empty soup pot took little time, and afterward she, too, went outside. By then Reed had abandoned his arm swinging. She found him standing straddle-legged beyond the well, gazing west into the purple and gold dusk. A hankering to be gone was written on his boldly etched features. She knew what he wished. And she knew, too, that if she didn't do something, he would light out. He was just itching to be free of her. Wanted to loosen his shackles and head for the setting sun, not once looking back. Like Papa, maybe like most men, she didn't know.

Tressie shuddered at the thought of being alone again. Of waking one morning to find this man gone, too. Somehow she had to prevent that.

A soft prairie breeze whipped away the last of the sweat from her body, and she lifted her arms to let the air play through the thin dress. She stood that way in silence for a while, then said, "We could walk down to the Platte in two or three days if we kept a good pace."

He didn't answer right away, just sighed and shifted his weight, hanging both thumbs into the waistband of his worn pants. She could almost feel him weighing her words, considering other possibilities. Finally he spoke. "And then what would we do?"

"Work a spell in Cozad, earn enough money to pay our way into Oregon Territory."

"Why ain't you just done that in the first place?"

Tressie rubbed at the hollow of her throat, unconsciously settling an open hand just above her breasts.

Uncommonly conscious of his studious gaze, she raised her eyes to his. "A woman alone can't go traipsing off to the goldfields. Do you know what would happen to me? I can't take care of myself all by myself, you ought to know that. I'm not big enough nor strong enough, and I'm too particular."

Reed chuckled. "Particular?"

Even when he was making her mad, she admired the way humor enhanced his solemn features. "Oh, yes, mister smarty. I'm particular, and I guess I have that right! I suppose you think that any woman ought to just be grateful for anything a man might send her way. And he could

be any kind of man, too, I reckon. With dribbles of tobacco juice running down his chin and stinking worse
than your old dead horse. Well, no, thank you, Mr.
Bannon." Before she finished Tressie knew she'd let herself get too worked up for her own good and said more
than she had intended. Reed was bound to make the most
of it. He enjoyed funning and he didn't disappoint her.

"And this man you might be looking for. Just how perfect would he have to be?"

He appeared to be getting a lot of enjoyment from the
conversation. Tressie wasn't sure whether to let go her anger and enjoy the moment or pursue her thought.

"I am not looking for me a man," she said. "Suit me just
fine if I never had to lay eyes on one again, but the good
Lord did see fit to put men and women on this earth for
each other, suited and needful as we are. So I guess I just
don't have much choice. But I'll tell you this, Reed
Bannon." Tressie rounded on him, propping her hands on
her hips. "I'm going to Bannack before winter sets in. If
you don't take me, then I guess I'll have to find me someone who will. If I stay out here, I'll die, and that's the
truth." With that she whirled and marched back toward
the cabin so he couldn't see she was about to bust out
crying.

Darkness had fallen to the ground, though the sky
gleamed like silver around early sparkles of stars. Tressie
heard only the roar of a wild fury that blotted out the
nasty burring of a rattler in her path. Quicker than lightning, Bannon hit her from behind, knocking her to one
side as the diamondback struck. She landed hard, gasping
to regain her breath. At first she had no idea what had
happened, but on rising to a crouch saw Reed Bannon

where he'd landed on hands and knees, facing down the snake. Without a weapon, no rock or stick in sight, he hunkered there like a granite rock staring head on at the thing. The rattler, already foiled by its first strike at Tressie, had coiled once again and renewed the chilling reverberations. She could barely make out the shadowy triangular head, swaying and darting one side to the other, forward then backward.

Reed didn't move, scarcely breathed as he calmly watched that snake make up its mind whether to let him live or not—and it not two feet from his eyes. Whatever fear held Tressie in its grip turned loose and she scrabbled around on the ground until she came up with a few rocks smaller than her own fist.

"Don't do that," Reed hissed between clenched lips. "Don't rile her."

She eased the intended ammunition to the ground. Whispered, "I'll go get the rifle. Just hold real still. I'll go get the rifle." Because she couldn't bear to turn her back on the terrifying spectacle, she scrabbled backward, using her heels to propel herself.

When man and viper faded into the rapidly falling dusk, Tressie stumbled to her feet and raced for the soddy. A smoldering fire cast towering shadows in the sparse room. Holding the heavy rifle in one hand, she fumbled at a cap with shaking fingers and dropped it. Muttering, she fetched another and managed to fit it over the nipple of the loaded weapon. Thank God for Papa's instructions.

Back outside in the blackening night, Tressie could barely make out Reed and, inches in front of him, still performing a deadly and noisy dance, the coiled rattler. She swiped across her eyes with the fingers of one hand, then snugged the stock of the heavy rifle into her shoulder. Reed took a ragged breath that spooked the snake. The head made a warning pass and he jerked to one side.

Squinting her left eye, Tressie sighted down the long barrel and looked into the indistinct coiled mass of death. It was a long shot, but there was no time left. She squeezed the trigger and flinched when the hammer ignited the powder with an enormous bang that exploded a ball out the barrel.

The body of the deadly reptile flew apart, bits of meat and hide scattering. In the echoes of thunderous noise Reed's words hung like a prayer. "Blowed her to hell, blowed her plumb straight to hell."

Tressie lowered the butt of the rifle to the ground and spewed out a breath. "And I'll thank you, Reed Bannon, not to call that snake a her one more time."

By then Reed had tottered back onto his butt. There he rocked, his laughter growing, pealing into the stillness of dusk on the prairie. It was hard, after a while, not to join him simply for the sheer joy of it. Never mind what she'd said wasn't the least bit funny, and that he was probably making light of her once again. Soon Tressie's merriment rivaled his as she stood over him.

As quickly as his laughter came, it went, and he lay back, covering his eyes with the crook of an elbow. The right arm with its wounded shoulder lay across his stomach, quivering.

When she could finally get her breath and speak, Tressie said, "We'd best get in the house before that snake's mate comes out to see what all the excitement's about."

He reached up toward her. "I reckon I'm going to need some help getting up. Must still be a might weak."

She took his hand, felt the trembling in his muscles, and hoisted him to his feet. The episode had frightened him more than he cared to let on.

For support, Reed's other hand spread flat and warm on her back, and she was ashamed that he could tell she wore nothing under the dress. Long ago her undergarments had shredded away. She shrugged out from under his sizzling touch. "You can walk on your own, Bannon."

He jerked his hand back, as if burned. "Sorry," he mumbled, and lit out for the house, leaving her to tote the rifle.

She'd hurt his feelings and she hadn't intended to. No need to be so sharp with the man. He had, after all, taken her place as a target for the deadly snake. And could well have died for his effort. By the time she got in the door, Reed had poked a straw from the broom into the fire's coals and relit the kerosene lamp.

She glanced quickly at him, then set to cleaning the rifle at the table.

Reed lowered himself in the cane-bottom chair opposite her and watched in silence. Then abruptly both started to say something, halted, started again.

"You go first," Reed finally said.

"No, you."

"Well, hell, woman. Can't I even be gallant?"

"Gallant?" An odd word to come from his lips.

Reed studied his blunt fingernails. "I was trying. You saved my life, and I wanted to say thank you, to tell you I appreciated your caring enough. Hell, you could have just come back to the house and waited. Sooner or later, me or that old snake, one would have give in. You might have been rid of me that way."

"I don't want rid of you. Besides, you were only in that spot 'cause you pushed me aside. What I want is to go with you, that's all. And you can see I'd be useful. Your shoulder wouldn't take to firing a rifle, even if you had one, which you don't unless you steal mine. I wouldn't hold you back or anything."

Anger flushed his bronze complexion. "And what makes you think I'd steal your blamed old gun . . . ? Never mind. How old are you, girl?"

"I'll be eighteen soon."

"Holy crow. How soon?"

"A few months."

"How many?"

Tressie jammed the rag deep into the rifle's barrel and tugged it back out before answering. She had a little trouble holding her temper with this man, and she certainly didn't want to tell him that she wouldn't be eighteen until the following February. Have him treat her even more like a child than he already did. "What difference does it make? I buried my mother after helping her birth a child, and it was dead, too. I reckon I'm full grown."

He leveled a hard look at her, the black eyes like chips of flint. He didn't want to sympathize with her predicament, she knew. When she'd told him, he'd simply turned away to keep from viewing her grief. That had been back when he still lay in the bed too weak to move about. And she'd brought him not only every meal but a vessel to relieve himself in. She'd seen enough that she ought not to cringe at bodily functions, male or female. And she hadn't. But Reed Bannon had been embarrassed by the situation, she could tell, and certainly was in no mood to say he was sorry over her troubles. They were in the past, and survival was here and now.

"It was better, you know," he whispered, and she gave him a quick glance. Moisture glinted in his eyes gone all soft and velvety. "The baby, I mean. Without your mama it would have died anyway, making it all the harder for you, loving it and all."

"I know," she said, and lowered her gaze once more to measuring out the black powder. What kind of man was this, anyway?

He cleared his throat and stood. "I'm not sleeping in that bed anymore. You take it, and I'll sleep on the floor. My shoulder's all but healed."

Tressie nodded. "You going to take me to town with you?"

"Dammit, girl!"

She bit her lip and rose, hefting the loaded rifle in both hands. After putting it back in its place, she blew out the lamp and went to the bed, where she kicked off her ungainly shoes and lay down fully clothed. She longed to sleep naked once again, yet she dared not with this man on the place.

Back in Missouri Papa and Mama had finally given up on civilizing their little mountain nymph. Papa would laugh and chide Mama to let her be till she got full grown. That would soon enough see her wearing clothing, he'd bet. The hint that he would take a hand at the proper time warned Tressie and soothed Mama some.

She wondered what this man would think if he knew that about her. It didn't matter, though. He would go soon and leave her here. She might have survived the wilds of the forest, but this punishing and unforgiving plain that stretched from horizon to horizon would kill her. She hated being able to see so far and behold absolutely nothing. What a lonesome feeling.

While Reed bedded down noisily on the floor, Tressie turned her back so he wouldn't hear her crying. With all her heart she wanted to curl up in Mama's rocker and pretend that wonderful soul's arms were wrapped around her, soothing away the hurt and fear.

Reed shifted on the floor and grunted in surprised pain. Tressie held her breath. He was awake, she could tell by the noises he made. She had never been more conscious of his presence in the cramped room. The muscles of her stomach tightened when he cleared his throat and spoke.

"I never knew women, so maybe sometimes I'm too harsh."

Tressie didn't reply, just took a noisy breath to clear her clogged nostrils.

"Aw, hell. You ain't crying, are you?"

She still refused to answer.

His lazy voice came to her out of the dark. "My mother, she died birthing me. They said I come right out into my daddy's arms, him a cursing every screaming breath I took for paining his woman so. He come in there to kill me, they said, but my grandmother wouldn't let him. Mama was a Dakota Sioux. Bright Fox by name. Pa was a trapper, and when she died he just rode away and left me with them. Never came back."

Tressie waited for him to continue, and when he didn't, asked, "And you were raised by Indians?"

"For a spell. Hell, I may look more white than red, but

I'm still a breed. I finally run off soon after I became a man. I was twelve." He shifted again and groaned softly.

"Reed?" she asked after a long silence.

"Huh?"

"If your shoulder is paining you, you could sleep in the bed."

"No, you stay there. I'm okay."

"I didn't intend to leave . . . just move over."

"Oh." The word huffed out of his mouth to overpower the silence. "Well, I don't know."

"I'm dressed and so are you. No sense in you hurting." Tressie's heart pounded up in her throat until she almost couldn't speak. She wondered what it meant that she was willing to use her body to get her way with this man. Did that make her a soiled woman or just a survivor? The sounds of him rising from the floor quickened her pulse. With shaking fingers, she unbuttoned the front of her dress as he lowered his body to the edge of the shuck mattress.

He lifted one leg, then the other before lying back. Tressie turned toward him and lay the flat of her palm on the taut muscles of his stomach. Reed sucked in a quick breath. After a while he put his hand over hers and she guided it to one bare breast.

The callused fingers explored a nipple. Tressie moaned and gazed into the reflections his eyes sent into hers. Those beautiful black eyes that revealed so much of his vulnerability. What strengths he might have possessed had been sapped away by his injury, but she could sense them like an underlying current that is felt without being seen. As he grew stronger would this man desert her, too?

She leaned forward and he licked at the nipple with the

tip of his tongue. Tressie shivered. Despite her well-laid plans to entrap this man, his first tender touches awoke a slumbering passion within her soul. Hard work and deprivation had disguised the woman growing inside her, and to deal with her awakening presented Tressie with a problem. She was about to enjoy what had started out to be a ploy to trick this man.

Reed licked his lips and tilted his head, studying her face closely in the firelight. With a quizzical look that defied understanding, he cupped her ear with one palm and raised to take her full lips to his. Tressie forgot her mission and melted into the warmth of his bare chest, a great joyful sigh bursting from her. She twisted both hands into his long hair and held on, her tongue meeting the probing of his, all warm and wet and delicious.

After the kiss he held her in silence, his breath a mist against her cheek. Oddly confused, speaking now of his earlier puzzlement, he said, "Tressie? I feel like we've been together before, but I can't . . . Did we . . . ? Did you . . . ?"

"Just a dream. Maybe we're fated." A favorite term of Grammy's. Folks were often fated for one thing or another, and Tressie could accept that. If she could convince Reed Bannon, maybe he could accept it, too. His continuous touch sent tendrils of fire crawling over her flesh and set her heart to pounding. She tried to remind herself why she was doing this, but her body continued to betray her.

Reed shivered and his warm skin rippled where her small hand lay. "Whatever we do, it's just from our needs," he said down in his throat. "That's all, you understand? It don't mean anything, Tressie."

Surely she couldn't do this. Not let this stranger be the first, the one who would steal her virginity forever. She closed her eyes, said a little prayer begging forgiveness.

"Oh, yes, yes, it does mean something," she whispered. It meant trapping him, putting him in a position that would keep him from leaving her alone and going on his way. She could make him want her so badly he'd have to take her with him. At the same moment, growing deep in her soul, she sensed an overpowering need to have him close as only a lover can be.

She leaned forward, traced with her tongue the laddering of his ribs, then delicately kissed the firm slant of his whiskered jaw. "Take me with you, please."

He spanned her tiny waist with both hands and murmured "Tressie," then turned his head so that their mouths locked.

A moan flowed from his throat to hers. His need, his almost helpless desire rose to surround her. Lost in her own passion, Tressie almost forgot why she had started this deception. She kept trying to remind herself that she was supposed to be seducing him into taking her out of here. Promising him more sensual joys to come if only he'd let her go with him.

With each groan of his rapture, Tressie rejoiced. She would make him want her so desperately that he couldn't possibly give her up. Yet she couldn't stop the heated thrum of her own passion.

He embraced her, held her close, his breath coming in great gasps. She had worked the magic, and in the process been caught up in it herself, desiring nothing but for this moment to last forever. What a strange and wonderful feeling this was, this wanting of another human being.

Tressie marveled at it, but at the same time knew that she had to control herself. She had to be in charge, had to hold back. This was neither the time nor the place to yield her virginity. And certainly not to a man who wandered around the country, probably no better than Papa when it came to commitment.

"Tressie, I need you. Please." He fumbled at her clothing.

"No, not yet. Not now." She pushed away, feeling his frailty and glad of it. If he had just held on a little longer, she might have given in. "Later, after we've left this place. I can't do it here, not in Mama and Papa's bed. We can go somewhere else."

Unexpectedly he grabbed her wrist, his strength surprising. What if he wouldn't stop? Maybe she couldn't overpower him in the throes of passion. Suppose he decided to force her?

Heart hammering in her throat, Tressie pushed hard against his chest.

He grimaced and sighed, letting go.

She had hurt him and was sorry, but at the same time relieved. She moved quickly away, turned so that she lay facing the wall until her breathing evened out and her own passion subsided.

So this was what it felt like to want a man. She wondered at the overpowering surge of desire that had exploded in the pit of her stomach, gripped her so that her breasts ached and a living warmth flowed through her being.

Beside her, Bannon moved and Tressie stiffened, but he was only settling. She wanted to ask him right out without preamble if he was going to take her with him when he left. Suppose he only thought her a child indulging in a game, seeing as how she had cheated him of his reward.

A tear leaked from the corner of one eye and she rubbed it away angrily. Why were men the ones who made all the decisions, when life affected the woman so harshly?

Three

The *squee-squee* of prairie hens announcing the coming of morning awoke Tressie before daylight. To her distress she immediately discovered that wasn't early enough, for Reed Bannon had gone. She scrambled from the bed and stood in the open doorway, staring toward the horizon. Through the distant silver glow of dawn moved a figure, and it could be no one but her bed partner of the previous night escaping as fast as he could.

"Damn you, Reed Bannon. Damn you to hell." The wind tossed the shouted words back in her face.

Hugging herself, Tressie thought of the night before and shivered. How could he make her feel the way he had and then just walk away as if it were nothing? The louse. He wasn't going to get away with this.

Back inside, she saw that his saddlebags were gone, stuffed no doubt with his few belongings of which she knew nothing. She dug through her own meager supply of clothing and came up with overalls and an old shirt of Papa's. Shrugging into them, she fashioned a poke from another shirt. She filled it with such supplies as she could find: half a bag of cornmeal, some salt, the last few vegetables from the root cellar. If Bannon had waited, they could have packed up a proper supply for the trip. How could he have run away without so much as a fare-thee-well? And after she had saved his life, too.

Tressie tied the poke, slipped it over the barrel of the Kentucky rifle, and strapped the possible bag around her waist. Black powder, balls, and caps were almost as necessary as food if they were to survive the long trek across the vast Dakota territory. At the door she stuck bare feet into the only pair of shoes she owned and laced them tightly because they were too big. As an afterthought she grabbed an old felt hat from its hook on the wall and plopped it onto her head. It would keep off the punishing rays of the sun.

She was almost out the door before she remembered Mama's few hoarded coins tied in a hanky and stuffed down in the bedding. Rustling around in the dry corn shucks, she retrieved the handful of silver and crammed the pouch in the front pocket of her overalls. Her gaze was caught by Mama's rocker and a sob tore from deep in her throat.

Fear of the unknown combined with the sudden attack of forlorn sorrow and threatened momentarily to keep her there, in the company of what she knew. But then memories of the previous winter intruded. The bitter cold of the stark and endless days and nights; and later the scratching and hoeing in the dirt to raise what scraggly vegetables would grow in this hellhole. And always the loneliness. Memories of that and the loss of her family chased her from the soddy without a backward glance.

She turned away from thoughts of the life she had once had, and toward the man making tracks across the prairie. If she ran at a decent pace she could catch him when he bedded down for the night. The infernal wind pelted her with grit and powdery dust, but she ran on, ignoring its sting. Past the well and then the graves, not giving either a sideways glance. Going and not coming back. What she left she would just have to leave.

For a while Tressie tried to keep Reed Bannon's shrinking figure in sight while she trotted, but too many times she stumbled over clumps of grass or into prairie dog holes. Finally she decided to follow by tracing his passing through the brittle tufts of grama grass. He had veered to the north, scuffing along and leaving a trail that, while not easy to follow, was temporarily visible. No doubt of where he was going. Headed a little north of west, just like all the others in their quest for gold.

Before Papa lit out for Grasshopper Creek, he had traced the way in the dirt of the soddy floor. Tressie's knowledge of geography was limited to the Ozarks and their long trek north into Dakota Territory. She had been to Cozad, where they bought supplies, and it lay fifty miles or more to the south down on the Platte River and the well-traveled Oregon Trail. Reed Bannon was going toward the gold strikes with no notion of either Cozad or the Oregon Trail.

A grumbling stomach and the climbing sun announced dinnertime. Stopping only long enough to tear off a chunk of withering cabbage, Tressie stuffed it in her mouth and marched on. She gnawed at the tough leaves, welcoming the bit of moisture they offered. How stupid of her to have walked right past the well without realizing she needed water for the journey. She could only hope that Reed had had better sense. The inside of her mouth turned to dust as the heat of the June day bore down. She would surely choke.

When she first heard the deep, earthshaking rumbling, she thought it was a buffalo stampede. She'd heard men talk of such, but had never seen for herself the sight of countless shaggy beasts on the rampage, carpeting the land from sky to sky in all directions. Kicking up dust so thick it blotted out the sun. They stopped for nothing. But then out here, there wasn't much to stop for. Except this morning there was Reed Bannon and Tressie Majors. Both easy targets. Their trampled bodies would scarcely cause a thud under the hooves of such animals.

As the sun slid farther west and there came no sign of buffalo, Tressie realized that the steady rolling and rumbling was a storm building to the southwest. Thunderheads boiled above masses of black clouds, swallowing up the tin-metal sky. The hot wind whipped around, shifted abruptly. She shoved the hat to the back of her head and studied the progress of the storm for a few precious moments. Her nostrils quivered, picking up the tart smell of rain. As quickly as that she shifted her attention back in the direction Reed had taken, and saw only vast emptiness. He was gone! How could she have lost sight of him so fast? By nearly running and not stopping for anything, she should have shortened the distance between them in the hours since her departure. Whirling, she looked back the way she had come. No sign of the soddy anymore. Tressie turned a complete circle, confused and frightened. The vast emptiness terrified her and threw her into a panic. She could wander around and around for days and not know it.

That, of course, was ridiculous. All she had to do was

use the sun to get her bearings. It traveled almost precisely east to west, having only this week passed the summer solstice. Still, the darkening clouds would soon blot out its guiding rays. She needed to find a landmark to head for before she no longer had anything to go by. Once rain fell, Reed's scant trail would be washed away. There was nothing on the hateful, treeless plains but grass. Making up her mind, Tressie pointed her nose a little north of the sun where it disappeared into the massive black clouds, and began to trot. After a while she settled into a faster pace, and only slowed occasionally to shift the heavy rifle from one arm to the other.

The overheated land turned somber and threatening and took on a sickly yellow hue. Rumbles of thunder shook the ground, distant fingers of lightning split the sky, and soon sporadic hailstones as big as marbles pelted down. They struck painfully at her shoulders, thunked solidly onto the crown of the hat. On she ran until the ice turned to rain and the thirsty soil drank its fill before turning to mud. The aroma of wet grasses and sweet earth raced with the scampering wind, north toward the Black Hills and back again. She swept off the hat and threw back her head to catch the welcome moisture in her mouth. All too soon she was gasping within the cold, wet embrace of icy fingers.

Thunder and lightning pushed the rain, the deadly charges erupting to split apart the lowering sky. Panting, Tressie dropped to her knees. She couldn't go on until this passed. She remembered seeing cows and horses killed by such vicious bolts of fire. Back in the Ozarks she often watched in awe as balls of flame zigzagged through the trees. Carrying the gun in the open was inviting sudden death.

Placing the filthy hat beside her so it would catch the rain, Tressie chose to lay low until the storm passed. Hugging the poke to keep it dry, she sprawled out in the clumps of grass. Tiny rivers flowed around her, and minuscule creatures came to life where there had been none. Where did they come from? Perhaps rained from heaven itself, for surely they hadn't lain buried beneath the ground all these dry months.

At last the brunt of the storm passed over, its noisy departure fading to a low growl and crackle. Soaked through, stomach covered with mud, Tressie rose to take a look around. To the west, feeble fingers of sunlight broke through the scurrying clouds. It made her feel odd to know that the galloping storm was probably drenching the deserted soddy at this very moment, soaking the soil she'd piled on the double grave. She rubbed at her eyes, muddying them with both fists. The knot in her aching throat broke loose in wrenching sobs. The burying had been hard enough, but now to think of them lying beneath the soil down there in the dark while rainwater leaked through the crevices, ran over her beloved face, the baby cradled in both arms, its tiny precious mouth that never uttered a sound. Tressie could scarcely bear thinking about it, and she folded herself into a ball, sobbing without control.

Nearly sick with grief, Tressie realized she mustn't give in. She took a deep breath and swallowed back the sorrow. "Don't be such a baby. Just get up and be on your way."

Staggering to her feet, Tressie gulped down the foul-tasting water caught in the bedraggled old hat. With a grimace she shoved it onto her head and moved once more into a steady gait across the barren plains. After a while she noticed the muscles in her legs were tightening up and the going seemed harder. How curious. She slowed to get her bearings and saw that the land had begun a gentle upward slope, so gradual that she hadn't noticed. That was the way of the high plains. Always fooling you, getting the best of you without any warning. She panted her way to the top of the rise and gasped in astonishment. At her feet stretched a luminous green valley through which a river meandered. Dotting its banks were trees that from this distance resembled folks gathered for a baptizing. And just disappearing into that growth moved a figure. It had to be Reed.

Tressie raised an arm, waved and shouted his name. Of course he couldn't hear her, but much like a child at play, she continued to cry out until her voice grew hoarse. He passed out of sight into the trees. Probably going right on across the river that could only be the North Loup. She pushed back thoughts of crossing the rain-swollen waters alone. Tressie had often heard talk of the North Loup. Rich folks, big business people, had all homesteaded the land along its banks before the Majors came to the territory. Some took as much as four and five sections and then paid poor folks to throw up a shanty and work land they would never own.

What a sight that river valley was! Lush islands of succulent growth along the banks of a sparkling silver ribbon that stretched for miles and miles.

Tressie found going downhill much easier as long as she kept her feet under her. The rifle rode hard on her shoulder, the possible bag banged at her hip, but on she ran knowing only that she had to catch up with Reed before dark. The sun would soon set. Surely he would stop for the night near water. The land leveled out and she slowed to a walk. In the river bottoms the trees and clumps of shrubbery grew in such thick masses she might walk within yards of him and not know it. She even lost sight of the far bank of the river and the valley beyond once she reached flat land. Not very good at judging distances, Tressie figured she could still be as far as two miles behind Reed. A long way with night approaching, and if he crossed the river and went on, then what? She couldn't much more than dog-paddle, and she certainly couldn't swim strongly enough to overcome a swift current.

The sun rested on the rim of the earth when she finally made the riverbank. Hunkering on her heels, she gazed into rushing sworls of muddy water, made angry by the storm. The current ran mighty fast, the froth and roar enough in itself to frighten her out of crossing, never mind that she couldn't tell how deep the murky water was. Crouched there in the dense shadows of early dusk, she probably was invisible to man and beast. Beneath the thick canopy of cottonwood branches would be an ideal place to spend the night, lulled to sleep by the chattering leaves. The forest along the riverbank reminded her a bit of the Ozark wilderness, and she'd spent many a night alone there cradled in the arms of the deep woods. But if Reed walked on into the night, she would never catch him. Exhausted and confused, Tressie bent to drink, unsure of what to do.

Above the roar of the rushing waters and the wind

through the cottonwood trees came the sound of galloping horses. Harsh shouts cut through the rain-washed air. Peering between thick underbrush, she made out several riders upstream and on the far bank of the river. Indians! Afraid to move, she clapped a hand tightly over her mouth. Fear dried her tongue so that it stuck to her teeth. Obviously the Indian party hadn't seen Reed, wherever he might be, for several dismounted and let their horses drink while they stretched and spoke casually. A couple even relieved themselves right out in the open. Spying on them sent a chill trailing up and down her backbone. She shuddered. Any moment they might spot her, and that would mean death or worse.

A hailing shout from the bank directly opposite her hiding place fueled her fear. Were there more of the savages? While the Indians were distracted, Tressie edged deeper into the brush. There she huddled as the men grew quite boisterous. She dared a cautious peek. Someone had joined them. A white man. She expected at any moment to see them fall upon him and scalp his hair right off his head. That didn't happen. A friendly visit ensued that seemed endless. Finally the Indians mounted up and rode off, everyone waving friendly-like. She squinted her eyes and glared at the man they left behind. It was . . . no, it couldn't be. But it was. The man who had spoken so casually with the Indians was Reed Bannon.

An explosive breath from deep in her lungs sounded awfully loud and Tressie hunkered back in hiding, terrified that the Indians would swing around and ride her way. She stayed there until her legs were tingly stumps and a cramp held her back stiffly. She'd dropped the rifle in her earlier haste, and so backed out of the brush at long last, bent on retrieving it. She bumped solidly into a pair of legs clothed in soaked britches.

Screeching, she tried to scamper back into hiding. A hand snatched her overall straps and dragged her to her feet. "You can come out now," the stern voice said. Letting out a yowl, she flailed at the air with clenched fists.

Her Kentucky rifle in one hand, the crossed straps of her overalls fisted in the other, Reed Bannon spoke in a soft voice, "Hush, girl. You want to bring them back? Hush, now. Thunderation, what are you doing here?"

"Reed? Is that you?" Blind panic dissolving, she peered into the familiar face. "Turn me loose this instant, Reed Bannon. Let me go! And give me back my gun."

She kicked at his shins with the heavy shoes. He dodged easily out of range, grimaced, and let go of her. The shoulder wound had to still be bothering him, but Tressie didn't care. She just landed on both feet with a grunt and glared at him, ready to do further battle.

"Behave yourself. Is that any way to treat the man who just saved your hide?"

"Oh, sure. After leaving me out on the prairie to die, you save my life. How gallant." She took great pleasure in throwing his words back at him.

He ignored it and continued to scold her. "For goodness' sake, I didn't leave you to die. You were safe there. You had a roof over your head, food to eat, water to drink. What do you have out here, girl? Indians and wild animals, that's what. Do you know how many men die crossing these plains? Not to mention the weaker sex. Now what am I going to do with you? Two days lost if I take you home. There ain't many women in the camps. Lord sakes, girl, how can I protect you?"

Tressie seriously considered leaping on him and giving him a good pounding. His eyes snapped and she changed her mind, speaking instead. "Forget that; I'll protect myself. You're not taking me back. Not unless you hog-tie me and drag me. If you do I'll just follow you again."

He snorted in derision. "Hog-tying you isn't such a bad idea." Though she could scarcely see his face in the darkness, she sensed him studying her. "What were you going to do come dark? Or suppose I'd a gone on when I spotted you coming down off that rise, instead of hanging around? Them Indians would have had you if I hadn't sent them off in another direction, and then what would you have done?"

"A lot you care. Taking advantage of me just like some animal in heat, then running off. I thought we were . . . we had . . . I felt like—"

"Bull hockey, girl. You lured me into that trying to weasel your way into my good graces. You think I'd want it so bad I'd take you along so I'd have it at hand?"

Tressie doubled up her fist and belted him dead on the point of his chin. The blow jarred her to the top of her head. She sucked at her knuckles and did a dance while Reed staggered backward. The jolt didn't actually knock him off his feet, but his eyes glazed momentarily.

"Woman, what's the matter with you?" he finally asked in an amazed tone.

Lips and tongue soothing her aching fist, Tressie looked up into his black eyes. Eyes that revealed more hurt than anger. She felt the tears coming and could do nothing but let them flow. Down both cheeks they poured and plopped onto the ground. Soon she began to bawl in earnest and slumped to a sitting position. With moisture-laden words she tried to explain her actions, but couldn't make herself understood. Weariness had defeated her.

"Aw, dammit to hell," Reed said, and knelt beside her. "I ain't never seen a woman cry as much as you. And I can't hardly stand it."

"Well, doe den. Dust doe."

He put an arm around her, swiveled to sit at her side, and hugged her. "Hush up trying to talk; it sounds plumb silly. I reckon you need to cry, just go right ahead and do it. But I want you to get it out of your system, you hear? You can't trail me across this danged prairie bawling like a baby. It just won't do at all."

She nodded and wiped at her nose. Did that mean he was taking her, or was he just having one of his jokes again?

"Here, hell, use this," Reed said, whipping off his disreputable bandanna. "Don't worry if you get it dirty; we can wash it in the river," he announced solemnly.

Tressie eyed the sweat-stiffened, dust-coated, tattered thing and giggled. Before long she was laughing as hard as she'd been crying earlier.

Grumbling, trying to keep a straight face, Reed snatched the bandanna from her outstretched hand, took it to the riverbank, and sloshed it around awhile. Then he wrung out the piece of worn and faded cloth and brought it back to her. Between laughing and wiping, Tressie got herself cleaned up and settled down, then handed it back. "Better wash it," she said.

That set them both off.

The merriment didn't last long. Reed sobered first, gesturing upriver. "That was an advance hunting party of Sioux yonder. They're looking for a herd of buffalo, scouting ahead of the rest of the tribe. They'll be here soon and we'll need to be gone."

"Be gone tonight?"

"No, tomorrow'll do."

Tressie could no longer make out his face in the falling darkness, and she didn't enjoy talking to someone she couldn't see. "Could we build a fire now and eat? I'm hungry."

"No. No fire tonight. We'll sleep here till dawn, then we need to get gone. We should cross the river, then camp, but all things considered, we'd best wait."

Tressie could hardly contain her joy. He was taking her with him. For a while she was content to sit on the ground and embrace that bliss. The feeling didn't last long, for she began to detect the most foul odor. She sniffed at the air. "What is that?"

Reed flared his nostrils. "I don't smell anything."

Tressie shifted and realized the stink came from the two of them. "Oh, I can't stand this," she said, and unfastened the overall galusses. "I'm going to take a bath."

"A what? You're going to do what?"

"Take a bath. It's us I'm smelling, and we stink." She leaned toward him, sniffed. "Yep, you can take a bath, too."

Reed frowned and made a snorting noise in his throat. "I knew I'd regret this before we even got started. Just where are we going to take this bath, Miss Priss?"

"In the river, where else?"

"In the dark and all alone?" Reed asked.

"Not all alone. You're going to take one, too. I can't swim, so you'll have to hang on to me so I don't drown."

Reed sighed loudly. "I just might hold on to you, all

right . . . till you do drown. How would that be? I ain't going in that danged river in the dark. If I was going to do that, we'd just ford her and be on our way this very minute. Now hush up this nonsense and get some sleep. We'll leave at first light."

Tressie climbed to her feet. "I'm taking me a bath before I lay down to sleep."

Reed made some settling noises as if pawing out a bed, then came his hushed whisper, so soft she could only just make out the words. "With the cottonmouth snakes?"

Tressie thought about that for a beat or two. "You're lying," she finally said, but not very strongly.

"Nope. Comes up a rain like this, washes 'em out of their nests around the banks. Sometimes as many as a hundred will be writhing and hissing in one spot. But you do what you want. I'll wait here to drag you out and bury you when they get finished. Frail little thing like yourself, probably a couple a dozen of the varmints latching on to your hide is all it'll take to do you in."

Tressie considered what he said, not sure if he was lying or telling the truth, but certainly not willing to go in the water alone. "Maybe I could just wet that rag of yours and wash a bit."

Reed emitted a long, drawn-out snore. After listening but not believing the sound of his sleeping for a while longer, Tressie was attacked by a vision of hoards of snakes, crawling up the bank and slithering across the ground to attack her helpless body. Feeling with her feet, she located Reed's curled form and nested down, spooned against his lanky backside. He went right on with his snoring, like he didn't even know she was there.

Tomorrow they would cross the river and head for Bannack. What awaited them there she couldn't guess, having never learned much about gold rushes and the like. But it would surely beat life alone in a prairie soddy. Wouldn't it?

Four

While Reed shouted instructions over the roar of the river, he lashed their supplies to a raft of cottonwood limbs strapped together with strips of vine. "All you have to do is hang on, keep your head above water, and kick your feet. I'll do the rest."

Setting his lips tightly, Reed refused to so much as glance in her direction. He had his doubts they would make it across the river. Maybe he could do it alone, but with this jackleg floating contraption and a woman half scared to death, he wasn't sure. If he had to abandon the supplies to rescue her, could he do it? He'd gotten pretty good at running away from his own fears. That had started a long time ago, and maybe he'd never stop, he didn't know. What he did know was that if he met the steady gaze of Tressie's shimmering green eyes, she'd see his doubt. Then they sure as hell wouldn't make it.

Tressie thought she knew why Reed wouldn't look at her. He resented having her along; she was holding him up and he wanted to abandon her. If she faltered, that's exactly what he would do, too. Just go right on swimming, dragging along the supplies and leaving her to drown. After all, why should he care? He might even be glad to be rid of her. Even though Tressie didn't really believe he was quite that coldhearted, she was determined to keep up, no matter what it took.

If only she'd learned how to swim. Who could know one day she would be faced with a life-or-death situation on the banks of the ravenous North Loup River? Paddling around in a clear woodland stream or pool was far removed from kicking off into that storm-swollen rush of water that slapped hungrily at her legs as if taking a taste of what it would ultimately consume. Tressie gulped past a lump in her throat and fixed her gaze on Reed's back. He'd taken off his shirt, and the blades of his broad shoulders stood up like flat paddles. The exit wound high on his right arm shone purple against the coppery skin. Suppose he wasn't strong enough? Would he truly let her go to save himself and the precious supplies? She wanted to ask but thought better of it.

He turned abruptly toward her, catching her gaze with those incredibly dark eyes. A wan smile rippled over the morose features. Without a word he waded into the angry current until it washed at the line wrapped around his chest and under his arms. The raft wobbled and began to move, tightening the lashings.

He shouted back at her, the words nearly lost in the noise of the river. "Don't worry, we can do it. Keep your mouth shut and hold your breath if you go under."

"Go under?" Tressie, already rapidly being dragged into deep water, set her heels and pulled backward.

"No, you don't," Reed yelled, and dove in, swimming with surprisingly powerful overhand strokes, towing both the small raft and Tressie right into the swift current.

Terrified, she clung to the ridged pole. "But why can't

I float on the logs with our stuff?" The question had no more than tumbled from her trembling lips than the bottom dropped out from under her. Forgetting his instructions, she opened her mouth to scream, got a mouthful of water, and went under. Clutching at the raft, she surfaced, choking and sputtering. Her mind turned black with panic. Where was Reed? What had he told her to do? She couldn't think. Surely he wouldn't let her drown, would he? They couldn't survive without their supplies, but he'd do just fine without her.

Tressie coughed out a mouthful of water and squinted her eyes. Up ahead she could barely see Reed, who continued to swim. He appeared more desperate now as he dragged at all that dead weight, getting absolutely nowhere. They were being washed downstream, helplessly tossed about like deadwood. Gasping and frantically struggling to keep her head above water, Tressie kicked out tentatively and felt just the slightest forward movement. She kicked harder. Her effort was actually helping. Swimming wasn't, after all, so much different than marching across the prairie. Slow and steady for walking, harder and more intense for a fast trot. She concentrated, paddled her feet vigorously, and felt a rush of jubilation as they began to move slowly forward. She was doing it!

Though the pitiful little raft and its crew continued to float east with the current, the opposite bank appeared to inch closer. It was rough going and the river gave grudgingly, until finally her legs and arms grew heavy as stones. If they didn't make it soon, she would have to let go so Reed could reach shore safely. Despite a valiant effort, her strength began to desert her as the icy cold took its toll. At the very instant when her hands began to slip from the wet raft, both knees struck bottom. The grating blow scraped away skin even through the soaked pants legs, but she scarcely felt the pain. They had made it! Tears filled her eyes. They weren't going to die. She shouted, laughed, gulped in another mouthful of cold water, and choked.

Though in shallower water, Reed kept crawling along the bottom, head down, heaving like a horse tied to a heavy load. The raft, still caught by the swift current, threatened to pull him back into the river and he shouted, "Help me, Tressie, hang on . . . push."

She raised her drenched face and with what little energy she had left, shoved the raft onto shore beside him and rolled onto her back. "It's okay, we did it, we made it," she shouted into the clear blue sky.

Still on his hands and knees, Reed coughed and rocked back and forth. Somehow he couldn't make himself stop.

She crept to his side, laid a hand on the tense muscles rippling across his back. "We made it. We're on the other side."

Tugging on the binding, she dragged the raft even farther up on the bank, out of reach of the hungry river. With a last feeble pull, she collapsed beside Reed. "We did it. We did it. I thought I'd drown, but we did it. I think I could swim now. Did you see me? I just started paddling my legs, kicking for all I was worth, and—"

"Tressie?" He said it wearily.

"What, Reed? What is it?"

"Shut up."

Rolling over onto her back, she gazed up into the inverted bowl of cloudless metallic sky and laughed. She laughed like the child she was, like the child she'd once been, and soon he joined her. They hugged each other, then tried to pick the knots loose that held him to the raft.

"Just slip it over your head," she told him while he went on doggedly working at the knotted vine.

Vexed because he continued to ignore her instructions, she knelt in front of him and wrapped cold fingers around his. "Stop, Reed. Just lift up your arms."

He stared at her a moment. She knelt there, all wet and shivery, and grinning like a little kid. Irresistible and very alive. With a soul-deep shudder, he did as she said. They had, after all, both survived. A great cause for celebration. And she had done her share. After she removed the knotted harness, her breasts brushing his goose-pimply flesh, he locked his arms around her in a bear hug. Gazing down into her adorable face, its features still a little tense, full lips trembling from the cold, he had the most insane desire to kiss her. Not the lustful kind of desire she had exposed in him when she'd tricked him into her bed and her arms. But the kind a man feels when he first spots the woman he might want with him always. Still he ought to pull back, for this one was no woman, but merely a child. He couldn't forget that again.

Tressie gazed up into the smoky eyes. For a moment she thought he was going to kiss her and decided she wouldn't mind at all, but at the last minute he didn't. They knelt there a moment longer, then lay back side by side to let the heat of the sun dry their wet clothing.

Later, feeling rested and jubilant, Tressie rolled to her stomach and propped her chin in both hands to stare at her companion. "Reed?"

He took a deep breath before answering. "What now?"

"How many rivers will we have to cross?"

"That's a question I can't answer. Never toted them up. I know one thing, though; I sure hope you can learn to swim before too many more."

"Well, I was swimming. Along there at the last."

He chuckled and rose to unlash the rifle and their belongings from the crude raft.

"Time we got moving," he said, peering at her through a thick fringe of lashes. "Drink your fill before we leave. I wish we had some way to carry water, but I guess we'll just have to hope the storm filled some sump holes along the way. "He hefted the rifle. "You want to carry this?"

Sometime that afternoon they shared a handful of shriveled raw vegetables, chewing as they walked.

"My feet are on fire," Tressie complained later.

"Yeah, but we'll get used to it. They'll blister at first, but after a while they'll harden up. Socks help. You got socks?"

Tressie laughed bitterly. "Where would I get socks?"

He grunted.

Late in the day they came across a sinkhole of spring water surrounded by a few brave shrubs and saplings. After drinking, both slipped out of their shoes and soaked their aching feet.

"How do you know where we're going?" Tressie asked.

"We'll hit the Niobrara sometime tomorrow and then follow it west into Wyoming Territory."

That really wasn't what she had asked, but she nodded, afraid to think about crossing any more rivers. "How come we aren't taking the Platte River Road?"

"No need to go south and then come back north," he muttered, and lifted his feet out of the water. "Time we got moving. We can make some more miles before dark."

As it turned out, they didn't make many more miles that day. Their blazing feet gave out at a watering hole some few miles west of their last stop. Tressie could feel her feet bleeding inside her shoes, and had continued to fall farther and farther behind.

Finally she stumbled to both knees and cried out, "Please, can't we stop? I can't even walk."

He turned and limped back to her. Kneeling, he took her arm. "There's water ahead. You have to go just a bit farther. Come on, girl, you can do it."

Rocking in agony, she cried, "How do you know that? Can't we just stop right here?"

He looked around, scanning their exposure. "No. We're too out in the open. Bait is all we'd be."

"Bait for what?" she wailed. "I never saw such god-forsaken land. Who in his right mind would be out here?"

"Bears. Indians. White scum. You name it. Come on, up you go," Reed said, and hoisted her to her feet.

She jerked her arm away. He was probably only trying to scare her, and it was working. "Okay. I can walk myself."

He grinned a bit, admiring her spunk. She could still argue with him, but he wasn't sure how much longer she would last. Anything could be out here, including things they couldn't see. He'd watched invisible sicknesses wipe out whole parties in a scant few weeks. Indians and wild animals weren't all they had to worry about. Barring everything else, they could simply starve to death.

He lifted his head and sniffed at the sweet smell of water carried in the wind. Tressie tottered along behind, each step a torture that drove spikes of black through her vision, blotting out the sun. But she couldn't, she wouldn't give up. Not even if her feet turned to stumps. She put her mind on other things. Wondering about Reed Bannon. How could he just find water the way he did? Must be something to do with his Indian upbringing. All she wanted to know was how far it was to Grasshopper Creek, not dreaming that she would have given up at that very moment had she known.

Tressie had lost track of the days when they reached the sand hills. And there, gazing out across the wavering sands, she wondered why she had bothered to survive the trek only to end up on the brink of hell itself. After the initial shock, she shaded her eyes with the brim of her hat and squinted into the distance. "I didn't know there was a desert out here."

"I guess there's just about everything you could imagine in this part of the country, with the exception maybe of oceans." Crossing his legs, Reed sank to his butt in the cool sand.

They had been under way since before dawn, and the rising sun hadn't yet warmed the earth, having just cleared the horizon at their backs. It would soon turn this world into a flaming hell.

Reed propped the rifle over one shoulder and studied the terrain in a way that had become familiar to Tressie. Legs spread apart, he would gaze off into the distance with every appearance of sleeping. It was an unmoving stance that usually accompanied total silence.

Tressie could only be so patient, and after a while she wandered away to explore their new surroundings. With a great scurrying and flurrying of sand, something leaped from behind a growth of scrub. Tressie yelped. The tiny rodent that had landed a few paces away regarded her with beady eyes, nose whiskers twitching. The animal resembled a mouse, but with a tuft on its long stringy tail. She got that much of a look at the strange creature before it bounded high into the air, kicking sand every which way. Giggling with delight, Tressie followed the animal's springy progress. Obviously totally unafraid, he would pause occasionally, seat himself on rather long hind legs, and tuck miniature front feet neatly under his chin. She would have sworn he was saying, "Well, come on, let's go."

What a delightful pet he would make. Each time she approached tentatively, ready to make friends, the mouse would zip away in a blur of flying sand, causing her to yelp once again.

Those squeals finally disturbed Reed's reverie and he went in search of her. His mind still on the best way of crossing the sand hills, he finally caught up with her, playing tag with a damned mouse. And having quite a time of it, too, he reckoned. How wonderful to be able to find enjoyment in such a simple game.

He watched her squat down beside a clump of grass to giggle in delight at the mouse's antics. Her hair, shagging over the collar of the rough shirt, flamed in splashes of early morning sun. Sometime in the past few days she had ripped off the legs of the overalls above her knees. While he admired the view, her willingness to expose so much of her body perplexed him. He'd never known a woman to do that. Well, at least not a woman like her. A respectable type.

Reed chuckled at his silent attempts to explain his own judgments to himself, and she turned at the sound.

"Did you see that?" she shouted, clapping her hands. "A

mouse, not like one I've ever seen. He jumps as high as a jackrabbit and has legs to match."

Reed let a frown of concentration fall away, and smiled at her. What a wonderful child she was. And how he wished he had gotten cleanly away from her. She would have been so much better off fending for herself at the soddy. He feared failing her. Having her along was a burden he wasn't sure he could shoulder.

"We'll shelter here the day, and cross the sands by night," he told her. "You ought to try to get some sleep."

The abrupt tone puzzled Tressie. The long harsh days on the trail had seeped all the funning right out of him. She hated that and wished for the old Reed back again.

The smile that died on her face put Reed to shame. "I guess I never realized how young you are, girl. . . . I'm sorry about what happened back at the soddy. I never should have done that to you."

She scowled fiercely. He looked so forlorn, she found herself regretting her earlier folly. At the same time she was unable to let his comment about her youth go unchallenged. "Not too young to make you want me. Anyway, it wasn't your fault."

His harsh and bitter laugh frightened Tressie. "No, you didn't make me. I do what I do. No one makes me. Or you, either, girl. Remember that, will you?"

Though she nodded, Tressie was far from agreement. She had been made to do a lot of things in her young life, and she was sure that wasn't over with yet. "You tried to make me go back home," she said with a pout.

"Yes, I suppose I did. But it was for your own good."

Hands tucked into the sagging waist of her overalls, Tressie said with a distinct twinkle in her eye, "And what we did, that was for your own good. Mine, too, for that matter." With that she trounced to where she had left her old felt hat on top of the pack of dwindling supplies. She crammed the dusty thing down on her head, picked up the pack, and headed for the sparse brush Reed had indicated for shade.

"Damn, girl, you are something," he murmured, but not loud enough for her to hear. He would never forget the way she had made him feel when they held each other, her teasing because she didn't understand a man's needs. Such enjoyment of the basic human spirit was quite rare. Recalling their romp, he suddenly regretted his decision to keep his hands to himself.

For three nights they walked, and Tressie was surprised at how much light the stars cast. A fingernail moon would appear in the western skies as they darkened, and before long she could see almost better than in the glaring light of day. Sedge, thorny cactus, and towering soapweed plants cast elongated shadows on the gleaming sand. Reed showed her how to eat the cactus fruit. Cutting open the spiny green leaves, he would dig out the meat and squeeze moisture into her mouth while she held her head tilted back. The stuff tasted godawful, right on the verge of being bitter, but by then she was finally convinced he knew more than she did. After all, they were still alive.

It was on the evening of the third day that they came upon the cougar and her twin cubs. The sun had dropped below the horizon, leaving a glorious orange sky behind. Strings of lavender-hued clouds lay like tattered lace along the horizon. Tressie had been tramping behind Reed, chattering on about nothing in particular. The ground was smothered in darkness, so watching her feet made her stumble smack into Reed's solid back.

He had scented the cat earlier and gone on the alert, saying nothing to her. Now he signaled her to be absolutely still. The female cougar, probably six to eight feet long and as tawny as the earth, was hunting. Stalking into the wind had kept her from catching the smell of humans. Muscles bunched over her great shoulders, she approached her prey in slow motion. At first Reed couldn't see what the lioness saw, but he did see something else that clutched at his heart. A pair of cubs wrestled in a depression off to their right. He and Tressie had strayed inadvertently between the mother and her young. As long as the cat concentrated on the kill, they would be fine, but if she caught their scent, she would charge. He didn't want to shoot her and leave the cubs to die. Hell, he wasn't even sure he could hit her with the muzzle loader of Tressie's. Marksmanship was Tressie's forte, not his.

He motioned Tressie to crouch low and make herself smaller. She did and he held a finger to his lips. Green eyes wide, Tressie nodded. Her heart hammered so loudly, the lion could surely hear it. Hugging both knees, she watched as Reed fingered a cap from the possible bag and readied the rifle for firing.

Why was he going to shoot such a gorgeous creature? Surely they couldn't eat it, and the cat was paying no attention to them at all. She wanted to shout a warning as the supple limbs of the beautiful lion propelled the lithe body forward inch by inch. Tressie could not control her sudden outburst when a rabbit erupted from nowhere and zigzagged across the prairie, the cat hot on its trail. Hunter and prey kicked up clouds of dust as they ran into the black of night, zipping this way, then that through clumps of crackly sedge.

Soon there came a scream of pure terror such as Tressie had never heard before.

"Oh, God, what was that?"

Reed tapped her bowed head. "*Hsst*, be still and back up. Real slow," he ordered, and almost stepped on her before she could make her trembling legs obey. Somehow getting to her feet, she scampered out of his way, ignoring his orders and clattering through the underbrush, kicking up rocks and debris.

The playing cubs, aroused by the noise, set up a burbling greeting, and Reed caught his breath. "Stop," he said sharply, and lifted the barrel of the gun, sighting it as the cougar came in sight, her limp kill hanging from strong jaws.

Tressie managed to quell her instinct to run, and did as Reed ordered. The cougar headed for her cubs, trotting so close by them, Tressie could see the flash of her golden eye.

Reed let out a smothered sigh and carefully removed the cap from the rifle, letting the hammer down slowly.

"Come on," he said, and headed on down the trail. He couldn't let her see how distraught he was.

Tressie stood there frozen, watching him stride away but totally unable to follow. Her knees were shaking so badly she couldn't take that first step. She was going to be sick, she just knew it, and he could wait for her. After a moment, the feeling passed and she trotted to catch up.

Several mornings later, when Tressie had begun to believe the sand would go on forever, enormous jagged rocks appeared, protruding from the hot gritty soil like bizarre ships at sea. As they prepared to settle in the welcome shade of one, a good place to spend the long hot day, Reed pointed toward the distant western horizon at what looked like ragged clouds growing from the flat land.

"There's Wyoming over yonder," he said.

Tressie strained to see. Her lips were dry; her mouth tasted as bitter as the cactus juice they'd lived on so long. The welcome sight perked her up considerably. This trip had already taken much longer than she had thought it would, and she was eager to reach their destination. "And then how far? How far to Bannack?"

He put an arm around her shoulder. "Ah, Tressie, girl. Let's just watch those mountains grow. That distance will be far enough to last us a long time. But isn't it good to see something besides sand and cactus?"

"Then how far to them?" she insisted, sweeping off her hat and drinking in the sight of the rugged peaks, hazy as they were. Reed was right; they were beautiful. She wiped at moisture forming in her eyes and unconsciously sniffed. It had been a long time since she had cried.

"Ah, girl, I know what you mean," Reed said, and took her in his arms, resting his chin on top of her head. They had been together so long he felt attached to her in the way he supposed one would a family member. They had avoided physical contact, but he thought it was mostly from exhaustion. Having made his secret vow of celibacy where she was concerned, he was glad of the harsh circumstance that robbed their bodies of energy. It made the vow easy to keep. She was still such a child and he a worthless deserter and coward, surely not worthy of her love.

Tressie settled against Reed's chest. She felt a welcome strength in his embrace and hugged him fiercely. The touch of his muscular body awoke in her an animal lust so strong she gasped. She ached to strip herself naked and lie with him out there in the open, celebrate their survival in a primitive, explosive mating. They were going to make it, and how wonderful that was. But then she thought of the way Papa had left them, deserted his pregnant wife and Tressie. Reed was no better a man, running like they all must from responsibility. How could she imagine giving her virginity to a man who wouldn't hesitate to leave her, who had tried once already?

Even as Tressie pulled away, Reed found himself wanting her. His arms felt empty, and every male instinct urged him to fold her up there against his aching chest. Why was his body betraying him even while he argued the stupidity of such a thing? A man should have more control than that. Perhaps that's all it was, an animal lust. They had been alone together so very long. Once they made civilization, he could find him a fancy woman, get rid of all these desires the way a man was supposed to. That certainly didn't mean taking advantage of Tressie Majors while she was so vulnerable.

The endless land rolled to the mountains in huge waves that demanded struggling up and stumbling down. It was as if the dunes had turned into a grassy, turbulent ocean. On the morning of the third day with the coming dawn nudging their backsides, the mountains greeted them like walls of granite blotting out the sky. Huge boulders were scattered about, and great arroyos cut scars into the red earth among a scraggly growth of greasewood and sage. This day, as the sun climbed the metallic sky, Reed made no move to stop for their usual all-day sleep. For a while Tressie trudged along at his heels, letting her thoughts wander. Reed spoke very little while they were on the move, and she had grown quite used to occupying her time with great fantasy voyages through fairy castles. But as the hours went by and he made no offer to stop, she grew tired of even those magical adventures.

Focusing on his ramrod-straight back where the shoulder strap of the possible bag cut across the blue flannel shirt, Tressie wanted to shout at him to stop. Stop right here! And then, quite abruptly, as if he'd heard her, he pulled up short.

She stumbled to a halt beside him. "What is it?"

"A wagon, just over yonder in the trees."

"Folks?" she asked, peering where he pointed.

"Don't see anyone, but there's water there, too. You stay here while I check."

"I'm thirsty. Real honest-to-goodness water? Oh, Reed, I want to go, too."

He put an arm across her chest quite forcefully. "I said stay here, now do it."

The tone brooked no argument, and she heeded him, though doing so made her temper flare. He took the rifle with him and approached the covered wagon with a great deal of caution. One corner of the canvas whipped and snapped in the wind, and the tongue lay on the ground, empty of horse or oxen. No child cried, no human voice spoke. Tressie smelled something on the wind, recognized blood and death, and began to tremble. Something or someone lay dead over there, and she was weakly glad Reed had made her stay behind.

A few moments later he waved for her to join him. She

did so with a great deal of reluctance. He stood between her and the campsite.

"Just a woman and man here. They're dead. No need you looking. Climb up in the wagon and see if you can salvage anything. Take everything we can use. I'm going to . . ." He hesitated. "Never you mind what I'm going to do, just git yourself up there. Clothes, tools, vessels of any kind. Gather up everything. We'll take all we can carry."

"Did the Indians—"

"Not now, girl. Not now," Reed said gently, and turned her with a hand on each shoulder.

Tressie climbed up and over the seat into the back of the wagon. If the Indians had done this, they hadn't bothered to raid, yet the pickings were very poor indeed. Obviously the family had begun with very little, or like so many had lightened their load as they went along until not much was left. There were some patchwork quilts and a blanket marked U.S. in one corner. She took those and added some plates, flatware, and two tin cups. There was no food. Hopping down from the tailgate, she added to her bundle a cooking vessel and a small hatchet. A skin pouch beaded with moisture hung on the side of the wagon and her dry tongue caught at the roof of her mouth. Just a sip to hold her . . . there'd been nothing but liquid squeezed from cactus for so long. She pried out the stopper and took several languorous sips, rolling the last drops of cool water around in her mouth before swallowing. After she patted a handful over her face and neck, she gulped down some more.

As she tied the corners of the Army blanket together, Reed joined her, looking pale and sick. "I'll take that," he

said. "There's a creek just yonder. We'll camp there tonight."

"So close to . . . ?"

"I'm sorry, we'll go up stream a ways. That's as good as
we can do. We need the water and neither of us can walk
another step, I'd wager."

Despite the incident, Tressie sank gratefully on the
banks of the bubbling creek when he chose a likely spot
out of sight of the wagon. After drinking of the clear water, she removed her shoes, or what was left of them, and
lowered her burning feet in the stream. With a sigh of
contentment she lay back, propping one arm over her
eyes.

He joined her, drank, and had just taken off a boot
when she sensed his alarm and stiffened almost at the
moment he hissed for silence.

She touched his arm.

"Shhh. Don't move."

She thought the Indians had come back for them. Don't
move, indeed. Tressie drew her body up tightly, tensed to
leap to her feet and run. She couldn't help it, every instinct
screamed run and hide, *fast*.

"Stay still. I'll get the rifle," Reed whispered, and he
hustled soundlessly backward. Tressie decided not to un-
cover her eyes. Every inch of her skin crawled until she
itched with the need to flee. She imagined a towering,
painted savage standing over her. Did they hack away the
scalp before or after they ravaged a woman?

Somewhere behind her the rifle went off with a tremendous *ka-whoom* that made the air thump against her
eardrums. Tressie screeched, Reed shouted, and she

scrabbled as fast as she could into a stand of scrub nearby to hide.

She could hear him muttering, "Damn, damn, damn," but waited, afraid to breathe or open her eyes or wiggle a finger or toe.

After a second or two, she heard, "Tressie? Where the hell are you, girl? I think I got him. Could you go look?"

"In here," she squeaked, and waved a hand into the open. "You go look. I'm afraid."

"Afraid of what, a dead deer? What are you doing in there? Oh, hell. You were right about that goddamned gun. Kicked the thunder out of me. Over there, girl, on the far bank, a mule deer. I think I hit him."

Tressie crept from hiding to see Reed sprawled on his back rubbing at his shoulder. She ran to him. "You okay?"

His grin was one of chagrin. "Got too excited, I guess. Let her kick the hell out of me. 'Course I'm okay. Git on over there. He might be on the move. Sometimes they do. Oh, Lord, can't you just taste the venison now? Hurry. I'm coming."

Tressie didn't stay to watch him struggle to his feet, but high stepped it through the shallow creek, already imagining the juicy flavor of a venison steak roasted over hot coals.

Tressie's experience at cleaning large game came in mighty handy that evening. Together she and Reed hoisted the young doe up by her hind legs, securing the swaying body to a good-sized tree branch. Reed produced a long-bladed knife, which Tressie used to remove the musk gland from inside the rear leg. She slit open the belly of the deer with a precision that made Reed stare in wonderment.

"Lord, girl. Where'd you learn to do that?"

She shrugged, trying to act unconcerned, but inside she swelled with pride. It was time she carried her weight in this venture.

"Go get the cooking vessel for the heart and liver, and you might as well build us a fire, too," she told him.

He threw her a cocky salute and marched off. They were both feeling pretty good, what with the prospect of a meal of fresh venison on top of their luck at finding water.

It was after dark before the meat was cooked. Tressie and Reed sat facing the fire and ate with their fingers from chunky cuts of venison he sawed off with the shiny knife.

Tressie fingered a piece off the tip. "Where'd you get the knife?" she asked.

"Off the dead man," Reed said, and speared a hunk of meat into his mouth.

Tressie gulped, the meat seeming to grow in her mouth. She gagged and made a valiant effort at swallowing the chunk of venison, but it wouldn't go down. Her stomach roiled. Hand over her mouth, she leaped up and ran for the woods, where she dropped to her knees and lost every bite of the delicious supper. Moaning, Tressie leaned against a tree and wiped her face. Reed was coming after her, his boots crunching through the leaves, and she felt ashamed. How foolish to be such a baby.

He knelt beside her, put an arm around her shoulders. "You okay? Too rich for you, I guess. Should have taken it easy. Ate too fast."

Let him think that if he wanted, she decided. It was better than the truth that she was just too queasy to handle eating from a dead man's knife blade.

He helped her up. "Come on, wash your face and get a drink. You can probably eat a little if you go slow and easy."

"I guess," she said, and went with him, but she was unable to eat any more of the venison. "Maybe tomorrow. Too bad it's so hot; the rest will spoil, I suppose."

Reed stirred and rose to his feet.

"Where you going?" Tressie asked.

"I'm gonna make us some jerky to take along. We'll take a cut or two of the meat as well. We can eat on it till it grows hair, then start on the dried stuff. Half-rotten venison never hurt anyone, I don't suppose."

Tressie had eaten her share of rotten meat. It was done when there was no other choice. That was just the way things were. She knew also that she would not suffer from her earlier revulsion again. It had been a momentary thing, brought about as much by eating too much rich meat on an empty stomach as anything.

Reed sloshed back across the creek carrying the other rear haunch from the mule deer. Squatting, he carved out a hefty chunk and began slicing around and around the piece of meat until he had a long, narrow, and unbroken strip of the brownish red flesh. He spread it across the branches of a nearby fallen tree. Then he cut and laced green limbs together into a drying rack, which he propped so that the smoke from the fire would filter through it. As he hung the meat, he said, "I don't do this as good as my grandmother, but it'll do. Now let's take a look at what you gleaned from the wagon."

Together they went through their windfall. The clothing was probably the most valuable find. Several pairs of britches and shirts, some woolen socks, a couple of full-skirted dresses, and a pair of bloomers. Tressie had mixed emotions about someone else's tragedy being their saving grace.

"Why didn't the Indians take these?" she asked.

"Indians? It wasn't an Indian attack."

"Well, then. What killed them? And what happened to their animals?"

He sharpened a small twig and picked at meat caught between his teeth. "Run off, I guess, or maybe a wandering band did take the animals. But I don't think so. They'd have taken the geegaws. The pots and clothes, this knife." He held up the blade, catching reflections from the fire that shot across the dark clearing.

Tressie waited for him to explain the dead couple. The aroma of cooking meat hovered around the campsite as the wind laid for the night. From the dark tree branches, a dove cooed and settled in. Still Reed kept his silence.

"What killed them, Reed?" she finally asked.

"A sickness," he said real low.

"Oh, God," Tressie clutched a pair of socks under her chin, ran her fingers over the quilt she'd spread out to sit on. A quilt that had once covered those two poor souls buried in a strange land with no family to mourn their passing. She wondered where they came from, if someone back home envisioned their loved ones living in the promised land. How dreadful. She cleared her throat, dropped the socks, and got up. An early waning moon appeared with languid grace and spread a mantle of silver across the land.

Reed glanced at her, his eyes gleaming unspoken questions she was afraid had no answers. At least not any she could give.

Rather than try, she whispered huskily, "I have to take a bath. No snakes this time, please. Just come with me." She reached down toward him, felt a great rush of warm desire as his hand closed over hers and he rose to his feet beside her.

Five

Reed sat on the bank to remove his boots, watching Tressie as if in a trance. What they were about to do was wrong, but he could no more stop himself than he could wish the golden moon out of the night sky into her arms. And the way she focused those moss-green eyes so deliberately on him, he knew she felt the same. It was like falling off a cliff. After the final step there would be no going back and nothing to grab hold of, and they had both made that step. He had no idea what had changed between them, what had removed the barriers. Maybe they just needed to celebrate being alive.

Tressie kicked off her shoes and took his hand. Even now, after he'd removed his boots, she feared he would back away from her. Together they waded into the cold water fully clothed. The stream bed was littered with smooth stones, some slick with moss. She grabbed at his arm to keep from falling.

Near a cutback of gravel, the unceasing flow of water had hollowed out a basin in the bedrock, and they came together there. The gentle rush of the whispering stream caressed her breasts, puckering the nipples. He cupped them in the palms of his hands.

Soon it will be too late to stop this, Reed thought, but he wanted her in every way. Today, tomorrow, and always. With an enormous sigh, he bent to her, lips slightly parted. Awash in desire, Tressie met the kiss with complete abandon. The mountains and the rising moon watched; the water murmured softly.

His hands swept upward to unhitch the galluses of the overalls she wore, and they slipped off. His fingers fumbled with the buttons of her shirt, and she enfolded his hands in hers. Inching back, Tressie slowly raised her eyes to meet his smoldering gaze. He brushed at her cheek, a question in the dark eyes.

She nodded. "Let me," she said, and began to undo his shirt, finally skinning it off his shoulders. The sinewy curves of his arms and chest gleamed in the moonlight. With trembling fingers Tressie combed the black locks away from one side of his angular face and kept her hand there, entwined.

"Girl, we ought not to do this," he said, but turned to bury his lips in her palm. His breath was warm, his tongue raspy against her skin.

"Oh, yes, yes, we ought." Tressie unfastened the familiar belt buckle and shoved his pants down into the water, fingers lingering between his thighs.

Nearly blind with desire, he struggled awkwardly with her shirt, finally ripping the fragile material. It came away in shreds, leaving her erect young breasts bobbing in the current, pale skin exposed to the soft glow of moonlight. Bodies water-slicked to a petal softness, they eased into an embrace. Both sighed, then cried out in their ecstasy of coming together. Up on the bank the fire crackled, and a whiff of smoke curled their way.

Reed tasted of her deeply, the flesh of her shoulders, throat, chin, ears. She felt him rise against her and knew that this time their lovemaking would be for real, not some fumbling attempt by a wounded man and a desperate girl. He wanted her, Tressie could feel the urgency of his desire down to the fingertips of his broad hands kneading at her back. A heated passion cloaked them safely in an imaginary cocoon.

Hands spanning her waist, he lifted her out of her overalls, holding her close. She locked her legs around his waist, their bodies molding together as if they had long ago been cut from one piece and were at last being put back together. He tried to be easy with her and the sharp pain of penetration faded as he waited for her to relax. She cried out and began to move with him so he could tell it was all right. The water cradled them; the moon and stars looked on.

Buried in her warm sweetness, he carried her from the creek. Kicking his britches from around both ankles, he knelt on the quilt beside the fire. Tumbling, their gleaming limbs tangled in the throes of their passion. Her lithe young body begged for more. In her first love's passion and loneliness, Tressie reached into the very soul of the man who had literally saved her from death. She would keep him with her always. Him and only him. Gone was all the memory of the very reason they were together in this wilderness. Gone the fears and doubts.

They slept wrapped together, naked limbs entwined like young animals.

He awoke just at dawn, but Reed couldn't arise without disturbing Tressie. She slept soundly, making soft purring

noises as she breathed. So he lay there, one arm trapped
under her head, thighs pinned by one of her legs. He considered the possibility of simply carrying her away with
him. Heading in the opposite direction, away from Bannack. And then what? Some soldier would find them, or
Reed would spot a familiar face, and he'd be off like the
coward he was. He had absolutely nothing to offer her.
He'd been a wanderer all his life, turning tail and running
at the first sign of trouble. Her father had been like that.
Why complicate things further?

He sensed her watching him and looked to see sleep-
smoked green eyes. "You look sad," she said, putting the
tip of one finger to his chin. "What is it?"

Unwinding, he tossed his head so that dark hair tumbled into his eyes. Tressie watched him shove it back impatiently, and sensed his withdrawal, his uncertainty.
"What's wrong, Reed?" she asked, and sat up. The quilt
fell from her naked breasts, but she ignored that. The be-
reft look on his face warned her that something was
wrong; she just couldn't figure out what.

"I'm sorry about . . . about last night."

"Sorry?" she echoed, hurting down in her chest.

He nodded, turned away from the sweet beauty of her.
"Put some clothes on." His voice sounded rougher than he
had intended and he regretted the tears that sprung to her
eyes.

Disappointment turned to anger and Tressie scrambled
away, dragging the pack of clothing with her into the
brush. She chose a dress salvaged from the wagon of the
dead family. It hung loosely and dragged on the ground so
that she had to lift the skirt to stomp barefoot into the
clearing. He wasn't going to do this to her! She'd given

him her own true self, something no other man had had. Wisely, Reed had made himself scarce so she couldn't tell him so. Just like a man.

By the time he returned, her initial fury had turned into a somber pout and she did her best to ignore him.

He held up a dripping wad of clothing. "Found these washed up on the bank down creek a ways, but they'll dry." He sorted out her overalls and his shirt, hanging them on the low limbs of a tree. "Sorry about your shirt. It must have washed away."

Tressie glared at him. How could he be so casual about something that had meant so much to her? Was he really just a rounder, a thief or worse?

Reed studied her face, pretty even when she drew it up in such a fierce frown. This wasn't going to be easy. She wanted what she wanted, and worried about the consequences later, if at all. Right now, he supposed she wanted him. Well, he wanted her, too, but had a little better sense about it than she did. One day she would thank him. Meanwhile, he tried to lighten the mood. "You look like a little girl in her mother's clothes," he said, and laughed when she tossed her head and stumbled on the hem of the dress in her haste to turn away. "We'll stay here a day or two before heading into the mountains. Rest up."

"Whatever you say," she snapped.

And that's the way it went that day and the next. They spent their nights sleeping apart on opposite sides of the fire. Tressie was glad when he told her they would leave the next morning. Traveling with his silences was much easier than remaining in one place with them.

She arose early the morning they were to leave, dressed

hastily in pants and shirt, and prepared johnnycakes for breakfast. They ate in total silence, each avoiding the other's gaze. Reed busied himself with the packs they would carry, and Tressie took the water pouch to the creek. Dumping what was left of the water—it had tasted brackish and old—she rinsed the container thoroughly before immersing it in the crystal stream. Bubbles floated to the surface, making small gurgling noises as the container filled. After fitting in the stopper, she lay the pouch safely on the bank and leaned forward to drink deeply. The icy sweet liquid tasted better than the finest apple cider or grape squeezings Grammy ever produced.

She raised her head and gazed toward the craggy mountains that cut into the indigo morning sky. The air smelled vaguely of granite and soil and pine forests, all tinged with the sweet smoke from their campfire. Arching her back, she stretched both arms, then ran the flat of her hands over her unbound breasts. Fingers curled loosely in her lap, she thought she could feel him there still, deep in that dark and wonderful secret place, all hot and wet and sweet. Pulses of desire kicked through her and she closed her eyes a moment. Damn him for making her feel so good and then turning away.

Reed hung back in the trees and quietly watched Tressie for a moment. The sight of her took his breath away. The pale golden light of early morning and the ugly clothing blurred her shape, but he could imagine each soft curve as if she wore nothing. She appeared as unreal as a dream. He smothered a desire to go to her, hold her close, tell her how he felt. It was no use, and he shook his head vigorously. What a fool he was. Wanting a woman he couldn't have because he didn't have the good sense to be a real man.

The sun continued its climb into the sky, and it was time they left. With an impatient backward glance, Reed returned to the campsite. Angry at his own weaknesses, he strapped on the bulkier of the two packs he had fashioned from the Army blanket. He would carry that plus his heavily laden saddlebags and the rifle.

Tressie surveyed the larger pack on his back while she pulled on socks and shoes. "I carry my own weight," she said, and hefted the smaller one. She grunted. "Ooof, it's heavy."

Reed squinted at her. She was speaking to him again, anyway. "They both are; mine's just lumpier. We'll take turns with the water pouch. That suit you?" His eyes sparked as he cast a questioning glance in her direction.

"I suppose. What's that smell?"

"Well, it ain't me," Reed said. "I bathed with you, remember?"

She ignored his teasing. It wasn't going to be that easy to get back in her good graces. "It smells like rotten meat."

"Not yet it ain't. It'll go over quick, but we can eat on it awhile. You've got it in your poke. Sorry, it just worked out that way. Once it starts to making us sick, we'll leave it for the varmints."

Tressie screwed up her face.

"It beats starving, girl, and I didn't come this far to do that. That's pretty desolate country yonder." He swung an arm up the slopes of the craggy mountains. "Nothing much lives there that's fit to eat."

Neither, thought Tressie, is rotten deer meat, but she didn't say anything. He'd kept them alive this long.

"What about the water? Will this be enough?" She held up the leather pouch with its wide shoulder strap.

"It'll have to be. It'll get heavy. We'll trade it off if you need to," he said. "Or, if you can't handle it, I'll take it."

Tressie jutted her jaw at him, dropped the wide belt over her head, and snugged the pouch under the opposite arm. He had to help her adjust the blanket pack and shrug into the loops he'd fashioned. He tried not to touch any part of her, not the satiny soft skin nor the downy wisps of gleaming red hair.

While he was kicking sand over the smoldering campfire, she heard him mutter, "Stubborn little colt," in a tone she thought to be regretful.

Tressie soon learned why Reed had insisted on a two-day stay to rest up before beginning their journey into the rugged foothills. Even when the land appeared flat the going was rough.

Once she remarked about that feeling and Reed laughed uproariously. "From here on out, everything's uphill. And if it's not, that's only because you're fixing to really climb."

Fear of the unknown made it impossible for Tressie to remain coldly aloof to her traveling companion. He was her protector if not her lover, she had to admit that. They were, after all, the only humans within hundreds of miles. Or so she hoped. It was hard not to imagine savage Indians around every bend.

They stopped to rest when the sun was high. As they sat against an outcropping of enormous boulders to chew on tough jerky, she asked, "Have you been out here before? I mean, because you seem to be so easy about everything."

Reed contemplated her question for a long time, as he always did. Staring off at the distant snow-capped peaks, he watched the young boy in his memories, mounted and riding faster than the prairie winds. Black hair flying, heels locked against the horse's sides, lithe body a part of the animal he rode. The Sioux were the finest horsemen alive. No one could best them. Once, not many years ago, he had heard a general call the Sioux "the greatest light cavalry in the world." How Reed wished he had a horse now.

He tossed his head and sharpened the images of the mountains to blot out those of so long ago. Those days, like all the others to follow, were gone forever. He no longer thought like an Indian, if he ever had. Perhaps there was no place for him, for he found life in the white world equally impossible.

He swung his head around finally and stared back the way they had come to answer her question. "Spent some time around Fort Laramie, but it was a long time ago, before I decided I was man enough to go east to help fight that crazy war. 'Course things here ain't changed much yet. They will, though, once folks get their minds off fighting and start moving west." He chewed thoughtfully. "No man will ever tame these mountains, though. Even the Indian makes of them sacred ground so they have good reason for not coming here."

"Then why don't we go on down to the Oregon Trail? It'd be a lot easier."

"We're headed to Grasshopper Creek, and that's north of here. North of Fort Laramie, too. No sense in going down to that place. You wouldn't like it anyway. We'll get through all right. Lots of men have. Special kinds of men. Mountain men, trappers, Indian holy men, the like. I got just enough of all kinds to see us through. Don't worry."

Tressie decided she never would find out why he shied away from any place there might be people. She herself wouldn't have minded visiting civilization once in a while.

Seeing snow on the higher mountain peaks surprised her, for it was most surely July by now. What would this country be like come winter? She prayed she wouldn't have to find out, but wondered if they would ever reach their destination.

Soon they began to spot enormous boulders layered one upon the other like peculiar growths. Reed pointed out copper-colored brush—mountain mahogany, he said—that grew in profusion. Once again he made cactus a part of their diet. Tressie never managed to consume the rank-flavored juice without making a face. It had such an odd, gingery flavor. Not at all like ginseng or sassafras tea.

"Swallow as much as you can," he said when she puckered her lips shut. "It's good for you. You won't take the blackleg."

Tressie did as he told her, regarding him with renewed respect. "What's the blackleg?" she asked, wiping her lips and watching him tilt back his head to drip the liquid into his open mouth.

"It's what happens when you don't eat enough cactus juice," he quipped.

"Do your legs really turn black?"

"Yep, after you suffer all sorts of other awful things. You get sores all over, you can't be up and around no time without wearing plumb out, and finally your legs turn black."

"Then what happens?" Tressie asked, eyes wide. He surely was teasing her, though she did know that there were some dreadful maladies just waiting to strike down perfectly healthy folks.

"You die," he said, and gulped down the final squeezings.

That so distressed Tressie that Reed changed the subject, all the while pulling his long hair into a tail at the back of his head and tying it with a length of rawhide.

"Longer we stay out here, the hairier we get," he said. "Might need to get haircuts, both of us." He rubbed at the full-blown beard. "Was I pure Indian, I wouldn't have to worry about growing face hair like this."

She dodged and laughed when he tousled her own wild locks. Despite the funning, she couldn't forget what he'd said about black leg. Tressie didn't want to die of anything, and certainly not something that turned your legs black, so she silently vowed from then on to drink the foul cactus juice every day.

The next night, following a grueling day of climbing after which Reed complained that they had only made five miles, Tressie awoke with cramps in her stomach, a swimming head, and burning with fever. No change of position eased the pain. She felt as if she were lying on one of those craggy outcroppings they'd struggled over the day before. Fear that she had the dreaded black leg disease made her numb with terror. She lay in total misery the rest of the night, alternately shivering with cold and burning up. When the cramps intensified, she stuffed a fist into her mouth to keep her moaning from awakening Reed.

Just at dawn he arose to wander away from the camp and relieve himself. When he came back, he called out to Tressie, "Up and at 'em, girl."

She shifted and groaned. "I can't. Oh, I hurt."

He knelt beside her and touched the back of his hand to her forehead. His dark eyes clouded and he stared off into the distance. Dear Lord, don't let it be, he prayed silently.

"I'll be okay," she whispered. "Just let me rest is all. Probably that old cactus juice, or that stinking deer meat."

He met her feeble attempt at humor with a solemn stare and a shake of his head.

Hit by another bout of intensely sharp pains, Tressie grasped her stomach and cried out. Gazing up into Reed's rugged features, which were wrinkled in concern, she imagined the sensual visage when they'd made love. Smiling at her, fine lips moving in silent words, dark eyes swimming with desire.

She reached up a trembling hand, cupped the bearded jaw, and gasped, "Oh, Reed, I've missed you so. Where have you been?" The welcome darkness swallowed her, but his name followed her into its depths.

Reed caught at the small hand and held it to his lips. They hadn't made love since leaving the creek campsite. Harsh reality kept coming between them. But neither had spoken of it since their argument down by the river. She looked so frail. God, he hoped she didn't die.

He knew he had to get Tressie to shelter of some kind where he could take care of her properly. He feared she had cholera, which was almost always fatal, but he had seen people live through it. He had to try. So he fashioned a travois of birch and alder, bound her and the supplies to it, and stepped into the harness.

Tressie lapsed into a frightening world where she pursued a man who looked and sounded like Papa, until he turned around to reveal fangs and drooling lips, head as bald as river stones. At times, when she was rational, there would be cool water on her brow and at her lips. She occasionally awoke to a jarring that bruised her down to the bone. Strapped into some kind of contraption, she was being dragged along. Once she remembered screaming for Papa to help her. Oh, how she needed him to save her from this torturous treatment, take her back home to Missouri so she could see Mama again.

All day Reed Bannon pulled the heavy travois. He pulled until every muscle ached, until his vision was clouded with weariness. Still he searched for a place where he could keep her cool and sheltered from the elements. Nights in the mountains were often wet and frigid. Sudden summer storms could drench the countryside. Before he found the trapper's cabin, he had begun to think he was back in the war. He began to have visions of stumbling through the dead and dying, heard their pitiful cries for mercy. Even when he spotted the cabin, his thinking had become so muddled from exhaustion that at first he saw no way to get her to it.

The crude shack clung to an outcropping on a trail that appeared to lead straight up the mountain's face. Its back into the bluffs, the cabin formed a fort of sorts, a place in which to stand off marauding man or beast. Despite its inaccessibility, the poor structure had four walls and a roof. Just what he needed if he were to save Tressie's life.

Water was another thing he would need, and a spring flowed beside the path, obviously born high up in the mountains.

Reed set down the travois gently. For a long while he stood there, stooped and contemplating, bringing himself back to full reality. He couldn't drag the travois up the narrow goat trail; it was too hazardous. He would have to carry her and all the supplies, which would mean at least three trips up and down the treacherous path. He was exhausted, spent to the point of collapse. Would this be where he finally failed Tressie?

From somewhere behind the mountain peak, thunder rumbled in ominous persistence. The breeze shifted, turned colder. He had to get her up there, and now. Before it rained. Failure could result in her death, something he wasn't willing to face.

Stumbling to her side, Reed untied the strips of rawhide he'd laced over her and the quilt wrappings.

She rolled her head, murmured, "Mama . . . Papa."

He touched her skin with the back of his hand. Burning up! He tried not to think that she was calling for another man who had failed her. After two awkward attempts, he managed to lift her while keeping the quilt over her feverish thin body. In his arms she seemed so tiny and helpless, and he became terrified of losing her, of standing helplessly by while the disease snatched her away. He didn't consider that she wasn't his to lose.

"Ah, Tressie," he whispered, eyes stinging with unshed tears. Her head tucked under his chin burned a fiery spot in his flesh.

A gust of cold, wet wind danced around the edges of the mountain crags, hitting him full in the face as he began his climb. He had to go slowly, placing each foot and testing the safety before taking his next step. If he started to slip, nothing would stop the both of them from tumbling over the precipice.

Rocks shifted and spilled from the edge of the trail, and he could no longer see his feet in the falling darkness. Time and again he had to stop and rest, leaning elbows against the steep incline to keep from dropping her. He tried to think of happier times, better times, but what haunted him were Tressie's huge eyes the way they had looked early that morning when she awoke and told him she was sick. They'd been filled with a fear he'd never seen there before. Not even the day they forded the Loup had she looked so scared. She thought she was going to die, and he couldn't let that happen.

One more step and Reed reached the cutback in the rocks where the cabin slouched. He fell against the sagging plank door and went to his knees inside, clutching her in desperation. The cabin was worse than he had thought. He had hoped for something in occasional use by a mountain trapper, but what he found was a deserted hovel. It stank of the droppings of various tenants. He had to chase out a family of pack rats. All other occupants had flown or fled with the opening of the door.

Reed had no choice but to lay Tressie on the floor. He would bring up the rest of their supplies first. Then he could get the place cleaned up enough to fashion her a bed near a crude mud fireplace at the back of the hut. He kicked away some rubble and lowered her gently, being careful to cover her before going down for the packs.

The next time Tressie regained consciousness it was to the view of a cobwebbed roof. She tried to turn her head and look around, but the slightest movement caused her head to pound thunderously. She squeezed her eyes shut and lay very still until the waves of pain passed. Swallowing tentatively, she opened one eye and let out a feeble croak, calling out to she knew not who.

A great shadow shut off the glare of sunlight pouring in the doorway and she covered her eyes with one hand to avoid the monster of her nightmares. A far-off cry came to her ears. Who had made that feeble sound? Was it the child? He needed nursing, and Mama was . . . "Mama, oh, Mama, ooo."

With one trembling hand she fumbled between her breasts, intending to unbutton her dress, but there was nothing but bare skin under a thin quilt. A warm wet cloth lay over her abdomen. She shoved the covers down with the flats of her hands, baring both breasts. "No, don't die. The baby's coming. See him? You mustn't die. Who will feed the baby?"

Reed stood in the doorway a moment longer, then crossed the room to her side. A blinding shaft of sunlight threw his features into shadow as he approached the bed where she lay. He wanted to gather her into his arms, but instead dropped to his knees, and with gentle fingers pulled the quilt up to cover her breasts. He remembered tasting of those lovely nipples, rosy, sweet, and burning with passion.

Tressie licked at dry, split lips. They stung. "Papa? Have you seen Papa?"

Sadly he shook his head, produced a water-soaked cloth and moistened her mouth. "You're gonna be okay, Tressie."

She remembered then in a rending flash like lightning

crashing across the prairie. "Reed? Where are we? What happened to me?"

Instead of answering her questions, he rose and went across the room to ladle her a bowl of broth from a simmering pot.

Sitting on the floor beside her, he blew on the spoonful of steaming liquid, then tilted drops into her mouth. After a few swallows, she clamped her lips and turned her head away.

"Good, that was good," Reed said, and wiped her mouth carefully. "You'll take more later."

Despite all the unanswered questions Tressie had, she dropped off to sleep. When she awoke again, darkness had closed in around the cabin, lit only by a small fire at the hearth. She was alone, and that frightened her terribly. It would be better to run away and hide somewhere, but she was too weak to get out of bed. She rubbed the palms of her hands over her cool skin. Naked. Naked under the covers. Who had taken off her clothes? And where was everybody? Mama, Papa? No, Reed. Reed Bannon, who had dragged her across the high plains and saved her life as she had once saved his.

The sound of his voice, his words falling soft and gentle on her soul, came as if through a dream. She recalled with sweet clarity the night they had made love. The water cold, their desire hot. His mouth warm and moist. His hardness so gently breaking the shell of her womanhood. Then nothing. He hadn't touched her again, despite them being thrown together in bath and bed night after night on the long trek. Tears leaked from the corners of her eyes, as if she were mourning a great loss.

Very carefully she rolled her head to look toward the

door. Crude skins of some kind hung over the opening that earlier had been uncovered. Except for the glow from a small fire it was dark in the room. Without a sound to warn of his coming, Reed pushed the skins aside and came in. Tressie bit at the back of her hand to keep from screaming.

"Awake again? Hungry?" he asked.

"You were gone. I was afraid." Though her voice was stronger, it still didn't sound like hers.

"Nonsense," Reed admonished, and dipped out another bowl of soup, this time adding a few chunks to the broth. "Since when are you afraid of anything, Tressie Majors?"

Something about the curt tone in his voice warned Tressie that things weren't as they had been before her illness, but she didn't catch on right away. She ate the entire bowl of soup.

"Think you can get up?" he asked when she had finished.

She tried to lift her arms and legs, shook her head. Not possible, too weak.

"Then I'll carry you," he said, and scooped her from the bed, quilt and all. "We're gonna get some of the stink blowed off you," he told her, and she heard the grin in his words, though she couldn't see his face.

He was just the same, after all. Tressie locked her arms firmly around his thick neck. Outside the door she gulped in a deep breath and gazed around at glistening stars in the vast purple-velvet sky. Far to the west hung a sliver of moon, so thin and fine as to be almost invisible. Cradled in its curve rested a bold star.

"Look at that, Tressie," Reed said, turning so she could

see it better. "Old man moon holding that bright young'un safe and sound. He'll come to no harm, I'd wager."

He lowered his head and made a choking sound down deep in his throat, and she felt the heat of his breath through the quilt on her bare flesh. Goose bumps raised and she tightened her thin arms around his neck.

Reed breathed in the scent of her illness, which was driven back now, defeated. She would not die, and he'd wager she would be wanting a bath soon. The notion made him grin despite his sorrow at losing her to something stronger than cholera. "Better get you back inside, girl. Just wanted you to see the world didn't go anywhere while you were away."

He had her back in bed before she asked, "How long, Reed? How long was I sick?"

"I kept track of the days, scratched 'em on the wall there." He grinned his full and familiar grin. "Somehow knew you'd want to know. Let's see here, there's five, six, eight marks all told. 'Course I didn't start them till I got you here, and that took all of a day and into the night. Reckon that makes nine or ten days and nights of fever." He turned his back on her for a moment and pawed at the floor with one foot. "I thought you were going to die there for a while." Then he faced her. "Should have known better than that, though, girl. You are tough as rawhide."

"What was it, do you know? Not blackleg?" She couldn't keep the quivering from her own voice.

"No, girl. Not that. Can't know for sure, without a doctor, but I'd say you had cholera, bad as it was."

Tressie clenched both hands over her mouth. "A miracle I'm still alive. You saved my life, Reed, you surely did."

"It was the water. I should have known better when we found them folks and buried them. Taking their water pouch . . . stupid, stupid. I plain didn't think. They must of got some bad water on their travels, some was still in the pouch, and we just filled it from the blamed creek and come on. That's the only way I can account for it. I burned the blamed thing in the fire."

Tressie felt her eyelids sinking, but she wanted to watch Reed longer. The way he paced when agitated, the way he threw his hair back from his face before gazing at her. He was looking more and more like the Indian that he was. His mother's tribe, the Dakota Sioux, had left their mark on him. She wanted to listen to the deep vibrating tones of his voice, lulling her into a security she'd never known with anyone else. But she couldn't stop the blackness from descending. This night she slept without dreams that she could recall and awoke feeling a great cleanness deep in her chest.

After breakfast he took her outside again, this time leaving her on a huge boulder near the cabin while he refreshed her sickbed. After he went back inside, Tressie unfolded the quilt and exposed her pale naked body to the warmth of the morning sun. She could then take in their surroundings, and what she saw made her gasp in wonderment. At her feet, stretching for miles, lay the country over which they had traveled. Cactus and golden and copper scrub and scraggly pine scattered amid building-sized boulders. A narrow and steep path with a treacherous drop along one side led up to the cabin. And at their back door rose the majestic mountains. All purples and blues and umbers, capped in a pure white snow that glistened brazenly in the warm summer sun.

Heat from the sun's rays lulled her and she leaned back on her arms, closing her eyes. He came upon her like that, and studied every curve and line of her before he spoke, trying to memorize them for later when they parted.

"Are you tired yet?" he finally asked, startling her into a tiny squeak of surprise. He gazed, as she had earlier, out across the vast panorama, a look of pure wonderment on his face.

"You frightened me," she whispered when she realized her bare body was exposed to him, if he cared to look.

"I didn't mean to. You ought to . . . I think it would be a good idea if you . . . Aw, hell, I'll just go back inside and leave you be till you're ready to come in. And would you put that dang thing over yourself before you call me back out here?"

Tressie watched him go, glanced down at her bony white body, and giggled. Not much there to look at, that was for sure.

That night she sat wrapped in the quilt, knees drawn up under her chin. "Could we stay here awhile, Reed? It's so nice having a roof and walls and a door. I can turn over in my bed without worrying about laying on a rattler or a scorpion."

He shrugged from where he sat cross-legged nearby. "No matter to me. You won't be fit to travel for a spell yet. It's you wants to find your Papa, not me. I got no place in particular to go."

"Why is that, Reed?" Tressie asked.

"Why is what?"

"Why is it that you have no place to go? Why did we cross country in the wilds like we did, instead of going on down to the Platte and the Oregon Trail? You still scared of the Army?"

He tucked his chin and appeared to study the floor. " 'Course not, girl. Don't be foolish. I just don't like people. See what happened to us when we come upon some that had already passed on? You come down with a sickness. Happens every time. Folks carry all kinds of sickness of the mind and body and spirit. Man's better off alone."

"Well, a woman ain't. A woman likes company."

"You got company."

She nodded and smiled at him. "And you're not alone."

He rose effortlessly, not uncrossing his ankles until he stood upright. Be damned if he was going to do what he was aching to do. Take that little girl in his arms and . . . But he couldn't even think of such. He said, instead, "And I think tomorrow you better put you on some clothes. Now that you're feeling so pert and sassy." He got out of there fast. No sense tempting fate.

Tressie didn't take well to Reed's leaving her to her own devices, in fact was downright angry about it. She fussed around the cabin, decided to air the bedding and the spare clothing, and was unrolling Reed's meager belongings when she found the exquisite deerskin pouch. It was wrapped carefully in brown paper and tied with a thong. Curiosity immediately got the best of her. And besides, he shouldn't have taken off like he did. Serve him right if she got nosy.

On unwrapping it Tressie gasped and gently touched

her cheek to the velvety feel of the fine leather. It smelled of tobacco and another elusive fragrance not unlike apples. An intricate beadwork design decorated one side of the small pouch, and stitched into the bottom were the initials RB, followed by a very unusual set of marks not unlike a brand in the vague shape of a tepee overcast by an arrow.

Tressie studied the small pouch, but could only guess at its significance. Probably belonged to Reed's Sioux mother, but why the RB? His initials. Perhaps she had fashioned it for him. But Reed said he had left the Sioux before his thirteenth birthday. Could he have carried this throughout all those years and even during the war, keeping it so well preserved?

She loosened the top and looked inside. Empty. How very curious. With a great deal of care she rewrapped the deerskin pouch in its brown paper and replaced the thong, trying to tie it in the precise same way. This was obviously something very important to Reed Bannon, and she tucked it back where she'd found it.

Tressie soon exhausted the few cleaning chores around the cabin. So when Reed continued to remain away from the cabin during the daylight hours, she began exploring. During the forays she wore men's britches and shirts because of their comfort and the ease with which she could scramble around on the goat trails. She was thusly dressed, her disreputable old hat crammed over her mop of hair, when she stepped around a sharp curve in the lower trail that led away from the cabin, right into the path of an Indian woman astride a small horse. Before Tressie could turn tail and run, a man's voice boomed out at her.

"You stay put, mister, or you'll be dealing with the wrath of the Lord. Move even to blink, and I'll blow your head clean off."

Tressie did exactly as the voice ordered. She stayed put.

Six

If the Indian woman astride the pony hadn't put an end to the standoff by letting out the most godawful holler, Tressie might have remained fixed to that same spot for an eternity. She had no wish to have her head blown off, and even if she might have chanced that, she was frozen stiff with fear. But the shrill ululating cry that came from the squaw sent Tressie kicking up dirt in a speedy retreat. She couldn't help running from the savage noise, even though all the while she expected a ball from the unseen man's gun to smash into the back of her head.

Running like mad, Tressie fetched up at the cabin, made a wide, almost uncontrolled turn, and threw herself inside. Seeking the darkest corner, she huddled there and listened. It was impossible to control her harsh breathing. Most surely the wild man would hear and blow her to hell, as promised.

After a while, when nothing happened, she reined in her galloping imagination. He'd mistaken her for a man. Maybe if she hurried and put on a dress he wouldn't kill her.

No, of course not. Not right away. First he'd ravage her. Tressie shuddered and hugged herself. He must be as big as a grizzly by the sound of his voice. And where was Reed, anyway? The very idea, leaving her all alone out here in this wilderness to face such dangers as wild Indian women and their giant protectors.

Just as she summoned up enough courage to creep to the door and take a look around, she heard laughter, the soft plodding of a horse, and men's voices. Coming closer, the words remained indistinguishable. Some kind of foreign lingo, she guessed. The woman said something rather curtly and two men laughed. Two men?

Tressie catapulted across the cabin and raced outside. There stood Reed with an apparition nearly twice his size, head covered all over in hair and fur. Both talking as calm as you please, sizing each other up, like men do on first meeting.

Relieved to learn she would not be shot, Tressie literally threw herself between the two, choosing as a target the large stranger.

Kicking out at his stump-sized legs, she screeched, "He tried to kill me."

"Whoa, lad," the man boomed. With a palm wide as her girth, he held fast to the top of her head so that she flailed away at thin air.

"I'm not a lad." Tressie kept swinging until she was panting.

Reed wrapped an arm around her waist and dragged her out of reach of the man. The Indian woman, who had dismounted from the pony during the fracas, watched in stoic silence, hands clasped under a tremendous belly.

"Behave yourself, Tressie," Reed grated into her ear. "Come on, now, he didn't know you meant no harm. Cool off. You'll hurt yourself."

Dizzy now, she slumped over his arm and gasped for air. He was right. She felt her knees go all wobbly and was grateful that Reed supported her, otherwise she would have fallen flat on her face.

"Okay, that's better," Reed said, but kept the arm around her nevertheless. "It's okay, Dooley, you're safe now. She's tamed."

"A real hellcat, ain't she?" the man called Dooley said. "And to think I mistook her for a lad." Both men laughed uproariously, and if Tressie hadn't been totally winded, she would have taken them on, one at a time or together. As it was, she settled for glaring at the man Reed called Dooley.

He surely had a face under that dusty-colored hair somewhere. She knew from the noise he made there was a mouth in there. Eyes, too, since he obviously could see. He wore a most disreputable outfit: wide-legged pants stuffed down in tall black boots, and a long-tailed jacket, under which there was a sweat-soaked white shirt gone to gray. She wondered why he wore the jacket if he was hot enough to sweat. He carried the longest rifle she'd ever laid eyes on.

"Your woman, I take it," Dooley bellowed. "Kind of peculiar in the eyes of the Lord to see a woman so clothed."

"What do you care?" Tressie gasped.

"Madame, if I hadn't lost my hat over a ravine just this very morning, I'd take it off to you for your sheer spunk."

The broad-faced Indian woman tugged at Dooley's jacket tail and said something in that peculiar tongue that Tressie had heard earlier. All the while her dark eyes watched Tressie with extreme interest.

"She wants to know if they can stay here the night," Reed muttered in Tressie's ear. "What do you think?"

"And get scalped in my sleep? And how do you know what she's saying, anyway?"

"She's Sioux. And not apt to scalp either of us, or anyone else, for that matter."

Tressie met the sloe-eyed stare of the beautiful young woman. Challenging yet anxious. She smiled and turned on Dooley with distrust. "What about him?"

"He says he's a trapper recently called to the cloth."

"What?" Tressie twisted to peer into Reed's face. "He's a trapper and a preacher?"

Reed nodded. "What he says."

"On my way to the gold camps to carry the merciful healing of our Lord to those poor hardworking souls lost to their Creator," Dooley bellowed.

"Sounds like a preacher, all right," Tressie told Reed, as yet unwilling to directly address the bear of a man.

"Well, then, we can surely extend our hospitality, considering this place don't really belong to us anyways. Dooley could just exercise his rights and toss us out."

Tressie gritted her teeth. "Rights? What rights?"

"The rights of the biggest and strongest," Reed answered under his breath.

Tressie contemplated heading for the cabin and the Kentucky rifle. "Just let him try. I'll equalize things."

"Whoa, now, girl. You've had just about all the excitement you need for one day," Reed said with a chuckle. "Dooley, let's just all go inside and we'll stir up a little something for supper. You're welcome, both of you. Ain't they, Tressie?"

Having caught a second wind, Tressie pulled free from

Reed's grasp. "I reckon," she grumbled. "But I hope they have something to add to the pot. He looks like he could eat himself a full-grown bear without burping."

Dooley roared with laughter. "I'd like to know where you got this little gal, Bannon. Seems she's a match for just about anyone."

"He didn't *get* me, Mr. Dooley. I *got* him. You tell your wife she's welcome to come inside and rest a bit, would you?"

Reed spoke softly to the woman, and the words sounded like the trilling of music. He turned to her, eyes alight. "Her name is Bitter Leaf," he said as if presenting Tressie with a new treasure. "And she's going to have a child pretty quick."

"I can see that, Reed Bannon." In spite of her sharp tone, Tressie sympathized with his enjoyment of being among one of his own. She decided that he might be a little proud of his Indian heritage despite claims to the contrary.

Tressie took Bitter Leaf's arm and guided her inside the cabin. She was a fragile little thing with eyes much like Reed's. Deep and dark with faraway mysterious lights. Tressie judged her to be no more than fifteen, though it was difficult to tell with her body so swollen with child. The men didn't follow, leaving the two women on their own.

For several awkward moments both women stood in the middle of the gloomy room eyeing each other, then Tressie gestured toward the crude table Reed had fashioned. There a wooden bowl held red and blue plums picked by Reed the evening before. They were small and tart but very tasty. Tressie dreamed of plum pudding like

Mama used to make, but they had no flour or sugar. Bitter Leaf shyly accepted one of the ruby red fruits and put it to her lips.

"I don't suppose you can understand me," Tressie told her, "but it sure is nice to have another woman around." She reached toward the girl's bulging belly. "My mama lost her young'un not long ago."

Bitter Leaf nodded without comprehension and chewed on her plum, allowing Tressie to spread an open hand on her stomach.

"Oh, my. It's moving a lot." Tressie shook her head vigorously. "Very healthy, I'd guess." She fanned both hands over the girl's stomach. Precious life penned up in there, and it grew impatient.

The girl reached out for a curly lock of Tressie's auburn hair. Then she cupped her hand and opened it wide, smiling.

Tressie nodded eagerly and admired her guest's hair in the same way. Babbling on, though she knew Bitter Leaf didn't understand, Tressie said, "You've never had a child before, have you? And I'll bet you're frightened half out of your wits. Well, I think maybe we should just see that you stay here until this baby is born. No use in you going through this with that galoot of a man out there. Little use he'd be, I'll wager."

Bitter Leaf's answering smile lit up her heart-shaped face and she babbled awhile. Tressie responded by giggling like a girl and Bitter Leaf joined in.

Reed came through the doorway about that time. "Well, I see you two gals are getting along okay. Guess what? Dooley has coffee and some flour and sugar. He'll share it with us for a few days' hospitality. Says he could smell that rabbit stew five miles down the trail. They ain't took the time to campfire cook for three days."

"Reed, her baby is due any day. She ought to stay here till after it's born. That savage out there can't birth this baby. He'll just let her do it on her own, and she's only a child herself."

Reed touched fingers to Tressie's upturned face. "If you don't beat anything, girl." Jerking the hand away, he cleared his throat. "I'll talk to Dooley. I'm sure he'll agree. But Tressie, you need to know she'll probably want to do it her own way, and it's best if you let her. You understand?"

Temporarily distracted by his closeness, she nodded, then mumbled, "Least I can do is hold her hand."

Reed moved away from her, filling her with regret. Ever since her recovery from the sickness, he had been reluctant to come too close to her. He seldom touched her or talked overlong with her. What had happened she had no idea. If she let herself think too much about his coolness, an unexplained sadness welled up, immediately followed by a stirring of anger. Venting either to such a stubborn man would be useless.

That evening over supper, Dooley told a strange and wondrous tale. It certainly explained the relationship between the mountain man and his devoted Indian companion.

He related how he had found Bitter Leaf in a village, the sole survivor of a cholera outbreak. "Everyone left her for dead, those that could leave, anyway. She was most gravely ill when I came across her. I doctored her until she recovered, and now she follows me. Thinks I'm a god or some such."

Even considering the man's unforgivable manners, Tressie decided she could understand how Bitter Leaf might feel.

Dooley slurped down great mouthfuls of rabbit stew before continuing. "That was quite a sight, finding her in that lodge. Her people dressed her for death before they left. She had on new moccasins, her legs were wrapped in scarlet cloth, she was covered in buffalo robes all stitched with porcupine quills."

"When was that? I mean, how long the two of you been together?" Reed asked, sopping out the bottom of his bowl with a biscuit.

"More'n a year ago now, I reckon. I performed the marrying ceremony so we ain't living in sin. Man gets mighty lonely wandering through this vast country by hisself. Itching, if you know what I mean. A woman who can put up with such is a treasure indeed. She's a mite puny and dumb as a rock, but young enough and awful purty, don't you think?"

Tressie watched the girl eat, eyes downcast, and shuddered. How dreadful to think of this man covering that delicate little thing. When she looked away, she caught Reed's gaze holding on her steady.

He took a quick bite of the bread and complimented her on the first baking she'd done for them. She nodded and said nothing.

The men began discussing the gold camps and what was going on in the mad rush the country seemed caught up in.

"It's a sad state of affairs out yonder," Dooley declared waving a great paw toward the door. "Females deserted or left because their man has died, sitting in their wagons weeping. Some holding dead children. Animals starving yoked to the wagon of an entire family of dead folk. Folks throwing their possessions along the side of the trail to lighten their load for the mountain trek, till they get so desperate they have no food or clothing. Some started out with nothing, thinking only of the gold they'd find at the end of the trail. Many knowing nothing about the countryside."

"What's the government doing about it?" Reed asked.

"What do you expect? Nothing, that's what. They could send out some troops, check out the trails, at least show folks the way and help them that's stranded. But they're for the most part caught up in that bloody war. Hell, even before, during the California rush, wasn't any better and there wasn't even no war then. Government men are a bunch a useless varmints, want to know what I think. They's a few private citizens helping out, though."

"What do you hear of the war?" Reed asked.

"Last word I heard, Lee had defeated the Union Army at Chancellorsville, but it cost him dearly. Old Stonewall Jackson met his maker there. Shot by mistake by his own men, I hear. Ain't heard much since, and I reckon that was early on this year. In May, near as I could find out. Been a bit out of touch."

Reed pursed his lips and said nothing.

"Young feller like you, how'd you miss it?" Dooley asked.

Tressie jerked a quick look at him. He sounded threateningly casual, and whatever answer Reed might have Tressie considered his own business. Besides, she was frightened of the unspoken answer to Dooley's question. She interrupted before more could come of the inquiry.

"Reed, we could use some water before dark so I can clean up the supper things. Would you mind?"

Obviously Reed welcomed the change of subject, and he gave her a grateful glance before he headed out for the spring where they'd been getting their water since settling in the cabin. He didn't ask Dooley to go along.

That night Tressie offered the only bed to Bitter Leaf, and after much discussion, only some of which she understood, it was decided she and Bitter Leaf would share the bed and the men would sleep on the floor.

During the week that followed, Tressie decided the two men had come to some kind of an understanding, for all talk was of the gold camps. No one made further mention of the war raging between the North and the South. Instead, the men hunted together, sometimes remaining out all day. She and Bitter Leaf searched for berries and edible roots and herbs known to the Indian woman. And they talked, using a crude sign language that both devised as they went along.

In awkward sign Bitter Leaf told Tressie that she had two older sisters and a brother who would one day be chief of their band. She had lost her mother in the cholera epidemic that had almost claimed her own life. This brought the two women closer together, for Tressie sorely missed her own mama. They exchanged words for "mother" and "family" and "love," and finally "sister," reverting to calling each other that in an affectionate way.

Nearly every day Dooley fetched his "squaw" and led her off to the woods. Tressie figured out what they were doing after Bitter Leaf returned with blood on her deerskin dress. Tressie wanted to kill the brute, sneak up on him in the middle of the night and bludgeon him to death with that gun he carried so proudly, as if it were an extension of his fearsome body.

She feared appealing to Reed. Such things were, after all, nobody's business. All she could do was comfort Bitter Leaf in her misery. She had grown so large with the child, and carried it so low, she could scarcely rise from the bed during the last days before the birth.

There were good times, too. Reed fashioned them all boots of deerskin and lined them with rabbit fur. Tressie cherished hers and knew come winter they would be invaluable.

The two men decided that as soon as the baby came and could handle traveling, the foursome would head northwest across the mountains toward the gold camps. The men could seek their fortunes while Dooley converted sinners, Tressie could search for her father, and Bitter Leaf would care for the child. It was a wonderful plan, according to the men. Tressie and Bitter Leaf saw no choice but to follow along, at least until they reached civilization.

While they awaited the birth, Reed withdrew totally from Tressie's company. Despite their plans, she feared any day to find him gone, leaving her to the mercy of Dooley's wishes.

In truth, Reed couldn't stand being around the two women. Though he approved wholly of their friendship, watching Bitter Leaf recalled to him thoughts of his own mother. The fact that this lovely young Indian woman soon would bear a child made the memories even more painful. Reed hadn't known how much he missed growing up without a mother until the big trapper and his wife showed up. Dooley Kling could well be his own father.

As for Tressie, every time he looked at her he experi-enced the sawtoothed ache of knowing he could never have her. And as she recovered from the ravages of chol-era she grew more and more beautiful. Her skin glowed with a healthy sheen, her hair grew into curls that ca-ressed her shoulders, her forest-green eyes flashed with life. And when she laughed . . . oh, dear God, when she laughed, he thought he would die from wanting her.

So he took to roaming the woods long after the day's game was slain and firewood gathered.

The night Bitter Leaf's baby would come, Tressie lay awake, torn between her excitement over the coming event and being on the way again in search of Papa. The Indian girl made no sound, simply shyly touched Tressie's arm, then slipped from the bed and squatted on the floor. Tressie followed and fetched the birthing bed, unrolling the cloth near the girl, who rocked back and forth with her arms clasped around both knees. A patch of moon-light flooding through the open door threw a grotesque humped shadow onto the wall.

In a flash of painful memory Tressie recalled Mama's birthing. How she had labored, sweated, and howled her anguish, and finally died in a room empty of her man, be-reft of his love. Bitter Leaf would have Tressie's love and support. Tressie knelt beside her and laid a hand on her back.

"There, there, sweet, sweet girl," Tressie crooned. "I'm here." After a while she moistened a cloth in cold water and placed it around Bitter Leaf's neck. The girl made lit-tle noise, just occasionally uttering low, guttural sounds that drifted away as if they'd never been.

By dawn, Tressie was tracking the contractions by the

pattern of small sounds, and knew they were very near the birth. She built up the glowing fire and put on a pot of water.

The clatter awoke both men. Dooley pulled on his boots and jacket—they all slept clothed in the small cabin—grabbed his long rifle, and was out the door. The coward.

While Reed tarried to lace up his hide boots, he watched Tressie's preparations nervously. "Will you be okay, Tressie?"

"Oh, I've delivered a child, if that's what you mean. It's her that might not be all right. We'll do the best we can. Women die doing this."

He flinched as if struck, and she remembered too late what he'd said about his own mother. "I know, Tressie. Can I do anything?"

"I'm sorry, Reed. You could bring some more water, then just keep Dooley out of here. I don't trust him to do her good." She poked another stick in the fire as Bitter Leaf bore down and grunted in earnest.

Indian women obviously were not used to much preparation, and Bitter Leaf had shown Tressie how she planned to birth the baby. Surprisingly it wasn't much different than Tressie had witnessed, except she had used scissors to cut the umbilical cord after tying it off, and Bitter Leaf would bite hers in two.

As the girl strained, sweat pouring off her body and muscles bulging, Tressie knelt in front of her and took her hands. She prayed this birth would be luckier than her mother's. Bitter Leaf pushed and panted and growled her way through each contraction, her face contorting, then going slack. She squeezed Tressie's hands so tightly the bones made cracking sounds.

Reed returned with the water. She sensed his presence before he spoke. "Is everything okay? Do you need anything?"

"She's almost ready. She just has to do this herself. I can only hang on and let her know I'm here. At least she has that."

"Tressie, girl," Reed said, and cupped a hand on the back of her head.

They stayed that way, watching Bitter Leaf, who never once looked up from her labors. When her water broke, it spread in a dark pool across the pine-board floor. Too soon the girl tossed back her head, tendons harsh against the sweaty skin, and let out the only cry she had uttered during the entire episode. She reached between her legs to support the head of the child as it emerged.

"Shouldn't she lie down?" Reed asked, watching in awe.

"This is her way." Tressie kept watch as Bitter Leaf cradled the squirming bloody baby.

"Look at that. Dear Lord, look," Reed said. He wanted to cry with the joy of it, like men weren't supposed to do.

"It's a boy. It's a baby boy. You should go now, Reed," Tressie said. She wasn't conscious of his leaving, only that he was no longer there.

Bitter Leaf lifted the child, still attached to her by the wrinkled length of cord, and smiled at Tressie.

Tressie positioned the child across its mother's stomach and tied off the cord in two places with string they'd fashioned from the sinew of one of Dooley's deer kills. Brown eyes swimming in moisture, Bitter Leaf bent to gnaw the cord and separate herself from her baby. Tressie then cleaned out the tiny mouth and blew puffs of air into the red face, just as Bitter Leaf had instructed. The baby gasped and began to cry.

"Well, Dooley, you have yourself a living, breathing son," Tressie said under her breath. But she didn't go call him to look. An animallike sound from Bitter Leaf caught her attention. The woman's face had gone purple with strain. She should expel the afterbirth easier than that.

The baby in Tressie's arms shivered and squalled, and she focused on him. He needed to be washed and wrapped right now. She was determined he wouldn't die; he just couldn't. The tiny fists flailed the air, spindly legs kicked, and he bawled lustily, bringing a sad grin to Tressie's lips.

"A wonderful sound, little one," she said, and kissed the wrinkled, blood-smeared forehead. Then she washed the baby with warm water, starting with the thick crop of black hair and ending with the delicate toes. The bath soothed him and he searched her face inquisitively with unfocused eyes. Wrapping him in a portion of the quilt she'd cut up into small squares, Tressie kissed each silken cheek, then held him close to her heart so he could hear the beat. Closing her eyes, she cradled him there for a long while, gently swaying. She wouldn't cry, she just wouldn't. With a sigh she turned to hand him over to his true mother.

The girl lay on the dirt floor curled in a fetal position. Tressie cradled the child in one arm and leaned down to brush long strands of Bitter Leaf's black hair from the sweat-covered face. The brown eyes were open and unseeing. For a moment Tressie thought the girl was dead, but felt then feeble breaths of air from her open mouth.

What was wrong with her?

A brutal contraction hit the girl, drawing her knees even tighter against her chest, and she began to hemorrhage, a mass of dark blood spreading around her still form. She groaned weakly. Tressie lay the child on the bed and knelt to tend to its mother. Another contraction exposed a tiny head awash in blood.

Tressie cried out. Bitter Leaf was having another child. She'd been carrying twins.

But it wasn't to be. The frail girl bled to death while struggling to birth the second child. Almost before Tressie realized what was happening, Bitter Leaf simply quit breathing. Tressie sat on the floor beside her, holding her hand while tears coursed down her cheeks. So much death everywhere. Would it never end?

She could hear the baby sucking at his fist on the bed, so she roused and went to check on him. From there she could see out the door. Dooley and Reed sat in the sun, backs up against a huge boulder out on the rim of the bluff.

An insane need to punish someone for what had happened washed over Tressie. She raced to the men. Reed struggled to his feet, but Dooley was past being able to rise. Both had been drinking.

"Tressie?" Reed said, and swayed a little, holding himself upright.

She ignored him, preferring Dooley as a target. The attack began fairly controlled, but grew quickly into mayhem. "I won't ask where you got that whiskey," she said, indicating the jug Dooley held between his legs. Then, so fast he had no idea it was coming, she kicked out, catching him just above one kneecap. Before Dooley could let out his enraged bellow, she grabbed the whiskey jug and flung it off the side of the mountain.

"While you sat out here getting drunk, your wife was in there dying. And it took her a long time to do it. You monster, you no-account animal." The tone of her voice rose with each word until she was screaming incoherently. She barely knew what she said, and certainly doubted that he understood any of the accusations. How could a man of his so-called convictions sit out here drinking while his wife bled to death? All men were alike, and women were meant to suffer because of it. She would never forgive Dooley. Him or Papa. Was Reed any better?

"Damn you all, damn you!" At that moment she longed to punish Papa every bit as much as she did this uncivilized animal of a man. Frustrated at her inability to further put into words how she felt, Tressie fled, ignoring Reed's bewildered expression of sorrow.

She spoke to neither man when later that evening they buried Bitter Leaf and the darkly still baby. Anger left Tressie exhausted, and she preferred to mourn in private, with only God and Bitter Leaf's surviving son as her witness.

Seven

*B*efore daylight he rose and crept in silence to the saddle-bags belonging to the breed. The breed put great stock in what he carried; there must be something of great value there, and there was no use in leaving it behind. Very quietly he carried the leather saddlebags outside. It was time to leave.

Before retiring, he had readied everything he would take, secreting the hoard in the woods where he also tied Bitter Leaf's pony. His Enfield rifle stood outside the door, and he eased to it, stepping carefully in the boots the breed had made. Made for quiet walking, they were. He stifled an insane desire to laugh.

No moon shone and it took a while for him to make his way down the steep path and into the stand of pine. He tossed the bags on his horse, mounted up, and rode off, heading high up into the mountains.

As if someone had shaken her, Tressie awoke abruptly. Predawn light touched the windows of the cabin, and she gazed down into the peaceful countenance of Bitter Leaf's beautiful son. Her mind was boggled by their predicament. There was no milk for him, and she had no idea how far it was to civilization. A trading post or farm would do, but either of those could be a day's walk or more.

She brushed at the tiny fist with the tip of a finger. "Caleb," she whispered. "Caleb Reed Kling." Much as she hated to add the distasteful surname, Dooley Kling was the child's father. And a boy should carry his father's name.

Before Caleb could set up a howl, she rose from the bed and prepared him a cloth soaked in sugar water. The rosebud mouth sucked noisily at the sugar teat, eyes closed and fists clenched.

Tressie sat on the edge of the bed. The men hadn't returned until after she had gone to bed. Except for the soft sounds of Caleb's suckling, the cabin was unusually quiet. Kling usually snored up a storm, and Reed wasn't the quietist man sleeping, either. They must be up and about already.

A distant bird song floated in the morning air, and she caught her breath at the beauty of it. Nature certainly wasted no time mourning the loss of one of its precious own. And perhaps that was the way it should be.

"Caleb," she whispered. "Sweet Caleb. I'll take care of you, baby. Don't you worry, you poor little fella. Not a way to start life, without a mama. But never you mind, I'll be your mama."

Reed stood in the middle of the clearing, not wanting to believe what his eyes told him. The Indian pony was gone, as were all of Kling's belongings. The man had lit out, leaving them with the little fellow and no way to ride out for help. The bastard!

He knuckled bleary eyes and paced around, hoping to

find signs of the man. Signs that he was wrong and the trapper had simply ridden out to hunt or set traps. But everything was gone. Things the man wouldn't have taken on such a trip. Dear God, what would they do now? Kling was just like Reed's father and Tressie's, too. Run away and deserted his own flesh and blood as if he weren't worth even a thought. Reed stood for a moment on the rim of the trail, staring out across the rugged mountain peaks. Sometimes even the toughest man felt like turning loose and bawling. Instead he trudged silently to the cabin to break the news to Tressie.

For a moment he hesitated in the doorway, gazing in awe. What a beautiful sight they were, this mother crooning to her babe. Tears stung at his eyelids. At times like this his hunger for her overpowered his better sense. They'd take the child and go away together. Anywhere she wanted. He would care for them both and love them. See that the tiny mite never had a day's regret about being unwanted by his callous father. He and Tressie could have other children together. Fear nudged at his heart, making it ache. Women were so fragile, and yet were forced to perform the hardest of all tasks in the world. Bearing children, these lovely beings endured a pain greater than any he could imagine. He hungered to go to her, gather them both in his arms and protect them forever.

Before he could make a move, Tressie sensed him standing there and glanced in his direction. He walked silent as no breeze at all to her side, and when she could see his face she noticed a glint of moisture in the dark eyes.

"How is he?"

"Oh, he's fine. No thanks to his daddy."

"Tressie, I'm sorry about the girl . . . and all." He shrugged and gestured to the outdoors, wondering again how to tell her of their plight.

"I know. Where is he? I'm not giving him this baby, you know. He can't have him. He's not—"

Reed took a deep breath and plunged. "He's gone. Left out, slick as a skinning. You don't have to worry about him wanting that little tyke."

"Oh," she said softly, and glanced down at Caleb, whose wide eyes studied her solemnly.

She still didn't realize the gravity of their situation, and Reed wasn't quite ready to tell her. He took a step closer and peered at the child nested in her arms. The baby gazed up at him with wide dark eyes. "Not so ugly this morning, is he?"

"Why, Reed Bannon, no baby is ugly." Squeezing her eyes tightly shut, she whispered, "There's no milk. What are we going to do? I couldn't stand it if he dies."

He didn't reply and she looked up to see him watching her with such an intent and tender expression that her mind flew back to the time she nursed him back to health. How he lay so helpless and hurt, depending on her. That tie tugged at her heart. He was hers, too, saved for what? To now save this child?

"Oh, Tressie," he said, and dropped to his knees. He touched her cheek with the back of one hand. "I wish I could have taken better care of you . . . of his mama. I just didn't know. . . . I mean I knew, but it didn't seem possible it could happen again. Like some kind of punishment. Dying just like my own mama. I was so sure that this time everything would be all right. That all I needed to do was keep Dooley out of the way. And I . . ." Reed leaned his head on her breasts beside the baby. He couldn't tell her the whole truth. How relieved he'd been when she'd made him leave; how he couldn't wait to run away like the coward he was. Just the same as he always did when things got to be too much.

Tressie shifted and embraced him. "What are we going to do now? That's what's important. We can't let Caleb suffer."

"Caleb?"

She nodded her head. "Caleb Reed, I thought. After my grandfather and . . . well. If that man doesn't want him, he'll not carry his name. We can call him Cale if you like. It has a nice sturdy ring to it."

Reed noisily cleared his throat. What was he thinking of? She sounded like they were going to take the baby somewhere together and raise him, a half-breed child. Reed jerked his hand away and climbed to his feet. "I'll find him some milk . . . somewhere. A cow, a goat . . . surely there's people somewhere. It'll be best if you stay here with him, and I go."

Her heart swelled into her throat and pounded there fit to choke her. What if he didn't come back? "Why can't we just go to Fort Laramie?"

Reed crossed the small room to sort through the remainder of the supplies. There was hardly anything left. It was a wonder the man hadn't taken it all, but perhaps he was afraid of getting caught if he prowled around inside the cabin. A little flour, sugar, and meal, a double handful of beans, and a water pouch. Hell, the bastard had even taken Reed's saddlebags. He grabbed the water bag and glanced up to see her watching him, waiting for a reply to her question.

"Oh, no, we can't walk all that way. It's at least two days by horseback to the fort. Once down off this mountain there's still the hot windy flatlands to cross. No, you'll be safer here."

She didn't like the idea one bit, but knew he was right. Caleb needed strength before he could safely make that kind of trip. For a long moment she studied Reed's searching eyes, which met hers without flinching. Did she trust him? What choice did she have? She shrugged imperceptibly and fingered her handkerchief pouch from under the mattress. "You'll need this."

Reed took it. "What's this?"

"To buy the milk," she said softly.

"Where did this come from?"

"What difference does it make?" she asked sharply. "Just use it."

He took the hanky, then busied himself tying the rawhide strands of the water bag to his belt. There were more important things to consider than why she had kept a few lousy coins a secret from him. He was guilty of hiding things himself, letting her believe they could actually save this newborn child. How could he tell her how slim the chance was of him finding milk or getting back in time? No, it was better if they each carried their own secrets.

Tressie never knew what to make of this man. First he was tender, then distant. She shook away the fleeting reminder that he had run before and could do the same again. Caleb fussed at the sugar teat. How much longer would it keep him satisfied?

Reed crossed to the door, careful not to get too close to the woman and child. He was afraid of what he might do should she reach out.

At the door he spoke without looking back. "I'll be as quick as I can. I'm leaving the rifle, over there in the corner. It's loaded," and he was gone.

For a long while Tressie stared at the empty doorway, until the sound of Reed's going faded. Birds trilled in the warming morning. Caleb had fallen asleep in her arms and she lay him in the middle of the bed. Then, without conscious thought, she dropped to her knees and rested her forehead on the mattress. She wanted to pray, but all she could think of was, "Dear God, dear God," and she repeated the words over and over with a longing in her soul such as she'd never felt before. Don't let this child die, too. Please don't.

She rested there until her knees protested the hard floor. Having no idea how much time had passed since Reed left unnerved Tressie. How long should she wait before deciding he wasn't coming back? What should she do then? Little Caleb slept on, but too soon he would awaken, and this time he would be hungrier. The sugar teat might not satisfy him, and even if it did, how long would it take a newborn baby to starve to death without milk?

Tressie stepped outside to gaze into the western sky, riffled with clouds that looked like clabbered milk.

As soon as Reed was out of sight of the cabin, he struck out for the river routes. There would be traders along that way. If he had avoided settlements on their trip in, he could no longer do that and save the child. Only a crazy man would think he could accidentally run across a stray cow or goat just waiting to be milked. By midday he cut a well-marked trail. Indians or white man traveled this way on a regular basis. And maybe even soldiers, though Kling had said they were mostly fighting the war. It was a big country, and the chances of him running across someone who knew him from his days with Quantrill, or later at Pea Ridge, or even the incident with the Union soldier, were nil. He couldn't help being nervous about it.

The trading post was nothing more than a log cabin with no windows and a lean-to where several horses were tied. Reed eyed a stout Indian pony wearing a saddle with a blanket tossed over it. Two long-legged duns and a red mare were also tied at the rail. In front of the post was a wagon and as Reed stepped up onto the plank porch, a man came out carrying a sack of feed over one shoulder. He loaded it in the wagon as Reed stepped inside the dark post.

The Indian who obviously owned the pony outside was squatted just inside the door. Two men visited with the storekeep, who stood behind a plank counter doling out his wares. It was too dark in the room to make out features, and Reed was glad of that. He glanced around at the shelves of goods. A wooden barrel in one corner held dry beans. There was a smell of feed and leather in the suffocating air.

The men at the counter, who had suspended their visiting when Reed entered, went back to their jabbering. Weather and hunting and talk of women. Then his ears perked.

"Hear there's a new commander down to the fort," one said.

The storekeeper, who had a nasal twang, replied, "Yep, heard the same. He come up from Missouri with a passel of soldiers. Gonna quieten down the Indians. It got to where the stages and freight wagons couldn't even get through. Savages killed a bunch a whites a time back. That all for you?"

The customer hefted his purchases and left.

Reed waited his turn, wondering who the Union soldier sent to quell the Indian uprisings could possibly be. Funny they'd take him out of the war, but then after Pea Ridge, there wasn't much war to fight. He figured it was just a matter of time now before Lee surrendered, if he hadn't already.

"Help you?" the storekeep said, and Reed realized the man was talking to him.

"Milk."

"In tins?"

"Whatever you've got."

"Only have three. Supplies overdue now."

"How about a bottle? You got a baby bottle?"

"Not much call for them." The man eyed Reed.

He nodded. "Still, you got one?"

"Easier if you was to ask for a wet nurse, mister." The man snorted and Reed realized it was meant for a laugh.

Reed drew out the handkerchief and began to untie the knot. "We'll make do, I reckon. How much?"

"Would a whiskey bottle do?"

"Not without one of those . . . whatchamacallits . . . a rubber nipple?"

"Well, I sure as toot don't have one of them." The man snorted out another laugh. He took the coins Reed offered, gave him a few in change.

Reed studied his hand a moment, thinking about the sugar teat. "I'll take that whiskey bottle after all," he said.

While the man rummaged around under the counter,

Reed asked, "You know that commander's name, the one who come to Fort Laramie?"

"Nope, never heard it. White-headed, they say. A mite too old to fight in a war, maybe. Good place to dump him. Fort Laramie." He held out a flat-sided empty clear glass bottle. "This do?"

"Owe you anything for it?"

The man studied Reed a moment. "Nah, it's okay."

When Reed left, the Indian was still squatted beside the door. He could have been made of wood. It was all Reed could do to walk past the fine pony without just jumping on its back and riding off hell-bent for leather. But if he did, it would have to be for high country, leaving Tressie to her own devices. She had enough troubles without him leading a bunch of wild Indians right to her door. So he expelled a deep sigh and headed back the way he had come, on foot. He couldn't help but wonder how long three tins of milk would last.

Tressie had grown used to being hungry on the trail, and so didn't notice that she hadn't eaten anything at all that day until late in the afternoon. By then her stomach ached with a need to be fed. She dared not leave Caleb to hunt; just her brief forays into the woods to relieve herself had made her nervous. Suppose he woke and started to cry and choked, or somehow managed to fall off the bed? She knew such thoughts were probably very irrational, but couldn't help it.

The stew pot had been scraped clean the day before, ever since she'd been too distracted to do much about it. Building up the fire, Tressie added a bit of water to the remaining cornmeal and made a couple of johnnycakes.

She ate them standing in the doorway, straining her eyes to catch a first sight of Reed returning. Caleb woke and she changed him, rinsing the soaked cloth and hanging it near the fire to dry.

He began to cry when sucking on both fists brought no results, and Tressie soaked the sugar teat in the last of the sweet water, mopping up every last drop before offering it to the screaming, red-faced baby.

She held him close, sitting outside the cabin on a boulder so she could see Reed as soon as he came up the trail. Caleb was satisfied for a while, then began to whimper and spat out the rag. He turned his head into Tressie's breasts, tiny mouth opened and searching. The incredible mop of black hair tickled at her arm, and his lips made wet spots on the bodice of her dress.

She could hardly stand it when he cried, especially when she couldn't get him to hush. Standing, she rocked him gently and walked back and forth in front of the cabin, tears streaming freely down her cheeks.

"Hush, darling. Don't cry so. He'll be back. He'll be back real soon." His little fingers kneaded at her useless breasts.

Suppose Reed didn't return, or found no milk?

"Oh, God, oh, God." Her prayer seemed useless as the burning sun slid behind the mountains to the west and left her and Caleb alone in the frightening dusk. The baby finally cried himself into a restless sleep in her arms, but she continued to hold him.

The grizzly showed up just at full dark, making all the noise in the world circling the cabin. Snorting, snuffling, his great claws slashed at the sides of the cabin. Tressie cast one frantic glance at the open doorway, over which only a skin hung. Some bears, she knew, weren't actually dangerous to humans. But others, like the giant grizzly, could slice a man in two with one swipe of its vicious paw, and often did.

Heart leaping into her throat, Tressie quickly wrapped Caleb and hid him in the far corner away from the door. Then she hefted the rifle and prepared it to fire. Even the powerful .50-caliber ball might not stop a grizzly, and she would have to reload and fire again before he could cross the room.

Of course, she could hit him between the eyes and maybe stop him. Tressie positioned herself between Caleb and the doorway, rifle butt snugged into her shoulder.

Outside, the bear grunted and knocked over something, then moved along the side of the cabin, coming closer to the door. Tressie patted the possible bag to check its location. She could scarcely breathe as she listened to the animal. There was no light inside the cabin, and so she could make out starshine through the window and around the skin hanging over the doorway. As he entered, the bear would make a perfect target.

The rifle grew heavy and the barrel began to waver. The muscles in her arms protested keeping the thing aimed. The bear stopped moving. His breath evened out, as if he, too, were listening for danger. Tressie held her own breath. What was he doing? Caleb hiccuped and Tressie jerked, her attention temporarily caught by the child at her back.

At that precise moment, when she was halfway between seeing to the baby and listening to the bear, the creature let out a wall-shaking roar and burst through the flimsy skin. On hind legs he stood taller than the doorframe, and the heat of his enormous body washed over her. His breath smelled fetid and he stank of his own waste. The tiny room filled with the taste and smell of fear and death. Caleb began to scream bloody murder, and for just an instant Tressie thought about joining him.

She bit at her lip . . . hard, tasting salt and blood, aimed the rifle, and squeezed the trigger. The hammer fell and nothing happened! Just that terrible snap that warns of a misfire.

The bear dropped to all fours and snuffled loudly, big head swaying back and forth as he surveyed this strange cave. She couldn't see his face—it was too dark—but she could make out a shape, and its enormity horrified her.

Without taking her eyes away from the looming shadow, Tressie fumbled inside the possible bag, found another cap, and replaced the useless one. All by feel. She wanted to shout at Caleb to shut up so she could think, but his endless crying gave impetus to her need to do this thing right this time. The animal obviously didn't see well, but he had to smell them, had to be making up his mind whether to eat them for his dinner or just rip them to shreds.

Tressie raised the rifle once again, curved her quivering finger over the trigger, and pulled. She couldn't help shutting her eyes when the thing went off. *Ka-blatt-boom-boom-boom*. The noise ricocheted around the walls of the small room. The bear bellowed and rose once again to his full height so that his head was up in the rafters. Tressie screamed and Caleb, who hadn't stopped screaming, got all the louder.

Reed, who had come up the trail to the cabin just in time to hear the gun discharge, added his own shouts to the cacophony. The bear literally knocked him aside as it crashed through the door. He climbed to his feet in time to see the staggering, lunging body go over the edge of the cliff, its wounded roar of pain following it down into the deep canyon. It was suddenly so dreadfully still inside the cabin that Reed just knew the wild creature had slain both Tressie and the baby. He hadn't really seen enough to know if perhaps the animal might have carried one of them off the cliff with him.

The heat of blood and the smell of black powder permeated the suffocating room. Reed crept through the doorway, feeling a gory dampness brush along the side of his face. The shredded hide dripped gore from the wounded bear. Despite the ghastly odor and the dreadful stillness, he sensed a living woman and child, as if he could hear them breathing or smell their particular odor. Then he realized why. Tressie was crooning very softly and the child's breath hitched as he cooed back to her.

They were alive!

Reed fumbled around and found a stub of candle. Brushing away the gray coals in the fireplace, he uncovered a glowing ember, lit a sliver of wood, and touched it to the wick. The golden glow sprung into all corners, revealing utter chaos. And in its midst the woman hunkered in the corner on her heels, rocking the baby. Singing, for chrissakes. She was singing!

Tressie was not aware of Reed's presence until he lit the candle. Even then she continued to soothe Caleb, who had cried so hard she thought he would convulse. She finally had him quieted, mostly because he was too exhausted to cry anymore, and could let nothing distract her. Reed was back and they were safe. At least for the moment. She didn't realize how really terrified she was until Reed gently took the child from her arms. Then she began to shake. She shook so hard she couldn't talk. She couldn't rise from her crouching position, even though it had grown uncomfortable. She could do nothing but huddle there and tremble. When Reed tried to solace her, she shook her head and shoved him away.

"The . . . the . . . bab . . . bab . . . feed him. Oh . . . oh . . . oh . . . kay?"

Reed nodded. She hadn't asked him if he brought milk, but just to feed the baby. He built up the fire and put on a pot of water to boil. He supposed the milk should be boiled, too, he didn't know. But it was in a tin. It should be safe. And the hot water would warm it. While the water came to a boil, Reed busied himself figuring out how to stuff a rag in the top of the bottle so that milk could be sucked through it. It would be messy, and not the best, but the child would get some. Failing that, they could always spoon-feed him.

Tressie was finally able to crawl out of the corner and struggle to her feet, but found her hands wouldn't stop shaking long enough to help Reed. So she sat on the bed, arms wrapped around her shoulders, and watched him. He poured some of the boiling water in the bottle, swished it around and dumped it on the floor, then washed the hunting knife and pried open the tin. With an unsteady hand he poured some in the bottle and added warm water. Not much, for the child's first feeding would have to be small. Tressie approved of Reed's motions. Once he looked at her and smiled and she was able to return the favor, if a bit shakily.

Some adjustments made the cloth nipple workable after

a fashion, and Caleb concentrated so hard on sucking that the furrowed expression on his little face amused both Reed and Tressie. It took the two of them to get half the feeding in him, burp him, and then get him to finish it off. He spit up some, but seemed to take well to the strange-tasting canned milk. To Tressie it smelled awful.

She lay him on the bed, put the dry makeshift diaper on in place of the soiled one he wore, then nearly collapsed beside him.

Reed sat on the floor beside the bed. "Well, I see you had a full day."

"Not too bad. How was yours?" she murmured, and grabbed his big hand in hers. Holding it to her lips, she remained that way for a while. Then he reached up and touched her cheek with the other hand. Tressie relaxed, and the next thing she knew it was morning. Caleb was gone from his place beside her and the cabin was empty.

She stretched full length, making her muscles and bones pop and crack. They were sore and she felt in bad need of a bath. The stench in the cabin was overpowering, and she knew she'd never get it out of there. Barefoot, she went outside into another sunny day. Did it never rain in this country? She didn't see Reed and Caleb anywhere, but after watching him with the baby last night, she didn't worry. He was probably teaching the boy how to cut trail, or maybe how to suck juice out of a cactus. Whatever, Tressie had only one thing on her mind.

The spring near the cabin didn't have a bowl deep enough to bathe in, but she could certainly wash off. Stripping out of her dress, she knelt in the cool wet moss of the bank and began to splash icy cold water over her body, beginning with her face and rubbing down over her breasts, flat stomach, and thighs.

Reed came upon her as she stood to finish washing. Caleb slept in his arms, and he nested the baby safely on his quilt in the crunchy dried leaves nearby.

He walked up behind her, eyes drinking in the delicate curve of backbone, the slight flare of slim hips, the long lean look of her exquisite legs.

Tressie threw her head back and ran her fingers between her breasts and down into the pale nest of hair. She shivered with desire at her own touch, and at that moment sensed Reed behind her. She turned and lifted her hand toward him, graceful fingers uncurling. He stepped forward, their eyes locked, and she eased into his arms.

With the thick fingers of one hand, Reed massaged the ridges of her backbone down into the cleft of her hips, and the other hand he spread in her thick auburn hair. Their lips met, tasted, hesitated, then drank deeply.

Tressie fumbled with the buttons of his shirt, pressing rigid nipples against his broad chest as she pulled away the fabric. Then the belt buckle, the buttons of the fly, freeing his manhood with one swift motion, then taking him in her fist. He was suffused in warmth, huge and tender, and her need tasted sweet and bright as the day.

Reed moaned against the thrust of her tongue in the warm recesses of his mouth. Lifting her effortlessly, he lay her on the cool moss, kneeling astride her. Nearby the baby sucked at his fist, smacking loudly. Tressie smiled and met Reed's eager lips.

"I love you," Reed told her between hot kisses, saying it into her flesh with a passion that surprised her.

His long black hair fell over her face when he lowered

himself to embrace every inch of her body with his, covering her with his need and his heat and his aroma. When he slipped inside her, she raised her hips to meet him and hung on. His lips ravished every inch of her—the pulse in her throat, the rosy tips of each breast, the satiny stomach—and she felt a quivering deep inside like a great starving beast rousing from a long slumber.

Still Reed held her tightly to him and tasted of her, making her wait for that final ride that would end all too soon. He rocked backward, pulling her into a sitting position beneath him, and she thought she would explode with the feel of him filling the core of her being. His manhood was throbbing inside her, exploring where no one but he had ever been. At last he rocked her backward, cradled her head on his arms, and brought her to climax, joining her with a shout that woke the baby.

He rolled to her side, laughing. Slick with the mixture of their perspiration, Tressie panted and coiled backward into his arms to rest. She felt him soft and satisfied against her backbone.

He said the words again then. "I love you, Tressie, I love you."

Tressie didn't know what to make of them. All she could think of at that moment was that she was not supposed to let herself love a man so like her traitorous father.

No matter how she felt in Reed's arms, no matter the bliss, her mind kept coming back to Papa's treachery. How could she dare trust a man so like him? How could she believe his declaration of love and return it when he might only be waiting for the right time to walk away and not even look back? He would wait until she was helpless, most vulnerable, then leave her.

He hadn't left her when she was so ill and he had returned with milk for the baby, yet she couldn't drive the insidious fear from her mind that he would leave her when she grew to trust him the most . . . just like Papa.

But oh, Lord, did Reed Bannon make her feel wonderful.

Eight

Reed fashioned a small pack, mostly things for the baby, and helped Tressie strap it to her back. He would carry everything else. There wasn't time to bemoan the theft of the saddlebags; he couldn't remember what had been in them.

He and Tressie had slept together, Caleb between them. Like a real family. He waited until dawn to awaken her, for she had risen twice in the night to feed the baby.

He lifted her hair to settle the pack. "Good thing there's not much left in the way of supplies. Makes less to carry. We'll take turns with the baby, if you like. I kind of enjoy toting the little tyke. He has such a damn-you quizzical look on that monkey face."

"I'm worried about him making the trip," Tressie said quietly.

Reed tested the pack, fingers lingering on the warm skin of her upper arm. "We don't have a choice. The milk will last only another day or so. We can stop at the post first, see if their supplies came. If not, there are other posts along the river. Once we get to Fort Laramie, we'll be okay. There are Army doctors and women there. A sutler's store, too. And a stage line."

Tressie was suddenly afraid. When they reached civilization, Reed would dump her the first place she'd be safe and take off, she just knew it. Even if he had told her he loved her in the heat of passion; she didn't really believe it for a minute once she came to her senses.

He noticed her silence. "What's wrong?"

"Nothing, I guess. I . . . what are we going to do? At Fort Laramie, I mean?"

"What do you want to do, girl? From there you can head west and find your father. That is what you want, isn't it?"

"Of course, but I thought maybe—"

He turned away. God, if only they could. He had other places to be, things to prove to himself. And she must finish her own quest. "Maybe what? I'd go along for the ride? Sorry. I've got other things to do. I'm sorry about . . . I mean, yesterday, I didn't mean to let that get out of hand." Perhaps his reply came out more harsh than he had intended, but he wouldn't take it back now.

"I know." She was utterly miserable. Damn him for apologizing for making her feel like a woman.

Reed studied her a moment, then circled around and put the tip of a finger under her chin, tilting upward so that she had to look at him. "You don't want me, not really. We both know why, don't we?" Silently he thought, one coward is quite enough for any woman.

She nodded and didn't say anything. He had told her he loved her, but it didn't mean he did. It had just been something to say. Otherwise he'd try to talk her into staying with him, for his own selfish needs. Again, she'd made a fool of herself where this man was concerned. But she wasn't sorry they had made love. She cherished the memory like she cherished those memories of home that kept her going when things were tough. No matter where she went or what she did, Tressie knew she would never forget the way Reed Bannon had made her feel when he took her body to his. When he had put his lips on hers, when he had touched her and looked at her with those bottomless eyes. He couldn't make that feeling go away by leaving her somewhere.

"Well," she said too brightly, "if you're ready, let's get going to Fort Laramie."

Caleb proved to be a tough little traveler. Though the tinned milk caused his stomach some trouble in adjusting, he was soon over that and bobbed along in a pouchlike sling strapped either to Tressie's bosom or Reed's chest.

The trip took the better part of four days. Of a morning Reed would boil enough water to last until they camped for the night. The heat of the sun kept the water warm enough for the baby when mixed with the milk. They lost some milk because Caleb couldn't drink an entire can before it soured in the dreadful heat. Replacement proved not to be a problem. Tressie was surprised at the trading posts in the otherwise barren country. It seemed trappers, miners, travelers, and even Indians were numerous enough to support such merchants. Her stash of coins dwindled, though, for things were expensive. She despaired of having enough to board the stage when they reached Fort Laramie.

Late afternoon of the fourth day Reed pointed out their destination. It was a disappointment to Tressie, that gathering of scattered buildings resting on a knoll that somewhat resembled a giant egg sliced in half. Thus situated on the wide plain, Fort Laramie squatted in the crooks of the Laramie and the North Platte rivers.

The icy cold, clear water, snowmelt from high in the mountains, curled around the western flank of the numerous plank and adobe buildings. Tressie hadn't expected the fort to be so large, with so many structures spread like boulders after an avalanche. The fort had no walls. Reed told her they had been torn down years before, not long after the Army took over the trading post from the American Fur Company.

"Hell, Indians ride right in among them now. It's become the laughingstock of this country, this fort that isn't a fort. Said by some to be totally indefensible."

Tressie's eyes grew wide at the tale. "But aren't there soldiers there? Won't we be safe from Indians?"

Reed only chuckled. He didn't expect them to be safe from Indians anywhere they went from now on, but he didn't tell her that. Oddly, that thought reminded Reed of the deerskin pouch he'd carried since leaving his mother's people many years earlier. And he remembered then that it had been in the saddlebags Kling had stolen. It had belonged, not to his mother but to his father, a keepsake of sorts that his grandmother assumed he might want. Reed wondered why he had kept it around so long, and felt a surprising relief that it was gone. He'd never been able to simply throw the thing away.

From the very moment they caught sight of Fort Laramie, Tressie hated it. Persistent dust, kicked up by heavy wagon and horse traffic, billowed into the endless wind. Crowds of ruffians milled about on foot as if they had no destination. She was, however, reassured by the sign of a few soldiers apparently on guard duty. There were also Indians and fur-clothed mountain men, traders and freighters, barking dogs and stomping horses, all making more noise than she'd ever heard in her entire life. Then there was the stench. Thank God for prairie winds.

Reed had suggested that she wear a dress so she would be decently covered, and to her mind that simply made matters worse. Every man turned to stare and comment as she followed Reed between the buildings. She saw few women. They were, Reed explained, officers' wives and they lived in the married men's quarters.

Reed left Tressie and Caleb in the sutler's store, where she spent one of her coins for a few cans of milk and, wonder of wonders, an actual bottle complete with rubber nipple. The kindly storekeeper found her a place to rest in the back room, and Reed set out to do his business.

Just the proximity of the men in blue uniforms made him extremely edgy. No doubt his description could be found on wanted posters in the States, but he hoped that with the war and the gold rush, the territories were being ignored when it came to law enforcement. It didn't matter, though, for the sooner he could get away from all these boys in blue, the better he would feel. Would he ever be free, or was he destined to run and hide the rest of his life for a series of very dumb mistakes? Maybe eventually Quantrill's riders would forget the man who deserted them at the battle of Lexington, and the Rebs, too, but he doubted that the Union Army would soon forget that he was a horse thief. He hoped to God he wasn't also a killer.

Spotting the Indian tepees on the outskirts of the fort, Reed decided that there he might find answers to some of his questions without risking his freedom.

The Indians were Oglala Sioux, mostly women and children, with a few less savory braves hanging around. They had set up a regular village upstream a ways from the fort and welcomed Reed because he spoke their language, even if he did sound like a white man.

A young boy, no older than twelve or so, fell in with Reed as he entered what the soldiers called "Squaw Town."

After the polite amenities were out of the way, Reed asked the boy, "Who commands the fort?"

"You are from the People?" the boy asked, sniggering behind a hand at Reed's accent.

"My mother was. Tell me about this place."

"They are here to kill the People. They say not, that they are friendly. Their Colonel Collins lies well." The boy grinned up at Reed. "But so do we, when it comes to the whites."

"This Colonel Collins, when did he come here? Where is he from?"

"They say he came from the white man's war, a place called Missouri, to make peace with us." The boy laughed like the sharp bark of a dog. "I wish I was old enough to fight them. Soon, though."

Reed shuddered at the expression of malice on the youngster's face. He could hardly blame the boy, yet the boy would one day die because of it. There was very little Reed could do about it. Very little anyone could do, really. The end of this great nation was coming as surely as the wind swept the plains. Once the Yanks licked the Rebs, they'd spit in their hands and head west, and they wouldn't stop until they'd cleared the territories of every Indian who wouldn't surrender. He wanted to tell the boy to put on white man's clothes and go on with his life away from all this, but he didn't. That was no answer. Reed knew that all too well. Sooner or later, you had to pay your dues.

Squaw Town was aptly named, for the only men there were small boys and very old men. From the boy's mother and sister, who worked for the soldiers washing and mending clothes and cleaning the barracks, Reed learned that the braves were elsewhere. This appeared to be an open secret, but one which they would not discuss in great detail. Perhaps the Sioux also realized their own fate and were getting ready for the last battles, gathering with other tribes to bring down on the white man the wrath of their spirit Gods. It would be a great and wondrous battle, and Reed wondered if he might not join them. Surely a way to earn his own warrior feathers?

At last he headed back to the fort. At the sutler's he found Tressie sound asleep on a pallet in the back room of the store, Caleb nestled in the crook of her arm. He struck a deal with the sutler, trading the Kentucky rifle for more tins of milk and enough cash to buy a stagecoach ticket to Virginia City for her and the baby.

"The Overland's got a hotel where she can put up for the night. Stage won't be in till tomorrow," the storekeeper told him. "You ain't going with the little lady?"

Reed shook his head. "Need a job for a while."

The sutler studied him. "You don't talk like a blamed Indian, but you shore look like one. Don't hire Indians except as scouts. You scout, do you? Track your own kind?"

Reed didn't like the man, despite his kindness to Tressie. He had a streak in him that prodded a man.

"Nope. I'll find something. Thanks for your kindness to the girl."

"Think nothing of it. She'll have a hard row to hoe, that one. Having that half-breed kid and all. She might ought to have drowned it, been better off."

Reed ground his teeth and took a step backward to keep from hitting the man. "Tressie. Tressie, girl. Git on out here," he shouted, not taking his flintlike gaze from the sutler, whose expression seemed to say, *Go ahead and hit me, see what happens.* Reed knew how tough these men had to be, and had no real desire to tangle with this one, who was broad as a bull.

Just as Tressie appeared from the stock room holding Caleb, the front door burst open and two soldiers came in. They paid no attention either to her or to Reed, but continued a conversation that had obviously begun out on the street.

"He is, too, a dirty Reb, I don't care what you say," one told the other.

"Quantrill is nothing but a killer. He ain't no soldier, on either side."

"Well, may be, but that just shows you don't know everything. He's a captain in the dang Confederate Army, I know that for a fact."

Reed's fingers tightened on Tressie's elbow and she glanced at him sharply. He seemed not to notice, but was watching the two soldiers with an intensity she found unnerving.

The smaller of the two soldiers, who wore an impressive black mustache, whirled on the one who had just spoken, a tall redneck farm boy, by the look of him. "Then you explain to me why, if he's a soldier, did he attack and murder all those civilians down in Lawrence? Tell me that, smart aleck."

"They was probably hiding bushwhackers or the like."

The short man hawked and spit in the direction of a large brass spittoon near the door. He missed, but paid that no mind. "You jest better get your loyalties straight, Nixon, afore the colonel hears you defending a no-account, back-shooting, baby-killing coward like Quantrill and his four hundred. I get any one of them in my sights and it's so long, you mealy-mouth coward. And I won't wait for him to explain he was just doing his soldierly duty, neither."

The tirade heaped upon the redneck soldier made his lantern-jawed cheeks redden, and he flicked a glance toward Tressie. " 'Scuse us, ma'am," he said, touching the brim of his hat with one finger.

Reed, lips drawn so tight there were spots of white around his mouth, ducked his head and turned his back to the two soldiers.

"Hey, you, Indian," the tall one said. "You hadn't ought to touch that little lady. You two ain't together, are you?"

Obviously the man was looking for a way to extricate himself from the embarrassment heaped upon him by his companion, and decided to pass it on to another victim. Reed was in the way.

Tressie looked up at him, watched with fascination the transformation from fury to docility cross Reed's face. Even the tone of his voice changed. "No, we're not together. I just helped her find her way to the fort."

The soldier touched the butt of a weapon strapped to his waist. "Then you best just move on. You got her here, didn't you? Now, little lady," the man said, and this time removed the hat to reveal a crop of red hair, "if I could be of assistance. You planning on taking the stage?"

Tressie nodded and shot a silent plea toward Reed. He turned and stepped away from her.

"Well, then," the soldier said, and offered his arm. "You just come with me. The Overland's got a hotel, and I'll see you and the little one are settled."

Helplessly, Tressie tucked her hand into the crook of the man's arm and, glancing once again at Reed, went with the soldier out the door and onto the dusty grounds.

"You hadn't ought to be traveling alone, ma'am."

"I—I know, but I—"

The man interrupted, "Where are you headed? California?"

"No. No, I'm meeting my husband in Virginia City," she finally managed.

"Not many women out there except for . . . well . . . uh—"

"Yes, well . . ." Tressie trailed off, hoping the man would just shut up. She wanted to turn around and look for Reed. Surely he was following her. Why had he acted like that? This man had no right to treat him like some savage Indian. He was more white man than Indian. Couldn't they see that? Of course, his hair had grown so long that it hung down between his shoulder blades.

"How long he been gone?" the soldier asked, and gazed pointedly at Caleb, riding on Tressie's left arm.

"Over a year," she said, then wanted to call the words back immediately, for she realized the blunder. The man could certainly count, even if he might have to use his fingers.

The freckled skin of his face flushed bright red, and the

soldier stared straight ahead, taking several more steps without saying anything. Then he stopped, took his arm from her grip, and pointed across the way. "Yonder's the hotel. I'd best get back to my barracks."

Tressie's mouth dropped open at his scathing tone. He muttered something about loose women that would lay with redskins and stomped off, beating dust out of his hat with swift thumps across one thigh.

"You knotheaded, loco, stump-kicking—"

Reed came up behind her and took her elbow. "Whoa, Tressie. That's no way for a loose woman to talk."

"You just let him talk to you like dirt and now you think it's funny he treated me the same?"

"Better get used to it if you're gonna raise Caleb. He got his looks from his mama, and he'll never pass for white, no matter what you do."

"You pass," she insisted with a stubborn set to her lip.

Reed looked angry again. "That's been my mistake, but it does keep a fella from getting his teeth kicked out in some quarters." His eyes flashed at her. "Think I ought to get a haircut?"

Tressie couldn't tell if the sparkle in his eye was mischief or irritation. But she was just put out enough herself to snap at him, no matter which it was. "Why should I care one way or the other? You're leaving us here and going your way."

He chewed on that a moment, all the while steering her toward the Overland Hotel. "True. It's best that way and you know it. Tressie, it's not like I'm deserting you and Caleb. I just don't see any sense to it. Helping you look for your pa in this big country when he—" Reed clamped his lips.

He might have rescued her, but he remained too stubborn to commit to her and Caleb. Well, good, Tressie thought. Fine. Just fine. I don't need him anyway. If they hadn't been stepping through the door of the establishment at that very moment, Tressie would have told Reed that she was tired of needing any man, and at that moment wished them all a good trip right straight off the edge of the earth, cowards that they were. As it was, she held her tongue on that subject, smiled at the clerk, and presented her stage ticket, acting as if Reed were a piece of furniture.

When she started to follow the clerk's directions on finding her room, Reed took her arm. "Tressie, wait a minute."

"Why? So you can tell me again how little you care what happens to me? No. You be on your way. Do whatever it is you have to do. Caleb and I will go to Virginia City and we'll do just fine, thank you. As for you and I, we're just about even on favors, so let's leave it at that."

With a feeling of deep loss, Reed watched her disappear down the dark hallway. Never in his life had he wanted anything so badly as he wanted a life with Tressie and Caleb. But he couldn't go with her. He was worthless to any woman, pursued by soldiers from both sides of that thankless war. Tressie would do better on her own. She was young and tough. Who would harm a mother and child?

Such thoughts reminded Reed of the story he'd heard about Quantrill's raid on Lawrence. Could it be true? If so, he thanked God he hadn't remained with the four hundred. Was Quantrill a butcher despite his motives? Reed had seen firsthand his devotion to the cause that translated into vicious debauchery at the battle of Lexington. Soon after, Reed left his command to join up with Ben McCulloch and his band of five thousand Indian soldiers.

At the Battle of Pea Ridge all hell broke loose. The survivors of that bloody fight scattered to the winds, no food, no boots, no clothing. Hunting the lines, stragglers from the near massacre of Rebel forces dug turnips and onions from abandoned gardens to survive. Many simply headed for home, calling the war over. Reed might have made it back to the front lines of the battling Confederate forces without incident, had it not been for running up against a colonel who remembered him from Quantrill's forces. Who knew he had deserted that band, and accused him of being a traitor. Reed had lost his weapon at Pea Ridge, and so he fled the accusations. Come next spring, outside St. Louis he stole a horse from a Union Army trader, who shot him in the back. Carrying the bullet in his shoulder, he headed north, but not before he shot a Union cavalry private who was in hot pursuit. Reed took that bullet with him right to Tressie's door. If not for her, he would have died. Should any of Quantrill's men ever find him, they'd kill him. On the other hand, the Union Army would surely hang him for the horse thief he was. Never mind what McCulloch's men would do.

Reed left the Overland Hotel and didn't look back.

Tressie asked for extra water, and bathed both herself and Caleb in the wash dish beside the lumpy cot provided by the Overland Stage Company. She paid no attention to the sagging mattress, for it felt so good to lie down on a real bed that nothing else mattered. The sun had almost gone down, and she was hungry, but both she and the baby fell asleep after he took some milk.

When Caleb awoke her to be fed, Tressie was surprised to see that it was dark outside. She could hear the call of sentries shouting their "All's well," and an occasional whinny or snort of an animal. Otherwise, the fort seemed to have settled in for the night. She had no way of knowing what time it was. She changed Caleb, rinsed out his diaper in the scummy wash water from earlier in the evening, draped the diaper over the foot of the bed, and fell back into an exhausted sleep. They were awakened by morning reveille. Tressie couldn't remember the last time she had slept so soundly or so long.

After changing Caleb and feeding him, she took her handkerchief pouch from her pocket and counted the few coins left there. How was she going to go so far without food? Perhaps the stage line provided food along the way, she didn't know. The idea of the trip across the rugged mountains terrified Tressie. And all the talk she'd heard about Indians being on the rampage. She wished that she and Reed could just walk to Virginia City. They'd done all right on foot so far, hadn't they?

Caleb whimpered and she touched a finger to his chin. "Such a good boy," she cooed. He kicked and waved his arms about. She was sure he recognized her and she hugged him. Her baby, her darling baby boy.

Certainly walking cross-country would be too hard on a newborn, but she was afraid that a baby so young wouldn't even survive the stage trip. They couldn't stay here, though. This filthy, uncivilized Army post had no facilities for a family unless the father was in the military. And then she surmised it would be mighty lean pickings.

"You've gone and got yourself between a rock and a hard place," Tressie scolded aloud. Caleb watched her with solemn dark eyes. She kissed his velvety soft cheek and he rolled his head to search her face with tongue and lips. He wanted a breast, this child, and she wished she had a full one to give him. That realization led her naturally to thoughts of Reed Bannon's lips at her breast. She flushed hotly and pushed those thoughts away. He was out of their life, and she would have to forget him.

Tressie couldn't have guessed how wrong she was, for when she stepped out into the morning sunshine, there stood Reed grinning at her like nothing had happened at all. Somehow he'd gotten a bath and had his hair cut. It changed him, made him appear more vulnerable.

She swept past him. He caught up, his long legs easily matching her own graceful stride.

Scowling, she said, "What do you want?"

"To wave good-bye."

"You could have done that without—without—oh, shoot."

"Slow down, you're jostling him. Look at the little tyke."

Tressie set her chin higher and kept right on marching.

"He's going to—oops, see there," Reed said, just as Caleb upchucked all down the front of her dress.

"Look what you made him do," she said.

Reed spread one large hand over his own chest and widened his eyes. "Not I, ma'am. Here, let me help." He reached for the baby.

She slapped his hand away. "Go away. Just go away."

Reed tilted his head and watched her blot at the mess with Caleb's spare diaper. He pointed. "There. A spot right there."

Glaring, Tressie wiped some more. Caleb began to cry.

"Oh, darling, it's okay," she crooned. "Now you've made him cry," she said to Reed.

"Don't be mad at me, Tressie. God, it's such a beautiful morning."

"How can you tell? Look around us. At the filth and noise and stench. How do people live this way?"

He shrugged. "Beats me. Give me the rag. I'll wash it," he said, grabbing the diaper and rinsing it out in a nearby horse trough.

When he came back, holding out the cloth so she could finish her cleanup job, their eyes caught, stumbled, and fell over each other. Tressie felt a flush growing up her neck and onto her cheeks. Reed grinned, his white teeth flashing like pearls against the golden brown skin. Obviously they were both remembering a hot night on a creek bank, and a shared bath.

"Damn you, Reed Bannon," Tressie said fondly. "Are you always going to be able to do this to me?"

"I hope so, girl. I truly hope so."

"Oh, why didn't you just keep on walking when you left me yesterday? I was good and mad at you and could have ridden out of here without any qualms. Now . . ."

"Now what, darlin? It'll work out. I got promise of a job with a new freight line following the Oregon Trail. I thought about never seeing you and the tyke again, and I just couldn't imagine it. So when I get enough money together I'll come along to Virginia City. I guess I'm just no good at saying good-bye, Tressie. I'll be there. Maybe by then you'll have decided to give up lookin' for your pa. Anyway, we'll see where we go from there."

"Why are you promising me that? All along you said we

wouldn't be together anyway. Now all of a sudden you're telling me that as soon as you can, you'll be there. You're just doing this so you won't feel guilty, Reed, so you can be on your way without feeling bad."

"Oh, I'll be there; I just don't know when. Tressie, we don't have enough money for both of us to ride or I'd go with you, I swear. I thought I could just walk away, but I can't. You and me, well, we'll just have to work something out. I promise I'll get there. It'll just take a while."

"How will you find us? Reed, don't do this to me, please. I'm scared enough as it is. Don't make a promise you have no intention of keeping." Tressie had a feeling she knew why men sometimes cussed a blue streak. She so wanted to do just that. He had put her in an impossible situation. She couldn't refuse to take the stage for Caleb's sake, yet if she rode away she had a feeling deep inside that she would never see Reed Bannon again.

"You're deserting me, too. Just like Papa did. No matter what you say." She backed off a step, hating what she was feeling.

"We ain't married, and it's not my fault what your papa did, Tressie, don't you see that? What I do will be strictly Reed Bannon, not Evan Majors. I'll join you as soon as I can, but I don't recall ever asking you to marry me or saying we would be together. I won't just desert you. I'll come and make sure you're okay. Then we'll talk some more. That's as best as I can do, Tressie. There are some things you just don't know about, and it's better you don't."

"Oh, you mean like the law is after you? And that's why you wouldn't follow the Oregon Trail and we had to take off through those devilish sand hills. What haven't you

told me, Reed Bannon? Why do you have to keep on running away?"

Reed studied her closely, and she didn't back down one
bit. Caleb sensed the tension and set up his own howl,
which they both ignored.

"You know, Dooley hit it square when he said that you're
a whole lot of spunky gal. You'll need it, 'cause you're gonna
have to be real tough to raise that Indian young'un in a
white world. And he'll have it even harder. I know that as
good as most."

"Damn you, Reed Bannon, you could be his father if
you weren't such a coward," she spat, and pushed past
him carrying the crying child.

She'd called it right that time, and Reed didn't try to
follow, but that afternoon he was there when she and Caleb boarded the stage. He kept his lips pressed tightly together and there was a glint in his eyes that turned them
to chips of hard rock. She didn't let him catch her looking
his way and spoke not a word, but climbed aboard the
high-wheeled coach so that her back was to him. She
wondered how long he stood in the dust kicked up by
the team before he turned and walked away. The thought
brought tears to her eyes, but she wiped them with determined swipes of her fingers.

Nine

The Bozeman Trail, according to the elderly gentleman who sat with Tressie, had only opened that year and already had attracted the attention of the Sioux, Arapaho, and Cheyenne, who earlier were content to concentrate their raids on folks traveling the Platte River Road farther south.

The portly man dressed in black, who introduced himself as Sir Harry Crenshaw, seemed determined to educate Tressie on the history of the territory. "Fools built this road through their sacred grounds, you know. Then when the savages naturally protested, the Army arrived to look out for us. Now they are astonished to find two routes to guard instead of one. Your colonial government has a sense of humor, but then I suppose it has to, given its propensity toward horrendous errors of judgment."

This Englishman, who because of his accent Tressie concluded actually spoke another language altogether from hers, occupied the choice seat on the stage with Tressie. Because of the baby, other passengers had deferred to her and let her sit with royalty just behind the front boot. Riding backward was disconcerting at first, but she and the privileged gentleman were less crowded.

Three passengers on the middle bench bumped knees with the three on the back one.

She was told the stage wasn't filled to capacity, but could not see where another body could be crammed. There were eight inside and four up top. When the driver set the coach in motion, Tressie gritted her teeth and gripped the floor with her toes through the bottoms of her deerskin boots. Despite the lingering heat, she had chosen to wear the knee-high, comfortable footwear under the long skirts of her dress. The incessant rocking and jouncing unsettled her stomach, and she worried about Caleb's digestion over the long trip. After all, they were still traveling on fairly level land. What would come when the stage coach climbed into the mountains, she could only guess.

Caleb spit up a lot, and it was difficult to keep the thick dust away from his eyes, mouth, and nose, yet he seldom complained. As the day grew hotter, the curtains covering the windows were opened to let in grit-thick air. Otherwise everyone would have suffocated.

The stage traveled hell-bent for leather, making her feel as if she had lassoed a cyclone and couldn't let go of the rope. No wonder these marvels of transportation could reach the West Coast in less than twenty days. The wheels scarcely touched the ground except when the contraption clattered to a halt. The only breaks allowed the suffering passengers were the four-minute stops to change horses. Other than that, passengers were allowed two rest stops in a twenty-four-hour period. When Tressie learned this, she looked forward eagerly to the first stop, where she and the baby could rest and wash up. She soon found out how far from luxurious those stops were.

The last to climb wearily from the coach, Tressie gratefully took the offered hand of her seat companion and, clutching Caleb, put her feet on each narrow step with great care. The only other woman aboard stood near the home station, splashing her face over a pan of water. She wore a handsome brown linen dress with a matching bonnet and gloves and fine button-up shoes, and carried a small leather satchel.

Sir Harry herded Tressie to the washbasin when the woman moved aside. He appeared to have appointed himself her guardian. After cleaning her face and hands, Tressie attempted to wash some of the dust from Caleb, who kicked and squalled at the touch of the cold rag.

The woman in brown had been watching Tressie closely since disembarking. In her worn muslin dress Tressie felt uncomfortable under the scrutiny. As Tressie moved away from the wash pan to make room for the other passengers, the woman approached. "He's awfully wee for such a trip, isn't he?" she asked.

With a cool nod, Tressie lay Caleb on the log bench set up on one end of the crude building. Did the woman suppose Tressie had other choices? She unwrapped his clothing and diaper and did the best she could to clean the poor little mite up before fastening on the spare diaper.

"My name is Kate Flanningan," the woman said, and wrinkled her nose through a hurried scrubbing of the dirty diaper in the water left from the passengers' washing. It wasn't until Tressie settled to feed Caleb that the woman began to chatter.

"I'm joining my husband in Virginia City. I've never seen the mountains. I suppose they're enormous. We've lived in St. Louis since we married, but Ezekiel grew tired of running a mercantile. His father owns a freight lines, and they're expanding into the West, so this seemed an ideal time for Zeke and me to make a change. Before we get set in a rut, his father said." The woman laughed nervously, as if wondering at the desires of such men.

"It sounds like an adventure," Tressie said, and propped Caleb over her shoulder to burp.

"I'm famished. What do you suppose there'll be to eat?"

"I don't know," Tressie replied, "but it couldn't matter to me. I'll eat anything that doesn't bite me first." She was glad Kate would rather talk about herself than ask more questions.

When they stepped inside the station, Tressie almost changed her idea of what she would and wouldn't eat. She reluctantly handed over one of her precious coins for a decidedly gray chunk of fried pork fat, mustard greens, a stale biscuit, and a cup of gritty coffee. She and Kate carried the poor fare back outside and ate it in competition with flies and assorted other crawling and flying insects.

Many of the passengers had brought along their own canteens of water. All Tressie had was a supply of boiled water for Caleb's milk. Afraid to drink it and run the baby short, she approached the stationmaster's son, a rangy, bucktoothed boy burned black by the incessant sun. He grudgingly fetched her a tin cup of tepid orange water that tasted brackish and reminded Tressie that she'd once contracted cholera from bad water.

Too soon came the shout, "All aboard. Awaaaaay!" and they were once again lurching along the trail.

Once under way, Sir Harry remarked, "During the next rest stop they'll let us lie down for a few hours. Undoubtedly, it'll be a miracle if we aren't all scalped in our sleep."

The remark did little to ease Tressie's mind. In the beginning she had worried more about Caleb standing up to the trip than anything else. Now she could add to that visions of hoards of Indian braves riding down on them, shouting and waving knives and hatchets. "I thought the Army was guarding the route," she said.

"This is the Powder River Run, child. We're for the most part on our way into gold mining country. Speculators and the like. Now who do you think is more important to the stage line and the Army: folks going to California and paying six hundred dollars for the privilege, or us poor misled individuals out seeking our fortune?"

Tressie sighed and leaned her head back to close her burning eyes. She kept Caleb's face shielded with one corner of his quilt. He had been so good. Sometimes he fussed, but mostly he slept. When he made no sounds at all, she worried.

She must have dozed, for when next she looked out the window she beheld the huge purple wall of the Bighorn Mountains. Then the trip got really rough.

Though it was only early September, the higher jagged peaks lay buried under mounds of pristine snow. When the stage wasn't struggling upward along the edge of a precipice, it was skidding almost straight down. It forded swift-flowing creeks and sometimes the passengers had to get out and push until the great wheels rolled free of thigh-deep mud. Tressie and Kate were spared, but not Sir Harry, who didn't seem to mind at all muddying his fancy clothing.

Once the terrified passengers spent the better part of an afternoon watching a long line of Indian braves ride the ridge above.

As the punishing trip progressed, Tressie vowed to never again deliberately get on board such a horrendous vehicle, not even for one single moment. She continued to vow this over and over as she crawled in or out of the stage, or tasted mustard greens and fried pork fat or rancid corn dodgers. Even walking and sleeping and eating on the ground was preferable to such torture. She found herself longing for the days spent with Reed Bannon on the trail. If it weren't for the constant sightings of Indians, and the nearly impassable, precarious trail, she would have climbed right down from that stage and set out walking, baby and all.

When the stage crossed the Bighorn River, the trail bent west, and Tressie felt that surely they would soon spot Virginia City. Caleb was out of milk, but tethered in the brush near a station stop, miracle of miracles, she spied a milk goat. She remembered Grammy telling of how goat's milk was much superior to cow's milk for folks with queasy stomachs. If Caleb didn't have a queasy stomach, he was doing much better than her. She was able to buy some, provided she would do the milking. That proved to be quite a task.

Kate Flannigan, with her adventuresome spirit, agreed to help. First they made a bed for Caleb in the shade out of harm's way. The escapade would require some elbow room . . . or, as it turned out, butting room.

The nanny obviously was used to men in britches, for when a gust of wind caught at Kate's voluminous skirt, the goat lowered her head and gave the woman a sturdy thump on the thigh.

After a few more attempts to approach in the normal manner, the women regrouped to discuss new strategy.

"It's clear," said a laughing Kate, "that we are going to have to trick the clever little beast."

"Agreed," Tressie said. "What do you have in mind?"

"Well, she has four sharp little hooves, and I don't relish being kicked by them. She has a hard head as well, and as far as I can tell, a good set of teeth. The milk faucets are well placed underneath for their own protection. We have to decide which one of us will do the milking, and the other will simply have to overpower the old girl and hold her down." Tilting her attractive head, Kate studied the goat, who swayed on spread legs, head down but with her devil's eyes alert.

"Do you suppose," Kate went on, "that the milk will come out if she's lying down?"

"We used to milk cows down home in Missouri, and it never occurred to me to turn one upside down. But I'd wager it wouldn't be a good idea. I think we just need to be real gentle and talk her into letting us have some."

"You can look at those eyes and suggest such a thing?" Kate took a few steps and saw that the goat was watching her. She dragged in a huge sigh. "Okay. I'll subdue the thing, you get the milk out."

Without waiting for a reply, Kate launched a mighty leap and put an armlock around the confused nanny's neck. Wrestling her to the ground, Kate panted, "Okay, bring the bucket. She's going to behave now, aren't you, sweetie?"

Tressie laughed so hard at the sight of Kate's upturned fanny, her splayed legs, and the goat's frantic bleats that she was momentarily unable to move.

"Might I suggest," Sir Harry said at Tressie's elbow, "that you find something to feed the poor frightened animal, and she'll no doubt let you have all the milk you want."

Wondering why she herself hadn't thought of that, Tressie turned to see the portly gentleman holding out a pan of dried corn.

"Would you two mind doing something?" Kate squalled, one arm around the nanny's neck. "If I turn loose, she's gonna get me." Eyes rolling, the animal had scrambled to her feet and was putting up a rather impressive tug-of-war, though her poor tongue hung out of her mouth.

"You're choking her. Let her go, Kate," Tressie called.

"More than glad to," Kate replied, and did so. The goat tumbled to her rear end, then staggered to her feet and eyed all three with obvious hate. A tremulous cry fell from her quivering lips, or what looked like lips to Tressie. She couldn't be real sure.

"I don't blame you, dear," Tressie cooed, and held out the pan of corn.

With one golden eye on Kate, whom she'd obviously settled on as the harbinger of all her troubles, the little nanny sidled up to the corn. Once she had buried her nose in it, all was forgiven and Tressie was able to milk her with no further incident.

Caleb slept through the entire incident, and as it turned out didn't really appreciate the effort. While Kate went to wash up from having rolled around in the dust with a goat, Tressie settled on a boulder in the shade to feed Caleb.

Before offering him the milk, Tressie removed all his clothing. Poor little fellow had developed a heat rash under his arms and in the backs of his knees. Fresh air would be good for him. With a feeling of great accomplishment, she gave him the bottle of goat's milk. Caleb was a voracious eater, and at first he slurped away with vigor. Suddenly a look of wonder, then disgust wrinkled his little features and he spat out the nipple.

"Come on, sweetheart, it's good," Tressie said, and again tried to get him to take the bottle. He tongued it away and set up a howl.

Tressie leaned down close and began to croon to the baby. Her clear young voice rang like bells in the mountain air. Caleb grew quiet and watched her intently. He was such a darling child. Tressie ran the tips of her fingers over his delicate features. How much like Reed he was. She knew those were the Indian features, but couldn't help admiring in the child what she admired in the man.

As Tressie continued to sing the lullaby she remembered from her own childhood, Caleb formed a delighted O with his little lips and his eyes drifted closed. Tressie offered the nipple once again and he began to suck without opening his eyes. Her mind hundreds of miles away in a log cabin in the Missouri Ozarks, Tressie cradled the child, bars of afternoon sun touching her hair and appearing to set it on fire. She thought of her own mother and her childhood, so brief and so enduring. Those memories would live in her dreams forever, and now she had a child to share them with.

For those brief restful moments, she thought not of her Papa's betrayal or that of Reed Bannon. She had buried her own dear sweet Mama, but the devotion passed to Tressie so lovingly during her own childhood flowed from her heart to encircle the tiny Indian baby. Tressie felt its strength as she had felt no other. Some ties, she knew, were never meant to be broken, and so they were as strong as the very earth itself. As durable as the mountains, as the trees, as the sky and the water. As lasting as eternity.

"I love you, Caleb, I love you," she crooned, bending to kiss the soft little cheek. With surprise she watched a warm tear fall there. She was crying for the first time from joy rather than sorrow, and how wonderfully cleansing it felt. "I love you, Caleb, I love you," she repeated like the words of a song.

The gold mining settlement called Virginia City was on the verge of one of the greatest explosions a community could experience. For the cry of *"Gold!"* echoed all across the mountains reaching out from the Far West in California and tumbling down the mudbound trails. Virginia City had become another Comstock, beckoning even the Forty-niners from that fabled strike. Those with enough gumption who weren't afraid of hard work would make a fortune there in the next decade.

On arrival, Tressie knew little of the excitement. Instead she was utterly exhausted, too tired even to be relieved that the grueling trip was over. She had no more than climbed from the stage than she had an immediate urge to flee the absolute tumult that greeted her.

Clapboard structures grew everywhere, and a great throng of humanity rushed to and fro as if on a commonly shared and death-defying mission. Men shouted and shoved and pushed each other. They laughed and whistled at their animals, whips cracked, and horses whinnied.

Kate Flanningan's husband met her, and though Tressie could see she didn't want to be rude, the woman was so pleased to see Zeke that one thing led to another, and they departed for their new home behind the freight station belonging to the elder Flannigan. The parting message from Kate was, "Come see us when you get settled."

It wasn't exactly that her newfound friend was deserting Tressie to the unknown. The woman simply hadn't been told all of Tressie's circumstances. It was too embarrassing, and so Kate had been led to believe that Tressie, too, had someone meeting her in Virginia City.

Tressie had changed into her only spare dress at the last rest stop. With her small bundle on one arm, Caleb cradled in the other, Tressie stood on the boardwalk and looked around. Diagonally across the street was an establishment with a crude sign announcing GOLDEN SUN SALOON. Tressie searched up and down her side of the wide street. What had she expected? Papa holding out his arms in greeting?

Being in such a place and alone was all extremely frightening for both Tressie and Caleb. He promptly let her know by puckering up his little mouth to protest. She gave him a hug and kiss. What would she do now? Where would she stay until she found a job? There was nothing left of her little hoard of coins. She'd had no bath since leaving Fort Laramie, she was hungry, and she was frightened. How could Reed have done this to her? The longer she stood there, the worse appeared her circumstances. Crude and dirty men were eying her, leering, circling. And her with a babe in arms. No wonder, either. She could see quickly that there were very few women on the streets, and most of them looked like the men.

Biting at her lips, Tressie glanced once up and down the boardwalk. Amid the drab and dirty prospectors, she spotted the most beautiful woman she had ever seen. A vivid flower abloom in the rawness of Virginia City. She was clad in a bright yellow full-skirted dress, and a matching parasol shaded masses of her blond curls. Appearing to float above the splintery boards, she drew near and caught sight of Tressie. At first she only hesitated, nodded, and went on by. Then she turned, openly inspected both the young woman and her Indian baby, and returned.

Under the scrutiny, Tressie bobbed her head, jostled Caleb to keep him happy, and dropped her chin to keep from staring.

"What's your name, child?" the woman asked. Her lips were painted crimson and she had the bluest of eyes.

"I . . . I'm Tressie Majors, ma'am."

"My, aren't you a pretty thing?"

Knowing the woman couldn't possibly mean her, Tressie gazed with pride at Caleb. "He sure is. His name is Caleb."

"Oh, my," the woman said with a chuckle. "I meant you, dear, but he is precious, isn't he? I'm Rose Langue, owner of the Golden Sun there." She gestured with the filmy parasol.

A dusty, disreputable old man staggered along the walk and veered toward Tressie, a string of drool hanging from one corner of his mouth. Rose took her arm, pulling her out of the way so that he stumbled off the edge of the boardwalk and fell to his knees in front of the team of standing horses.

"Git yore ass up out of the dirt," the stage driver bellowed, after which he slapped the reins on the horses' backsides and set them to moving with a mighty shout.

The unfortunate old man barely scrabbled out of the way in time to keep from being trampled.

A couple of men riding by on horses set up a banshee howl. Caleb joined them, screwing up his little brown face in the process.

"Oh, sweetheart," Tressie said, and jostled him gently.

"This is no place for a baby, Tressie Majors. Where is your man?"

Tressie had already thought up a story, and gave it now to this beautiful saloon keeper.

She told her concocted story. "He came out to stake his claim and I followed along as soon as the baby was born. We didn't want to miss a chance, and his brother had already found gold. He could only hold the claim for so long, you see."

Rose studied her with pursed lips. "Indians don't usually file claims. In fact, it might not even be legal."

"Oh, my husband's not an Indian." Caught in her lie!

Rose whooped. "Then, honey, there must have been one in the woodpile, 'cause this child sure ain't white."

Tressie jerked away from Rose's hand, still resting on her arm. "Let me go. Leave me be. I have to go now."

"Oh, you mustn't be so quick to anger, child. You'll soon learn that what few women are here just find it natural to mind each other's business. It helps us endure . . . well, you understand. Here, let me take you and—Caleb, is it?—somewhere where you can get cleaned up. Then you can send word to your husband and he can come get you there. You can't just go wandering around the streets. Do you have any money?"

"Yes," Tressie said, jutting her chin at Rose.

"How much?"

Too tired to carry on with the lie, Tressie lowered her head and didn't reply.

"Honey, this is a gold camp, despite its efforts to look like a real town. A girl like you has no business on the street alone. Now, you just come on with me. We can talk some more. You look plumb wore out."

Tressie admitted she was. She could no longer put up any resistance to such an offer, and so followed along docilely. Together the two women dodged in and out of the masses of mankind that had recklessly gathered in the midst of this wilderness.

Dust choked the brazen glare of sunlight, sifting a grimy coat onto her perspiring flesh. Tressie welcomed the cool shadows thrown by a store with a crude sign that read GENERAL MERCANTILE. Caleb kicked and squirmed in her arms, and she felt suddenly and overwhelmingly weary. Like a cloak worn for weeks, exhaustion dragged at her. Even without a mirror she knew what she must look like in her bedraggled dress and hide-bound feet, with hair that hung to her shoulders in lank strings. What did this lovely woman see? This woman with her white teeth and skin as pale as milk, her jonquil-yellow dress like captured sunlight, must surely be a vision and Tressie asleep and dreaming.

Caleb squirmed and bellowed. Rose waited a moment in the door of the Golden Sun Saloon until Tressie caught up. "You'll be wanting to feed that little one and get cleaned up. Come with me." Together they went to a staircase at the back of the cool dark saloon. Tressie paid little attention to her surroundings as she dragged one foot, then the other up the steps. All she wanted was a bath and bed, but would gladly settle for the latter.

Rose chatted amiably as they climbed. "There aren't many women in a gold camp, nor in the territory, for that matter. There's a great demand for young, pretty women like you."

Tressie was too tired to ask for what, or even think about it much. She could only envision taking a bath and sprinkling on some of what this woman wore that smelled so wonderful, then collapsing on a soft bed.

Caleb's squalling dragged her away from the near stupor. "I'll need some milk for the baby."

They had reached the top of the stairs and Rose halted. "You're not nursing him?" Her tone asked what manner of woman this was, but she kept her mouth shut on the criticism.

Tressie stammered, wondering if it wasn't time she told the truth, but was unable to rouse enough energy to do so. "No. I have no milk."

"Then I'll send one of the girls to fetch you some. Do you need anything else?"

Tressie shifted Caleb and gazed morosely at Rose. "He needs diapers and something to wear, but I have no money." Tressie would go without and not ask, but she couldn't let pride force the baby to suffer.

Rose waved the words away with an impatient, white-gloved hand. "Maggie? Maggie, come here," she called toward the landing where a door stood ajar.

A perky dark-haired girl perhaps a year or so older than Tressie poked her head around the jamb. Rose went over to her and they talked for a few minutes, the girl glancing surreptitiously in Tressie's direction. She wore only a black body corset that shoved her tiny breasts high and held up long dark stockings. After a while the girl nodded and disappeared back into the room. Rose directed Tressie to another room along the hall, ushered her inside, and shut the door with a click.

Caleb found a fist and snuffled as he sucked loudly on it. "My poor little one," Tressie crooned, smoothing the crop of sweaty black hair.

Rose guided her to a lounge covered in red velvet and Tressie couldn't even object that she was dusty before dropping onto it with a great sigh. Immediately she saw the bathtub. It was the most marvelous contrivance she had ever laid eyes on. One end curved into a backrest with blue and gold curlicues. The inside of the tub gleamed like rich cream. It was at least four feet long. How wonderful it would be to lie there up to her chin in hot, soapy water. Never mind the heat or the soap. She would settle for water.

At the very moment she completed the thought, a muscular young man came through the door carrying two large buckets of hot water. Steam rose up around his thick arms. He barely nodded at Tressie, poured the water in the tub, and left. By the time she had unwrapped Caleb and removed his soaked diaper and clothing, the man had the tub half filled.

He left without a word, and Tressie sat there holding her naked baby and staring with longing at the tub. She dared not disrobe. He might come back and find her that way. Besides, no one had told her the bath was for her.

A soft tap on the door ended her ruminating. The girl called Maggie, now wearing a ginger-colored dress, the bust cut as low as the corset she wore beneath it, came in with some parcels and a bottle of warm milk.

"Miss Rose said to tell you she will bring you some clothes before you finish your bath. These things are for the baby." The girl bent over and tickled Caleb's bare belly. "He's a sweetheart, isn't he?"

Tressie smiled.

Caleb kicked and swung his doubled-up fists. What passed for a grin dimpled the fat cheeks. Tressie and the girl both laughed. "He's my tough little brown nut," Tressie said with pride.

Maggie pinched Caleb's chin and made baby talk for a minute, then stood up abruptly, as if remembering a pressing chore. "I'll leave. You must be worn out."

Without giving Tressie a chance to thank her, the delicate woman minced from the room, slamming the door behind her. Tressie waited no longer, but peeled out of the soiled dress, kicked it into the corner, gathered Caleb from the red velvet lounge, and took him with his bottle into the tub with her.

The rising steam gave off a delicate fragrance. On a stand near the tub were towels, washcloths, and a bar of pink soap. Tressie leaned back and sank as deeply into the water as she could without submerging Caleb, who sucked greedily on the bulbous rubber nipple. This was heaven. Whatever Rose Langue had in mind would be fine, as long as she and Caleb were sheltered and fed. Tressie was so tired of living on the edge of disaster, she thought she might do anything to be free of want.

She wouldn't think about what the girls here did for a living. That pretty Maggie with her tiny breasts all but bursting full-blown from the neck of her dress. And beautiful Rose. In the back of her mind, she knew what they were. Everything had a price and she expected this luxury was no exception. She ignored the niggling little voice of warning and dreamily lathered the sweet-smelling soap over first her baby, then herself.

Ten

"They call them hurdy-gurdy houses," Rose explained. She took Tressie's hand and led her down the flight of rough stairs to the room below. "That's because we have dancing girls but no gambling. The men can buy tickets and dance with the girls. They are also expected to purchase drinks for themselves and their partner. Of course, the girls are sometimes willing to, shall we say, consider other favors. That's what the cribs are for, along the back."

Tressie placed her hand on her bare chest and felt the heat of her flush. The dress, loaned by one of Rose's girls, left too much uncovered and she hadn't even wanted to venture from the room. But Rose had been so kind, she simply couldn't be rude to her. Tressie scarcely remembered coming through the saloon the evening before. She eyed it now from the bottom of the steps. Two kerosene chandeliers with multiple globes hung from the high ceiling. A bar ran along one wall just inside the door. At the back, near where she and Rose stood, was a dance floor. At this morning hour, only one couple, a scantily dressed woman and a young fellow in a flannel shirt and baggy pants held up by suspenders, shuffled around on the hardwood floor.

A few men leaned on the mahogany bar. Spittoons were lined up under the bar, but the floor was badly stained with near misses. A mirror hung behind the bar, flanked by paintings of naked, quite hefty women. The room was very narrow and dark, the only window being in the front wall. It had a red velvet drape pulled to one side and tied to let in a few rays of morning sun. In the corner under the window, an old man slept, his legs splayed out in front and a disreputable hat tilted over his eyes. A white beard lay on his chest like a massive rug.

"Not too fancy," Rose said in an apologetic tone. "Cleaning up after men is easier forgotten than worked at." She shrugged, smiled at Tressie, and took her arm. "It's a living."

Tressie heard the tinkling notes of a piano, and gazed in awe as one of the girls pounded out a lively tune. The shuffling dancers, who had sat down to have drinks, rose and went back to circling the dance floor, this time with more vigor.

"We just moved in a few months ago," Rose assured her. "I'm only just getting started. Hell, this town is fixing to rise from the dirt like a crop of rain-soaked corn. It's gold, Tressie. Gold that's causing it all. And I'm getting my share without ever leaving the comforts of home. These men are desperate for female company, and those that have nuggets and dust will pay anything to get it. You're a pretty little thing, if a bit thin, and you can stay right here, live good like the rest of my girls."

Tressie watched the man on the dance floor cup his partner's bottom in two dirty hands and wiggle his hips to settle her securely into his suggestive gyrations. The girl laughed down in her throat and leaned her head back so that he was looking down the front of her scanty bodice.

"I couldn't do that," Tressie said, and turned away.

Rose tossed her blond curls and laughed. "Of course you can. What's he really getting, anyway? A touch, a feel, and a dance. All for an occasional buck's worth of whiskey for him and his dancing partner. Anything else he'll pay all too dearly for."

"I don't even like whiskey."

"Oh, our girls don't drink whiskey. Theirs is tea or watered-down coffee. But he pays whiskey prices."

Tressie tilted her head to whisper in Rose's ear. "Oh, my goodness. I wouldn't know what to do. I never . . . I just couldn't . . . well, I just wouldn't, that's all." The idea of letting total strangers fondle her, do to her what only Reed Bannon had done, was abhorrent. And most especially these filthy men who didn't look like they ever bathed.

Rose studied Tressie a moment with narrowed cornflower-blue eyes. "How old are you, child?"

Tressie had to think a minute. Finally, "I guess I'm going to be eighteen in February," she finally admitted.

"Then stop acting like a child. You're a grown woman with a child. Since I've seen no sign of a man, I'd guess that story to be pure fabrication. So that means there's only a few choices for you out here. You haul their ashes or you take in laundry or you cook in some sweatbox. And end up wed to some worthless pilgrim who works you to death. Here Caleb will have a warm bed and all the attention in the world. He will never want for anything. Maggie already loves him and the other girls will, too."

Tressie didn't bother to try to explain her earlier lie.

"And all I have to do is let these disgusting men do whatever they want to me?"

"They just fumble and poke around. Most times they're too drunk to do much, and are happy for feelies. And they pay in gold, girl. Think, Tressie, think."

Tressie shuddered and nodded. She fingered the fine fabric of the borrowed dress she wore and the glittery combs that held her auburn hair. Such finery tempted her sorely. What did she have to lose but her respect? And suppose one day she found Papa. What would he think? And Reed Bannon, the only man who'd loved her, touched her. No, she couldn't do it! She simply couldn't, no matter the consequences.

Eyes tearing, she shook her head. "No, I can't, ma'am. I just can't do it. We won't starve; I'll find something. Oh, I'll pay you back for what you've done. I'm sorry if you thought—"

Rose sighed and put her arm around Tressie's narrow shoulders. She hated to lose this one, a real beauty who only needed fattening up a little to attract the men like flies to carrion. If it weren't for the little one, Rose thought she just might have entrapped Tressie after bringing her this far. Instead, she frowned at her own lack of fortitude and guided the young girl back up the stairs. Sometimes you hit color, other times . . . well, other times you came up empty.

"Never you mind, child. We girls have to stick together. God knows there's few enough of us to stand against all of them. I have a—uh—friend, Jarrad Lincolnshire, who owns a big mining company outside of town. He's needing someone to cook three squares a day for his pilgrims. But Lordy, Tressie, I wish you'd change your mind."

"I won't have to . . . ?"

"Huh-uh, never. Jarred's got daughters your age. He'll see the men leave you be. Get changed so you don't look so inviting and we'll ride out there before business around here gets too brisk."

They rode to the mine in a fine black buggy with gold and red wheels and a shiny leather seat. Wearing elbow-length gloves of soft deerhide, Rose held the reins of a dainty-footed red mare who pranced and tossed her head proudly. There had been no rain in months, and the mare's hooves kicked up puffs of powdery dust. Rose produced two white lace hankies sprinkled with rosewater to hold over their noses for the dusty ride up the mountain.

The gold mine operations took Tressie's breath away. Coiling up the side of the hill like a giant snake were great wooden troughs. At the top, pivotal nozzles, each manned by two or three miners, spat water against the cliffs. Earth and debris tumbled into the troughs to be washed all the way to the creek bed at the bottom. Tressie guessed that the gold was sorted out by the miners who labored at intervals along the wooden ditches. It was an impressive operation, and certainly beat panning gold on a creek bank.

A log building and massive tent had been erected in a flattened-out area on the side of the mountain. There, Rose reined in the mare. A grizzled old man took charge of the buggy after helping Rose and Tressie down. Before they took more than a few steps toward the log structure, a veritable skeleton of a man who was at least six and a half feet tall ducked through the door and headed for the women. He greeted Rose with a gigantic bear hug that purely lifted her off her feet.

When she could get her breath, Rose introduced him as Jarrad Lincolnshire.

He took Tressie's small hand in his long-fingered one. "So very pleased to meet you, my dear," he said with an accent such as Tressie had never heard. He softened his r's and dropped his h's a bit like the Englishman on the stage, but with a little less harsh inflection. He, like Sir Harry, was obviously a well-bred gentleman. Tressie hadn't expected to find such men on the frontier. To meet up with two in such a short span of time was even more surprising.

She just knew her mouth dropped open when she stammered out her reply. "Uh, yes. Thank you, I mean. . . ." She couldn't help being such a silly fool as she looked up and up into the man's gaunt features. He had a long jaw with sunken cheeks, wispy silver hair, and the palest blue eyes Tressie had ever seen. A pair of bright red suspenders held up pants that were ash gray with thin black stripes. He wore a white shirt with ruffles down the front and fine leather boots that covered his knees. When Tressie couldn't stop her unashamed gawking, he threw back his head and laughed infectiously.

Rose chided him. "Now, Jarrad, don't make light of the child. She needs work, and knowing you were in dire straits here since Jacob kicked the bucket, I thought maybe she could take his place and cook for the men. I know she looks a mite frail, but take my word for it, she's not. Wait'll you hear her tale—"

Lincolnshire shushed Rose, not letting her finish telling what little Tressie had related during their ride to the mine. "Well, girl, hit on hard times, have you? Can you cook?"

Tressie nodded and continued to stare up at the man.

"And strong. You must be strong. I really prefer a man for this job, Rosie, you must know that." He shrugged his narrow shoulders, took note of Rose's exquisite moue, and went on. "It's hard work and long hours. I suppose one of the men can keep firewood cut for you. Other than that, the whole job falls on you. Stoking the fire, cleaning up after, and the like. You understand?"

"I can cut my own wood, sir," Tressie murmured, feeling totally out of control of this situation. "I have a baby; he'd stay with me." She cast a hard look at Rose, for she would brook no nonsense about Caleb remaining at the Golden Sun in the care of those "loose ladies."

Lincolnshire hooked bony thumbs under the suspenders and rocked on his heels. "And no man. You poor wee thing. How old is the child?"

"Almost a month now. His name is Caleb and he's Indian," Tressie said, hedging on Caleb's age just a bit while jutting her jaw at him.

"Holy God, child. You lay with one of those savages?"

Tressie glared, tightening her lips. No one must ever know Caleb wasn't hers. She had nightmares about self-righteous women coming to steal him right from her very arms. Or worse yet, a tribe of Sioux sneaking into her room and plucking him from his bed so they could turn him into what Sir Harry called a "bloody savage."

Lincolnshire became distracted suddenly and turned to Rose Langue to lift her pink fingers in one hand. Bending deeply, he touched them to his lips, and the look of tender love that passed over the woman's exquisite features embarrassed Tressie. She gazed all around, not used to such an open show of affection between two people. It was clear that this man's being married and a father of daughters, as Rose had said, made little difference to the Golden Sun's proprietress. She was madly in love with him.

Lincolnshire led them into the huge tent. "This is where the miners take meals, and yonder is where you'll cook."

Tressie's heart lurched. He was going to hire her. Immediately on the heels of that realization came doubt. Could she do the job? She had never cooked for more than four or five at a time, and that with Grammy on one side and Mama on the other.

The mess tent was big as a barn. To take her mind off how many men she would be cooking for, Tressie gazed around. The canvas sides were rolled up in the heat of day, but it was still suffocating inside. At one end were piled sacks of supplies, crates, barrels, and a tremendous cast-iron stove. Logs had been notched together to form a bar between the cooking and dining areas. Crude tables and benches, cut from logs hewn on one side, filled that section. It looked like a hundred men could eat here. Tressie decided to ask, but hated to interrupt the soft murmurings between her new boss and her new friend. Since Lincolnshire hadn't kicked her out when she told him about Caleb, he would obviously let her keep the baby here with her. That's all that truly mattered.

He finally turned his attention back to his new cook. "I prefer my help to remain on premises except for time off, and ye'll have little of that. Ye have a place to live, little one?" he asked abruptly.

It took a moment for Tressie to realize he was speaking

to her, for he had once again focused a gaze of rapture on the blue eyes of his paramour.

She finally stammered out a reply. "No, I—"

"We'll fix you a place behind the kitchen. It'll be warm there come winter."

Rose broke in. "You intend to winter here? I'd venture most plan to leave out and return in the spring. It's not fit for man nor beast in these mountains once the blizzards come."

Lincolnshire chuckled. "We'll not be going out. We're here for the duration. This is a settlement, woman. It's no longer a primitive gold camp. Soon there'll be all manner of businesses in Virginia City. At this very moment we're taking fistfuls of nuggets the size of my big toe from the placers. As long as the water keeps running, we'll work them. Come spring I intend to sink shafts into the mountainside. There's bound to be veins of gold ore as big as my leg beneath this earth."

"Suppose your men won't stay and work the winter?" Rose asked.

"Ah, the most will. It's good pay for the pilgrims who missed out on their own claims. Well, we shall soon see at any rate, shan't we? Meanwhile, little lady"—he addressed Tressie once again—"I'll have you a cot set up. You go with Miss Rose and fetch your things and the child. We'd all fancy us a home-cooked meal this night. That give you time to settle in?"

"Not so fast, Jarrad," Rosie said. "You haven't agreed on wages, and you'd better pay her well."

Again came the magnificent full-blown laugh from the English gentleman. "Or you'll take it out of my hide in other ways?"

Tressie found herself gaping again. How different were these miners than men she had known in Missouri. To say such things right to the face of two ladies. But then, back in the Ozarks, no one would consider Rose Langue a lady.

The two haggled over Tressie's wages until they came to a settlement that sounded to the young woman like more money than she might have seen in a lifetime of farming the prairie soil. And that was every month! Lord, Rose was right. There were better ways than with a pick and shovel to take gold out of these hills.

Tressie had yet to learn that with high wages came higher prices, especially in this town inaccessible to transportation much of the year. She found it out soon, for Rose proceeded to talk Lincolnshire out of a month's wages in advance so Tressie could buy badly needed clothing and bedding for herself and the baby. Rose took her shopping in Virginia City before they fetched Caleb for the short buggy ride back out to the Lincolnshire mine.

In the general store, Tressie fingered the few bolts of fabric piled on hastily constructed shelves. There was little to choose from, and she had no idea if she would have time to make the dresses she would need. She wanted at least two so that she would have one to wear while the other was being washed and dried.

Rose stood beside her, pretty mouth puckered while she draped swatches of fabric under Tressie's chin. More than covering the body was obviously important to the blond beauty. She finally reached a decision.

"This blue looks the best on you. One of my girls, Lissa, is right handy with the needle. We'll take some measurements and she'll sew you up two frocks from this.

Later they'll have more to choose from. Freight lines will be forming fast, each trying to beat out the other to service these gold camps. And I think Virginia City will grow enormously in the next few years. Why, there may come the day when you'll see Paris fashions on these very streets. Wouldn't that be grand?"

The woman's enthusiasm was catching, and soon Tressie felt lighthearted and hopeful. Perhaps there was a future for her and Caleb here. One day maybe Reed would come, like he promised, and they could be a family. And Papa, what about him? Did he look like the rest of the men out there on the streets, with their stern and grizzled faces and filthy clothing?

Gaiety dashed, Tressie trailed along behind Rose, who carried the bolt of cloth as she picked up items and lay them back down. Rose chattered and Tressie only half paid attention. There were so many goods here she could scarcely imagine having a need for them.

"A large crate will have to do for Caleb's bed. A cot won't be sufficient to sleep you both." Rose fingered some soft red flannel. "We can cut blankets from this, and here, this bleached muslin will do for his wraps. At least at the camp there will be hot water for you to do a regular wash. Jarrad didn't skimp on hauling in equipment."

"Ma'am," Tressie finally said to Rose. "I don't understand why you're doing this for me. You don't know me, and I can't ever pay you back for all this. It's too much, just too much."

"Oh, don't be silly," Rose said. "We're too few, we have to stick together. If we don't help one another, then these darned old men will just get the best of us, and we can't have that, can we? Now, do you see anything else you need?"

Tressie glanced shyly around, afraid to touch any of the geegaws, for fear they would stick to her fingers. She had no need for such pretties, but my, how beautiful they were. A box of ivory combs with stones like diamonds adorning the curved top caught her eye, and she held both hands behind her back to keep from touching them.

Rose saw the look of wonder on Tressie's lovely face and dipped into the box. She came up with a creamy-colored comb with aquamarine stones the color of Tressie's eyes. "Just one pretty won't hurt. My treat," she said with a smile.

"Oh, but I couldn't," Tressie objected, clenching her hands tightly to keep from reaching for the wonderful comb.

"Now, don't take on. Just bring that darling little boy in for me to visit with once in a while, and consider me well paid."

How strange a woman like this could love babies so and do the things she did that were meant only to bring life into the world. And do them for pure enjoyment. To think about the waste made Tressie sad. A memory of Reed Bannon lowering his mouth to hers made Tressie tremble. Women did what they had to do, she supposed, and she wasted no more time on judging Rose's motives, whatever they might be.

The storekeeper, a cricket of a man with a completely bald head, cut and folded the blue fabric to Rose's specifications and totaled up the items they had piled on the counter. Tressie gasped at the total and watched the man weigh out the gold which Lincolnshire had given her for advance wages. Their purchases took over half of it.

"Don't worry," Rose whispered in her ear. "You'll not want for anything. You'll have plenty to eat, a roof over your head, and a bed. Are you sure you won't change your mind and come back to the Golden Sun with me?" she teased.

"I'm sure," Tressie said solemnly while she watched the storekeeper wrap her purchases in brown paper. "We'll do just fine out at the mine, Caleb and me," she told Rose, and picked up the package. "And besides, all those men, maybe one will have run across . . . uh . . . my husband in his travels. He has to be out here somewhere."

Rose gave her such a look of dismay mixed with pity that Tressie turned away, unable to accept the woman's judgment of her actions. Rose certainly didn't know all there was to know, anyway.

Out on the street, dodging through the hustle of humanity, Tressie continued to search the faces. "Wouldn't it be something if he just walked into that tent one day to eat and there I was cooking? Oh, Rose, wouldn't that be wonderful?"

"Oh, sure," Rose muttered. "That'll happen just about the day Jarrad Lincolnshire makes an honest woman of me. Here we are. Throw your stuff in here and wait. I'll go over and fetch Caleb. Those girls of mine have probably spoiled him rotten by now and you won't be able to put up with him. Just wait here."

Tressie climbed into the buggy, caught up by Rose's bitter words concerning Jarrad. Rose might cherish her lifestyle, but clearly she dreamed of marrying Lincolnshire. How sad that was for all concerned. Not only his wife far

across the ocean, but Rose and Jarrad as well. It was clear
that the two were terribly fond of each other, but all those
other men that Rose allowed to . . . Tressie couldn't even
let her imagination near that subject. Instead she gazed
around with interest.

The town was fit to explode with sights and smells and
sounds. Hammering came from every direction as wooden
shacks were constructed and privies thrown hastily up behind them. What a sight to see: the actual birthing of a
town. Tressie thought she was going to enjoy very much
working at the mine up on the side of the hill, where she
could look down on this miracle as it took place. There
seemed to be little planning, yet spaces were being left
between rows of structures. There roads formed, winding
around to accommodate more buildings.

One day, Reed Bannon was sure to ride into this town.
And he would hear she was at the Lincolnshire mine
cooking and come to fetch her and their baby. Tressie
sighed and gazed through a veil of tears into the brittle
blue September sky. What a foolish dreamer she had become.

Eleven

Caleb flourished in the open-air atmosphere of the mess tent. Many of the miners who worked for Lincolnshire became fond of the child, and it wasn't unusual for one of them to fetch him from his makeshift cradle on the floor beside Tressie. The baby would often spend mealtimes being passed around at the crude tables. His mother soon learned not to worry about him as she served up the generous meals provided the men for four bits. Since the laborers had come hoping to stake their own claims only to become disillusioned for one reason or the other, they gladly worked for wages: $6 a day in gold that was equal to $12 in greenbacks, if there had been any such thing in the territory, which there was not. Coins worth twelve and a half cents and referred to as "bits" were in good supply. Saloons priced their mugs of beer at a bit. It was convenient. The "pilgrims" who worked for Lincolnshire were paid in gold. Men with their own claims were taking out up to $150 worth of gold a day. The Lincolnshire mine daily fetched out that much for each and every man who toiled there. It was a bitter lesson well learned that the owner takes the lion's share.

Tressie didn't have to worry about collecting the cost of

the meals she served. She had but to cook, serve, and clean up after the meals. Lincolnshire had an accountant who kept track of such things as room and board for the miners. He ran, in essence, a company town. A man could board for $1, take his meals for less than $2, and have the equal of $3 left of his daily pay. Prices were high because of the gold strikes, and no one got rich except those who struck gold on their own claims.

Tressie learned all this before she had been cooking in the mess tent a week. She also learned what hard work it was feeding twenty or thirty men three times a day. What appetites they had! She would no sooner finish all the scrubbing up from breakfast than it was time to cook dinner, and the same again for supper. She soon found shortcuts, such as cooking all the potatoes for a day during the morning, or cooking enough stew or beans for two days in the big iron kettle, then keeping it at the back of the stove with a low fire going all night. At long day's end, she often fell asleep while crooning to Caleb in his crate beside her cot. But it was honest work that didn't ask her to sell her self-respect, and she was glad to get it.

Lincolnshire didn't charge Tressie room and board like he did the miners, and soon she had amassed quite a nest egg of gold, which she kept squirreled away in the deer-hide pouch Reed had fashioned for her on the trail. There was rarely time to ride into town and spend what she was earning. Tressie worked seven days a week, for though the miners laid out on Sunday, they still had to be fed. Many of them, however, were absent from Saturday night until the wee hours of Monday morning, out doing their cele-brating in town, dancing at the Golden Sun or gambling at the Busted Mule, or bedding the girls anywhere they could find them.

From the perch on the side of the hill Tressie watched in awe as the town of Virginia City mushroomed. Stone buildings soon outnumbered wooden ones. And what a wide variety of businesses there were: bathrooms attached to shaving and hairdressing saloons, a physician and surgeon's office, a Chinese laundry where the dirty wash water was panned daily for stray gold dust. Though Tressie didn't go into town much, she kept abreast of the news, for the miners were wont to gossip and exchange stories while at the table.

Some even brought in copies of the first newspaper in town, the *Montana Post*. In December, Tressie was awed to learn that an honest-to-goodness theater would be presenting the play *Faint Heart Never Won Fair Lady* and planned many more thereafter. She couldn't go, but Rose did and told her all about it during one of their weekly visits.

On that occasion Tressie's beautiful blond friend alighted from her carriage, holding her full, brightly colored skirts up out of the muck while she strode through the center aisle of the cook tent to where Tressie spent the better part of her days. There she picked up Caleb, who sat propped into the corner of his sleeping crate, and parked herself nearby to chatter.

"I wish you could have been there last night, Tressie. I never saw such shenanigans in my life. The theater was so full you could scarcely wiggle. And people stomped and cheered and laughed and cried, all at the proper times, of course. Folks were only a little more rowdy than a sophisticated city crowd. And after the play they had this wonderfully funny presentation of songs, and Tressie, a grand overture by a real orchestra. It was delightful."

Caleb gnawed at Rose's finger and crowed with delight.

Watching him with adoration, Tressie smiled at her friend. "Did everybody go?"

"Goodness, no. Some of my girls managed to get someone to take them. I went with Jarrad, of course. But the whole town couldn't have gotten inside. They say we're nearing a population of ten thousand souls. Can you imagine that, Tressie? Ten thousand folks all in one place out here in this wilderness?"

Tressie could not.

"What flabbergasts me," Rose went on, "is that they seem to be here for the winter. I truly thought we'd close down, but here it is December, colder than the hubs of hell, if you'll excuse my swearing, and business is going full tilt. I don't know about you, but I'm ready for a warmer climate."

Rose shifted Caleb across one knee and jiggled him, laughing at the expression on his round little face. Abruptly, she said, "I may just travel back to St. Louis till spring."

The idea distressed Tressie. Rose was the only person she felt a true kinship to, and the thought of going without her Sunday afternoon visits for several months was not a happy one. With the sides of the mess tent now staked down against the brutal cold and wind, Tressie felt like a prisoner enclosed in a dark and very lonely cave. She could no longer gaze out at the mountains while she worked, nor catch a whiff of pine-scented air.

Tressie turned back to the bubbling pot, stirring at it with a wooden spoon. Rose was right, the weather here had little to offer. Living under such primitive conditions was made all the more difficult in subzero weather. Despite her disappointment, she couldn't blame her friend for seeking the more genteel offerings in St. Louis.

"I'll miss you," Tressie finally murmured without glancing at Rose. Her own desires, she knew, were written on her face for all to see. A home and hearth, a bed for Caleb, and a man to love them both. Still, this place wasn't too bad, and the huge cookstove kept her little niche quite cozy, despite the cold of the floor.

A new man came in around Christmas, taking Tressie's mind off her friend's departure the previous week. He hailed from over Bannack way, Tressie heard someone say. Anxious to question him, she hurriedly piled fluffy sourdough biscuits on a platter and took them to his table.

"Excuse me, sir," she said, placing the platter upwind to make sure he caught the fresh aroma. Men about to be well fed were more pliant. "How long did you work in Bannack?"

"Till she begin to run out," he replied, helping himself to a biscuit.

"Run out?"

"Hello, yes. She's been all but panned out. Figgered it was time for me to git up and dust. Some come to Alder Gulch, hit it big. Me, soon's I earn a stake I'm heading to Idaho Territory. Ever one's all but deserted them claims for up here, but I reckon they's color to find there yet."

"Did you ever meet a man called Evan Majors? Sturdy brown-haired fella with broad shoulders and big hazel eyes?"

The miner squinted and dug at his dirty beard with black fingernails. He appeared to still be thinking as he poked his stew-filled spoon into a hidden opening in the grubby hair on his face. "No'm, can't reckon I did. But they's lots of miners wandering around. Some ain't such miners, either, don't know a shovel from a rocker." He slapped the table to loud guffaws. "For ever one who strikes, they's a hunnerd go away empty-fisted. Reckon I could have some more of that stew?"

Tressie took his bowl. "And you're sure you never run across a man name of Majors."

"Could be, but I don't recollect."

Tressie hustled away, gravely disappointed. The gold had panned out in Bannack? Where would Papa have gone from there?

That night Caleb awoke her, coughing deep down in his throat. By morning he was running a fever and turning nearly purple with fits of coughing.

"It's the croup," Tressie told Lincolnshire, who daily stepped into the kitchen for a few words with her.

He peered at the red-faced child. "I don't know. Looks and sounds bad to me. Maybe you ought to take him down to the doctor. There's a new healing man in town, seems to be the talk of the place. I'll send someone to bring him up here. That'd be best."

Tressie felt a deep-seated fear growing inside her belly until she quivered with dread. She propped Caleb over her shoulder, which seemed the only way he could get his breath between choking spells. She cooked breakfast that way, stirring the heavy pots of mush and pans of fatback and dipping the helpings out with one hand. The men, exhausted by fighting the brutal subzero weather while working the sluices, took pity on her plight and helped themselves to coffee and seconds on the mush.

The ill-fitting boots Tressie had bought in town when the weather had turned nasty dragged heavily at her heels as she paced back and forth near the stove. She crooned and cried, beside herself with worry. "Oh, Caleb, sweet, sweet child. Don't die, please God, don't let my baby die."

She told herself it was only, after all, the croup. All babies had that in the winter, didn't they? And if she had some of Grammy's plasters she could steam it right out of him. She hoped the fancy town doctor knew those cures and would come real soon to administer some. Where in these godforsaken mountains would they find comfrey for cough syrup, or mustard for plaster? That would break up Caleb's congestion right away.

After she cleared the breakfast things, she put on a wrap and stood outside in the brittle cold. Caleb had exhausted himself and slept fitfully in his bed, propped up by a pillow to ease his breathing. After a while a large black buggy arrived pulled by a big-footed dray, and Tressie tried to see the man hidden under the shadows of its top. Jarrad Lincolnshire caught her attention when he rode up astride his shaggy red gelding just behind the doctor. Rather than send someone else, he'd gone himself. Tressie felt a flutter of fondness for the odd man, despite his dishonest intentions toward her friend Rose.

As Jarrad dismounted, a huge man unfolded himself from the buggy's seat. Both were bundled against the bitter wind so that only their eyes showed. Tressie couldn't remember ever seeing a bigger man than this doctor, unless it would be Dooley Kling. She pushed away any thought of Caleb's father and scurried inside ahead of the two men.

Bending over the sick child, she touched his cheek

with her own. The boy was burning up. She noted the wheeze deep in his chest and turned frightened eyes in the direction of the doctor. The bear of a man took his time unwrapping himself from an enormous buffalo-robe coat.

"He has such a high fever, Doctor. And his breathing is rattly. I'm so afraid he—"

The man's brittle stare caught at her, held on for a brief moment, and she gasped. She knew those eyes! She scanned the other features. Brashly sculpted into sharp planes, the bones of his cheeks and nose were like granite, reminding her of someone. She studied the clean-shaven features, the sand-colored hair cut neatly away from his ears and up off his white shirt collar. Tressie shook her head and pinched at her temples with thumb and fingers. She was mistaken. Such foolishness came from worrying over the baby, she decided.

Caleb choked and gasped, causing Tressie to forget her wandering suppositions.

"Tressie, this is Dr. Abel Gideon. I told you about him."

The big man nodded and said, "So this is the young fellow who's in dire straits. We'll soon have him fit again. Now, ma'am, if you'll just move aside and let me examine him."

Tressie hovered nearby, Lincolnshire holding her arm in his long fingers as if she needed his support. Gideon was so large he blocked out all view of what he was doing as he worked over Caleb, who gasped for breath between hoarse screams.

After what seemed an endless wait, Gideon finally turned from the child. "I've given him something to purge the poison. After he's cleaned out proper, give him this."

From his bag he produced a bottle of brown liquid. "It's nasty stuff." The doctor actually chortled gruffly. "If it doesn't taste bad, it can't be good medicine."

Tressie glared unforgivingly up at the insensitive doctor.

In return, Gideon slapped his massive girth with the flat of one hand. "Yes, well, he'll take it if you pour a few drops over sugar. Do that every four hours and make sure he drinks a lot of water."

"He won't eat," Tressie said with a quiver in her voice.

Gideon's glance shifted to her breasts in a flicker she barely noticed. "Do you need some relief?"

"Me? I'm not sick."

"The milk, I mean. Surely if he's not suckling . . ."

Tressie could have sworn the man leered and reached for her bosom. The feeling was so real she took a couple of steps backward. What was it about this giant that so disturbed her? For God's sake, he was a doctor, here to heal. Hadn't Jarrad said he had a good reputation in Virginia City? For some reason she couldn't fathom, she decided not to explain her situation to this man. It was really none of his business. Instead she merely turned away. Let him take her actions for whatever he wanted.

He laid a heavy hand on her shoulder. "Forgive me, ma'am, for being forward. I understand. But if you do need relief—for the child may not nurse for several days yet—I'll be glad to assist."

Tressie kept her back to Gideon until she heard him rustling into the heavy coat. "Plenty of water, now. That's very important. And keep him wrapped and near the stove to sweat out the fever. Don't let a breath of night air on him. It could be his death."

Tressie nodded. She could well remember Grammy

cautioning about the dangers of night air, and it eased her mind to hear the same warning coming from this doctor. Perhaps he was as good as they said. She looked at him and asked, "How much do I owe you?"

Lincolnshire said, "It's okay, Tressie. I took care of the doctor."

"You can't pay my bills," she said rather sharply.

"We'll take care of it next pay period, child. I wouldn't think of paying your bills. You just stop fussing and take care of the wee mite. I'm going to get one of the men to help out here in the kitchen. You just tell him what to do and he'll do it. We've fewer mouths to feed, at any rate. How'll that be?"

Tears filled her eyes. Lincolnshire being so kind when she was so near collapse from work and worry touched her heart deeply. While bundling Caleb into the quilt, she was struck with a vivid memory of Reed Bannon, gazing out at her from down in those soft dark eyes, saying, "You're sure something, Tressie, girl."

She buried her nose in the bundle and felt the heat emanating from the sick child's body. "No, I'm not, Reed Bannon, I'm surely not." In her concern about survival, Tressie hadn't let herself think much on Reed. But now thoughts of him washed over her unbidden, right along with the sad realization that he was never coming back to her. She knew that with a sudden certainty that made the baby's illness that much more threatening to her sanity. First Papa, then Mama and the baby and now Reed. All had deserted her. She had nobody. Nobody but this tiny child, and she so feared he would not live.

Nothing Doc Gideon did for Caleb seemed to help. Tressie tasted the strange brown medicine, but it wasn't comfrey. Caleb vomited and voided his bowels so many times after the doctor left that Tressie just knew there could be nothing left in the child's system. But that's what the doctor had intended. Two, three, four times she heated water and washed the soiled clothing, bedding, and diapers. A clothesline behind the stove hung full constantly.

It was a nightmare that she prayed to be over. The baby's wrenching cough continued, and it tore at Tressie's heart. She'd get a teaspoon of water down him, only to have it come back up. He screamed until it seemed he would choke to death. She couldn't bear his suffering, and so continued to carry him over her shoulder, bundled in blankets. When not coughing, he wheezed and rattled down deep in his chest.

Lincolnshire sent word to the Golden Sun that Tressie needed someone to help out. Though a young miner lent a hand with the cooking, Tressie hadn't slept or eaten in days. Several of Rose's girls set up shifts, over Tressie's objections, to care for Caleb so she could get some rest. But Caleb only wanted his mother, and so they soon gave up. Tressie missed her friend Rose sorely, longed for her restful presence.

Doc Gideon came every evening, but Tressie could tell he knew less about what to do for her child than she herself did.

Jarrad Lincolnshire came to Tressie on the morning of the third day of Caleb's illness, sat on a crate near the hot stove, and drank a cup of coffee. Tressie knew he had something to say, feared that he would be firing her.

Instead, he said, "There's another doctor in town. A homeopath name of Dr. Monroe. Perhaps we should get him up here to take a look at the wee lad." He placed the empty tin cup on the corner of the great cast-iron stove and studied Tressie with soulful eyes. "You yourself are looking quite peaked. Are you getting any rest at all?"

She waved a hand at him and shifted Caleb to her left shoulder. He dragged in a great wheezing breath, whimpered, and grew quiet. "It's not me, it's my baby. He's not getting any better. The purging is only making him weaker. The fever comes and goes. And all the man does is poke and prod around on him and give him more of that bitter medicine. I don't think I can stand much more, and neither can Caleb. What is a homeopath?"

"I don't suppose I'm quite sure, but many of our townfolk swear by the man. He preaches cleanliness and the proper food. Says humans can't live like this, all shoved together without proper—uh—sanitary facilities."

Tears formed in Tressie's eyes. Eyes that gritted with weariness and threatened to fall shut at any moment. "Cleanliness is next to godliness," she murmured, and sagged back against the counter at her back.

She felt strong arms supporting her, guiding her to her cot, but she still wouldn't give up the baby. "Fetch this doctor for me, please," she whispered to Lincolnshire. "Someone has to help Caleb. If he dies, I can't go on. Please save my baby."

In a dark haze Tressie cradled Caleb, rocking back and forth monotonously, unaware that Lincolnshire had gone to bring back Dr. Monroe. Her next conscious act was that of trying to keep someone from taking Caleb away from her. A face, round and red-cheeked, hovered over her, his soft hands pressing her to lie back on the cot and pulling a quilt up over her exhausted body. The doctor had Caleb now. He would make him well.

She spiraled into a well of dark mystery. A place where Reed dwelled, waiting for her. Telling her he hadn't really ever deserted her, but had always been there watching over her and Caleb. And she screamed at him to leave her be. To stop fooling with her. It hurt so much to love a man who could do such a dreadful thing. Just like Papa. He came, too, laughing and calling her his sweet little honey. The pain and anguish ripped at her. Too much to bear, losing them all. Take me, too, God. Take me, too, she cried.

Once she opened her eyes and thought she saw Reed, hovering over her, touching her cheek with icy fingers. "Oh, Reed, our baby," she whimpered. "Take care of our baby." He didn't reply, and when she awoke again, daylight had come and she was alone. Alone like before, alone like always.

The empty mess tent was deathly still except for the snapping and whipping of the canvas in the brutal howling wind. She moaned and rolled over, dropping her hand off the edge of the mattress to touch Caleb, who was sleeping in his crate beside the bed. The crate wasn't there; nor was her baby.

A dreadful melancholy filled her, and she felt as if she had been immersed in a tank of icy water. "Nooooo," she howled, raising herself and fighting a wave of nausea and dizziness. Her cry was a thin wail of despair. "Where's my baby? I want my baby."

She was finally able to swing her legs off the bed and settle both feet on the dirt floor, only to find someone had removed her shoes. She still wore heavy wool socks over cotton stockings; her woolen skirt was twisted up around her waist to reveal unbleached muslin pantaloons. Shakily, she came to her feet. A wrap was draped over the crate in which Caleb should be sleeping, and she grabbed it up. The mess tent was empty. Tressie staggered toward the doors, pushed her way through, and gasped.

The brutal cold sucked her breath from her lungs, leaving only brittle emptiness. She could see nothing but a wall of white. Snow blew thick in the air; it covered the ground and drifted around the huge tent until she stood knee-deep in the stuff. Pulling the wrap up over her head and clutching it at her breasts, Tressie battled her way through the snow, feet growing absolutely numb after only two or three steps. She drew the wrap over her mouth and took shallow breaths to fight the fiery spasms of pain in her lungs.

Where is everybody? She thought she shouted that, but the words froze before they left her mouth. Turning to go back into the tent, she discovered that it had disappeared behind her. She was left stranded and alone, completely surrounded by a world that had gone deathly white.

Tears of distress turned to icicles on her cheeks. Where was her baby? Where was everyone? Why had they left her all alone?

"Tressie? Tressie, are you there?" A voice that was only an echo bounded on the vicious wind.

"Help! Help me!" she shouted.

The vision wrapped in furs came out of nowhere, slammed into her in his haste, then caught her by the shoulders. A tall and sweetly familiar figure whose name she couldn't think of at all.

Lincolnshire lifted her into the blessed warmth of his

fur-robed body. "What in God's name are you doing wandering around in this blizzard? Come back inside where it's warm."

Tressie lost all control over the sounds that boiled from deep inside her. Wet explosions of incoherent pleas. In her mind, she knew what she said, but could not herself understand the words that came from her mouth. "Someone's taken my baby. Caleb. I have to find him. Please save me, save Caleb. Don't let him die, too. I have to take care of him. I have to look for Papa . . . and Reed . . . and Caleb. Ooooh, please."

She pummeled her rescuer with cold-numbed fists as he carried her back inside.

How could she explain the baby's death to Papa? She would never forgive him for letting Mama and the baby die. For making her bury them out on the plains where the rain and wind and sun and snow could get to them. Their flesh, their very being. "Why did you leave me? Why did everyone leave me?" she cried into the damp, musky-smelling fur. "Oh, God, I'm sorry, sorry, sorry."

She was afraid to let go of this man who cradled her like a child, rescued her from the cold. She feared she would fly away into that ugly black hole that seemed the only safe place to be now. Sudden warmth washed over her; hands chafed at her feet, then at her hands. They laid her back and covered her up to her chin. She dozed. It was not yet time to awake and face the terrible reality she feared awaited her.

All too soon someone shook at her shoulder, touched her cheek, called her name so that she was forced to open her eyes. She looked up into the kind face of the homeopathic doctor she barely remembered. "Lord, you gave us all such a fright."

"Where's Caleb? Where's my baby?"

Another face appeared, far above that of Dr. Monroe. The long and lean-jawed Jarrad Lincolnshire. "My dear child, you could have died out there. Whatever were you thinking of?"

Neither of them had answered her question. With frightened eyes she watched each in turn. Something terrible had happened to Caleb, and they weren't going to tell her. Filled with a deep and abiding anguish from which she feared she would never recover, Tressie began to cry.

Twelve

Reed was thinking of Tressie when the band of Crow rode out of the sun, whooping madly, their ponies' tails flaring like banners. Even when standing flat-footed on a windless day, he'd never been much of a marksman. Atop a freight load on a careening wagon, he'd be lucky if he could hit sky. But he damned well better try. Reed belly-crawled toward the rear of the bouncing wagon and aimed the Henry from a crouch. Dismissing memories of Tressie bathing naked in the early dawn, he pulled off a dozen shots into the twenty or so charging savages. Six braves tumbled into the churning dust.

The Henry repeating rifle, even with its drawbacks, was a wonder indeed. Firing a few more rounds in rapid succession, he shouted a war whoop of his own, and the remaining braves split in two groups, coming up on both sides of the wagon. Reed countered by scrabbling backward into the seat beside Chim, using the freight as a shield against a rain of flying arrows while he reloaded.

Old Chim lashed out at the mules, but they were giving everything they had, the wagon rattling and banging and shaking along the rutted trail. Reed raised his head to see the two groups gaining. One young brave had actually leaped from his horse, catching the lashing across the freight to spring to the top of the load. Reed aimed and fired twice. The brave, whose eyes Reed saw clearly at the moment he squeezed the trigger, toppled backward right under the hooves of one of the Indian ponies. Feet tangled up in the fallen brave, the pony and its rider somersaulted.

Reed rose to his knees and fired rapidly, swinging the barrel of the gun as he did so. He counted three mounted braves when the band reined up and let the wagon go.

He wanted not to think of the thing he had just done. Killing always left a bad taste. So he thought instead that they'd nearly bought it that time, him and the old man. He shifted to a sitting position on the seat beside Chim.

The driver hadn't slowed down the stampeding mules, giving them one hell of a wild ride. Maybe he didn't realize the Indians had given up.

Reed glanced in his direction, intending to tell him, but instead muttered, "Aw, hell, Chim," and touched the slumped shoulders. An arrow had caught the old man in the back, midway down his left side. Angled like it was, and him bent forward to urge on the team, sure as hell it had pierced his heart.

Reed stowed the Henry and laced the reins through his own fingers. Bracing his boots on the footboard, he hauled back, feeling the muscles in his back and shoulders bunch in protest. "Whoa, there. Whoa, you ornery devils," he yelled.

The body of the driver bounced like a rag doll. Reed went for the brake as the mules slowed and finally came to a halt. Old Chim slid sideways and would have fallen to the ground if Reed hadn't dropped the reins and caught at the old man's arm.

"Aw, hell, Chim," he repeated as he held the lolling head against his shoulder.

He and Chim had established a friendship of sorts, neither talking much, but exchanging some innermost feelings nevertheless. Reed would miss the old codger, who had been as tough as a saddle when it came to handling a team of stubborn mules. He had a muleskinner's philosophy about life, too, and it had been his words, though he would never know it, that kept Reed from riding to St. Louis and insisting the Army punish him for his earlier lapse.

He'd told his tale to Chim about a month after they started hauling freight together for the Dacota Company. To Reed, getting the horse-stealing incident off his chest became more necessary as time passed. He wanted to go to Tressie, but not carrying that kind of baggage.

The banty-legged muleskinner had grinned up at Reed. "Tarnation, boy. If they was to hang ever man who run from that war, or shot a damn Yankee in the process, they wouldn't be enough rope in all the Americas, and most certain not airy enough trees. As for stealing a horse, hell, you're half Indian, ain't you? Means you jest plain didn't know no better." Chim had chuckled and spat into the dust then, casting Reed a knowing look with squinted eyes.

Reed remembered that and other similar conversations as he strapped the driver's body down for the ride to the post at Powder River. There he would notify the freightmaster for the company and see what they wanted

him to do with the rest of this load consigned to the Bighorn River trading post.

The small Dacota Company ran three mule-drawn
freight wagons out of Julesburg down on the Platte River.
This one followed the Bozeman Trail, supplying the growing network of trading posts as far as the Yellowstone
River. There were plans to extend the run into the gold
strike country over Alder Gulch way, and that's why Reed
had opted for riding gun on this one. He might be ready
to head for Virginia City come spring, and what better
way to go than doing a job he was being paid for. Another
arm of the Dacota freight line ran the Platte River Road
to Denver, and the third followed the North Platte over
Rattlesnake Pass to supply trading posts scattered through
the area. Reed wouldn't have had that run for all the gold
in Oregon Territory, for on that treacherous trip a guard
and driver were killed an average of once a week.

The larger freight companies traveled in caravans and
used oxen to pull the loaded wagons. They were less apt
to lose men to Indian attacks, for they could circle up at
night and form a miniature fort. But Reed wasn't a
bullwhacker—a job that took immense cunning. It was
said some could flick a fly off a bull's ear without ever
touching the beast with the eighteen-foot-long whip. Reed
had no desire to be around those big dumb oxen for any
reason. And he figured all he'd manage to do with that
whip was put out his own eye. Besides, big companies
tended to hire experienced men.

He'd got on with Dacota because they were a small in-
dependent with some firm contracts, several oversized
buckboard wagons, and a desperate need for help. Unlike
most mule trains, whose drivers rode the left wheeler

animal—one of twelve—rather than the wagon, Dacota kept it cheap and simple. They put a driver and a guard up top, the freight covered with canvas and tied down behind. Now that Chim was dead, Reed was afraid the company would cancel this run through the months of January and February, what with the snow so deep to boot. There'd even been talk the owners were thinking of selling out to the giant of western freighting, Russell, Majors & Waddell out of Leavenworth, Kansas.

At the moment Reed had more to worry about than rumors. He seated himself beside the lashed-down body, pulled on Chim's heavy gloves, and once again took up the leather reins. Slapping them briskly, he set the animals to moving. The wagon rolled forward in jerks and fits, finally picking up speed as the mules hit their stride.

At the post Reed told his story, then waited in the small Dacota office, hat in hand, for the verdict.

"We ain't got no choice," freightmaster Cord Wiggett squeaked. He was small in stature with a tinny voice, a bald head, and the roundest baby face Reed had ever seen on a full-grown man.

Reed bunched the gloves in one hand. "But I'm not a driver. I rode shotgun."

The little man balled his fists on the scarred wooden desk. "You want to keep your job, don't you?"

Reed nodded and sighed, giving over reluctantly. "I'll not go into Powder River country without a guard, job or no. Get me a marksman to watch our back and I'll do it."

If it wasn't the Arapaho on the warpath it was the Blackfoot or Crow, with an occasional Sioux band joining in. Reed couldn't blame them much. Watching the white man swarm all over their land was surely a mite fearsome.

He'd probably be right there among them had he stayed with his mother's people. Killing white men along with the rest. Likely he'd have been a mite more accurate with bow and arrow than he was with a rifle.

By dawn the next morning, Reed found himself back up on the wagon seat. He dragged in a long breath and slapped the broad leather reins over the backs of the mule team.

Seated beside him was a young sharpshooter who went by the name of Brett Scoggins. He was as eager as a pup and just about as clumsy, his feet and hands being sized way too big for his compact body. But the boy could hit anything he could see with his sparkling blue eyes, and he saw a far piece. He carried a cud of tobacco in one cheek and already his teeth were staining brown. He couldn't be over eighteen, Reed had decided after watching him stumble all over himself climbing aboard. Reed soon found he preferred driving to banging around on his backside with both eyes peeled in all directions at once.

Reed deeply regretted having sent Tressie and Caleb to Virginia City alone. But he still didn't see how he could have done any different. He was haunted now with fears of her fate. Damn it, why couldn't he just have hooked up with her? Her vengeful notions and Reed's own past be gone to hell.

The boy was blathering on, something about Quantrill's latest activities. Reed pulled himself away from fond memories of sun-splashed hair and spring-green eyes, the warm softness of rosy-tipped breasts. This kind of dreaming could get a fellow in deep trouble.

"What'd you say, Scoggins?"

"I just asked if you'd heard about Quantrill."

"You mean Lawrence? Yea. That was a long while back, wasn't it?"

"Yeah, but then they raided Baxter Springs, Kansas. Killed sixty-five Union soldiers."

Reed shrugged. Killing soldiers was war, pure and simple, the way he looked at it. Now, that thing in Lawrence, all those women and babies, that was shameful, and he would be forever grateful he'd left that bunch before they got started on such as that.

"Rumor is they're headed for Kentucky to regroup. Hope they don't do no killing down there."

"Why should they? They're Rebs through and through."

The boy snorted. "The hell they are. They ain't nothing but a bunch a outlaws, and ought to be hung out to dry. Skinned alive."

Reed twitched his lips into a smile. The boy was obviously repeating what he'd heard around Fort Laramie from the soldiers there, who for the most part champed at the bit to be involved in the war and resented having to police the frontier. They made up for it by jawing. Still, Reed didn't much like this talk. If someone ever came along who could tie him in to that bunch of border raiders, he could well be hung himself.

Out here in the territories, law was a sometime thing, mostly carried out by bands of vigilantes who dealt out swift justice at the end of a rope draped over the nearest tree. They didn't ask a whole lot of questions, either.

Brett poked Reed with the butt of his rifle, startling him out of his reverie. "Hey, I asked what's your hurry?"

"Huh?" Reed dragged his attention back to the job at hand to see that the mules were galloping flat out, their long ears laid back in protest. He eased back on the poor beasts. Best not to wreck a wagonload of this size. The trail was hazardous enough in such weather, though traffic did keep the ice chewed up so traction came better.

Reed caught up with a stagecoach toward midday and the two traveled together till dark, when they reached a rest stop where both could lay out a few hours. Reed left his companion unhitching the mules and went inside to fetch coffee. He and Chim would have made camp, but Reed saw no need here. He and the boy would bed down under the wagon, but they might as well take a meal from the station master. Inside the cramped log cabin, Reed hung back until the stage passengers were served. There was a woman among them, and Reed studied her intently.

She looked exhausted, beaten down by the trip. He couldn't help but wonder what a woman was doing in this punishing country. She'd be worn out and dead before she reached forty, he'd allow. How was life treating Tressie and the baby? He hoped they had found work and shelter.

The boy had little to say as he and Reed ate their simple fare, then rolled up in blankets and canvas on the cold hard ground. Such silences as were common in the mountain wilderness, filled up easily with unwanted thoughts.

Suppose men had taken advantage of Tressie. Closing his eyes, Reed was beset with visions of her gentle beauty ravaged by some brutal man . . . or worse, men. God, how could he have been so callous? He should have remained with her, protected her, loved her.

Reed muttered aloud and turned over. Beside him Brett grunted and shifted to settle close, sharing the warmth. When Reed finally did fall asleep, he dreamed of Tressie, but every time he reached out for her, she drifted off, trailing a sharp laugh that grated painfully in his ears. He awoke shivering from the cold and his regrets.

Both drivers decided to keep the two rigs together, Reed bringing up the rear, until they reached the trading post on the Powder River. Such a joining would double their chances of getting through in one piece.

When they reached the Bighorn Mountains, the traveling group discovered that snow had drifted along the trail until it touched the horses' bellies. The coach soon bogged down. Reed halted the team of mules, looped the handful of reins over the brake handle, and jumped down. A few miles back he'd tied his hat down with a woolen neck scarf and donned a buffalo-hide coat, for the temperature had been dropping all day. He felt much like one of the large animals himself as he plowed his way forward to the stranded coach.

Liberty McFee, a scabrous but competent driver whom Reed had met on previous occasions, was already down surveying the situation. Canvas sashes had been drawn over all the stage windows, but as Reed passed the coach, one lifted at the corner. He caught the glance of a pair of feminine eyes. Their look of fear clutched at his gut. He didn't even know if the lady on board was accompanied by someone or had come alone, but he experienced a sharp twinge of sympathy for her. Their predicament was bad enough for a man. How must she feel? How must Tressie have felt when he bade her good-bye and walked away? Reed turned, wanting to reassure the woman, but she had lowered the flap. The door opened and three men crawled down, capturing his attention.

For a long while the men stood around, hip deep in the powdery snow, and contemplated various solutions.

Liberty scratched at his bearded chin. "Didn't have a lady aboard, I'd say dig in for the night, but it's only a few miles yonder to a rest stop. I'd sure like to git her there." He squinted up into the bright white sky. " 'Sides, I'd say we're in for another snow come nightfall. Hell, we could be here till spring thaw. I say let's walk 'em out if we kin."

Reed eyed the snowfield completely obliterating the trail. Up ahead he knew lay a sharp curve around a rocky outcropping, then the trail wound into the lee of the mountain. These drifts out here in the open ought to give way in the cut where the wind should have swept the snow away. "I'm with you, Liberty. We can make it around the bend into that draw, it ought to be clear. I'll unhitch the mules and lead 'em. With nothing to pull, them lop-eared stubborn sons a bitches can wade anything. We'll break trail, then come back doing the same. We should then be able to pull both the coach and the wagon through. And if not, we'll carry your passengers into a more sheltered place to bed down for the night."

Everyone agreed, Liberty adding with a chuckle that if those six runt mules couldn't break trail alone, he'd un-hitch the horses, too. It didn't take long for Reed and Brett to unhitch the mules. Reed walked behind, urging the team through the deep snow. He left Brett on the wagon seat to keep an extra eye out for marauders, though in this weather he didn't expect any trouble unless it be from wildcat or bear, both of which preferred the long shadows of evening.

Reed couldn't help thinking of the woman on board the stage. Her presence continued to take his mind back to Tressie Majors. Why, when he finally did meet a woman he could truly be happy with, did everything have to be so troublesome? Life sometimes was mighty wearisome. Just thinking about her, what with all this frigid weather, made his gut ache and his manhood hard as a damn icicle. Tough as life was on this relentless frontier, a man needed a woman to bed down with, a woman who could keep him warm and cozy and satisfied. Lord, how good it would feel. . . .

The mules rounded the outcropping in their relentless single-minded way and broke from the deep drifts onto frozen ground swept clean by wind, just as Reed had said. Relieved, he hauled back on the team, shouting, "Whoa, you ornery cusses." By damn, he'd been right. The storm had bellowed its way right up this draw and blown all the snow out into the open, leaving the trail as slick as a skinned possum. And in the quiet of the cold afternoon, he made out a tall plume of smoke rising from a chimney hidden in a grove of enormous pines up ahead. They would make it.

With the already frigid temperature plunging, it was decided everyone would spend the night inside the station. The mules and horses were put up in a lean-to and fed. Reed, Brett, and Liberty completed that chore. The storm Liberty had predicted earlier stirred noisily, then blasted down out of the Bighorns with a ferocity unknown by flatlanders.

Crammed in the small log dwelling, one woman and nine men huddled as close to the fireplace and as far from the walls as possible. While the wind careened and blasted at the structure with a vengeance, they all tried to sleep, propped against each other for warmth and because there wasn't room for all to lie down. When dawn awoke them, they found they were stranded. Drifts all but covered the log cabin, and it took most of the morning to tunnel a path from the door to the attached lean-to and feed the animals.

The ungainly boy Brett took it upon himself to see to the only female among them. It was touching to watch him arrange private facilities for her needs and stand guard at the blanket-draped corner.

The blizzard blew itself out late that afternoon and just at sunset, a flare of golden light blazed across the pristine world. Reed stood shoulder-deep in the dug-out path, having come from haying the animals, and gazed in wonder at such a sight. He had never seen anything quite so breathtaking as the snow-covered ragged mountain peaks reflected in shards of brilliant orange and pink light. Such virgin beauty brought a huge lump to his throat and filled him with a yearning that stung at his eyes.

Dear God, would he never find a home and hearth?

The Indians came the next afternoon, one riding in slowly, the others hanging back. The single brave, whose pony plowed relentlessly through the snow, looked gaunt. Reed stepped out, holding the Henry loosely in one hand so the brave could see he had it, but wasn't pointing it. Not yet. The small band looked cold and hungry and, if no one started anything, would probably go away if given food.

The proud Dakota Sioux dismounted with agility, paying no attention to the snow. He wore a buffalo robe around his shoulders, and hide boots. Touching his chest, he told Reed his name was Eagle That Hunts.

Reed touched the flat of one hand to his own chest and uttered for the first time in almost fifteen years his own Sioux name. The action surprised even himself. He thought he might have forgotten how to say Wolf Who Runs in Sioux, but the syllables rolled off his tongue sweet and clear.

With a look of pleasure on his regal features, the brave said, "We came looking for food. Your smoke brought us." The man touched the side of his nose and sniffed.

Reed nodded. "What little we have, we'll share with you. There are many of us inside."

The brave immediately caught the subtlety and cast a quick glance over his shoulder. At a border of tall pines, where wind had swept the snow clear, eight braves sat their ponies. Reed thought he saw the stock of a rifle but couldn't be sure, they were so far away.

He held up a hand. "One minute. I'll pack something," he said, and backed through the door, closing it swiftly.

"What do they want?" Liberty asked.

"They're hungry. Look half starved." Reed shook his head. "I don't know. We can share with them, and they might just decide to kill us and take it all, or they might go away. If we don't offer anything at all, they'll for sure kill us and take it. But it ain't mine to offer. I just vote to give the poor souls some food. This I know for sure: They're hungrier than we are."

A couple of the male passengers murmured in agreement, but two others, who looked pretty wild to Reed, objected. "Hell, I say we shoot the sons a bitches. Among us we got enough guns. Why should we give them food? Blamed red savages."

The other nodded, then took another tack, glaring at Reed. "How do you know how to palaver with them redskinned no-goods, anyway? I ain't sure we should give a breed a vote in this anyways."

Liberty, usually quiet but easy to rile, hefted his rifle, a well-worn Springfield. "Hold up, hoss. We ain't having any of that fighting amongst ourselves. We all get a vote in this, and that's 'cause I and this here gun say so. This feller is right, and he knows. We got a fifty-fifty chance if we share, none at all if we don't. They'll just wait till dark and burn us out. Hell, they ain't fools to ride in against armed men holed up like we are."

The woman made a soft sound down in her throat and Brett patted her arm. "We do need to think of the lady and what's best for her," the boy said.

One of the wild ones guffawed. "We all know what's best for wimmen."

Brett launched himself on the fellow, who shook him off like a pesky fly. He fetched up on the floor with the woman kneeling beside him.

Reed stepped in. "Fighting among ourselves won't solve our problem. And they aren't going to wait forever for a decision. Do we give them some food or not?"

The man who had knocked Brett to the floor made a move so quick and unexpected that no matter how Reed thought about it later, he didn't see how he or Liberty could have stopped him. Bulling his way through to the door, he jerked it open, lifted his rifle, and shot the unsuspecting brave who waited beside his pony.

Reed launched himself against the shooter, but it came too late to help their situation. He had been right about seeing a rifle, for a shot rang out almost immediately, and the bullet cut a chunk of wood from a log just above where he grappled with the other man. No one had to urge either of them back inside.

The Indians attacked late that evening, waiting until

deep blue and purple shadows crept across the glistening snow.

Reed had gone to feed the animals when he heard the commotion. By then it was too late. Several of the raiding band had cut through the low roof and, once inside the cabin, made quick work of their massacre. Several shots were fired and the woman screamed, an unholy sound that was cut off abruptly.

He had his Henry and he managed to pick off a couple of the braves as they came for the horses, but then they were on him.

Why they didn't kill him, Reed never knew. But he came to his senses half frozen and thinking he'd gone blind, for it was as dark as the hubs of hell when he dragged his eyes open.

As he scrambled and fought to rise, he discovered he was covered with snow. Frantically he searched for a way out, digging with hands that were numb with cold. Then she came to him, in a vision as clear and plain as if she were really kneeling over him. And she reached out her hand, touched his cheek, her green eyes flashing with great spirit. Her fragrance washed around him; her passion filled him with warmth.

He shook free of the snow and climbed to his feet, stumbling a few steps before righting himself. Reaching out to embrace her, he almost wept when he saw that she had gone.

A quivering deep down in his gut told Reed he was on the verge of freezing to death, and he hugged his arms tightly around his own middle. No matter what was inside that cabin, he had to go there or die. Somewhere off in the distance a wolf howled, sending a fresh spate of shivers through him.

He got his bearings, at last able to see in the reflection of starshine on the white world around him. The Indians had taken all the animals; they would probably eat the mules. He started toward the station, dragging one hand over the high ridge of snow alongside the path. The nearer he got to the cabin, the more he dreaded going inside. But he had no choices.

The smell of death hung hot and brackish, though it was as cold inside the cabin as out. Reed built up a fire quickly, then set to his grisly task. He knew he would never forget the sight that greeted him there, and for the first time in his life was glad for his experiences in the war. This task was made a little easier for it; not much, but a little. Even at that, he was sobbing by the time he dragged out the last body. For it was that of the woman, and she had been shot in the temple. Brett had protected her to the last. Poor kid, poor damned brave kid.

With tears freezing on his cheeks, Reed covered them all over with snow, not knowing anything else to do. Back inside, near exhaustion, he discovered the lump on his head and the blood that had dried over the back of his coat. More hungry than vicious, the Dakota had hit and run fast, settling for the horses and leaving Reed for dead without bothering to finish him off. Well, perhaps they had been right. He was probably as good as dead stranded out here in the middle of the winter with no food or a mount. But he had traveled afoot before, half starved and beaten, and by God, he could do it again.

By morning he had burned every shattered stick of furniture in the place along with a great deal of the wood supply stacked in one corner. But even a huge roaring fire couldn't keep the demons at bay, and that night Reed was faced with some of the worst demons of his entire twenty-six years.

They attacked from every dark and dreadful corner of the scene of this slaughter. The young boys who defended their homes and their women against armies from both sides of the brutal war. The dead and dying from the battlefields. The brave Indians he had fought alongside of at Pea Ridge who had died for a way of life they didn't even understand. Doomed from the outset, the red man took sides when in reality he should have been defending his own right to the land where white men spilled each other's blood. And as if that weren't enough, Reed's guilt over sending Tressie and the boy away alone grew into the most formidable demon of them all. He loved her with all his heart, and he couldn't have her, but that was no excuse for what he had done.

Well, he didn't care anymore whether she could be his or not. He was going to her, and no matter what happened, he would be with her. Chances were no one would ever come to the frontier looking for a no-account deserter and thief. Even so, all he knew was that he had lived for a reason, and it wasn't to wander around lonely and bereft seeking something he might never find. What he really needed he'd already found, and like an idiot let it go.

He scarcely slept. At first light, he set out to salvage what he could. The Indians had ransacked the cabin, taking all the food and clothing. They'd stolen the animals. But they hadn't even bothered with the freight wagon. Reed could hardly believe that, but supposed that in all the excitement they hadn't seen it nosed in behind the stagecoach back in the trees. It had been nearly dark. Whatever the reason, he was able to dig out enough food and clothing to suffice.

As prepared as he could be, Reed took one final long look at the cabin, and began the treacherous walk out.

Thirteen

The last day of March in the gold town of Virginia City, Montana Territory, dawned clear and brittle, but with a hint of spring. The deep snow, previously frozen so hard horses walked on top of it, glittered with moisture. The path to the mess tent, with shoulder-high banks of winter-long snow, turned slushy underfoot during daylight hours. It wasn't warm yet, but it soon would be. Tressie could taste spring, smell it in the bite of afternoon breezes, feel it on her skin so that she experienced sudden urges to strip out of her long johns and woolens.

That evening of this perfect final day of March, Lincolnshire set out to coax Tressie into accompanying him on the half-mile ride into town the next day.

"Just what you need, child," he told her, presenting the idea as she prepared supper for the crew.

Tressie lifted her shoulders and sighed. "I'm content here. I don't want to go anywhere. There's nothing wrong with that, is there?"

He held up broad palms. "I know, I know. You're perfectly all right. That's precisely why you don't speak for days on end, nor eat, either, for that matter. You're a walking-around skeleton. What you need is some female company and a shopping trip. Surely you have accumulated some funds. Where would you have spent anything?"

Tressie couldn't help but grin at his manner and hold up both hands in supplication. "I give up, I'll go to town. Anything to get you to stop blathering at me. You sound just like my father used to when I'd misbehaved and was pouting over my punishment. I'm really fine. It's just hard, that's all, getting over . . ." The words choked off, and she couldn't go on, couldn't yet speak of Caleb, whose tiny body lay in the cold of the storage tent not fifty yards from where she and Lincolnshire talked.

It was almost too much to bear, thinking of the chubby, brown-skinned child she had loved with all her heart and who was now forever lost to her. She was never to hear his laughter, or see him walk and talk and call her mommy. Too soon the ground would soften and she'd have to bid a last farewell to the child she would never see grow up. For come spring thaw, those who hadn't made it through the harsh winter would all be buried. Tressie attempted to soothe the heartache by imagining Caleb with Mama, frolicking in fields of daisies, flushed by a warm and constant sun in a place where she would someday join them.

Of course Lincolnshire was right that she needed a change. She just wasn't sure that a trip to Virginia City would help. Even now, after all this time, she dreamed of the day Reed Bannon would come strolling up over the rim of the hill, dark eyes dancing, and grab her up in his strong arms. Kiss away the loneliness and share her grief, take her somewhere far from this place of silenced dreams. For only the precious memories of him had kept her from dying of a broken heart during the awful months since Caleb's death. She no longer thought of her quest to find Papa and exact revenge. Too much heartache had numbed her senses so that she wondered if she could even remember his face.

Still trying to get out of the suggested shopping trip, Tressie protested weakly one more time. "Maggie visits sometimes. She's a friend. And soon Rose will be back from St. Louis. I'll just stay here and fix a big supper for everyone."

But nothing had worked. Just by looking at Lincolnshire she could tell she was making no headway at all. He was determined, and what was worse than a determined Englishman, Tressie didn't know. The man always got his way without ever raising his voice even the tiniest bit. Everyone wanted to please him. It was easy to see why Rose loved this tall foreigner with the odd voice and winning ways.

The object of her contemplations propped himself on an empty wooden barrel and chewed on the end of a sulfur match. "Do you ever think of finding yourself a good man, child? There are plenty in this country who would fall all over themselves to be wed to the likes of you. All they see, after all, are girls like that Maggie. A prostitute. Most would aim higher."

Tressie swung on him, ready to do battle. "Is that how you feel about Rose, too?" Perhaps only she understood how deeply Rose loved this aloof Englishman. He certainly had no idea. And even if he had, she wondered if that would stop him from taking advantage of that love. He had a wife and two daughters in London, and had no intentions of deserting them for a mere prostitute. Why couldn't Rose see that?

His gray eyes leveled on her. "And what would you know about Rose and me? Whatever we do, it is private, and not your concern. She does her job, that's what I pay her for, and it's nothing for you to even think about." He paused and scuffled one booted toe smartly on the frozen floor. When he spoke again, his voice grew soft. "Now look at us, having words over such trivial things. What are you preparing for the evening meal?"

Tressie wanted to snap at him that anything to do with Rose Langue was far from trivial, but held her tongue and turned quickly to stir at the simmering pot. "Venison stew, what else?" She shrugged away a vague grin and sneaked a look at Lincolnshire. Did he only miss the beautiful blond saloon keeper in his bed, or were his earlier words of derision simply a smokescreen? She wanted to believe he held Rose in a special place in his heart, but Tressie knew how fickle men could be when it came to women.

"Perhaps we can find something to add to the larder in town. Men are apt to be getting tired of deer meat. I'll take a hindquarter of venison and we'll barter, maybe come up with a freshly cured ham," Lincolnshire said. Then he unfolded his six and a half feet, slapped his thighs through layers of woolen garments, and said, "Be ready to leave right after breakfast in the morning. The men can finish off that stew for dinner tomorrow. Just put some more water in it."

Tressie finished her chores quickly the next morning. Despite her earlier reluctance, she found herself actually looking forward to riding into town with Lincolnshire. She laid it to the weather. Who wouldn't welcome the chance to escape this mess tent when the sun shined so gloriously?

When Lincolnshire arrived she covered her head and shoulders with a black woolen shawl and followed him to the buggy. He helped her in and bundled her up in buffalo robes for the short trip down the side of the mountain into Virginia City.

The clever Englishman had put two men to work early in the winter constructing heavy skids for the buggy. The sled proved quite innovative and was copied quickly by several other townspeople. Soon the ground would grow too mushy, and the runners would have to be replaced with the black-and-red-spoked wheels.

Once settled in the nest of warm robes, Tressie gazed in awe at the world of glittering ice and snow. The majestic peaks skirted by gigantic pine were surely a most gorgeous sight to behold and she didn't want to miss anything. How could God have created such wonder, only to smite down an innocent child before he could enjoy that world?

Brilliant spring sunshine struck the blue-white jagged peaks, throwing spines of light in rainbow colors that changed with every shift of the sled across the icy terrain. Below, the town of Virginia City lay nested in drifts of pristine beauty that would soon give way to spring flowers. The boardwalks had been shoveled clean, leaving doorways accessible. These brave souls who tread on new ground, regardless of the danger, had managed to dig themselves out a burrow and carry on a somewhat normal daily life in this harsh wilderness.

Tressie almost wished winter would go on forever. Her life here would truly be over once Caleb was laid to his final rest. She would be free to leave. Where would she go, and what would she do? A sob escaped her lips. She could not ever be more than two or three thoughts away from Caleb's terrible death. Not even when Mama died had Tressie felt this lonely. So soon Reed had come to fill the void. But now she had nothing. Even her only friend Rose had deserted her. What kind of life was this, anyway?

"Do you think the Overland stage is running?" she asked Lincolnshire as he drove to the livery to leave the rig.

"I've no doubt of it. They're a hardy lot, those stage drivers. Only the worst blizzards hold them up for any time at all. Them and the freighters keep the trails broken pretty good. There are so many people out here now, Tressie. My God, can you imagine a country this size being peopled from coast to coast? It absolutely boggles the mind, it does. All working and buying and eating and wearing clothing and boots and building houses. 'Tis amazing what you colonists have accomplished in this raw world."

Tressie wasn't always sure precisely what Lincolnshire meant by some of the things he said. Often she simply listened to the eloquence of his voice and ignored the meaning of the words.

The tall Englishman climbed down and went around to offer assistance. Tressie burrowed from under the robes and took Lincolnshire's hand. He didn't settle for that, instead plucking her from the seat as if she were a will-o'-the-wisp. Before she could gasp, he had deposited her on the boardwalk, leaving her feeling a bit giddy.

After regaining her composure, Tressie murmured,

"Thank you," and began to look around for something to do or say. She knew her face was flushed, could feel the heat overpowering the cold of the day.

She wore the blue dress of the fabric Rose had chosen on their first shopping trip together. The floral design had begun to fade, but she hadn't found the energy to care. Because the weather was still brisk, she wore woolen long johns underneath and knee-high boots over woolen socks. The shawl was draped over her pinned-up hair and around her throat. Gloves covered her small hands. Only her flushed cheeks and sparkling eyes were exposed.

Lincolnshire held his hands at her tiny waist for a moment after settling her on the boardwalk. He regarded the gaunt loveliness of her young features with a deep sigh of longing. She reminded him a little of his youngest daughter, Leslie, and he missed his family so. Perhaps this spring he would make the long trip back to London. Try once again to convince Victoria that she and the girls would be comfortable here in this wild new country. He would build them a house such as had never been seen in this place. It would be as near to a castle as possible. He could send stonecutters into the mountains and . . .

He let the thoughts break off when Tressie, in an effort to turn his avid attention away from her to something else, asked, "Do you suppose they're still fighting the Civil War? How long can it go on?"

"I wouldn't care to guess, but indeed they are still fighting. Do you not look at the *Post*? The war still rages. And they care little for the needs of us out here in the territories. We are not in the States, after all. We live by an entirely different set of laws."

Tressie did not read the local newspaper, had little interest in anything printed there. Before Caleb died she had enjoyed eavesdropping on the miners, listening to their talk of hangings and battles and gold strikes. She scarcely cared enough to do such a thing anymore. Consciously, she couldn't remember any specific happenings since that ugly January day when Lincolnshire had rescued her from the blizzard, only to inform her of the child's death. And her not able to ever hold his dear body in her arms again.

Lincolnshire tucked her gloved hand into the crook of his left arm and together they strolled along the boardwalk.

A price slate on the mercantile caught her eye. Flour at $27 a hundredweight and eggs at $1 each were chalked in. "I thought things like flour and sugar were made in the East and shipped out here. Wouldn't those trading routes be affected by war?" Tressie asked.

"We get much of our trade goods from Salt Lake City, or by boat up the river from St. Louis," he told her absently. He appeared to be paying very little attention to Tressie, and she wondered if he was thinking of Rose.

Abruptly Tressie caught sight of something that made her jerk backward on Lincolnshire's arm and gasp. Coming toward them, seeming to take up all the width of the boardwalk, was a bear of a man wrapped to the ears in a buffalo robe. "It can't be," she cried. "Dooley Kling?"

"Who?" her companion asked, watching the blood drain from her face, leaving her white as the snowcapped peaks.

The man came closer, and Lincolnshire nodded. "Afternoon, Doctor." Then to Tressie out of the side of his mouth, "Are you ill, child? Whatever is wrong?"

Tressie continued to watch the mountain of a man who

had lifted his bowler hat in greeting and stepped around them on the street side to go on his way.

"Oh, no. Oh, Lord, for a minute I thought he was . . . Who was that man?"

Lincolnshire gazed at her in concern. "Why, that was Dr. Gideon. You remember, he took care of Caleb?"

That's who the man had reminded her of from the first: Dooley Kling. But of course he wasn't. Tressie nodded and swallowed hard against a rising nausea. For a moment she could have sworn the man was Dooley Kling, all wrapped in furs like that. But Kling wore a beard and was filthy dirty and wrapped himself from head to foot in animal skins. Dr. Gideon had no facial hair but a neat mustache. Only their size was the same.

She took one last glance at the back of the fur-coated giant and let Lincolnshire lead her into the mercantile store. Warmth from the stove hit her flush in the face, but she continued to shiver, thinking of meeting Dooley Kling face-to-face. A man she hated as much as one could hate any human.

Tressie pretended a composure she didn't feel, and languidly poked among the items on display. Her insides continued to quiver as if she suffered from the ague. Lincolnshire evidently took her strange behavior as long as he could, then, exasperated with her silence, whispered in her ear, "What was that all about, anyway? Do you not remember the doctor at all?" He was looking at her as if she were demented, and Tressie attempted a smile.

"Of course I remember him. It was the coat, I suppose. I only saw him . . . I just . . . that is, he reminded me of . . . oh, I don't know. I guess I'm just not used to being around so many people. It's so noisy and dirty here, and from up on the hill it's so pretty."

"Who is Dooley King?" Lincolnshire picked up a thimble and twirled it around on his pinky finger, pale eyes pinning her.

There was no use resisting. "Kling, not King. Dooley Kling. He was Caleb's father." She pointed the statement and her chin at Lincolnshire like an accusation.

He backed off, fast, as if embarrassed for both of them, and became very interested in bolts of cloth.

Tressie had no idea if Rose had told Lincolnshire anything about her situation, past her need for a job and a home, and she certainly had no intention of doing so.

After that brief and terrifying episode with Dr. Gideon, Tressie began to take walks every afternoon between dinner and cooking the final meal of the day. In comparison to feeding twenty to thirty men, the eleven who had stayed on for the winter seemed easy, and she found herself with some free time. So, wrapped only in a shawl, for the sun warmed daily, Tressie would circle the compound around the mess tent, then stand above the town gazing down and thinking of Dooley Kling. She hadn't been able to get him out of her thoughts since mistaking Dr. Gideon for him.

Behind her, on the mountainside, the fiercely powerful jets of water ground away at the rising terrain, blasting out great chunks of earth and ore. Lincolnshire's use of hydraulic mining, scoffed at when he had the equipment hauled in, was a great success. Even now, with work curtailed for the winter months, the sluices carried hundreds of times the amount of gold an individual miner could ever hope to pan.

As the weeks went by, rushing headlong toward spring, a longing took root in Tressie's heart and soul. A longing so profound and melancholy that she found herself unable to resist. Day after day, as the sound of Dooley Kling's monstrous voice haunted her, Tressie thought more and more of those sweet weeks spent with Reed Bannon. Even the worst of them were better than any since. As a child she had longed for love, and now the dark-eyed and gentle Reed Bannon began to walk with her in her dreams. She had no idea what was happening to her, but a birthing of spirit soft and clean as the touch of falling snow began to nourish a faint hope in her breast.

On a day when the ice-blue sky was laced with fingers of gold, Tressie left the huge tent at the Lincolnshire Mines on foot. It was a Sunday afternoon, settling day in Virginia City, the day all the miners went to town with their gold to settle their debts and make their week's purchases. All places of business, including the saloons and hurdy-gurdy houses, were wide open. It wasn't unusual for many of the men to carry their Saturday night carousing on into Sunday without bothering to sleep between.

Tressie waited until Lincolnshire rode out on his favorite shaggy black mare before starting down the muddy road into town. He would have taken her to town had she asked, but she didn't want to answer any questions. And she certainly didn't want him trailing along after her. This was to be a day of discovery and decision, and she needed to do it without help.

As her booted feet sank into the mire left behind by melting ice and snow, Tressie breathed deeply of the smoky, warming air. She thrived in the high altitude, enjoyed its arid embrace, the smell of pine and the sight of jagged precipices. What an exciting wildness of spirit dwelled here. If only she could find Reed, they could live high up in those mountains the rest of their lives.

So engrossed in thought was she that the approaching carriage drew up beside her without her noticing.

"Tressie, Tressie, child," cried a familiar voice, bringing her out of her reveries.

To her delight she looked up into the face of Rose Langue, nested in white fur. How wonderful to have her friend back again. Tressie hoisted herself into the carriage and crawled into the luxurious fur robes, both women laughing and exclaiming over each other.

Rose called out to her driver, "Take us back to the Golden Sun, Enoch."

"Yes'm," he replied, and clicked his tongue at the fine black mare pulling the rig.

"When did you get back?" Tressie asked.

"Late yesterday, and I must confess I'm still exhausted by the trip. I couldn't bear to be away when spring erupted. No sight is quite as glorious as watching these mountains come to life. How have you been, dear?" Rose found Tressie's gloved hands with her own and clasped them. "Maggie told me of your loss. I'm so dreadfully sorry about the child. He was so lovely. I have to confess I cried. Are you recovering?"

Tressie's eyes teared, but she nodded. She did, after all, have to get on with things. All thoughts of wanting to be alone this day vanished. Rose was just the tonic she needed. The older woman's presence would soothe even the saddest of souls, and it was difficult to remain depressed when she was around.

"And now, what is this story I hear about you? Jarrad says you hardly leave that dreadful mess tent. Don't do that, child, don't withdraw from life. You're so young, you must move on. Fall in love, have some fun before it's too late. Goodness knows, there's little enough pleasure. But you know how I feel about taking pleasure where it comes." The sound of Rose's glorious laugh warmed the dark corners of Tressie's mind.

She squeezed her friend's hand. "Oh, Rose, I didn't realize how much I missed you. I haven't realized a lot of things for a long, long time. And then when Caleb died, I guess it all just got wiped out. I don't even know where I've been these last months, and I can't remember anything but sorrow. What am I going to do now? What?"

Rose embraced Tressie, held her head to her shoulders. What a sad life this child had lived so far. How to teach her to enjoy what was left? To take huge bites and savor each and every one as if it were the last, and have absolutely no regrets. She patted Tressie's head. "What do you want to do?"

"If I knew that, I'd do it."

Rose chuckled. "I doubt it. You're too timid, child. Even if you could come up with a plan, you'd wallow it around until you found some reason not to carry through. For once in your life, do something just for the hell of it."

Enoch pulled up the mare. "We here, Miss Rose."

"Yes. Come on, Tressie. Let's go in and have a hot toddy and catch up. I'm anxious to hear all the news since I've been gone." To Enoch she said, "Don't unhitch the buggy. You'll be taking Miss Tressie back later."

Rose's gay mood was catching, and soon Tressie was chattering away as she and Rose swept into the Golden Sun Saloon and up the wide staircase.

Settled on the matching chaise lounges, holding steaming cups of lemon water dashed with honey and whiskey, the two women delighted in their reunion.

"We went to the theater at least once a week," Rose said. "It was such fun. And the new fashions. One must wonder, what with the war dragging on so, how merchants could possibly think of things like feathered hats and fur muffs, but in St. Louis they do. I brought you something that will perk up those sad eyes, child."

Tressie relaxed and sipped at the toddy, feeling its fire all the way to her marrow. This was precisely what she had needed. A giddy, devil-may-care afternoon in which absolutely nothing mattered. "You shouldn't have, but I'm glad you did," she told Rose. "Oh, it's so good to have you back. I've missed you so. Does Mr. Lincolnshire know you're here?"

Rose tipped her glass up and drank lustily. "Yes, indeed. We had our reunion last night. Most of the night, in fact, if you must know. He hasn't changed. Just as randy as ever. I think my absence has done wonders. He couldn't leave me alone."

Tressie flushed and changed the subject. "Why didn't he tell me you were here? I saw him at breakfast."

Rose chuckled. "I asked him not to. I wanted to surprise you by riding out this morning, but you turned the tables on me. What were you doing on foot on that dreadful road?"

"I'm not sure. I just knew that I had to do something today or I would explode. Everything's coming to life,

Rose. And I'm fit to burst inside with a need for something, and I don't even know what it is. Yet, when I think like that, thoughts of Caleb and having to bury him intrude. And about the time I get them put back in their place, Reed Bannon crops up. Oh, Rose, why are men such jackasses?"

Rose whooped and set her glass down on the round table between them. "Might as well ask why the moon shines, or the snow falls. That's just the way of things, and the sooner we face it, the better. Who is this Reed Bannon, and what did he do to you? Is he Caleb's father? What's been going on while I've been off having a good time?"

Tressie had deliberately never mentioned Reed to Rose. There never seemed to be the appropriate time, and she was ashamed to admit to her brief fling. Rose did think her so chaste in her ways. But now she blurted out the whole story, glossing over nothing.

Rose listened raptly, never interrupting as Tressie wound down. "And even right up till he put me on the stage I thought he might come along, but he didn't. He just stood there watching me and Caleb ride away. I know he loved me as much as I loved him. I still do love him, but it does no good at all. He's gone for good, and I still miss him. Oh, Rose, I'm so ashamed for being such a fool."

"Hogwash. Men have a way of fooling women, no doubt of it, but if you truly love a man, well, then do what you have to do to get him and keep him. If you lose . . ." She shrugged ivory shoulders.

"I suppose. And I guess I've lost this time, Rose. I'm tired of it. I don't care if I ever see another man."

Rose stretched and stood. "Well, sweetie, I wouldn't go that far if I were you. Just keep your mind on straight, that's all. But don't give up on all men. They can be downright enjoyable."

"Is that how you feel about Lincolnshire?"

Rose flushed and touched her bosom lightly with the flat of a hand. "Of course, what else? There's no need in loving the man, now, is there?"

But Tressie no more believed her friend than she believed the end of the world was at hand.

Rose bustled over to a huge trunk sitting on end and open to reveal an array of colorful costumes. She fingered through them, selecting a shimmering cobalt-blue dress that might have been plucked from the spring sky. Yards of material draped softly away from a softly gathered bodice that fastened up the back. Billowy long sleeves and high neckline were trimmed with ribbons and tiny pearls.

Tressie gasped in disbelief. She had never seen anything so lovely.

Rose lifted it up under Tressie's chin. "Perfect," she murmured. "Undress. Get out of that dowdy rag."

While Tressie disrobed, Rose spread the dress across the bed and rummaged around until she came up with a corset. "Everything. Down to the nubbin, girl."

"Rose?" Tressie asked tremulously as she slipped out of her bloomers.

"Yes, sweetheart," Rose said, eying the corset thoughtfully.

"Could I have a bath first?"

"Well, my darling, of course you may. Let me get you a robe and I'll have some water brought. Why am I so thoughtless? I'll bet you've been bundled in long johns all the winter long, haven't you?"

Tressie, who had never gone a day without a bath before coming into this uncivilized country, nodded mutely. "I just grab a quick wash first thing in the morning. A bath would be heaven."

Rose tossed Tressie a lavender robe as luxurious as any the young woman had ever seen and left the room. Soon buckets of hot water began to arrive carried by young men who glanced only furtively in Tressie's direction before dumping them into the marvelous tub. Rose didn't return while Tressie lolled up to her neck in fragrant bubbles.

Rubbing the thick cloth over a bar of scented soap, Tressie cleansed her body, using slow, languorous strokes that awakened every fiber of her being. Her skin tingled and she grew warm and flushed. When she finished the wash, she sank down until water lapped her chin and closed her eyes. Absently, she trailed one finger over her breasts and down past her belly button to the nest of fine reddish hair.

A sleeping desire awakened there, reaching and throbbing with exquisite pain. She touched its swollen head and cried out. Here, after months of stumbling numbly through her days, Tressie Majors found herself astoundingly alive.

Rose returned to discover her young friend lying dreamily in the cooling water. "Let's wash that lovely head of hair, too," she said. "If you're finished, that is."

Tressie agreed she was and Maggie came in with fresh water to help.

"It's grown a lot over the winter," Rose remarked as she

combed out the tangles of curls. They fell past her shoulders. "We'll do it up after you get dressed."

Tressie stood before the looking glass, scarcely able to believe her eyes. The glorious blue cloud of a dress, her hair fastened at the top of her head and cascading down around her face in bouncing curls, the touch of color Rose had applied carefully to her skin. Where had that radiant creature in the mirror come from? She'd thought her dead and gone.

"Oh, Rose. Look at me. Oh, thank you. Thank you." Tressie pirouetted and glanced into the mirror over her shoulder. She took a step or two, then became conscious of the rug under her bare feet. Lifting the dress carefully, she wiggled her toes. "What about these?"

"Oh, slippers, yes, of course." Rose fetched several pair and they were all a little tight. Or perhaps Tressie only thought so because for so long she had worn outsized shapeless footwear. She would grow used to these, she determined, and took a few mincing steps.

"Let's go downstairs, let everyone have a look. What do you say?" Rose enthused.

"Oh, I don't know," Tressie said in a small voice.

Hands on hips, Rose said, "You don't mean to tell me you're not going to let anyone see you after all that hard work. Nonsense." Grabbing Tressie's hand, she dragged her across the room and to the top of the stairs.

The saloon was crowded with miners, including some Tressie knew from the Lincolnshire Mines. Rose clapped her hands loudly. "Attention, everyone. I present, straight from her debut, Miss Tressie Majors."

Every eye turned her way and Tressie wanted to run back to the room, but Rose wouldn't let her. Instead she urged her, step by careful step, down the long staircase while everyone in the room cheered and shouted and held up dripping mugs of brew. Tressie had an idea she was blushing wildly, but there was no stopping Rose.

Just as Tressie put her foot down from the last step, the batwing doors swung open, letting in a tall man who stopped when he caught sight of her. The hanging lamp cast a shadow from the wide brim of his gray hat so that she couldn't make out his features. But when he swept it off and said, "My God in heaven," Tressie nearly fainted.

Her heart slammed against her rib cage so hard she could scarcely breathe. Then she just stood there, arms limp at her sides, as Reed Bannon crossed the room in huge strides and captured her trembling body. She would have fallen had he not wrapped her in a vigorous embrace.

Fourteen

When Reed saw Tressie standing there, all clouded in sky blue, little smudges under her eyes, their green shining like she'd been through hell but was coming back anyway, he nearly whooped with the glory of it. He forgot he couldn't have her love. He just stumbled forward, losing his hat as he wrapped her up in both arms, snugged her tightly just where she belonged, against his thundering heart.

Tressie clung to what she could. Fingers threaded through the shaggy black hair, her head resting against a shoulder as hard as iron, as giving as feathery down. The joy of such a miracle spread through her sweet as honey. "Oh, Reed, it's you. Oh, Reed," she said into the unfamiliar beard.

To cheers from the miners he danced her around the room. In the borrowed slippers, her feet scarcely touched the floor. He smelled of the trail and damp woolens worn too long, but she didn't care. She could only repeat in a somewhat dazed mumble, "You came back, you came back."

"You bet I did, darlin'. Oh, Lord, you're lovely as spring. Do you know how much I've missed you?" He plopped her down on the far end of the bar and backed away a step to gaze with awe, never breaking contact: spanning her waist, grasping her hands, touching fingertips to the flushed skin of her face.

She sobered as a wave of anger swept over her. "Where have you been? Where did you go?"

Drawing her close, he kissed her tightened lips to another wave of applause and shouting. At last Reed realized he was performing for an audience and lifted her down. He captured her hand and ignored the frown creasing her forehead. "Go? Where did I go? Away from you, and I'll always be sorry for that. Come on." He tugged her toward the dance floor, where two or three couples swayed in the dimness.

But she couldn't stem the fury growing inside. Born of grief and loneliness and despair, it spewed out at him in a bitter tirade. "No. I don't work here, Reed Bannon, and I'm not at your beck and call. You want a whore, buy a ticket and I'll fetch one of the girls." Justly deserved, those words. They were payment for deserting her, for making her go through Caleb's death alone, for taking back his love when she needed it the most. He had to be punished; he couldn't just return like this free of blame, expecting her to take up where they'd left off. Nothing was the same, nor would it ever be. And he had to realize that before they could seek a way to go on.

To Reed's total dismay, Tressie whirled and, lifting the billowing blue skirts, raced up the stairs. She flew past Rose, who was rooted in place near the banister. The saloon owner let her go, studied the tall dark man. Eyes cloudy with pain, he extended one arm and seemed to freeze that way. Rose went to him. Taking his limp and unresisting hand, she led him to the bar and bought him a beer. She was afraid that if he left now, Tressie would never forgive him or herself. Rose intended to lend a gentle hand, guide circumstances just a bit in the direction she thought they should go.

"My name is Rose Langue, and I own this place. And who might you be?" By now she had guessed his identity, but he needed to tell it.

In a voice hoarse with surprise, he said his name. After lifting the glass to take a hefty swallow, he shook his head as if perplexed. "Thank you."

"She'll be all right," Rose said.

He shifted a quick look around, taking in the scantily dressed women lounging around the dance floor. "Quite a place," he remarked, then cleared his throat. "She doesn't—"

"Lord, no. Not her." Rose laughed robustly. "Not that I didn't try, mind you. No, she's been cooking up at the Lincolnshire Mines."

"Then, what?" He gestured into space as if he could bring back the earlier scene with all its poignancy.

"We're friends. She's had a rough time, what with the baby dying and all. I—"

The woman might as well have struck him physically with such news. He would have staggered had he not been leaning on the bar. "Caleb? He died? Oh, dear God. My poor Tressie. What happened?"

Rose squeezed at the beer mug with both hands and motioned toward his empty glass.

He shook his head, feeling sick. "I don't understand. What happened?"

"Get her to tell you," Rose said. "She needs to talk

about it with someone who cares." She paused and pointed a shrewd look at him. "You do care?"

"Hell, yes, I care. I've been looking for her since I realized what a mistake I made sending her off like I did. If it wasn't for . . . well, for my own stupidity, I—"

"Did you know her papa?"

Reed shook his head vigorously. "No. And I hope to God I never do, the bastard. Leaving his family out in the middle of nowhere to starve to death. Wonder she didn't die out there, too, and him not even caring enough to come back."

Rose pursed her lips. "Maybe he couldn't. Did you ever think that maybe he's the one who died?"

Reed snapped his head around. "No. I never once thought that. What I did think was that she'd ruin her life looking for vengeance. She loves the scoundrel, and that's double trouble. She deserves better than me; I ain't much better."

"So you just took the coward's way out and deserted her just like he did."

His own thoughts, thrown back at him so precisely, fed Reed's self-contempt so that he was forced to defend himself against this strange woman's judgment. "Now, you wait a doggone minute." Reed half turned to face Rose, and when he did he saw Tressie, standing at the top of the stairs, stiff as a ramrod, looking down at him.

He drew a ragged breath and Rose glanced over her shoulder. She shoved at him. "Go on to her. Go upstairs and shut yourselves up in my room and get this hashed out. If you don't, you'll both always be sorry."

Tressie watched Reed cross the room in long strides, his intent stare ever on her. Tears leaked from the corners of her eyes, but she ignored them. His cave-dark gaze caught hers, sending a shimmer of desire through her. He came up the steps, reaching one hand out to her before he ever reached the top. She gave him her trembling fingers and he lifted them to his mouth. The moist warmth of his tongue sent a surge of elation straight to her heart and she smiled through her tears. The corners of his generous mouth twitched, dimpling both cheeks.

"Oh, dear Tressie. My sweet darlin' Tressie." He folded her into his arms. "I'm so sorry. I never meant to hurt you, I only wanted what was best, I truly did."

"Shh, shh, it's okay, Reed. I know, I know. It was just so awful and dark without you."

The terrible dread lifted from his mind and heart, and he dared to hope. "Rose said to use her room. Where—"

"This way." Tressie pulled him through the door, backing up against it to shut out the world.

At the sound of the latch, both turned suddenly shy. Alone, shut away from prying eyes, they weren't sure what might happen next. Tressie gestured toward one of the chaise longues. "Sit down. Tell me where you've been, what you've been doing."

Reed rubbed both hands down the front of his shirt, disrupting clouds of dust. How trail-weary he looked and felt. Mud covered his boots, had splashed up the legs of pants tucked into their tops. He looked at the brocaded fabric of the longue. "I can't. Look at me, Tressie."

She did, seeing a broad-shouldered, well-muscled man who could use a bath. Otherwise he was the finest sight she'd beheld in recent memory. "I see you, Reed. Come over here to me."

He did, but sank to the floor and let her draw his head

into her lap. With caring fingers she traced the line of his strong whiskered jaw, flitted her touch over his lips, and then brushed the hair off his forehead. Reed closed his eyes and sighed.

"Would you like a hot bath?" Tressie whispered in his ear.

Reed couldn't help laughing. How like her. "Oh, darlin', you and your baths. It would be great. I feel like I've got half the territory hanging on my britches. But I'm too tired and happy to move."

"Oh, you won't have to move much. Just lift your head so I can go see to the hot water. You stay here and rest." She slid from under his weight and patted the chaise. "Put it there, and I'll be right back."

He grabbed at her hand. "Tressie?"

She turned sparkling summery-green eyes on him, waited.

"Don't go very far. I don't want to lose you again."

"I won't," she said, then kissed the tips of two of her fingers and touched them to his lips. "Be right back."

Reed was half asleep when the buckets of hot water began to arrive. He watched in amazement as the steaming tub grew rich with bubbles and deep with water. Tressie followed the bearer of the last two buckets. She carried large towels, a washcloth, and a fresh bar of plain white soap.

Kicking the door shut, she put her load down on a chair near the tub and came to him, fingers going to work on the buttons of his shirt. "You still dressed?"

As her fingers reached his waist and pulled the shirt from his pants, Reed took her wrists in his gentle grasp.

"You'd better let me finish that, or we'll never get me in the tub. I swear, woman, I've missed the hell out of you."

He caught her lips to his, tasting, savoring. Though their bodies didn't touch, Tressie just knew her heart would explode right out of her chest.

With reluctance she eased back, said into his mouth, "The water is getting cold."

He nodded. There would be time for everything now. He crawled to his feet, shucked out of the britches and underclothing, and walked naked to the tub. With a grateful sigh, he climbed in, lowering himself delicately, for the water was still hot. When the bubbles sloshed around his ears, he let out another long-drawn breath. "Oh, that's fine. Real fine."

"Rest awhile," Tressie advised. "From the looks of you, it'll take a good soak to get all that grime off. What you been doing, wrestling buffalo?"

The time would come, Reed knew, when he would have to tell her about the Indian massacre. How he felt that he'd been nothing but a coward, that he should have been able to save his companions. Most men would have been braver, would have figured out something to do before the affair got totally out of hand. But just now, all he wanted was to luxuriate in her company, touch her, get his fill of her exquisite beauty. To have found her again was unbelievable. He splashed water over his face and scrubbed at the itchy beard. Leaning back, he closed his eyes. He hadn't felt this good in months, perhaps not since the last time he'd shared a bath with Tressie.

She was content to remain on the chaise longue and watch him for a long time. All signs of exhaustion drained from his features as he relaxed in the bath. There was something different about him, but she couldn't put her finger on it. A sadness or haunting about the eyes. Other than that he looked much as he had when they parted, except for the beard. After a while she couldn't stand the room being between them and went to sit in the chair near the tub, holding the towels in her lap.

He fluttered his long lashes open to gaze at her. "Come here," he whispered. A smoky, sensual tone that sent shudders into her innermost being.

She glanced down at the lovely blue dress, then began to undo the buttons with trembling fingers.

When she had reached as far as she could both up and down the back, he said, "Here, I'll do those."

She let him, then crossed the room to skin from the dress and petticoats, spreading them out flat on the bed. She was taking her time because she wanted him so badly and that felt so good. Finally, down to a corset and pantaloons, she returned to him. He worked at the lacing, at last releasing her from the tight bonds. Her gasp of relief brought nervous laughter to them both.

Embarrassed now, as if she'd never stood naked before him, she said shyly, "I'm not sure I'm made for such as that."

"Women will wear anything," he remarked, and turned her around to gaze with delight. Smooth creamy skin, round firm breasts, rosy nipples. So familiar, so exquisite. Tongue caught between his lips, he hooked his thumbs in her bloomers and eased them down as far as he could reach.

Struck by the delicate loveliness of her young body, he could scarcely speak, and scooted up straight in the tub to make room. "Get in here with me, can you?"

Tressie only hesitated a moment. Her flesh throbbed with a need for him, the renewed desire a living, breathing thing. She imagined his rigid maleness made slick by the hot soapy water, thought of how it would feel slipping deep inside her aching body. Before this very moment Tressie had never realized how much of her suffering had been tied up with missing Reed Bannon. She wanted never to let him free again. Wanted to touch him, to love him, to make him cry out with passion and desire and need. Wanted to rid herself forever of the pain of not having him.

In a hurry, she wrenched off the shoes and stockings and posed that way briefly, giving him a good look. His tongue rolled out and moistened his lips. She touched it with the tips of her fingers, felt his hand rippling across the flesh of her belly as he reached out to her.

When she lifted one leg to climb in the tub, he laid his palm on the inside of her thigh and brushed at the bristle of pubic hair with one thumb tip. Her heart thundered and she bit at her lip, overcome by ecstasy. His thumb explored some more and she eased into the tub, holding his hand in place with the pressure of both thighs.

Under the bubbles she caressed his legs, working upward until she had him firmly in hand. Reed growled and cupped her breast gently, kneading the nipple in a languorous motion. Bending forward, he lapped the rosebud into his mouth. He would never let her go again. Not for anyone, not for any reason.

A yearning grew within his soul, his mind, his body, to overpower the doubts he had about himself. By giving herself to him she proved her love, and he embraced that gift, hoping to God he could live up to the expectations that were bound to come with it. A blinding passion temporarily drowned the fears lurking just beyond his need for this exquisite woman and he reached out.

Tressie slid forward, guided him into her, and held his mouth at her breast a moment longer. His arms tightened; he moaned, then cried out. Together they rocked in pure ecstasy.

"This must be the way it feels to be born," she murmured just before the world went from a shadowy black to a pearlescent white that consumed her in its purity.

For long moments afterward, he felt unsure of where he was. Did he even want to return from that intense and all-encompassing world? Then he began to stir, clinging to her, finally rewrapping his arms, this time around her shoulders because she was slick with soap and he couldn't seem to hang on. Her breath tickled at his ear and he turned his head so that their lips met.

Slipping both hands into her hair, he loosened what pins were left there and fingered its fiery tresses free. "You are the most lovely thing in this world."

"Thing? Thing?" she breathed back.

"Yes. Yes. Of all the things: mountains, rivers, plains, and oceans, women, children, clouds, sky. All things."

"Oh, Reed, I love you. What are we going to do? It's still the same, isn't it?"

"No. I won't let it be," he said almost harshly, then grinned into her face. "Look at you. All wet and bedraggled, like a newborn calf." He wanted only to keep her from thinking those thoughts, and he would do whatever it took.

"A newborn calf? Well, sir, that does it." Tressie wanted to go along with this all the way. She had no desire to go back into that blank nothingness of her existence up to this moment. "It's time I scrubbed your ears. There's a crop of grass sprouting in there. And this hair, all over you. Just look at that."

She went to work on him, using the washcloth and the bar of white soap. Lathering the thick black hair, she mounded up the suds into peaks that turned him into a mystical being with glistening eyes. He grimaced, made a face that caused her to howl in delight. She soaped up the beard and giggled when he sputtered flecks of foam.

"Lift your arm, you," she said, still chuckling. She washed in mock severity, first one arm, then the other. Then came his chest, and the lower she went, the more intent became their concentration.

"O-ho, what's this?" she finally asked. "You ought to be ashamed of yourself, sir. Some modicum of control would be called for in this situation."

"In this situation, madam, there can be no modicum of control," he retorted. "If you want this bath finished, I suggest you start at the other end and work your way up. Then when you reach—uh—the critical point once again, I'll be clean and we can . . . well . . . we can take care of this rising problem."

"An animal, that's all you are," she scolded, and pivoted, straddling his legs so her back was to him. It took a while to wash his toes because he claimed to be ticklish, causing quite a wrestling match that sloshed water everywhere.

They reached the critical point some time later, and the water grew cold around them before they finally slaked the desire each had for the other.

Crawling from the tub, they moved to the bed. There, wrapped in generous towels, they lay in each other's arms.

"Rose may want her room back sometime soon," Reed said while twining a curl of her hair around his finger.

"Um-hum, I suppose."

"Where do you live?" he asked.

"Up at the mine, in the back of the mess tent, behind the cookstove."

"Oh, Tressie, my dear sweet girl. I'm so sorry." Tears tickled at his throat and he swallowed their burning saltiness.

"It's okay. It's not so bad. It's warm and I have plenty to eat and a place to sleep. But we couldn't both—"

"What can we both do? We can't take advantage of Rose's good graces much longer. And I don't have any gold dust."

Tressie grinned and raised to one elbow. "I do."

"What? You have gold dust? Been out panning, my child?" he asked sotto voce.

"No, but I get paid in gold for cooking up at the mine, and other than a few clothes, I haven't needed much. It's hidden in my mattress."

"Oh, Tressie. Some things never do change. First you give me a bath before bed, now you tell me you still keep your poke in the mattress."

"Well, it's as good a place as any ... Wait a minute, how did you know I kept it there before? I never told you, and you were gone before I took it out. That reminds me, you louse. It's time you told me what you've been up to."

"I will, darlin', I will. Just as soon as we get out of here. What did you have in mind?"

She shrugged and sat up, holding the towel over her breasts. "A hotel, I guess."

"And let you pay for it? How low can a man sink?"

"Depends entirely on how badly he wants what he wants," Tressie shot back smartly.

"You should be ashamed of yourself, trying to buy my favors with a few ounces of gold."

She grinned and tugged at a hank of his shining and damp black hair. "I just can't resist a thing of such beauty."

Just as he lunged for her and she darted away, dropping the towel at her feet, a knock sounded on the door.

"It's Rose," came the woman's lilting voice. "Come to claim what's mine. Are you decent?"

"Not so you would notice," Reed shouted, and Tressie threw her wadded towel at him.

"Give us a few minutes, Rose," she said, and shook a finger at Reed. He laughed and rolled off the bed.

They dressed amid the confusion of trying to help each other and Reed's bemoaning putting his dirty clothes back on.

"You could send them out to the Chinese laundry and we could parade through the saloon with you wrapped in a towel," Tressie suggested as she urged him to button up her dress, the plain muslin one she'd arrived in, not the blue one Rose had bought her in St. Louis.

"What about that . . . that other thing—you know." Reed cupped his hands under her breasts and shoved them up.

"That's just for special occasions. Only women who have little to do would go around strapped into one of those things."

He tweaked her breasts before going back to his buttoning job. "Special occasions, huh? Oh, well, of course, this isn't one of those. And just what is it you expect to get done? Other than just walk from here to that hotel, where you'll be coming right out of this again?"

He took her upper arms in both hands and turned her around to face him. Her hair hung loose to her shoulders, the damp curls fringing her wide eyes and framing the delicate features. "Oh, Lordy, how did I let you get away?" he asked, and kissed the tip of her nose.

"Put on your boots and let's give Rose back her room," Tressie said, and she picked up the scattered towels and straightened the bed coverlet. She hung the blue dress in Rose's armoire. It would keep there very well.

While Reed shoved his feet into the high-top muddy boots, Tressie twisted her hair into a knot and pinned it securely. Immediately tiny ringlets escaped and she poohed at herself.

"Looks fine to me," Reed said with a chuckle.

"Well, look what poor judgment you have."

He regarded her somberly. "Yeah, I guess you're right there."

"Oh, Reed, I was only teasing."

He knew that, but was thinking of the massacre at the stage station, something she couldn't possibly know about. "I know," he said. "I'm starved. Do you suppose that gold dust will spread far enough to feed us?"

"How about some venison stew? We have to go back up to the mine, and I left some on the stove."

"Sounds fine to me."

That night in the hotel room Tressie told Reed about Caleb's death, reluctantly speaking of it for the first time.

She glossed over her reaction, other than to tell him she thought she might die of grief for ever so long.

"And you kept your job?"

"Oh, yes. Jarrad Lincolnshire has been very good to me. That's not to say he's good to everyone, though. He treats Rose disgracefully, and she continues to let him. Sometimes I think the blindness we women suffer when it comes to love is our worst curse."

"No worse than ours, my love," Reed said. "Perhaps he, too, is blinded in a way that prevents him from treating her properly."

"Don't you dare make excuses to me for a man you don't even know."

"It's not excusing him. It's just I'm saying sometimes behavior has reasons behind it that make perfect sense, if only we knew them."

"Well, he's cheating her. Married and cleaving to his wife while using Rose's feelings for him. Why doesn't he just pay someone he doesn't know if he must satisfy his lust?"

"Yes, indeed. That is cheating her, but perhaps she's willing to take whatever she can get."

Tressie wiggled around and lay staring up into the darkness for a moment. "We're no longer talking about Jarrad and Rose, are we?" she finally asked in a soft voice.

"It's okay, darlin'. No one held a gun to my head. I ran because I was afraid of my feelings for you. Ran more than once, as I recall."

"And I wouldn't let you go. But, you see, that was different. I needed you to rescue me from . . . from—"

He hushed her with a kiss, beginning on her bare shoulder and moving over her neck to her lips. It was too dark in the room to see each other, but she could make out the glitter in his eyes, like sparks of life in a dead place.

Could she abandon her search? Give up the one thing that had kept her going when everything crashed down around her: her rueful need to see Papa suffer as much as she and Mama had during those long months alone on the plains in that remote soddy? Cut off from the world, abandoned by the one who had pledged to care for them. Could she then take up with a man who might well do the same thing to her? A man who already had left her once. She lay stiffly beside him. Maybe it was possible that Reed was right, and the reasons for behavior ought to soften the consequences.

"What if I stopped looking for him? Then what?"

Reed held his breath. Dear God, he didn't dare make yet another promise he might not keep. This wasn't fair to either of them, and yet he loved her, thought she loved him.

Tressie heard the hesitation, even though he spoke almost immediately, huskily, "Can you?"

"I can try."

"Only try? Tressie, hate eats you up. I know, believe me. If you keep after your pa, keep looking for him in every face you see, keep dreaming of revenge for what he did, you'll never be happy, we'll never be happy. I've run most of my life, and I'm afraid I can't give you what you want, either. I don't know the answer, I don't, except you've got to stop hating your papa. Think of something else to do with your life."

She waited a long, long time before answering, and there were tears in her voice when she did. "I want to be married to the man I love. Have his children. But not until I find Papa and make him pay for what he did. He the same as killed Mama, and he didn't care one whit about me, either. Do you know what that's like? To know someone you love dearly doesn't even care what happens to you?

"And then you go off and Caleb dies . . . oh, I'm so confused, so frightened. Please understand, Reed. If our love is true, it will last through this. If you can't help me find him, well, then you just don't love me enough, that's all. And I don't want to find that out after we're married and have children.

"Please, Reed, I have to find Papa. I just have to. Damn his soul to hell."

"Ah, Tressie, love, you don't mean that. Don't even say it. You have to forgive him. Please forgive him."

It suddenly became very important to Reed that she let go of her hate of her papa. He could see it standing between their love like a great bank of storm clouds, hissing and spitting at any move they might make to be happy. He would follow her anywhere, he knew, but his prayer would be not that they find her pa, but that she forgive him.

Dear God, if Tressie couldn't forgive her own father, what made him think she ever could overlook the awful things he himself had done?

He held her tightly, felt the heat of her tears, and came close to joining her in the sobbing.

Reed fell into a deep and troubled sleep, eventually walking a familiar trail that led him through bloody snow to the door of a cabin. It all came back. The smell of blood and death, the sight of the helpless slain, the sound of the woman's scream, growing in intensity until he could dwell there no more. With a shout he lunged bolt upright in the bed. His breath came in jagged gasps and he was covered with sweat.

Tressie touched the hunched back, kneaded the knotted muscles, then crept around until she could hold him in her arms.

"Oh, God help me," he said, and grabbed on to her.

"Shh, shh, it's all right. It was only a dream. I'm here, you're here." Tressie rocked him until he stopped shaking, then lowered him back onto the pillow.

Somehow they would have to get through this together. She would not give him up again, but neither would she stop looking for Papa. There simply had to be a way.

Fifteen

Jarrad Lincolnshire eyed Tressie with regret. "We'll miss you, girl. Are you sure this is what you want?" He aimed a stern look toward Reed Bannon, who stood a few paces away, hat in both hands. His face appeared younger without the beard, the mouth more defined and stubborn. She was glad he had shaved.

Reed scowled and returned Lincolnshire's glare. The two men hadn't hit it off at all, and Tressie was secretly glad. After Reed's making excuses for a man he didn't even know, it served him right to find he disliked that man. Still, despite the relationship between the Englishman and her best friend Rose, she herself couldn't feel anything but grateful to him.

"What will you do?" Lincolnshire asked.

"We're heading up Bannack way. Maybe do some prospecting," Reed injected gruffly.

"Taking her with you? That's no life for a woman. Gold camps are barbaric, unsanitary hellholes," Lincolnshire said. "Let her remain here while you get this out of your system." He didn't wait for Reed to reply, but turned to Tressie. "Be reasonable, child. Don't let your heart rule your head. He'll work you to death."

Tressie was amazed at Lincolnshire's reaction. She knew he was fond of her, but this was totally out of reason. He was acting more like her father than an employer and friend.

Touching his arm, Tressie beseeched with wide green eyes. "You don't understand. This is what I want. I need to get away from here. We'll be okay. Reed will take care of me, I promise you."

"Tressie, come on," Reed urged. His face was blotched dark with anger, yet he held back from voicing it. Perhaps in deference to her feelings for this man and what he had done for her and Caleb. Still she had to wonder if he ever cared about a thing enough to explode. If he did, she'd never seen it.

She remembered how sometimes Papa would go into a blue rage, face turning red, fists clenching. On a few occasions he'd actually thrown things. Once he'd scared her half to death by shaking Mama quite roughly when she'd disagreed with him about something. What, she could no longer even remember. Men's anger was generally a frightening thing to see, for they often took it out on their woman. Even so she loved her father, and his few lapses hadn't changed that. But she didn't want to go remembering things about that life anymore. There was no purpose; it was gone for good, thanks to Papa. Would she never forgive him?

Lincolnshire jerked her back to the present with stern words. "And what about the funeral?"

Tressie clasped both fists tightly against her mouth. She had blotted that from her mind as surely as if Caleb had never existed. Being with Reed had renewed in her a happiness she didn't want to lose. Mention of the funeral yanked her back to a sorrowful reality. "Oh, oh. I never thought . . . when? When are they going to do it?"

"This coming Saturday: Everyone will be there."

Tressie nodded. "We'll stay for that." She didn't look to Reed for confirmation. There was no question in her own mind.

"Of course we will," Reed echoed. "Until then, Tressie will be staying at the hotel, that is if you can get along without her."

"Oh, but—" Tressie began.

Without giving her time to finish, Lincolnshire whirled and left the tent. They could hear his boots squishing in the thick mud as he walked away.

"I could have helped out till he found someone," Tressie said.

"No need," Reed replied. "It's best this way, don't you think?"

He was probably right, so Tressie didn't argue further.

Late that Friday afternoon, upstairs at the Golden Sun, Rose told Tressie that Maggie had a dress she could wear to the funeral.

Tressie thought it puzzling that Maggie would be the one who could come up with a suitable outfit, but Rose was too busy keeping peace at the Golden Sun to explain. In fact, Maggie was in great demand on the dance floor and it was a while before she came upstairs to talk to Tressie.

The dress she produced was black with a high neck and long sleeves. The girl offered it with tears in her eyes and Tressie mistakenly thought she regretted offering it.

"Oh, no," Maggie replied when asked. "It just brings back bad memories."

Tressie took the dress. "Bad memories. It's so beautiful, but so . . . well, not you."

"It belonged to my mother. My parents came west with Brigham Young. That was in 1847. . . . I was three. My father and his three wives died. The older children were given out to other families, all except me. I was sick and, they thought, dying. One of the elders left me and my mother's belongings out on the trail with a letter explaining what he had done and why." Maggie paused and touched the dress with trembling fingers.

"Heavens, Maggie. What a terrible thing. What happened? I mean, how did you get here?" Tressie decided there must be nearly as many tragic stories as there were women in the West.

"Little girls are prized by some," Maggie said with a bitter twist to her mouth. "We are never too young, I think, to pleasure some men."

"Oh, Maggie," Tressie said, and put her arm around her friend.

"It's okay. I killed the bastard," Maggie spat. "Just as soon as I was old enough, I waited till he went to sleep after having his way and I shot him in the ear with his own gun."

The two embraced for a moment, but Maggie shed no tears. Tressie felt the despair in the girl's thin body, and thought she understood more about Maggie's desire to care for Caleb when he was sick. Abandoned herself at a young age, she must have felt a certain compassion for the suffering of all children. "What happened then?" she whispered.

"I was fourteen. I managed to get a ride with a family heading for California. But before we could cross the mountains, the woman caught me and her man out in the woods and run me off. Called me a whore." Maggie pushed away, sighed, and gave Tressie a crooked grin. "And so, since that was what I was, I decided to make the most of it. So here I am." She spread her arms wide. "Oh, shoot. Everyone has a sad story, don't they? Let's see if that dress fits. You need to look your best for the funeral."

Maggie didn't appear at the burying. She had given Tressie the only suitable dress she owned. Spring had busted wide open, and the warm weather saw the town filled nearly to bursting with strangers. They, as well as those whose faces were familiar, all attended the mass funeral. After all, such occurrences were social events on the frontier where everyone welcomed any chance to come together. Tressie stood near Caleb's open grave. Reed held her right arm firmly, Jarrad tucked into her left with Rose next to him. Everyone stood ankle-deep in mud.

Dr. Gideon preached the sermon. It turned out he was a preacher as well as a medical doctor. Holding his stovepipe hat upside down, Bible open across it, the large man began in a melodious voice that carried over the heads of the crowd like the great roar of an avalanche.

As he intoned the service, Tressie steeled herself. A piece of her heart was going in that grave with Caleb. She couldn't help but remember another grave on a windy plain, and prayed this would be the last time she would have to endure such a painful loss. Reed's steadying touch was all that kept her from falling apart. It was almost like losing Caleb again, watching that tiny coffin lowered into the ground along with the others, as one by one the departed of that past harsh winter found their final resting place in Virginia City's cemetery.

Reed eased an arm around Tressie as he felt her sag against him. Of all the hardships a woman endures, losing a child must be the toughest. And Tressie at eighteen had already seen too much death. Though this child was not born to her, he couldn't help but think that caring for Caleb so deeply had made him her very own. God, how he regretted not having been here to help her when she needed him so.

His gaze shifted toward the preacher, a mountain of a man who reminded him of Dooley Kling. It was the size more than anything, but the voice struck a chord, too. Reed hadn't wasted much thought on Kling since the man had taken off and deserted his own baby back in the mountains. More important things had intruded. He did, however, still resent Kling's theft of the soft leather pouch he had carried with him since leaving his mother's people. It was all he had left of his past. Why had the man taken such a valueless thing?

Tressie buried her face in his chest, shoulders quivering as she cried, and Reed turned his attention back to her. Damn, he hated her having to suffer.

As the crowds drifted away, their voices carried off by a brisk chill wind, Jarrad Lincolnshire and Rose Langue lingered, loath to say good-bye to the young woman they'd grown so fond of.

Ignoring Reed, who remained at Tressie's side, Lincolnshire said, "I fear for you, dear child. There's no telling what will happen to you, out there amongst all those heathens."

Before she could defend their decision, Reed said, "It'll

be all right. We'll both do just fine. I'm going to make a place for her." He turned his dark gaze to Rose. "I promise I won't let anything happen to her. And we'll come back and visit sometime."

Rose cocked her head and studied the tall, dark-skinned man. "You're going to try to find Evan Majors, aren't you? That's what you're really up to, a fool's errand."

Tressie glanced quickly at Reed. They had neither spoken of Papa again, as if in keeping quiet both could make his ghostly presence go away. She knew Reed was right about her need to punish Papa. His silence now spoke volumes. He would be there even though he didn't agree.

"I just can't stop looking for him yet. It's not Reed's idea, don't blame him. I have to know why Papa left, don't you see? I have to find out what made him do that to us, so I can make sure it never happens to me. Oh, Rose, please understand."

The muscles of the arm Reed held around her tightened into rock-hard knots. "Come on, we have to be getting started," he said softly.

Tressie went along, picking her way through the mud. Rose and Lincolnshire followed. In her most secret self, Rose envied Tressie the love of a man like Reed Bannon. Jarrad Lincolnshire had announced that he would return to London soon to visit with his family. If things worked out, his wife and daughters would return to this new Montana Territory with him. He would build them a home. A castle, he said.

And what will I have? Rose had wanted to ask, but she hadn't. After all, she had expected nothing, why should she now complain? There were other men. She wiped at hot tears that flowed without warning down her cheeks.

As always, she would survive. She wondered how much longer that would be enough.

That night in the hotel room, Reed, in the midst of planning their departure, asked Tressie, "That man, that Gideon. Do you know him well? I can't get him out of my mind."

"I've often felt the same. He took care of Caleb, but I didn't know he was a preacher, too. Isn't that strange?"

"More than strange. He reminds me of Dooley Kling. How long has he been in Virginia City?"

"He arrived after I did, I'm not sure exactly when, though. But you know, he reminds me of Dooley Kling, too, except . . ."

Reed glanced up from the list he'd worked steadily on all evening. The lamplight brought out the rich coppery tones in Tressie's hair and softened the grief on her features. In her white nightdress, gathered around her neck with a delicate blue ribbon, she was so lovely it made his heart ache. And made him not pay enough attention to what she had just said—not at that moment, anyway.

"They're right, you know," he murmured, and chewed on the end of his pencil.

"About what?"

"You'll be in great danger out there with all those miners so starved for female company."

"I'll not wait here while you look for Papa. I won't be alone anymore." The idea he might leave her was terrifying.

His heart leaped up in his throat. "I won't leave you. I just thought . . ."

"You don't even know what he looks like."

"It's too hard a life, Tressie. This prospecting. Who said

anything about your father?" He almost choked on the words.

She began to cry, making no sound at it, but turning loose a great flood of tears.

"Aw, hell, darlin'. You know I can't stand that." He unwound himself from his chair, put down the pencil, and went to the bed where she sat. When he got there she threw herself at him, hanging on and sobbing.

"If you leave me again, I'll die," she wailed. It was all too much. Tressie felt her world spiraling away from her. She would promise anything, do anything, to go with him.

He held her close, big hands patting clumsily at the loose braid she'd put in her hair. He could not hurt her more than she'd already been hurt. "It's okay. I won't leave you. We'll go together, and we'll find him or what happened to him. And when we do ... well, then ..." He didn't know what else to say because he still wasn't completely sure of her love for him.

But she was, and she finished for him. "Then we can be free to start over."

In silence he nodded. All he knew for certain was that he could not watch her ride out on her search alone. She would do that, despite anything he could say. And so he had little choice but to go with her. Worrying about her out there alone on the trail among all those rough miners and whoever else might be at large was much worse than worrying about a Union soldier one day running him down, or some of Quantrill's men stringing him up.

From outside the hotel room, gunshots and shouts erupted.

"What in the hell is that?" Reed said.

They rose to go to the window. Down in the muddy

street, men in ever-growing numbers rode horses and shouted and fired off their weapons. About that time, there was a huge commotion out in the hallway, and Reed, followed closely by Tressie, raced to open the door.

"What the thunderation is going on?" he asked a be-whiskered man scurrying along, fastening his pants in haste.

"The war, man. It's the war. They say it's over. Lee surrendered today. I'm not sure where, but they say the war's over."

Reed staggered backward, pushing the door shut. So it was over with at last. Much as he hated the killing and the futility, the raping, burning, and looting, Reed had dreaded this day. For now would come the most devastating of wars. Union soldiers would cover up the West like a gigantic and hungry ocean, and the Indians, who up to now had managed to hold their own, would be wiped from the face of the earth. How tragic there wasn't room for both the red man and the white in this great country. But he sensed the massacres coming and knew he had no choice but to come down on the white man's side. Though he felt a deep affinity for his mother's people, he truly did not belong with them. Not in body or in spirit.

"Reed, are you all right? Isn't it wonderful? Now all those boys can go home." Tressie tugged at his shirtsleeve. "What is it? You're pale as a sheet."

"Nothing," he said softly. "I'm okay." Taking both her hands in his, he raised them to his lips and gazed intently into her shining, summer-grass eyes. "I was just remembering something I hadn't thought of in a while. But it's okay, that's in the past. We have to look to the future now, for sure. There'll be legions of folks moving west as soon as they get over this war. We haven't seen anything out here compared to what it will be. We need to be on our way, find what it is we want."

He led her back to the bed. "Here, sit. I just thought of something. Back when I was working for Dacota, I heard about this stage driver—tough old coot, as I recall—who died. And guess what?"

Tressie was confused. Why was he talking about some old stage driver dying?

"He was a she. They didn't even know it till the undertaker went to . . . well, you know. . . ."

She turned disbelieving eyes on him. "And so?"

"And so, that's what we'll do. We'll cut your hair, though God knows I hate to see those gorgeous curls shorn, dress you up like a boy. We'll get by with it, and the men won't bother you. What do you think? It's perfect."

Tressie gaped at his ear-to-ear grin. "A . . . a boy?"

"Yes, don't you see? You can be my little brother."

"Are you serious? You can't be. I'd never get away with it."

"Sure you would. Who would pay that much attention anyway? No one truly looks at anyone. How do you think that old coot got away with passing for a man . . . all her life, Tressie? We'll just be doing it for a few months, until we make our way through all the gold strike towns. Once we find your pa, then you can become my girl again. It'll work—you'll see."

His excitement was catching, and Tressie rose to look at herself in the wavery mirror above the washstand. "Too bad I can't grow whiskers," she joked after a moment's perusal.

Reed came up behind her and locked his arms around

her waist. "Well, don't get too carried away. I'm not sure how I'd feel kissing someone with whiskers."

She turned in his arms and rubbed up against his chest. "I don't see why; it doesn't bother me in the least," she murmured, and raised her mouth to his.

Tressie went to see Rose the next morning while Reed used her gold to outfit them for their journey. She promised to meet him at the mercantile in time to buy some clothing suitable for herself. "I just want to tell her good-bye," she said as she took leave of Reed.

The town was still in an uproar over the news of the war's ending. Some men, grateful for any excuse to celebrate, had spent the night in one of the several saloons, gambling, drinking and whoring. It had been an all-night party that hadn't ceased yet, but was losing momentum as the revelers grew too drunk to walk.

Weary horses, tied to hitching rails for many hours, had left piles of manure along the edges of the main street of town. The stink was overpowering.

In the Golden Sun, several girls held up exhausted miners as they shuffled around the dance floor. Rose and her bartender, helped out by her livery man, Enoch, were busy dragging unconscious patrons out onto the board-walk in order to clean up the place.

"Isn't this something?" the blond saloon keeper called out to Tressie. "I haven't had so much business in one night since the Alder Gulch gold strike. Maybe we ought to have the end of wars more often." Allowing Enoch and the bartender to finish up, Rose took Tressie's arm and they went upstairs together.

"I can't stay but a moment. I just came to say good-bye."

"So you're going anyway?"

"Surely you never thought I wouldn't. I love him, Rose. He's gentle and kind and good to me. Why would I not go with him? Besides, he came up with a great idea, one that should make you happy."

Rose hugged her friend. "It'll take a humdinger to make me happy with you going out there in that wilderness, child."

"Don't worry about me. He's got a plan that will keep me as safe as any man in the camps. I'm going to cut all my hair off and go dressed as a boy. I'll be his younger brother."

Rose stared in dismay. "That's the craziest thing I ever heard. You'll no more resemble a man than I would, if for different reasons. A young boy would be no safer, I'd wager, than a young girl."

"Of course I would. With Reed, no one will even look twice at a younger companion who looks like a boy. It's a wonderful idea," Tressie finished, but tears glistened in her eyes. "Please wish me well, Rose. I don't think I can stand leaving with you feeling like this."

"Oh, child," Rose said with a sigh. "It's just that I worry so about you. Of course I wish you well. I just don't understand why you and he don't homestead some land and forget all this other nonsense. You don't have to traipse all over gold country looking for that no-good. Just let it be, is what I say."

"I can't, Rose. My mama died and Evan Majors, my papa, well, I won't leave it at that. He'll learn what he did, face me and tell me why, or I'll die trying. Reed says I'm wrong, but he's going with me anyway. He says—"

"Oh, he says foot," Rose said, and paced across the

floor. "If that's not just like a man. Damn their hides anyway. I don't understand why they just can't accept what we offer without all this man stuff. It's got to be so and so. Or this way, or that." Rose began to cry.

Tressie rushed to her and put her arms around the heaving shoulders. "Whatever is wrong, Rose? Is it that Jarrad Lincolnshire? What's he done this time?"

"He's going back to England. Leaves next week." Between sobs Rose told Tressie about the mine owner's plans to set up his family in Virginia City. "And I'm afraid if she won't come back with him, I'll never see him again," she finished with a wail.

"Well, I wouldn't want to share a man with his wife, that's for darn sure," Tressie said. "But I guess you know what you want just like I do. I wish you'd think more of yourself than to let him ruin your life."

"I'd take what I can get and be grateful for it, from Jarrad Lincolnshire. I wish I didn't love him so." Rose sobbed, wiping at her eyes. She had never meant to let her feelings show so plainly. There were plenty of other men, and she could have any of them she wanted. How foolish to mourn the loss of one out of so many.

"Oh, Rose," Tressie said softly, "forget about Jarrad Lincolnshire. He has a wife and children that he loves. He uses you for his own pleasure, and when it comes right down to it, he'll choose them over you." She wondered that she could see so well what her friend should do, but her own decisions came with so much difficulty. All she knew was what she had to do, not what she ought to do.

But though Tressie begged and pleaded, all Rose Langue knew for sure was that she was losing the man she loved because he didn't return that love. She simply couldn't admit that he had been using her for his own pleasure.

As Tressie started to take her leave, Rose remembered the blue dress and pulled it from the closet.

"Oh, Rose, would you keep it for me? When this is all over, I'll come back and get it."

Rose silently rehung the dress, then embraced and kissed her friend.

"I'm going to miss you something awful," Tressie whispered.

"Me, too, but you take care of that big man. He'll need plenty of tender loving care. He has a grieving heart, so you be good to him, you hear? And if he ain't good to you, you let me know and I'll see he pays."

Tressie nodded, but could say no more, for her throat was clogged, her heart overflowing with emotions she could hardly bear.

Fear remained beneath the anticipation and excitement, and then there was, of course, the love she felt for Reed. At the same time, leaving Caleb behind caused a new burden of grief to add to that she carried for Mama and her young'un buried on the plains. So many memories trailed behind her. All at once she wanted to be gone, even though it meant saying good-bye to Rose, the only true friend she had ever made in her adult life. It would be almost as bad as when she left her childhood home.

Would she ever see Rose again? She didn't know, but as she walked beside Rose down the long staircase, she sensed that a whole new adventure was beginning to unfold for her.

Picking her way across the muddy street, she saw Reed waiting outside the mercantile. He hurried to meet her, lifted her out of the mud, and deposited her with a laugh on the boardwalk. "Careful, girl. That quick mire will suck you right under."

He had a sparkle to his eyes, a need-to-be-gone look that brightened his sculptured features. The feeling was contagious and she laughed back at him.

Inside, they picked out some britches and shirts from the boys' clothing in stock.

Reed plucked a hat from the top of a stack. "Try this. See if you can stuff those locks up under it. I hate like hell to have to cut them. Maybe we can poke 'em up, like this," he said merrily, trying to get the unruly ringlets to stay put.

She shook her head. "It's no use. If I just put my hair up, suppose my hat comes off. Everyone would see immediately. Even if I braided it. No, we have to cut it. That's the only way it'll be—" She broke off and tilted her head at the mirror. "Besides, it won't be so bad. It was short when you came to the farm. I must not have looked too awful."

"Awful? Why do you think I took off like a scalded dog the first chance I got?" he teased.

"Well, mister smarty, it wasn't because of my hair, I'd wager. Was it?" She gouged at his ribs, making him holler. "Was it?"

"Must've been your winning ways, then," he allowed in all seriousness.

"Add some shears to our supplies, if you didn't already. You can have the privilege of chopping it all off, soon as we make camp. Meanwhile, I'll just twist it up, like this."

Both were so absorbed in their plans that neither saw

Dr. Gideon until he stood at the counter near where they talked.

"Mrs. Majors, what a pleasure to see you," the big man boomed.

Reed, who had been looking at Tressie, whirled.

Gideon took a few steps toward them. "And your friend here. I don't believe we've met. I'm Abel Gideon. You must be the little one's daddy. He had your eyes, I believe." Gideon glared at Reed so intently that it made him squirm. What was going on here? He'd be damned if he'd correct this man's assumptions. It was none of his business anyway.

"Reed Bannon," Reed growled, and stuck out a hand.

Gideon's nostrils flared and he ignored the hand, saying, "Sorry about your boy."

"Thank you. Are you ready to go, Tressie?"

She nodded wordlessly and followed Reed up front, where they paid for their purchases, adding a pair of scissors to the stack of clothing.

"What was that all about?" Reed wondered aloud.

"I don't like him a bit. I don't think he's a very good doctor, and I wish I'd have gotten someone else for Caleb. Gideon makes me all crawly inside. He looks at me like he knows something about me he shouldn't."

"I get that same feeling. Ah, hell, I think we're just looking for troubles where there aren't any." Reed shrugged, and grabbed her hand. "Come on, I want to show you something you're going to love."

He led her to the livery stable. Standing there gazing at the two of them with soft brown eyes was a tiny gray donkey, long ears swinging forward in greeting.

Tressie rubbed the soft but prickly nose. "Oh, is he ours?"

Reed nodded. "Yep. Every stubborn foot of him. This time we go in style, darlin'. He's going to carry everything. And that's not all." He led her to a stall in which stood two horses. "This time we ride. And I bought lots of socks, too," he finished as he went to the far wall where he'd piled all their belongings.

Tressie eyed the smaller of the two roans. "Ride? Well, I'm not very good at that. I guess you'll have to teach me." Then, unable to contain her excitement any longer, she danced into Reed's arms. "Are we leaving soon?"

He smiled down into her ecstatic features and nodded.

Tressie shivered. The adventure was about to begin, and despite the purpose of their trip, she could hardly wait.

Sixteen

They headed west out of Virginia City, following the Ruby River. Nearby was the famed Alder Gulch strike. Everywhere, as far as they could see, men panned for gold. Gaunt-framed, hung with faded flannel shirts and patched trousers, hands puffy from constant dipping in the cold streams, the gold seekers scarcely resembled men who might have in their pokes thousands of dollars worth of gold. Greasy slouch hats shaded them from the sun, but nothing would ward off extreme bouts of homesickness, dysentery, or scurvy. They had to wonder if it was worth it.

Occasionally there would be three or four men manning a cradle, rocking the wooden contraption while pouring water over gravel dumped in the hopper. Fascinated, Tressie slowed her mount to study this particular operation. Suppose one of them came up with more than a little dust settling around the riffles in the foot. What would he do if the washing uncovered a $5,000 nugget? It had been known to happen. Yet she'd heard miners talk enough to know that many rarely did better than break even. Some not even that. Those were the ones who had given up and gone to work at mines like Lincolnshire's.

Soon Tressie and Reed entered Nevada City, a place not very different from Virginia City. Both had come to life as gold camps with the Alder Gulch strike. Slowly the pair made their way among the dirty-haired, foul-bodied men who all looked much the same. Had Papa become one of them? Tressie wondered if she would even know him if she saw him.

For the most part, Reed asked the questions. In bars and other business establishments, she would wait outside while he inquired of the owners and customers. Had they ever run up against Evan Majors? Did he trade there, or had he ever passed through headed for somewhere else? To every question the answer was a disinterested shrug or shake of the head.

On the trail she did the looking, giving everyone they spotted a quick once-over. And on they rode. No place could be home until they ran down Evan Majors. Until Tressie made her peace.

Near Adobe they made their first camp. When Reed pulled up, Tressie slipped from the saddle with a soft moan. The ground appeared to buckle under her and she swayed on spraddled legs. The gentle mare swung her head around as if to say, *I'm the one who does all the work, and you complain.*

Tressie patted the sweet little animal on the rump and chuckled.

"Sore?" Reed asked with a crooked grin. He felt great after a day in the saddle. "Just think, at least it's not your feet that hurt."

"Oh, yes, you can laugh," Tressie said, rubbing at her bottom. "I suppose you're just perfectly okay."

Reed threw a leg across the saddle horn and slid to the

ground. "I'll have you know, ma'am, I was born in the saddle, and damn glad to get back in one, too."

"Show-off," she grumbled, and lifted the stirrup to unbuckle the cinch.

"I'll do that," Reed said. "But just this one time, and that because I feel sorry for you." With competent fingers he loosened the girth and dragged off the saddle.

Tressie punched him lightly with a doubled-up fist. "I'll teach you to laugh at me, you lunkhead."

"Oh, yeah? When's my first lesson?"

Tressie half turned, but the laugh that bubbled up from her throat was choked off. For a split second she caught sight of a fleeting shadow moving through the edge of the trees. On closer inspection, she could see no one was there. A finger of fear walked up her backbone as she peered into the gloom of the woods.

Reed came up behind her. "What? What is it, honey?"

"I don't know. I thought . . . I guess it was just my imagination. Never mind, I'm just being silly. I'll be okay if you give me something to do. Shall I unpack Millie?" She'd named the dove-gray little animal Millie despite Reed's protest that the donkey was a jack, not a jenny. Her reply to that had been that she would not call such a lovable little thing Jack.

Reed suggested Billie, she came back with Tillie and they compromised.

All the while she laid out supplies, Tressie continued to experience a creepy feeling that they were being watched. But as dusk turned to night and no campfire glowed nearby, she told herself her nervousness was only because she feared someone might find out she was a woman.

When Reed approached in his light-footed way, she

yowled in surprise. "Don't come up on me like that. Whistle or something," she said.

"You mean like this?" he asked, and let out a shrill whistle that set the horses whinnying. Before she could object, he raced to her side and grabbed her up in a bear hug. "God, it's good to be able to hold you. Doesn't it feel good?"

He was impossible, and she was soon playing light right back at him. While they were both in that mood, he cut off her curls, and it wasn't so bad. It was only a condition for keeping her safe, after all, and they were able to laugh at her shorn appearance . . . at least a little.

When she fetched the frying pan, he took it from her. "Tonight you rest, I cook. After all, you are a poor pilgrim, and you need to get used to this hard life." A grin danced his features into life, but he sobered quickly. "I warn you, though, girl . . ." He paused, tousled her short hair. "Uh, I mean lad, you'll carry your weight after today. I'll not have any shirkers in this outfit. Besides, men don't lay around and let other men do all the work, like some women."

Tressie launched herself at him, knocking the frying pan aside. They ended up rolling around in the dirt, tickling and shouting, finally coming to rest wrapped in each other's arms.

"What would people say about this?" Tressie teased, kissing him lightly.

"Who cares?" Reed said, and returned the kiss but much more soundly.

"They'd say," she managed when she came up for air, "that either I'm not a boy, or there's something bad wrong with you, that's what they'd say. Now let me up and let's us get respectable, at least till the fire's out."

Later that night, as they lay together wrapped in blankets to keep out the cold night air, Tressie cried. She didn't know it was going to happen, had absolutely no warning. The hot tears just began to flow, silent as the fall of snowflakes. Worse, she couldn't tell Reed why. It was all wound up in Mama and Papa, the babies, the loneliness of the past few months, and the joy of being with him. And so he held her close until she slept, wondering with dread if he was going to be able to make Tressie happy. She had suffered so much for one so young, and he didn't know what else he could do that he hadn't already done.

Tressie awoke before dawn and turned to snuggle against Reed, but the pile of blankets and the saddle where he had lain his head were empty. She sat up and rubbed at her eyes. In the wind came the smell of salt pork frying and the heavy smoke of fires. Men camped everywhere as they swarmed from one gold camp to another in search of the sun-bright ore. How would she ever determine Papa's whereabouts? It would have been easier to find him in a city like St. Louis, where folks pretty much stayed put. This immense country was fairly crawling with prospectors who moved on at the least whim.

Tressie struggled into her boots and hightailed it for the woods before day broke. Maintaining the facade of being male was harder than she'd thought it would be, for eyes could be anywhere and boys did their private business in a much different way than girls.

Squatted in the bushes, britches down around her ankles, Tressie giggled. She guessed men did have to do it this way at least once in a while, but how easy it was for them the rest of the time. Just unzip and let 'er fly.

Tressie got back to camp at about the same time as Reed, and together they built up the fire and cooked breakfast.

Sopping up the last of her mush with a sourdough biscuit, Tressie said, "There's a lot more prospectors than I expected. Do you think we'll ever find him?"

He shrugged. "Well, we can sure say we gave it our best. If he's here to find, we'll find him. If not, well then, we'll just . . . just get on with it, I reckon."

"With what?" she asked, giving him a squared-on look.

"Why, our lives, of course." He paused in his chewing and eyed her steadily. What did she mean by that? Had she changed her mind?

"I don't mean that. I mean, what are we going to do? Homestead some land, get jobs in town, prospect? We don't either one exactly have a calling."

Her insistent question brought Reed a feeling of relief, and he let out a sigh. "Well, I know how to ride; I've worked for a freighting company. With this country growing like it is, there'll be a great need for moving things from one place to the other. I'm afraid I wouldn't make much of a farmer, though."

She set her tin plate down and picked up a cup of steaming, black-as-mud coffee. "Then you'd like to stay here, in the mountains?"

"I expect." He looked up. "Unless you'd like to go elsewhere. With the war over, these boomtowns will likely become permanent settlements. There'll be churches and schools as well as businesses of every description. Hell, look at Virginia City already. The world is marching West, Tressie, and we're already here."

She nodded, his excitement catching hold of her. The only other place she would want to live would be in the Missouri Ozarks, but what with all her people gone on, these mountains would suit her just as well. "Maybe we'll strike gold," she said with an impish grin. "And then we'll be rich and we can go anywhere we want and live anywhere we want."

"That's a fair dream," Reed said, and rose. "Time we broke camp. Oh, I made an early morning round asking questions. A feller camped yonder"—he pointed toward a draw—"he said he run up against a man name of Majors a few months back. Panning down near the Bitterroots. I thought we might head that way."

"Oh, Reed. Why didn't you tell me earlier? Did he say it was Papa? Did he talk to him? Was he . . . was he okay?"

Reed stopped and hung his head for a moment, not wanting to turn around and see her face. He knew full well what hate and love all tangled up with vengeance could do. His own pa's actions had come near ruining Reed's life, had chased him from one place to another like a pursuing demon.

He drew in a deep breath, said softly, "Now, Tressie, don't go getting your hopes up. He couldn't remember if that was his first name or last, nor much about him, except that he thought he hailed from the high plains. That's the onliest reason I'd say we even try to find him. It could be a wild goose chase, and I think we should keep checking out every man we meet, not just rush off after this one."

Tressie knew this was true, but still couldn't help being anxious to learn more. "Where is this Bitterroot? And how would we go about finding his claim after we got there?"

"Bitterroot Mountains. Assayer's or claims office in the nearest town, I would reckon," Reed muttered. The tone of her questions just plain scared him. His sweet little gal turning all mean and single-purposed lent a dread to his own soul. He had no solutions, though. In his experience, folks had to do what they had to do.

"Well, then, let's get moving," Tressie said, and started cleaning up their breakfast things while Reed packed and saddled their mounts.

At Twin Bridges Tressie took the time to write to Rose Langue, explaining what they had learned and where they were headed. She left it for the eastbound stage.

They spent the night outside of town and the next morning headed south for Dillon, the next settlement of any size. Reed had grown just plain grumpy as the days wore on. He even took to sleeping across the fire from her. Or if she complained of the cold and moved to his side, he would turn his back, presenting his stiff haunches for her to warm up on. Having come up with no cure for Tressie's problems, Reed felt helpless and that made him angry. Why was he so danged scared to assert himself? Be a man? He feared he knew the answer to that.

Tressie resented being at the mercy of this man's changing moods, and she'd be darned if she'd beg him to talk to her or put his arms around her. If he had a mad on, then let him keep it. Besides they were hot on Papa's trail, and she had other things to occupy her thoughts.

Like what would she do if she walked up on him face-to-face? She'd supposed a confrontation would mean she could vent all her hate. Watch his face crumple in shame when he learned what his leaving had caused. Now she wasn't so sure.

The trail wound deeper into the mountains and grew more steep and difficult. On their third night out after learning Papa might be in the Bitterroot Mountains south of Dillon, Reed had had enough talk about what she would say and do to the man. He decided to tell her so and to hell with the consequences.

He waited until after supper that evening to bring up the subject. Then he like to not got started, his tongue was so tied up. He picked at his teeth, shifted from sitting cross-legged to leaning back with his head on his saddle, then back to a sit.

"Something bothering you?" Tressie asked. "You're acting like you've sat on an anthill or something."

"I was just thinking about—"

"You seem to be doing a lot of that lately, and little else," she snapped.

"I expect I have. Girl, have you changed your mind?"

"Changed my mind about what?" Tressie drew lines in the dirt, then gazed at the fire. She could feel him looking at her, his gaze boring icy holes in her flesh.

"About us." A short, barked retort that was the closest Reed ever came to raising his voice in anger.

"Well, I have to admit, thinking about being around someone who can go for a week without so much as a good morning, dear, does give me pause."

He snorted. "That isn't what I meant, and you know it. Do you wish you could take back your promises to me so you could concentrate on paying back your pa, if and when we find him?"

Tressie swirled the stick and flipped a cloud of dust into the fire. Torn between love and hate, she was utterly miserable. She wanted to trust this man, yet all she could think about when she looked at him was Papa's betrayal. Creeping ever into her thoughts was the question, would Reed desert her, too? If she trusted him too much, left herself at his mercy, would she one day wake up to find him gone? Such doubts put their love in peril and caused her to question many of her own motives.

"It just isn't fair," she wailed at last. "I love you, Reed. With all my heart. But when I . . . when you said . . . oh, darn it, help me."

He stared into the fire, his somber eyes darker than the night and glinting with moisture. "I can't help you on this one, Tressie, girl. This is exactly why I wouldn't just grab you up and run away with you, though Lord knows I've wanted to enough times. And then I think of all the times I've run away when the going got tough. I think of seeing that faraway glint come into your eye when you think of your pa, and I get scared. Scared of what you'll do, scared of what I'll do."

Tressie had begun to cry softly. "You won't just leave me out here all alone, will you?"

Reed cleared his burning throat. The poor little thing. He wanted to take her in his arms, do his best to convince her that their love was stronger than his cowardice or her need for revenge. All he could do was say brokenly, "I swear I'll stick by you, Tressie. I'm so tired of running. But I understand how you feel, I truly do. I just wish . . . well, hell, I wish we could."

"Then quit acting like you're mad at me all the time. It's awful lonely riding all day every day without a word out of you."

"I'm not mad at you. I just can't take . . . touching you, being around and knowing that we can't . . . I love you, Tressie, and I don't want to hurt you. I promised I'd help you find your pa, and I will. But dang it, girl, you're gonna have to quit snuggling up to me. Till this is over and we get married, things between us will have to be strictly business. Or we can forget all this and make us a life."

Tressie gazed longingly into his moist dark eyes, saw the love and goodness there, and almost gave in. But she couldn't. She kept remembering her mama crying night after night, remembered her own pain at being abandoned, and then the worst thing of all when Mama lay in labor screaming out Papa's name over and over, and him not there. No. She would not give up. She shook her head slowly.

"I can't have a life till I find Papa. Till I can see his face when I tell him what he did. How much he hurt Mama and me. No matter what we did or where we went, I'd always think about it. And you're right, Reed. It'll eat me alive, and so I have to find him. Get rid of the pain and the hate. I loved him so much, Reed. I love you so much. Can't you understand what I'm saying? Please be patient. Please."

He nodded miserably. He supposed in a strange sort of way he sympathized with her, even though he didn't understand her decision. It cut deeply into his heart until he wanted to throw something, or ball his fists and scream his disappointment to the heavens. Instead, he said in a flat voice, "Well, if you can't give up this crazy idea of yours that you have to pay back your pa for what he did, then you're not ready for a life of your own. Hell, maybe I'm not, either.

"One thing's for sure, we can't keep rolling around in bed together. It ain't right, and besides, ain't no telling what could happen; then what would we do?"

She stared at the ground and knew he was right. A lump swelled in her throat that she couldn't swallow past. If she gave up looking for Papa and married Reed, they could have a life out here in the mountains, or go farther west. It was a wonderful fantasy.

She grinned up at him, a sad little grin that made her look about twelve. "Okay, but when it's cold can I sleep with you?"

"Dammit, girl, that's asking too much. Just get closer to the blamed fire if you're cold." It was the harshest tone he'd ever used with her, and he felt terrible as the words tumbled past his tongue. But a man could only be tempted so far.

As summer wore on and they rode in and out of gatherings of prospectors who all had the same answers to their questions about Evan Majors, Reed and Tressie developed a camaraderie that extended beyond their sexual and emotional feelings for each other. Reed had kept his promise to talk to Tressie, and she was like a child who went to bed on an argument and upon wakening forgot all about it. They were friends, at ease with each other, and it felt good.

Occasionally she would ask, "How much farther to Dillon?"

And he would reply patiently, almost always the same

answer, "We'll just have to ride till we get there. I haven't been over this way in years. Besides, these gold strike towns have sprung up where once there was nothing."

Another time she asked, "Where did you live when you were a little boy?"

That set him off on another tale. "Oh, we were plains Sioux. These mountains were too tough for wintering. This is where the gods live."

Tressie looked out across the panorama of rugged peaks, deep valleys, and gigantic pine reaching for the sky. "I'm not surprised. The gods sure did know what they were doing, saving this for themselves."

They had been following a downward trail all day, and Tressie soon grew weary of such a challenge to her meager riding skills. It was hard not to hang on to the horn, a thing Reed had cautioned her more than once not to do.

"It makes the animal's shoulders sore after a while," he told her every time he noticed her hands bunched over the horn during a particularly sheer descent. "Use the stirrups to hold yourself. Sit back easy and balance on the balls of your feet. Your mount knows what she's doing."

"It wouldn't be so hard if I couldn't see where we'll fall if she stumbles," Tressie said. Climbing had been a lot easier.

Reed couldn't help laughing. "We could tie your bandanna around your eyes."

After a while, she responded, "No, I guess I wouldn't like that, either."

Once they took a cold noonday meal sitting on a huge boulder on an overhang that gave them a bird's-eye view of a distant river valley. Virgin long-needled pine clung to the steep and rocky incline. Just below the swaying tops were clusters of brown cones.

"This must be what a bird feels like," Tressie said. "I could almost reach down and pluck one out of the treetop."

"Better not. You'd roll for a hundred miles if you lost your balance."

Tressie breathed deeply of the sweet air. "Isn't it lovely?"

Wildflowers of every color and description sprouted from seams in the hard rock. Overhead their blossoms swayed in the gentle breeze, hanging upside down as if it were a quite natural condition. Reds and purples, whites and yellows, the blooms exuded a luscious fragrance that sweetened the mountain air.

Suddenly Tressie heard something—a branch cracking, rocks scattering—and she stiffened. "Reed."

He held up a hand. "I heard. Be still."

The mare danced and rattled gravel underfoot; Millie curled her lip to reveal long teeth and emit what could only be called a laugh. Reed's large roan gelding called out shrilly. There was an answering whinny.

"Someone coming up the trail," Reed said.

"What will we do?"

He glanced at her and saw that she was afraid. "Do? Why, nothing. We're out here. It stands to reason others are, too, and with no more underhanded motives than we have. We'll stay to the side until they pass; the trail is narrow."

"Are we meeting them or are they coming up on us?"

Reed cocked his head. "In this country, it's hard to tell, but I think it came from down yonder behind us."

Tressie shuddered. Something about another rider on their back trail bothered her, as if someone were spying on them. That, of course, was silly. But she had never shaken the earlier feeling that they were being watched. It came and went with regularity, though she'd actually never seen anyone.

Both listened intently for quite a while, but nothing more was heard. No rider or his animal. Finally Reed shrugged and slid off the boulder. "That's funny. I didn't notice a way off this goat trail the way we came. Ah, well. Sound travels strange up here in this thin air. Could have been down below on another trail, I suppose."

He sounded puzzled, and that bothered Tressie. He made few mistakes on the trail. If he said someone was riding up on them, then it was probably true. So why hadn't that person come on? There was only one reason that she could think of, and that was that the person on their trail was staying behind them deliberately. Following. Spying.

It was nearly dark before they found a place to camp for the night, and both were kept busy until after they settled down to eat their meal. Reed had chosen a stand of pine nested up against a steep outcropping of sienna-colored rocks the size of ships. Back off the main trail a ways, the needle-covered ground offered a soft bed, the heavy branches overhead a shelter from the chilling dew that fell nightly. They carried plenty of water, but a plus for this campsite was the small spring bubbling from a crevice in the rocks to run merrily over moss-covered gravel and spill noisily down the side of the mountain.

They ate hungrily and in silence until Reed opened a can of fruit with his knife. Spooning up a golden peach, he sucked at the sugary syrup. "Couldn't resist buying these. Nothing better than peaches in a can. Too bad we couldn't bring more."

Tressie grinned at him. "It's time we had a treat. Back home we grew these on trees." She tasted her own, licked her lips. "Good, all right, but if you think these are good, you ought to have tasted ours. I still miss home." She decided she didn't want to talk about that anymore and said, "If we'd stay in one place long enough, I'd cook up some of those dry beans."

"There'll be time for that later," he said.

"When we get where we're going," she said like an echo. "Reed, I wish—"

"No more than I do, Tressie. No more than I do."

"Yes. Well, if you don't mind, that water is mighty tempting. I think I'll take a bath."

He slurped up the rest of the thick juice and put his plate down. "And I think I'll just take a look around. Check things out a bit. You need me, just give a holler."

Reed had no intention of sticking around to watch Tressie bathe, not with things the way they were. Besides, he wanted to check out their back trail. Ever since hearing that horse whinny earlier in the day, he'd expected someone to ride up on them. Or at least to hear other signs of a traveler. But there'd been nothing, and that was plumb strange.

For the first time since setting out from Virginia City, Reed pulled his rifle from the scabbard. Tressie noticed him going armed to scout the area. So he was taking their earlier mysterious visitor seriously.

In the gathering darkness she fetched a bar of soap and went to the spring. There she sat to remove her boots, then slipped out of her men's britches and flannel shirt. Both smelled of sweat and the trail. She would wash them after she bathed. Standing, Tressie unwrapped the tight binding from around her chest. She stretched, pale skin glowing in the half-light. For a moment she rubbed her hands over the itchy flesh of her breasts and squirmed when the nipples puckered. She wanted to make love to Reed, and the thought caused all kinds of problems with her young body. Ignoring the pain/pleasure urges, she bent to wet the bar of soap and began to lather it over one ankle and calf.

In the utter stillness someone giggled. She heard it distinctly and whirled, soap cupped in both hands between her breasts. Reed couldn't giggle like that if he had to. A stranger was watching her.

She shouted Reed's name as loud as she could, at the same time charging for the camp and something to cover herself with. She had almost reached the pile of blankets when the shadowy figures stepped from behind the trees like ghosts magically becoming visible. There were seven of them, and they looked to be no more than fifteen or so. Indian boys wearing very little clothing. The light from the campfire set their naked bodies to gleaming as if they were coated in grease. Perhaps they were.

Tressie stopped in midstride. She couldn't get to the blankets, so she turned to go the other way where she could hide. One of the boys yipped and leaped quickly into her path. She screeched again, and the soap went flying from her hands. The boys really thought that was funny. They kept shouting curt words to each other, nodding and laughing. One cupped his hands over his crotch in a crude gesture. That they found even funnier.

The boy nearest her moved quickly and grabbed her by the arm. She jerked away, shouted, "No!" He smacked her with the flat of his palm between the breasts and repeated the word "No!" sharp as a rifle's fire. The blow jarred her teeth and she staggered backward.

Eyes flitting from one looming shadow to another, Tressie screamed Reed's name once again. Where was he? Was he going to let these savages have their way with her? They were only boys, but their intention was obvious. They wanted to do more than just play games.

The boy who had smacked her reached for her hair. She dodged and he raised the other hand as if to hit her, so she stood still. He filled his fist with her short locks and shook until her teeth rattled. Immediately he gestured toward her breasts. The question became evident.

"I cut it," she whimpered. With two fingers she made a sign for scissors and held it to her head. "Now let me go, you indecent little savage, before I give you a lesson in manners." Tressie couldn't have explained why she said that. They didn't understand her, that was evident, but it felt good to stand up to them nevertheless.

From out of the darkness came Reed's steady voice. "No, let me." The demand was followed by a sharp retort from the rifle. The bullet chipped at the trunk of a pine inches from her tormentor's head.

Reed tried out his Sioux on the boys, ordering them to leave his woman be, followed by a vivid description of what he would do to their private parts if they didn't. Later he wasn't sure if it was the gun or his words that sent the young braves on their way. They'd evidently hidden their horses up the trail, for soon after they lit out, the pounding of hooves signaled their departure.

Tressie stood there a moment, rubbing at her aching head and trying to catch her breath. When she did, it was to turn on Reed. "Where were you? What took you so long? Those nasty little savages could have killed me."

It was so dark under the pines that only the firelight revealed her naked body. And he was halfway through answering her accusation when he pivoted from watching the boys leave.

"At least we know who we heard earlier—"

Catching sight of her drove the rest of his reply from his mouth. Taking one giant stride, he folded her up in his arms, kissed her long and hard, then pushed her away.

Tressie scarcely responded to the kiss before it was over. She held the back of her hand to her mouth, tears glistening in her green eyes, and struggled against the swell of passion in her loins. "Reed, I—"

"Put some clothes on now, before someone sees you," he said. It took all the willpower he had to walk away from her, standing there with her arms stiffly at her sides, the glory of her exquisite body open to the shadow and light thrown by the flickering fire. He wanted her as badly as he ever had wanted anyone or anything in his entire life. There were times when he thought he could make her choose between him and her need for vengeance, but he couldn't bring himself to do it. So he would just walk away, like always.

Seventeen

That summer of 1865, Rose Langue wasn't sure whose leaving devastated her more, Jarrad's or Tressie's. Her life had been forever changed by both. Jarrad she cursed for making her fall in love with him and totally disregarding her feelings; Tressie she blessed for showing her that youth and courage and beauty of soul still counted for something in this jaded old world.

Once Jarrad Lincolnshire took the stagecoach east where he would board a ship for England, Rose found other men boring, infantile, and most of all dreadfully depressing. She finally quit dealing with them altogether, letting the hurdy-gurdy house and girls like Maggie earn money for her. There was no place where Rose felt entirely comfortable anymore. On Jarrad Lincolnshire's arm, her presence had been accepted in places like the theater and the posh eating establishments in town.

Virginia City continued to grow, becoming more and more sophisticated. Families were moving in, which meant the influx of women and children other than the wives of rich merchants and miners. A middle class had developed, and for that schools and churches were needed.

Rose would have liked to attend church services and mingle with these wives and mothers, but of course she couldn't. So she had herself a small house built on the outskirts of town somewhat removed from the Golden Sun. Out back she began a flower garden and hired the son of the Chinese launderer to help out. He would carry bucket after bucket of water to her tender new roses, plants that had been shipped on the stage all the way from St. Louis. The day the first delicate pale pink petals of the pampered Radiance rose unfolded, Rose buried her nose in the fragrant flower and cried. How rare to have had a hand in bringing such beauty to this raw and ugly town.

Soon she had not only roses, but a variety of blooming shrubs, including the gracious mountain laurel. By the following spring she hoped to see lilies, jonquils and tulips, bulbs she had already ordered from Pennsylvania.

One day in early August Rose left her little garden and went in the house by the back entrance just as someone tapped on the front door. She had grown accustomed to an occasional visit from one of the girls at the Golden Sun, who on their time off liked to visit her rose garden and take a glass of lemonade with their friend and employer. Rose encouraged such visits, for they filled a corner of her lonely life.

Wiping perspiration from her face and pulling off her work gloves, she opened the door. To her surprise a young man stood there, rumpled black hat in hand, a nervous smile playing around his finely drawn lips. He tipped his head forward slightly in a nod, loosening golden hair that fell over his ears. "Ma'am? I'm sorry to bother you, but I was told to bring this to you."

"What?" Rose asked, seeing nothing but the hat held in both hands across his belt.

Obviously flustered, he met her gaze squarely while flashing snowy white teeth and digging around in his pockets. "It's here, somewhere."

Rose couldn't help but return his smile. For some reason she had always had this effect on men, and she had grown to accept it and take advantage of it. Lately such thoughts had not entered her mind. She grieved for Jarrad as if he had died, and a widow in mourning did not raise her eyes to those of other gentlemen. But this one . . . well, he was a most impressive young man. Noteworthy.

He continued to finger through the pockets of his black pants until he finally came up with a flat package wrapped carefully in brown paper. He held it out to her, blushing furiously when her fingers brushed his in passing.

"What is this?"

"A tintype, ma'am."

She picked at the string with long fingernails. "I'm afraid I can't untie this knot. Won't you come in?" Rose asked, and stepped back out of the doorway, still studying the parcel. "Would you like some lemonade? And I'll let you unfasten this while I fetch it."

The young man glanced around at the charming room with pink and white chintz curtains that matched throw covers on the delicate furniture, at the exquisite hand-painted glass shades on the kerosene lamps, at the dainty doilies and antimacassars, and he shuffled his booted feet.

"I don't know, ma'am. I couldn't rightly set on any of this fine furniture. I might mess it up."

Rose laughed heartily. "Well, then, if you're a country

boy, why don't you just come with me out to the kitchen? I think we'd both feel more at home there. And the chairs are . . . well, sturdier."

Without waiting for an answer, Rose regally led the way through the arched doorway into a yellow and white kitchen. Sunlight splashed the three windows that framed the lovely rose garden out back. The young man gasped with delight.

"You like it?" Rose asked, and fetched a pitcher of lemonade from the wooden box alongside the dry sink. She knelt and unwrapped a block of ice in the bottom of the box, chipping off several slivers for each of two glasses, which she then filled to the top with frosty, shimmering lemonade.

"You'd never know coming up on it from outside that it would be so . . . so, well . . . so womany," he said.

Rose dimpled with pleasure at the compliment and handed him his glass. "What's your name, and who sent you here with that?" She gestured at the packet now lying on the oiled tabletop.

He cleared his throat, as if only now remembering his mission. "Uh, well, I'm Ben Poole, and I—" He broke off and took a sip of the cold drink. "Ramey, over at the Busted Mule, he said you would want to see this." The boy gestured at the still-wrapped package.

"Well, then, I'd appreciate it if you would unwrap it for me," Rose said, and sat in one of the two chairs. "Sit, Ben. Sit, and show me what you've got."

It was a hot day, and perspiration ran from under Rose's heavy golden hair, piled high in enormous curls. She plucked a wisp of white linen from her bodice and blotted at the moisture at her throat and across the swelling of her breasts peeking from the low-cut neckline.

Ben Poole blushed again and tried to take his eyes from her long enough to untie the knot on the small package. He was having a very hard time doing either.

Rose felt a certain amount of pity for the young man, who obviously hadn't been around any women save his own mother. He no doubt was the victim of rampaging desires he had no idea what to do with. He was certainly at that age, maybe sixteen or seventeen. He could very well have been her son.

"Ben, show me the picture. Then I want you to go over to the Golden Sun, tell Maggie I sent you especially to her. She'll be good for you, son. Take care of those urges you're experiencing. You don't want me, I'm old enough to be your mother. And besides, I'm retired. Maggie, she's just about right. She can show you things you've only imagined, if that. And you tell her, Ben, that she's paid. I'll take care of it."

As Rose spoke she looked straight into the boy's dark blue eyes, saw a flare of desire there, then the embarrassment quickly covered by the lowering of his long, dark lashes. Ben went to work diligently and soon had the string off. He handed the package to Rose without unwrapping the paper or meeting her steady gaze.

"Thank you, Ben. Now, finish your lemonade and you can go."

He took a long two or three gulps, then asked, "Maggie?"

"Yes, that's right. And thank you for this."

Ben took another sip, then snapped his fingers. "Oh, Ramey, he said to tell you that if you wanted to know anything about that, you should come see him. Said some fella turned up with it, tried to use it as stakes in a poker game. Ramey, he knew you would be interested, seeing as how you was friends with this girl."

Rose's heart leaped into her throat and she ripped back the paper. There, in shades of sienna and cream preserved for all time, was the likeness of Tressie Majors with an older woman. The girl's hair hung in the long curls of childhood, adding a certain innocence to the familiar features, but it was Tressie, perhaps at the age of fifteen or so, and probably her mother.

"Who had this, do you know?" Rose felt faint, the tight corset squeezing at her until she could scarcely breathe.

"Look on the back, ma'am. See, there, Ramey said it says something, I forget what."

Scrawled in black ink on the back of the tintype were the words "Beloved Almyra and Tressie."

"Oh, my goodness," Rose whispered. "Oh, my dear goodness. It must have belonged to Evan Majors."

"Majors, ma'am?"

Rose glanced up at the boy. "Oh, never mind. Ben, you run along, now. And don't forget Maggie, won't you? Run along. And thank you. Thank you so much."

Ben stood, downed the last swallows of lemonade in noisy gulps, and hurried from the room. Rose sat there staring unseeing out the windows into her rose garden long after the front door banged closed.

"But where did he get it, Ramey?" Rose asked the owner of the Busted Mule that very same afternoon. She hadn't even waited for Ben to get out of sight on the street in front of her house before heading for the gambling saloon.

"Oh, he had a story to tell, all right, and it's a doozy. Near as I remember he found it on the dead body of a prospector down around Sugar Flats. That's near the divide, Rose."

Rose nodded impatiently. "I know where Sugar Flats is. The man he found it on. Was he a tall fella, brown hair?"

"Nah, he said he was an old codger, bald with lots of whiskers. Reason I remember, he was a laughing about this old prospector being so old he probably just died of old age right in the midst of what he was doing. You know, took one step, fell down the next?"

"Did he have a name?"

"Who?" Ramey asked, and poured them each a mug of dark beer.

"The old prospector, who else?"

Ramey frowned. "Fella didn't say. You sure are het up over this, Rose. It's only a likeness of that gal what cooked up at the Lincolnshire Mines last winter. What ever become of her, anyways?"

"She rode out to hunt for her lost pa. Did you read the back of this?"

"Yep, I did." Ramey's close-set brown eyes sparked. "Say, you thinking that old prospector was this little gal's pa, dead and gone on?"

Rose sighed. "Of course not. Evan was . . . is a younger man. But where did this old man get the tintype, Ramey? That's what I want to know. Is this fella that had it still in town?"

Ramey shrugged. "Beats me. Tossed him outta here when he run out a money and started making such a fuss over us not using that there for ante. You might try up at the mine. He muttered something about getting himself a job to get a stake. Onliest place I know of a man dumb as a stump can earn him some wages."

Rose finished off her beer. "Thanks, Ramey. I really appreciate this. That boy, Ben Poole? Where'd he come in from, do you know?"

"Purty good kid, ain't he? Come up from down South somewheres. Served in the last year or so of the war down there. His people was all massacred, so when the war finished up, he just got on his horse and rode. He tole me he just rode till he couldn't hang on no more, then slid off into the dirt. And that's what he looked like when he come in here, too. Flat rode to a frazzle. I needed a boy to sweep up, so I hired him."

"But he's only fifteen, sixteen years old. He served in the war a year?"

"Oh, hell, yes. Along at the last they had kids no older'n twelve taking up arms. Those was desperate days for the Confederacy, I reckon." Ramey took her mug and rubbed at the bar with a rag. "Damn glad that hellish killing war come to a end. Such pure foolishness. Killed off too many of our young'uns. And fer what? I ask you that, Rose, fer what?"

"It's been my experience, Ramey, that man will always fight man, one way or another. It's just in their nature, like they were born with a killing club in their hands or something. There'll be other things to fight over, I'd wager. Well, I think I'll ride on up to the mine and see what I can learn. You be good to that Ben Poole, you hear me? I hear you're not, I'll take him away from you. I could use me a good-looking swamper. My girls'd treat him real good, too."

Ramey chuckled. "Hell, Rose, they'll treat him real good anyways. Good luck to you."

Rose thanked Ramey and stepped from the darkness of the saloon out into the blazing afternoon heat.

Her next stop was the livery stable, and she waited impatiently while Grainger harnessed her black mare to the small buggy. Then she thanked him, let him help her up into the seat, and headed for the Lincolnshire Mines. This part was not going to be easy. Rose hadn't gone near the place since Jarrad had left back in late April, and doing so now, she feared, would bring back many painful memories. But she'd set herself a task and she had no intention of backing out. If Evan Majors was dead, Tressie needed to know it, but she certainly didn't need rumors of his death to add to her troubles.

The last Rose had heard from her friend Tressie was a letter that said she and Reed were headed south to Dillon and on to Lima in the Bitterroot Mountains. Rose intended to run down the man who showed up in Virginia City carrying a tintype of Tressie and her ma. Maybe she could bring an end to this fruitless search of Tressie's. At least that sweet girl could find happiness, even if it wasn't in the cards for Rose.

Hauling at the reins, Rose stopped the horse outside the office of the Lincolnshire Mines. She could almost imagine the gangly Englishman bursting through the door, holding out his arms to her, lifting her down and embracing her. Tears pooled in her eyes and overflowed the corners. She wiped at them angrily. It was time she got over the hurt of losing Jarrad to that upper-class snob of a wife who considered herself too good for this country.

Jarrad's bookkeeper looked up from his desk when Rose

walked in. He was a little bit of a man with a bald head and prissy mannerisms. His mouth was forever pursed as if he'd tasted something bitter.

"Well, Miss Rose, we haven't seen you in a while," he said in a high voice.

She thought he wore his pants too tight. "Hello, James."

The man stared up at her as if wishing she weren't there, but too wary of his station to say so. "Could I perhaps help you with something?"

"Yes, I hope so. Did you hire a man this morning? A little the worse for wear and desperate for a job."

James raised his pen from the open ledger. "They're all that way, ma'am. What was his name?"

"I don't know. You can't have hired a dozen, so it couldn't be too hard for you simply to answer my question," Rose said sharply. She resented the condescending manner in which this little man had always treated her.

He blinked like an owl, but answered her question. "We hired two today, I believe."

"And where might I find them?"

He smiled. "Up on the side of the mountain, working. Otherwise, they'll be fired come suppertime."

Rose sighed. Dealing with this man was frustrating and she resisted an urge to shake his misshapen teeth from his parsimonious little mouth. "Do you know their names?"

"Of course," he said, and stared at her.

"Have you heard from Jarrad?" Rose asked sweetly, taking another step into the room.

The man had no way of knowing the status of that relationship, despite Jarrad's having made no secret of the reason for his trip abroad. For all James knew, Jarrad and

Rose would take right up where they left off when he returned, with or without his wife. So he probably better watch his step with this trollop.

"I believe he's returning within the month," James said. He took a deep breath. "One's named Phonse Cray, the other is Will O'Shaunessy. I believe the one you want is Mr. Cray. Will worked for us up until last month and just returned, so you would know him, probably. Cray is a stranger in these parts. He rode up from Sugar Flats, I believe."

"He's the one," Rose said, catching her breath.

"Well, I'm afraid you'll have to wait until the whistle blows. That'll be eight o'clock. Perhaps I could tell him you wish to see him."

Rose glanced around, sensing the presence of Jarrad Lincolnshire in every piece of burnished furniture in the room, in the paintings on the wall and the tidy placement of things on his desk. "Did he say if he was bringing Victoria and the girls with him?" Rose asked softly.

"I'm afraid he did," James said with a sniff. "'I'm surprised he didn't let you know. Mr. Lincolnshire is bringing the missus and the youngest daughter. The eldest married a while back. He only wired to say when they would arrive and ask that we obtain a place for them in Widow Mooney's rooming house until he can make other arrangements." James watched her closely and Rose held her chin high, determined he wouldn't know that her heart had just broken into a million pieces. She hadn't known until that very moment how much hope still dwelled within her. It was one thing to carry on an affair with a married man whose wife was conspicuously absent, quite another when she lived near at hand.

"Will that be all?" James asked when she continued to stare at him.

"What? Oh, yes, James. That will be quite all. Cray, you said? I'd appreciate it if you would ask him to call on me tonight. It's most important."

"I can do that." The little ferret smirked.

Rose slammed from the office. She wished she could shake the hateful little sneak till he rattled. Anger drove her now. So Jarrad was returning with Victoria on his arm. How long, she wondered, would that arrangement last? Well, it was definitely over. She'd not satisfy his lustful appetite while he kept that woman in a style she would demand while offering nothing in return. At least a prostitute was honest. She gave for what she got, up front. Wives, on the other hand, held out for what they wanted, giving grudgingly and making sure their husbands knew how it pained them.

Rose lashed at the mare with her whip, hanging on when the buggy jerked into motion.

Cray arrived at close to nine o'clock, when remnants of the summer sun touched fingers of purple clouds with brilliant orange fire. A fire in the sky that faded into darkness as Rose and he spoke, sitting at the kitchen table where earlier she had entertained young Ben Poole.

The man Cray, who said his first name was Phonse, was a soft-spoken man whose life's work would be to fail at everything he tried. That was so evident in his manner that Rose felt immediately sorry for him. The tale he told excited her enormously, though.

He spoke like a storyteller, as so many of his ilk, and she listened closely to what he said:

"It was along about dusk when I rides up on this poor

old fellow. Lying like he was sleeping beside a fire he hadn't yet built. I'd been doing some prospecting myself, see, over Dutch Oven way. So I welcomed a friendly face, maybe share some grub. When I turned him over, I saw he was dead, his eyes all bulging near out of his head, his tongue hanging out his mouth. There weren't no one around. If he had a mule it had wandered off with some of his stuff. I found that "—he gestured at the tintype that Rose had placed between them on the table— "and some other stuff. But nothing worth much, you understand."

Rose felt disappointment. "Is that all?"

"I didn't take nothin' valuable, I said."

"I'm not saying you did. I'm looking for the man this belonged to. I don't care what you did or didn't take. Evan Majors is his name, and I need desperately to know how to find him. He would have been carrying this picture, you see. How did this old man get it? Where had he been? If he had other things, we might be able to find out. You could help me. I'd be most grateful." She eyed him carefully.

He moistened his thick lips and leered at her.

"With money," she said quickly. "I'd pay well for the information."

"Sure," he muttered, the leer fading. "Well, I could use some gold."

"Oh, it'd be gold," Rose said quickly.

"How much?"

Rose studied him. Did he know something or was he simply trying to swindle her out of what he could?

"Depends on what you have. You show me, tell me what you know, and I'll pay you what it's worth. You can ask around; I'm an honest woman, and I wouldn't cheat you. Not someone like you."

"They ain't no law can do nothin' to me, even if you was to tell. I'd just say you was lying, you see?"

Rose clenched her fingers together in her lap and nodded somberly. "I think you can understand that I don't hold much with the law."

Cray laughed and rubbed under his nose with a grubby finger. "I reckon I know what you mean. Well, I met the old codger right out of Copper Springs a ways. He'd been working at one of them mines they dig right in the side of the mountain? With this feller who had that picture. Feller also had him quite a cache of gold, and he told the old man all about hisself over the time they worked together, you see. Men get like that, lonely, you see. Anyways, they got close, and traded secrets. You know how it is: If I die you get my found, if you die I get your'n? Me, I don't never tell no one nothing. I die, mine can rot right along with me, seeing as how I ain't never got nothin'.

"Anyways, this old man had got what belonged to the other fella, and now he was a fixin' to tell me all about it so if he died I could get it. He'd buried it near his camp, you see."

Rose couldn't wait for the drawn-out tale to continue. "He got what belonged to Evan because Evan died?"

"Lady, I don't know who Evan is. This fella had this"—he pointed at Tressie's picture—"the mine caved in on him and some others. So the old man took all his belongings and lit out. He said he didn't like working in no blamed cave, anyway. Would rather set on a creek bank and pan gold as to be buried like some damned mole."

Rose drew in a deep breath and let it out slowly. At last.

If this story was true . . . She glanced at Cray. "What other belongings were there?"

"Hey, that ain't none of your business. You got what you want. I ain't giving you no more."

"I ain't . . . I'm not asking for them. I only would want to look, make sure that this is the man I'm looking for."

"Well, you ain't gonna. I told you the truth of it. The old man give me everthing of his and the other fella's, and I aim to keep it. You said you'd pay me; now I want my gold." Cray slammed a gnarly fist on the table, making the muted likeness of Tressie and her ma jitter.

Rose jumped and rose from her chair. "I'll get it for you." She went in her bedroom, glanced at the door to make sure the man couldn't see her, and dug out her cache of gold from its hiding place in a secret drawer behind her nightstand. She removed several nuggets and replaced the heavily laden pouch with care. Her heart battered at her rib cage so hard she could scarcely breathe. If only she could get the man to tell her a few more facts, but it would seem to be enough that Evan Majors had been the man killed in the cave-in.

She lay the nuggets near the man's hand curled on the tabletop. He stared goggle-eyed, and when he reached for them she covered two. "Did the old man tell you anything else about this friend? Where he was from, how long he'd been out here, his name?"

Cray obviously considered his chances of taking the nuggets from her before answering. "Alls I remember is that he had a name like one of them fellas in the Army. Not colonel or captain, but something like that."

"Major, or perhaps Majors?" Rose asked.

"That were it. That right there were it. Now, can I have

them?" He clutched three nuggets tightly and eyed her pale hand covering the other two. He was about to grab them.

Rose slid both across the table and stood. She could hardly wait for her visitor to leave so she could write a letter to Tressie. God, she hoped it would reach her, traveling in the wilds of the mountains. It had to, it just had to. Rose could think of nothing more important than letting Tressie know that she could end her wild vendetta, begin her life with that nice Reed Bannon.

How strange that the news of a death could carry with it so much promise. Just thinking about it gave Rose hope for her own happiness. One thing she knew for sure, she wouldn't find it with Jarrad Lincolnshire or any other man like him. She just might find it within herself. Anyway, she felt as if she could finally seek the serenity of a fulfilling life.

Eighteen

Outside Dillon, at the junction of Beaverhead River and Rattlesnake Creek, Tressie and Reed discovered the sign, all but grown over in weeds and sagging badly. She nearly wept when Reed wiped it clean and read it aloud, precisely as it was printed:

"Tu grass Hop Per digins 30 myle Kepe the Trale nex the bluffe."

Tressie bit at her lip, let her gaze wander across the enormous land. "Grass Hopper diggings? That's Grasshopper Creek, near Bannack, isn't it? Where Papa was headed." Had he followed these crude instructions? And what had he found at the end of that thirty-mile trek? If he ever made it there at all, that is.

"Best move on," Reed said, "check it out."

Tressie nodded and made a soft sound to the mare. So attuned to each other had they become that no commands were ever necessary. As they followed the trail to Bannack, Tressie took a look over her shoulder. Farther south in the Bitterroots someone named Majors waited, if they could believe what they'd learned. Maybe they shouldn't make this detour to Bannack.

"Do you think there's anything left of the town?"

"Hard to say. I hear she's nearly deserted, that everyone fled to Alder Gulch when they struck color there, but who knows? Bannack was declared the temporary headquarters of the new territory of Montana so there was something there. But last December it moved, I hear to Virginia City."

Tressie didn't say anything for a while. She wanted to ask more about this wild new territory, but was soon enthralled once again by the beauty of the majestic mountains.

Nothing came of their trip to Bannack. It was, like Reed had thought, a sleepy little town on the verge of death and nobody there had ever heard of Evan Majors. It took another day to ride back out to the main trail and once again head south, this time toward Lima in the Bitterroots and yet another search. She prayed it, too, wouldn't be fruitless.

Occasionally they met up with travelers on the trail, some headed north, others south. None roused any suspicion and Tressie began to believe that her earlier fears of being followed were just her imagination. Everywhere they went, everyone they talked to, listened patiently to their queries about Papa's whereabouts, then shook their heads. Had Evan Majors vanished off the face of the earth? It began to seem so.

On a peaceful, very hot afternoon, Reed said they had to be very near Lima. Hope grew once again in Tressie's heart. It was time this was over and done with. In her mind she practiced what she would say to Papa, how she would vent her hatred, make him sorry.

Despite her anxiety, her need to see this finished, Reed insisted they not push the horses but let them set their own pace. All of a sudden a great whooping and hollering echoed from the trail ahead. Rounding a bend, the couple spotted a gang of riders coming at them. Before they could meet up, however, the riders veered off the trail and headed through the woods.

Shouts of, "There's gonna be a hanging. A hanging," reached Tressie's ears and she stared wide-eyed at Reed.

Several wagons overflowing with people, including a few fancy women, emerged out of the cloud of dust left by the riders. They too made the turn into the woods.

Tressie and Reed waited there a moment, watching the crowd disappear from sight.

"Well," he finally said. "Looks like the whole town is here. Could be we might learn something, but it's up to you. A hanging isn't exactly a pretty sight."

Tressie gulped down a knot of nausea. "How far are we from where Papa was supposed to be?"

"That'd be Lima right up the road, I'd judge. Probably closest to his claim . . . if the man we heard tell of is your pa. Tressie, you know we can't be sure of our information."

She shrugged and nudged the mare into the woodland trail. "And that's what we came here to find out. Reckon we'd better get to it."

As they walked their mounts, a rider came up on them from behind. A latecomer, and in a hurry, it appeared. Reed hailed him.

"Who they hanging?"

"A Major something-or-other, I hear," the man shouted, and kept right on riding, whopping at his horse's butt with a wadded felt hat.

"Reed? Surely that couldn't be—"

"Stay here," he said. "Wait right here. I'll find out."

"I can't. Suppose it is him. You wouldn't know the difference. No, I'm going with you."

"Tressie, dammit. I can find out. You don't want to see this."

"If it's him I'll make them stop," she said, and quite abruptly nudged the mare with both heels. Not accustomed to such handling, the small horse laid back her ears and took off at a gallop. Reed could do nothing but spur his gelding on to keep up.

Tressie tightened both knees, shifted her weight to the stirrups, and let the mare have her head. Surely this wasn't Papa, for he'd never do anything that would get him hung. A wanderer he might be, but a lawbreaker? Never. There'd been some mistake. Still, she couldn't take the chance. Maybe it was another Majors. The name wasn't all that unusual. Some men even carried Major as a first name. Then there were majors in the Army. All sorts of possibilities occurred to her by the time she broke from the woods into a small clearing, Reed right on her heels. There she saw a sight that nearly stopped her heart.

Beneath a towering, gnarly old tree stood a circle of armed men, rifles at the ready. In their center the unlucky victim sat astride a bony horse, hands tied behind him, a noose around his neck. The man's head was tilted back so that he appeared to stare upward at the thick branch holding the rope.

All Tressie could see was a crop of dusty brown hair and a disreputable old shirt. It could be Papa. Screaming "Noooo" in a long, drawn-out wail, Tressie spurred the mare through the milling crowd, scattering the vigilantes.

Heads swiveled, including that of the unfortunate man

about to be strung up. She caught a glimpse of a pale face, rolling eyes, a mouth opened wide, before his horse let out a disgusted snort and bolted. The noose tightened, jerking the rider out of his saddle. He swung back and forth in a wild arc, legs kicking frantically, his entire body jerking and twitching. Women screamed, men shouted.

Tressie leaped from her horse, her intention to grab the hanging man's feet, but the nearest vigilante outguessed her and tackled her around the waist. Both thumped to the ground in a great cloud of dust. Because of her clothing he thought she was a young man, so the rowdy treatment came as no surprise. It didn't make her any happier, though, and she kicked and screeched, clawing at the face of her attacker as they rolled around on the ground.

Rifle in one hand, Reed leaped from his galloping gelding into the melee. He took a moment to make up his mind whether to rescue Tressie or try to save the man dangling at the end of the rope. He chose the unfortunate man, grabbing him by the legs. Maybe if the fall hadn't broken his neck, he could keep him from being strangled by the tight noose. But it was obvious as soon as he got a good hold that the man was dead weight. It was too late to do anything for him.

Reed let go and turned to Tressie, who sobbed in frustration because she couldn't break the ironclad hold of her captor. Waving the rifle around like a saber, he said, "Turn her loose now, mister."

A man in black holding a Bible whined, "Hell, I didn't even get to say the words. What kind of a hanging is this, anyway? Send a man on to his maker without the words."

"Shut up, Brother Dawson," a gangly fellow with a bobbing Adam's apple said. He then pointed his rifle at

Tressie while two cohorts hauled her to her feet. "Now, just what the hell's this all about? We just might have us another hanging here if you don't explain yourself real good, young fella."

One of the men holding on to Tressie shouted, "Hank, disarm that other one 'fore he shoots someone." Then, turning to Tressie, he said, "Now, mister, you've got some explaining to do. You understand that you caused this here hanging, 'fore he was even ready to send the major here on. There was words needed saying. We was about to find out what he done with the goods he stole. Suppose you explain why you didn't want him to talk."

"Who was he? What was his name? I want to see," she cried, struggling to get free.

The man called Hank held his rifle on Reed, having disarmed him as ordered, and everyone stared at Tressie.

"Where's the sheriff?" Reed asked.

The one with the Adam's apple snorted. "Hell, we ain't got no sheriff around these parts. You break a law, we take care of it. No need for a sheriff. And you two is about fixing to taste of our law if you don't do some fast talking."

"You shouldn't have hung him without a trial," Tressie wailed, now convinced it was Papa swaying in the breeze.

"The major? Didn't need no trial, boy. The man robbed the general store, took a whole blamed case of peaches plus some other stuff. Done it right under the nose of half the town, then shot the onliest two fellers with the guts to try and stop him. We run him down with a posse and brung him here to the hanging tree. Now if that ain't swift and fair justice, I don't know what is."

Hank agreed, "A trial's a flat waste of time. Now, what's your reason for trying to save his ornery hide?" He addressed the question at Reed and nudged him with the barrel of his rifle. "You in cahoots? You and this green un?"

"Now, hold it," Reed said. "We don't know a thing about a robbery. We're looking for a man name of Evan Majors, and we heard a feller named Majors was being hung. We just came along to see if they were one and the same, that's all."

Adam's apple grinned, showing a gap between crooked front teeth. "Why you looking for this Majors fella?"

Reed glanced at Tressie for help. She wiggled and kicked at the shins of her two captors. "I'm his daughter," she yelled in frustration. "And if these two would let me go, I could tell right quick if that's him."

Henry widened his eyes, then twitched his head in her direction and the two men let her go. "Keep your eye on that one," he said, and walked with Tressie to where the poor hanged man dangled. Sweeping off his hat in a belated gesture of respect for the dead, Henry gazed up into the purple, bloated face of the dead man. "Should a said you was a she," he muttered. Then, "That your pappy, ma'am?"

For a moment Tressie couldn't force her eyes upward to look. Her heart thumped painfully in her throat and she felt dizzy. If it was Papa, she supposed she would faint. If it wasn't, she might faint anyway, because she'd never looked at a hanged body before. She wished Reed were beside her.

Ever so slowly she raised her eyes. Past the scuffed boots, toes turned inward toward each other, up over the ripped knees of the britches and a gray shirt that had once been white. Around the neck, the noose cut into the flesh and the head tilted unnaturally to one side. There was the mouth, tongue protruding, the nose with a thin trickle of blood running from one nostril, then the eyes, bulging and frantic. A widow's peak divided the long brown hair that hung in dirty strands around the dead face.

"It's not him," she whispered huskily. "Not him, not him."

She felt her knees going out from under her and dark flashes obscured her vision so that the swaying body faded. Then, like a bolt of light from an overhanging black cloud, Tressie realized that she had actually precipitated the hanging by riding through the crowd shouting at the top of her voice. She had hung this poor soul!

Throwing her hands over her face, she began to bawl quite loudly as if her heart were broken.

Reed, still held at gunpoint, took in the pitiful sight and, not having heard her earlier comment, thought the hanged man was indeed Evan Majors.

"Listen, you hunk of lard," he snarled at the robust fellow poking the rifle in his ribs, "you let me go take care of her, or I'll carve you up in little pieces and feed you to the crows." His knife appeared in one hand so quickly that Hank, an unfortunate vigilante who hadn't wanted any part in this hanging anyway, staggered backward, jabbering, "He's got a knife. The breed's got a knife. Look out."

Reed barreled his way through the surprised crowd to Tressie's side. By this time she had sunk to her knees in the dirt, continuing to cry. Hank, who hadn't yet caught on that she was a woman, stared in dismay at such an outburst from a young man.

Reed dropped to his knees, still holding the knife.

"Honey, I'm sorry. Dammit, I'm so sorry. But you'll be okay. It's over with, anyway." He gathered her in his arms and there they knelt, swaying back and forth gently, while high above, the killer and thief, a major and deserter from the Confederate Army who had never been any closer to the high plains than Fort Laramie, did a little swaying of his own.

Tressie struggled to explain to Reed that the man wasn't her father, but she felt so bereft at having caused the man's hanging, she could do nothing but babble.

The folks who had attended the ceremony meandered around awhile, not sure if they had been cheated of their afternoon's entertainment or if maybe the show they saw hadn't been even better. After a while, when it appeared that nothing else was going to happen, most of them wandered away, including Brother Dawson, who muttered his disappointment while cramming a tattered Bible into his saddlebag. Henry, who seemed to be in charge; Jake, the man with the Adam's apple; and Hank Norton, the bumbling fellow Reed had pulled a knife on, considered this entire thing unfinished, so stuck around to put things to rights.

The three vigilantes watched Reed and Tressie for a while, eyeing each other with disbelief.

"No sense at all in two fellows acting like that," Hank finally said with disgust.

"One's a woman, fool. Reckon they had anything to do with the major's shenanigans?" Jake asked.

Hank Norton gaped. "Well, that breed pulled a knife on me. He would have scalped me, too, if I hadn't got away from him."

"That's a load of bull, Hank. You didn't get away. You was so scared you shook loose."

Henry and Jake laughed at poor Hank's expense.

All three turned in expectation when a wagon rattled into the clearing. "It's Clete, come to claim the body," Henry said.

Jake gestured toward Reed and Tressie, who were still wrapped in each other's arms beneath the hanged man. "What do we do about them?"

Hank shrugged. "Aw, hell. One hanging a day's enough for me. Leave 'em be. You ask me, them two fellers got enough troubles as it is." He turned and waved at Clete as he went to his horse. Henry and Jake, discussing the downright plain stupidity of their friend Hank, stayed to cut down the body for the undertaker. Then they, too, left the clearing.

Reed was afraid he would never get Tressie settled down, but he really didn't mind holding her in his arms. He paid no attention as the undertaker's wagon clattered away, leaving him alone with her.

Awkwardly he rubbed at her head. "Shh, honey. Everything's going to be all right. Stop crying now, you'll be sick."

She hiccuped and said damply, "I killed him, I killed him."

"You did no such thing, darlin'. They hung him."

"But if I . . . if I hadn't . . . rode in . . . like . . . like I was . . . oh, Reed. I made them go ahead and hang him. Maybe he wouldn't . . . they might have changed their minds."

"That's nonsense, Tressie. Pure and simple. Come

on, now, dry your eyes and stop this. You didn't hang any one, and most especially not Evan Majors. I'm sorry he's dead, but you didn't kill him."

"Oh, not Papa. Reed, that wasn't . . . I mean, the body . . . it wasn't Papa. Oh, goodness, no." She began to cry again, but softer and more controlled.

Not Majors? Confused, Reed hugged her some more, though his knees were getting mighty tired of kneeling in the rock-encrusted dirt under the hanging tree. What a day it had been, and now to learn that they still hadn't found Evan Majors, when he'd thought for sure . . . Reed sighed. Would he never have this woman, or was he destined to trail around all over the West for the rest of his life searching for this man she both hated and loved? He wasn't sure he could take much more. Enough was enough.

"Come on, girl, get on your feet," he urged, and hauled her up with him. "We need to have us a talk, and I don't reckon this is a good place to do it, right here under a hanging tree. Let's find us a camp for the night, what do you say?"

Seeing the distressed look on his face, Tressie tried to get hold of her emotions. "I'm sorry, it was just such a shock. First thinking we'd found him, then finding out it wasn't him at all, then thinking I'd hanged him. You have to admit, Reed, it was pretty upsetting."

"Oh, it was that, all right," he muttered, and went to fetch their horses, which were munching listlessly at green leaves on low-hanging branches nearby. He had a good hold on both bridles before it occurred to him how funny the entire situation had been, when you got right down to it. And what had all those folks thought about him and Tressie busting up their pleasure and then carrying on so? Stories of the hanging of Major whoever-the-hell-he-was might grow into one of the most oft-repeated tales in these parts for years to come. He was chuckling when he returned to where Tressie waited.

Keeping a low profile, they rode through Lima and continued on another hour or so before camping on the edge of a stream far enough away from the main road so they couldn't be seen. Reed still wasn't sure some of the vigilantes might not reconsider the day's events and decide to come after the two of them.

Before dark Tressie waded upstream until she was completely out of sight of the camp. The creek curved away from an outcropping, and she wandered along a smaller stream. Breaking through a thick undergrowth of brush, she approached a cavelike shelter. A waterfall tumbled through a hole high above into a hollowed-out basin. The perfect place to bathe.

Stripping out of her clothes, Tressie waded in up to her knees, leaving deep footprints in the smooth black sand along the water's edge. She eased down, submerging all but her head. Idly, she fingered through the sand, fisting up handfuls and washing them away just beneath the surface of the water. The last rays of the setting sun penetrated the thick trees and fell across her hand momentarily flashing on something. She dug it out. Holding the rock up to catch the last of the evening's light, Tressie gasped at the golden sheen. Surely it couldn't be gold. She turned the nugget, which was about the size of the end of her thumb, rubbed at it. Then the sun was gone and she could no longer see much of anything in the isolated glen.

Heart beating high in her throat, Tressie clutched the mysterious rock as she hastened into her britches and shirt. Without binding her breasts or even buttoning the shirt all the way, she ran back toward camp, carrying her shoes.

Reed had a fire going and she approached him as speechless as she'd ever been. She wanted to babble or shout or something, but nothing would come out of her mouth but a squawk.

Seeing her so frantic, Reed thought for a moment something was after her. A bear, maybe, or some crazed vigilante set on hanging them both. He grabbed up his rifle.

Tressie panted to a halt in front of him and held out the nugget, eyes flashing in the light from the blazing fire.

Reed took it. "What is it, Tressie, girl? Cat get your tongue? What is this?"

She still couldn't say anything, just danced from one foot to the other and watched him.

He gave the nugget a closer look, put the rifle down and bent closer to the fire. "Where did you find this?" he asked, pulling out his knife to scrape at the surface.

She turned and pointed, looked back at him, finally croaked out, "Is it gold?"

Reed rubbed the nugget against his teeth, looked at it again, then nodded slowly as if in a trance. "Show me where you found it," he said softly. "Was there anyone else around? A camp or signs of a claim?"

"I don't know, I didn't look, but I didn't notice anyone."

Truth was, they hadn't seen signs of panning since before they took their inadvertent part in today's hanging. Gold fever hadn't yet made its way this deep into the mountains, or maybe no one had run across anything. Men tended to hunt where there was easier access. It was like the old story about the fishing hole. Find a good place to fish, even if you didn't catch anything.

Reed refused to believe Tressie could have accidentally found a valuable gold deposit. Probably just the one nugget, something they could sell for a few months' expenses. But you never knew, and he had to see for himself.

"Take me there now," he told her.

Dropping her shoes, Tressie headed back into the creek. "You can't get there following either bank, it's too wild, you'll have to wade the water," she told him. "I was just taking a bath, sitting there playing in the sand, and there it was. It's back in a cavelike place under a waterfall."

Reed's own heart pounded. Gold was often washed down from higher in the mountains. Beneath a waterfall was a perfect place to find nuggets like this. Still . . . "What color was the sand?" he asked, feeling as if his tongue overflowed his mouth.

"The prettiest black you ever saw," she said. "Here, in here. She led them along the creek. I almost missed it in the dark. Reed, you don't suppose there's snakes in here, do you?"

"Snakes?" he asked incredulously. "Snakes? You have found a gold nugget the size of your thumb and you're worried about snakes. Good Lord, Tressie. Do you realize we might be rich?"

"Oh, Reed, do you think so? Truly?" She wasn't sure how she felt about that. If they had to stake a claim and work it, then she would probably never find Papa. They wouldn't even look anymore, and his fate would be lost forever.

By the time they reached the waterfall it was so dark neither could see anything. They stumbled around in there for a while, then gave up.

"We'll come back first thing in the morning and take a good look," Reed said finally. "It's been here all this time, it ain't going anywhere. Oh, Lord, Tressie," he shouted, and pulled her close.

She nestled into his arms, trembling a bit in the knee-deep water. The warmth of his body washed over her and she hugged him tight. He lowered his head and she raised her face, finding his seeking lips in the pitch-black. Her arms snaked around his neck and he wrapped her up in a strong hug, shuddering a bit himself.

In the summer darkness, frogs and crickets, night creatures of all kinds, filled the air with their song. At that moment, when they were eerily suspended in a darkness that shut out time, Tressie decided that she wanted nothing but this man, holding her close, protecting and loving her for the rest of her life. Nothing frightened her when he held her like this, and when he pulled away it was as if she had lost her natural hold on things. Why then couldn't she just put her hate and need for revenge behind her? Give everything to Reed Bannon, and take everything he offered in return.

"Ah, Tressie, I do love you so," he whispered. "Let's get back to camp."

Holding hands, they made their careful way along the creek, and it took a long while before they spotted the campfire, burned down some but still glowing like a guiding star in the depths of the wilderness.

As they approached the camp, paying more attention to each other than to their surroundings, a twig snapped and gravel scattered near the camp. Reed froze and pulled her behind him. He had left both the rifle and his knife in camp with his saddlebags. They had made plenty of noise as they approached, and an intruder in their camp couldn't have helped but hear them coming.

"Get down on your knees in the brush there," he whispered to Tressie. "Don't move, don't come out for anything. You understand?"

Throat locked tightly, she nodded vigorously and obeyed.

Reed crouched down and made his way around the edge of the clearing, out of the glow of firelight. Pausing behind the trunk of a large tree, he stared at their campsite until his eyes ached. Nothing moved. The horses were hobbled at his back, not where the noise had come from. Someone had been snooping around, but whoever it was appeared to have lit out when Reed and Tressie returned.

What in the hell was going on? Why would anyone be snooping around their camp? They didn't have anything worth stealing, unless it was Indians wanting the horses. Or maybe Henry or Jake had had second thoughts and decided to check them out further. That was surely it. But why didn't they just do it openly?

After waiting a few more minutes, Reed called out to Tressie that everything was all right.

She approached the firelight cautiously. "Who was it?"

"I don't know. I didn't see anyone, and nothing has been disturbed. The rifle's right where I left it; so is everything else."

By this time Reed had convinced himself that his ears had played tricks on him, and one of the animals had simply moved around, making him think someone was prowling on the other side of the camp.

"What was it you wanted to talk to me about?" Tressie asked, settling down close to the fire to get warm.

"What?" he asked absentmindedly.

"You said we had to talk, back there after the . . . after the hanging. What about?"

"Oh, that," Reed said. He thought of the nugget and what it could mean, of how he felt holding her. The discussion about stopping this insane search for Evan Majors could wait until they checked out Tressie's discovery. If they decided to file a claim and pan some gold here, it would be settled for a while anyway. He really dreaded telling Tressie that he had no desire to keep traipsing around the country after a man who obviously didn't want to be found anyway.

She sidled around the fire and snuggled up against him. "Then let's sleep together tonight, Reed. I don't want to sleep alone."

He put his arm around her, pulled her head to his shoulder. Sometimes a man just couldn't fight anymore. The darkness around them seemed not so harmless as he wished. Something or someone lurked out there. He felt that as he'd never felt anything before. Who or what it was, he had no idea.

"No," he said, pulling her up into his lap. "I don't feel like sleeping alone, either." He slipped one hand inside the front of her partially buttoned shirt and caressed her breast.

She gave herself to him slowly, their love as sweet and warm as a summer night.

Nineteen

*H*idden in the secret darkness of the woods, he ran clumsy fingers over the beaded leather bag. He could almost taste victory sweetening the bitter hate he'd carried like a loathsome burden. It wouldn't be long now. The first time the breed left the woman alone . . . well, that would be too bad for her. He would steal her just as Race had stolen Bright Fox. And kill her the same, too. Well, nearly the same. It would do Reed no good to deny he was Race Brannigan's whelp. Changing his name didn't make it so. He would pay for what he and his daddy had done, pay good, for the rest of his miserable life.

The big man settled quietly against the trunk of a tree, keeping his eye on the couple lying beside the campfire. Like a cat over a rat hole, he had them now, and there was time to play.

Anxious to take a good look at the place where Tressie had found the gold nugget, Reed dragged her out of the mound of blankets at first light. He didn't even want to stop for breakfast.

"Later, we can eat later," he told her, grabbing her hand and heading for the stream as soon as she was dressed.

"Reed Bannon," she panted, "slow down. You'd think you were a gold-hungry prospector, the way you're acting."

Reed only laughed. But it was true that he saw in the gold find a possibility of being with the woman he loved for the rest of his life. No more running from ghosts, no more seeking what wasn't there to be found—her runaway pa, Reed's misplaced pride. They could have a home and family someplace out West. Maybe California, even. If only less . . .

"In there," Tressie cried, hauling him up short.

Together they pushed through the brush, following the trickling stream of water that flowed into the main branch. At last they emerged into a small clearing fronting an overhanging bluff. She pointed at the falls tumbling through a hole in the slab of rock at least twenty feet above their heads.

He gaped at the secluded glen. "How in the world did you find this, girl?"

She shrugged. "I don't know. I wanted a good place to take a bath in private, so I just kept looking. Come on."

Together they waded into the indigo pool of water. Her footprints from the evening before were still visible in the black sand on the bank.

She squatted and ran her fingers through the grit. "I just dug up a handful and sifted it, like this," she said, and did so. Another nugget peeked out, smaller than the first, but quite impressive. "Reed, look. My goodness, look!"

He laughed sharply and jerked his head all around, thinking that surely something couldn't be right about plucking nuggets up as if they were common stones. Then he filled his own fists and, opening both hands beneath the surface, let the black sand drift from his palms. In the crystalline water, flakes of gold floated toward the bottom like glittering rain.

"Good Lord," Reed said prayerfully. He glanced all around again. He expected at any moment for someone to leap out and shoot them for trespassing on their claim. But there were no signs anywhere that a human had ever been near this place. He'd been in this country long enough to know a claim such as this would be marked and well protected.

As if mesmerized, Tressie continued to stare at the two nuggets she now held. "What do we do? Good heavens, what do we do?"

"Stake our claim, now. Ride into Lima and register it, then come back out here and start panning, my girl."

"But Reed, you don't just go out one night to take a bath and end up finding gold. Not like this."

"Well, this time I reckon you do, darlin'." He pondered on that for a bit, then leaped high into the air, tossed his hat, and whooped. Droplets of multihued water arced in a rainbow around him. Coming down with a tremendous splash, he reached for Tressie and pulled her into a bear hug. "Someone has to be first, and I reckon this time it's us."

Clutching the nuggets in one hand, Tressie raised her gaze to meet Reed's. His shaggy black hair, wetly plastered around the harshly chiseled face, the depth of his eyes soft as a velvet night, the joy that transformed his somber features, all made her forget everything that had gone before in her life. What this discovery would mean to their lives she had no idea, but seeing him so happy filled her own heart with a joy as warm and sweet as summer honey.

She cupped one side of his face in her palm and tilted his mouth down to hers.

"Oh, girl. Sweet girl," he said. "None of this is worth a thing if I don't have you." He'd let it all go, he knew. In a minute. If only he could keep her this way always.

Tressie tasted the fire of his passion, his need for her, and ran her tongue around the soft inner flesh of his mouth. His manner allowed such trust. No rough hurtful play with this man. In Reed's tender embrace it was easy to push memories of Papa's betrayal aside. It was even easy to say it didn't matter, that she didn't care if she ever found him. Until, that is, one came awake in the wee dark hours of morning haunted by memories. You didn't forget a cruelty, a vow for revenge made over a grave, no matter your excuse.

Reluctantly they parted.

He licked her tangy taste from his lips and gazed down into her dazzling green eyes. "I guess we'd better get to business, huh?"

Beneath his grin she caught a glimpse of troubled sorrow. Before she could explore its meaning, he turned away. They set to work marking the outer perimeter of their claim by stacking a series of rocks in each of four corners.

"Now what?" she asked when they had finished.

"I've never done this before, but I'd guess we'll have to pace it off, see how far it is from the creek and the main trail."

"Who goes to town and who stays here?" she asked.

"Considering our last confrontation with folks from

Lima, I'd guess that to be the most dangerous of the two jobs, so I'll do it. But I think we have to have something to show, so I'll take the gold to the assayer and he'll tell us what to do next."

Tressie giggled. "I'll bet come tomorrow morning there'll be men panning this creek just like they were at Alder Gulch when we passed there."

"Word of gold does get around."

They waded out to their campsite hand in hand. "You know," Tressie said, "Papa might hear about this. Wouldn't that be something if our strike made him come to us?"

"Dammit, can't you forget your hate for two minutes at a time?" Reed was immediately sorry for his outburst, but her words had successfully shattered the plans he was making for their future. He had struck out in defense of his very life.

She stopped in the middle of the creek. "Well, no, I can't, Reed Bannon. He killed my mama, and so it's a little hard to just make his memory disappear forever."

"It seems he did a pretty good job of that himself, without your help," he said.

She watched him stride out of the water and into camp. No matter what happened, even uncovering gold nuggets that would choke a mule, she and Reed seemed destined to fight over her mission. She chased after him. "If that's the way you feel, why don't you just stay here with your precious gold and I'll go on looking for him by myself."

"Don't be dumb. You wouldn't last a week out there alone."

"Oh, yeah. Well, that's just what you think. I was taking care of myself when you found me, and I can just go on doing it. I don't need any old gold to make me happy. You can just keep it all."

"You try to leave, I'll hog-tie you, girl," Reed said softly. "I mean it, I will. I ain't letting you loose out here in this godforsaken land all alone, and I don't care what you think."

"You wouldn't dare, Reed Bannon," Tressie said, facing him and trembling with rage.

"Oh, yes I would dare, and it would be for your own good."

"Well, we'll just see about that." Tressie whirled and started tossing her belongings haphazardly in a pile on one of the blankets where they'd slept together the previous night. Speechless, Reed watched her fold, roll, and tie the blanket. She hefted her saddle, but found she couldn't carry both, so dropped the roll and headed for the mare who grazed nearby. He could hear water squishing in her clothes as she walked.

"Tressie," he commanded, chasing after her. The mare eyed them both with rolling eyes and backed away.

Gritting her teeth, Tressie shushed the frightened animal and tossed the saddle on its back. Anger masked her reasoning. Fear that he would let her go almost made her sick, yet she could see no way to back down now.

"You know I won't . . . can't let you do this," he warned in that steady and soft voice of his.

"Then don't," she thought she said aloud as she went right on working with the cinch.

"You didn't put her blanket on," Reed said.

Tressie thought she would choke with the anguish that instantly overpowered her. She whirled, doubled up her fists, and began to cry. "Why did I ever have to meet you?

Why didn't I die there with Mama? How could he do that to us? I hate him, hate him, hate him, and I want to tell him so. I wish he was dead. Do you hear me? I wish he was dead, dead, dead."

Reed took two steps and caught her in his arms. She remained stiff and unyielding, shaking with pent-up fury.

Even though she didn't respond to him, Reed hung on to her rigid body. "You don't mean that, darlin'. None of it. Just quieten down, now. You've got to forgive yourself, do you hear me? You can't go on blaming yourself for all that happened. Girl, listen to me, would you?"

"No, no. It wasn't my fault, it wasn't."

"I know that, but you don't. That's why you just keep up this crazy fighting with yourself. Tressie, let it go now, you hear me? Let it go so you can live. So we can live."

She felt her legs go weak. "I don't think I can," she whimpered.

Filled with compassion, he lifted her, curled one arm under her knees, and carried her back to where they had slept together. He figured if he didn't weaken, he'd win this tough woman/child one day. She sure did set high standards for herself, standards no human could ever live up to. He decided if they didn't settle this question of Evan Majors's whereabouts, she never would be able to live with herself. If he ever got his hands on the man, he'd shake him so hard his eyeballs fell out in the dust, then he'd make him tell Tressie how sorry he was for the wicked thing he'd done. Then he'd kick him all the way up to the divide and off the other side.

Tressie lay where he had placed her, watching him steadily with moist eyes.

He kissed the corner of her mouth and experimented with a teasing tone. "Do I have to tie you up now?"

She rolled her head back and forth. "You wouldn't anyway."

"No, I wouldn't anyway, but dammit, you sure did give me a scare. I was thinking I was going to have to do something. You're your own worst enemy, girl, I'll swear if you ain't. Could be you left home too wet."

She giggled weakly. "What an awful thing to say."

"Well, sometimes I think you still need someone to tell you what to do."

"You said no one can make us do things, that we do what we want."

"Oh, sure, throw that back at me. You know exactly what I meant. Whatever we do, and that includes your ill-begotten papa, is our own fault. We can't go laying it off on other folks, blaming them for our own weaknesses. One of these days you'll understand that."

"Oh, I understand it," she said primly. "I'm just not sure I agree with it. And anyway, what makes you so almighty smart?"

Reed rubbed at her jaw with the ball of his thumb. "Oh, I'm not so smart. I've done plenty of dumb things. Things I wish to hell I could take back. And I have to live with them. I wish I deserved your love, Tressie. Truly I do."

"Oh, Reed," she said. "You do, you do."

He looked away, staring out across the creek. "Well, maybe someday I will. Now let's get busy. We need to move the camp closer to our claim and get down to some serious panning."

She sat up, throwing off the earlier distress.

They spent the rest of the morning moving camp, actually managing to joke with each other as they worked. Using a small hatchet, Reed cleared saplings from the forest floor near where the stream flowed from under the overhang. There wasn't room beneath the bluff for the animals, a campfire, and sleeping arrangements, so they hobbled the mule and both horses across the main stream in a small field of lush grass.

When Reed returned from stepping off the claim they would file, Tressie had dinner cooked: fried fatback in dandelion greens with johnnycake alongside. They divided the meal, and Reed dug in, smacking his lips.

She enjoyed watching him eat. "After we finish I'm putting some beans on to cook. We'll be here awhile. I can start fixing decent meals for you."

"This is pretty decent," he said. "I was starving for fresh greens. Wouldn't a little vinegar be good on them?"

"Put it on your list," Tressie said, and took another bite.

He glanced up quickly. "List?"

"For when you go to town to file our claim. That gold is surely worth enough to buy us some vittles."

He grinned at her with a silly look on his face. He'd forgotten they were rich. "Yeah, I expect you're right. Oh, and Tressie, I know we're all alone out here, but maybe you ought to do something about . . ." He gestured with his spoon at her chest.

The flannel shirt she wore was unbuttoned halfway down, revealing much of the lush pale beauty of her breasts. There was little left to the imagination. Flashing her eyes mischievously at him, she fingered two more buttons loose.

"Aw, hell, girl, don't do that."

Carefully placing her empty plate on a rock near the fire, she rose in a sensuous movement, at the same time releasing the button at her waist. The baggy pants slid down her long, lean legs to bunch around trim ankles.

"Tressie," he warned, poking a last bite of johnnycake in his mouth and rising. "We've got work to do."

The shirt, all that covered her body now, came off in one slick motion of her arms. She stood there before him, the opulent jade forest at her back, the music of the waterfall playing around her. Sunlight danced with shadows over her erect breasts and flashed in her auburn tresses.

"Reed," she said softly. "Come here or I'm coming after you." She trailed a finger between her breasts and down past her belly button.

"You little savage," Reed groaned, and took off his shirt slowly, matching her eroticism with some of his own. When he stood naked before her, still not making a move in her direction, she cupped both hands under her breasts and lifted them, twitching the nipples with both thumbs.

Reed swayed and held his ground, gazing at her from half-closed eyes. A craving of such intensity invaded Tressie that she was nearly knocked to her knees. She staggered a bit, saw him through a haze as if only imagining his presence. It was hard to tell where the sheen from his bronze body became rays of woodland light. Hands hanging loosely at his sides, he shifted his weight, cocking one lean hip. A breeze lifted his long black hair. He was like something from an erotic dream. Beyond his appearance, she knew he possessed an inner radiance and kindness of spirit that made him very special.

When she could no longer stand being parted from him, she lifted one arm and bade him come to her. He did, taking her hand in one of his while running the other over her body. Gooseflesh followed the journey of his fingertips across one breast, down the curve of her tiny waist, and into the downy mound between her legs.

Dropping to his knees, he placed his warm lips against her flesh, flicking out his tongue as he moved ever so slowly downward. Tressie arched her head backward and cried out while his tongue performed maddening pirouettes within her innermost being. When her legs would no longer support her, she slithered down the length of him, until they knelt body to body. He smelled of musk and the leather of their saddles, and a wild unnameable fragrance that triggered an overpowering passion in her. His moist flesh embraced every inch of hers as they lay back in the cool green moss. When he lifted her lithe body unto his, they slipped gently into the shallow water. The quivering waves washed between them, lapping, lapping, licking away their juices.

Reed poised on the very edge of an ecstasy so supreme as not to be bearable. He would kill for this woman. He would die for her. These things he knew with a certainty he had never before experienced. He would do anything to see that she was happy. Even leave her, if that's what it took, for he had never felt so totally one with another being on this earth. She dwelled in his soul and she would forever be there, even if he never saw her again. But he knew, too, that he would do almost anything to keep her with him.

He dreamed that night of the running. Running from his mother's people and their primitive rites of passage, running from the war and that all-too-savage rite peculiar to the white man, and worst of all running always from

himself and what he feared dwelled in his innermost recesses that made of him a coward. He awoke drenched in
sweat, panting and reaching out for her, fearful that she
had somehow followed him into that terrible dream world
and seen what he truly was.

In her sleep she made a soft sound and snuggled into
his grasping arms, tucking her head against his chest. He
feared the day he would have to tell her his dark coward's
secret. It was a long time before he went back to sleep
again.

The next morning Reed saddled up his gelding, stuffed
into the front pocket of his pants the drawstring pouch
filled with gold they had found the day before, and kissed
Tressie.

"I'm leaving the rifle with you," he told her. "I'll be back
as soon as I can."

She clung to his hand a moment, then put it to her lips
in a farewell. "I'll be okay. You just be careful or you'll end
up in jail, after what we did to their hanging."

His dark eyes glittered. "We? I was only an innocent by-
stander." Seeing her glowering look, he continued, "Ah,
don't you worry, they'll be cooled down by now. Besides,
we're a long way from the Army and the law. I'll be fine."

"You've got the list of supplies?"

He nodded, patted his shirt pocket. "I love you, girl.
Now, don't worry."

"No, no, I won't." She backed away as he mounted, remained there watching him leave until the horse had
crossed the creek and plodded through their earlier campsite toward the road to town.

With a sigh Tressie leaped playfully through the water

and back toward the gold claim. She had decided to pan for more gold during the hottest part of the afternoon, then go searching for edible plants in the cool of the evening. She didn't know much about roots and herbs in these mountains, but if she were back home in the Ozarks there would be a harvest of fruit ripe by now. Blackberries hanging in thick clusters on their wickedly thorned bushes, huckleberries that grew low on spindly plants, and the sweet, ground-hugging dewberries. She recalled the tart red plums she and Bitter Leaf had so enjoyed last summer. Maybe she could find some of those, too. First, though, she would put beans on to cook.

All caught up in readying the hot coals, placing the pot of water just so, and looking over the dried beans, handful at a time, Tressie didn't hear the man enter the clearing. He came up on her so quiet she had no idea he was there until his massive arm locked around her from behind. The cloth sack tipped, spilling beans around on the ground. He lifted her completely off her feet, squeezing so hard she gasped for air. In her ear his hot, fetid breath whistled harshly.

"Behave, girlie, or I'll break your back, and I can do it, too." He exerted more pressure to convince her and she crumpled over his arm.

When she came to, very little time must have passed, for he was carrying her in the same position, headed for the small pasture where her mare and the mule were grazing. Tressie shoved and clawed at his hairy forearm, kicking out with both bare heels. He just laughed at her, a huge booming sound that echoed off the bluffs and peaks.

"What do you want? Let me go. Are you crazy?" These questions she blurted out between painful gasps for air.

She feared passing out again. Had he come to steal the claim, take away their gold?

He made no reply, just grunted and shifted her around so that she could no longer kick him. He tucked her under his arm like a sack of feed, her head faced forward and her legs stuck out behind. She looked down at his massive feet, encased in deerskin boots wet from wading the creek. His smell was that of rancid fat.

"Stop it!" she cried. "Who are you? Leave me alone!"

Tressie suddenly shut up, for she saw with amazement that her saddled mare waited alongside a leggy black that must belong to this man. When and how had he done that? He had to have saddled the mare while Reed was still in camp, for there hadn't been time since he rode out. My God, was this the man who had been following them? The one she had sensed but could never see?

He tossed her into the saddle so roughly that one thigh struck the horn painfully. "Straddle her. Do I have to tie your legs together, or are you going to behave?"

Tressie thought later that if she'd had better sense, she would have suffered less, but she lashed out, never having been wise when it came to controlling her mouth. "Behave? I'll hit you over the head with a rock first chance I get."

So, of course, he bound one ankle, drew the rawhide under the mare's belly and bound the other. Then he tied her wrists to the saddle horn. Drawing the thong tight so that she cried out, he said, "There, now, that'll keep you."

It was at that moment, when he stood at her mount's shoulder looking squarely up at her, that Tressie recognized the man. And this time it wasn't her imagination, like with Dr. Gideon. Or all the other fleeting times when she'd thought she saw someone familiar who reminded her of this monstrous man. This was Dooley Kling, who was just like Papa. A man who would desert his wife and child without a backward glance. But what was he doing here, and what did he want with her?

"You . . . you filthy killer," Tressie spat.

"Hush, girlie, or you'll wear a gag, too, and it'll be as tight as this gawdamn thong. You understand?"

Eyes filling and fear boiling from down deep in her stomach, Tressie nodded so hard her teeth clacked together. He hadn't come for the gold claim but for her. But why? And what did he intend to do with her?

After he had her trussed, Kling went back to the camp on foot and Tressie watched with puzzlement while he scratched in the dirt with a long stick. As she watched, Kling kicked over the pan of water and scattered the dry beans all around. He wanted Reed to know that something bad had happened to her. She wondered why, but didn't ask when he came back, for fear he would do as promised and gag her.

They rode the main trail, but not for long, for Kling soon cut off to the right and headed up what appeared to be nothing more than a goat trail. They were fast headed into high country. In front of them, snow-covered peaks cut jagged lines against the blue sky. It was dry season up there, but soon torrential rains would begin, rains that before long would turn to ice and snow. Tressie feared she wouldn't live to see it unless Reed could somehow track them. He was good at that, like he was good at a lot of other things on the trail. And oddly enough, Kling made no effort to hide the signs of their passage.

They stopped the first night in a small meadow filled

with white daisies surrounding a mirror-still lake. On the fringes of the forest golden aspen chattered in the breeze. The wind that touched her skin carried a misty tang from the high snows.

Kling unlashed one ankle and her wrists, then shoved her out of the saddle. With an outraged cry she tumbled to the ground in a heap. For a long while she lay in the brittle grass and rubbed at her tingling legs. When she could finally move them, she struggled to stand. It took all the effort she could muster. They had been riding almost all day without a break, though he had given her water twice.

"I have to go," she said thickly.

"You ain't going anywhere."

"No, I mean, I need to . . . please don't make me wet myself."

He studied her through squinted eyes, then finally nodded. "Do it there, where I can watch."

"No, please," she cried.

"Do it or forget it," he said, but did finally turn his back when she unfastened her britches and stood there glaring at him.

After hobbling the horses, Kling built a fire and boiled some coffee. He threw her a hard chunk of bread to go with the mud-black brew, and she swallowed both gratefully. She had to stay alive, any way she could, because as careless as this man was, Reed would catch them in no time.

She tried to imagine Reed's return to camp, his complete and utter distress at finding her and the mare gone. Would he ride out immediately or wait until morning? During the long, endless night, huddled without a blanket on the hard ground, Tressie pictured, over and over, Reed setting out to rescue her. She had to survive for when he caught up to them.

At the general store in Lima, where the stagecoach delivered mail, Reed presented his list for supplies. The dark-haired, bespectacled storekeeper was friendly and nosy. Reed had about decided that out here on the frontier the two went together.

"You staying around these parts?" the man asked, fetching the first item off the list: two cans of peaches. Reed grinned widely. He hadn't read Tressie's list, and was pleased that she remembered what high stock he put in the syrupy golden fruit.

"Staking a claim down south."

The man raised brown eyes, widened them. "A claim? Gold? Say, ain't you the fellow who come to the hanging . . . you and that other fellow what turned out to be a girl raised such a ruckus?"

Reed glanced around the store. An old man sat in a straight chair, head nodding as if asleep, and a young man about Tressie's age pawed through some overalls. "Yep, I reckon that was me and my . . . uh . . . my partner."

"Partnered with a girl and you're gonna pan for gold, are you?" The man snorted to show what he thought of such and pointed a narrow finger at the list. "Is this bacon? If so, I ain't got none."

Reed twisted to read the scrawl. "Looks like bacon, but you can put in fatback instead."

The storekeep nodded. "That I got." He went to a large wooden barrel and dug around in an assortment of salted meats till he came up with a chunk of pork fat. "You fellers names?"

"What?" Reed said, staring through the window at a rider in the street. He rode stiffly erect, one hand on his thigh as if he'd been in the cavalry. That made Reed unaccountably nervous.

"Names. What names do you two go by?" the storekeeper insisted.

"Oh." Reed thought about using a fake name, but couldn't think of one. Besides, like he'd told Tressie, they were a long way from the Army and the long arm of the law. "Reed Bannon's my name . . . and—"

"Bannon. Why, ain't that a crazy coincidence?"

Reed felt the hair on the back of his neck prickle. So they did know him after all. Would this man draw a hogleg pistol out from under the counter and hold him for the vigilantes?

The man did go under the counter, but it was to pull out a stack of envelopes. "A letter come here for you just last week. Says General Delivery, Lima, Territory of Montana. Used to be Idaho, you know. Plumb strange how them government fellas keep a changing the names of places. One week I live in Oregon, the next Idaho, now it's Montana."

Reed chuckled at the little joke, overdoing it somewhat in his relief that he wasn't going to be the next man strung up to the hanging tree outside of town. He reached for the letter, wondering what in the world it could be. The only person who had any idea where they were headed was the pretty blond lady friend of Tressie's who owned the saloon in Virginia City. The letter Tressie had sent by stagecoach when they turned south must have made it to the Golden Sun Saloon after all.

Though anxious to read this letter he now clutched, Reed stuffed it into his shirt pocket. It might be addressed to him, but that was just because of the situation, and he knew it was really for Tressie. He'd let her read it aloud for the both of them when he got back to camp.

Meanwhile, he had to get to the assayer's.

"Say," he said to the storekeeper, who continued to lay out items from the list, "would you mind finishing that out while I go to the assayer's?"

Despite several references to the interrupted hanging of Major whatever-his-name-was, by midafternoon Reed had completed his business in Lima. He rode back into camp with the mysterious letter burning a hole in his pocket. He had unsaddled his gelding and toted the two sacks of supplies into their new camp alongside the gold claim before it dawned on him that Tressie's mare was missing. That's when he saw the mess someone had made in camp and found the message scratched in the dirt nearby.

Twenty

At first Reed couldn't make out what was scrawled in the dirt. He saw the scattered beans, the overturned pot. Even then, for a split second longer, he considered that she had simply gone somewhere on her own. It didn't work. An intense fear for Tressie nearly blinded him. For a long while he just stood there staring down, not fully comprehending much of anything but that he had lost her. He had left her alone and unprotected and lost her. Coming back to his senses, he dropped the supplies and fell to both knees, tracing the gouges in the dirt with trembling fingers. R A C E. Race? What kind of race?

It wasn't until he spotted the beaded deerskin bag that the name of his hated father slammed at him like a thrown rock. Race Brannigan. How he'd hope never to be forced to think of the name again. He snatched up the bag, inspected it thoroughly. Yes, there it was, the peculiar symbol worked into the beading in the lower right-hand corner. This was the bag his grandmother had given him so long ago, the one Dooley Kling stole when he lit out and abandoned his newborn child. But what could Dooley Kling and Reed's father possibly have to do with this? Father and son wouldn't know each other if they met face-to-face in broad daylight. Reed didn't know how or why, but Dooley Kling had been here and had left this cryptic message. And it was somehow connected to Reed's past. To his own father and mother.

His first impulse was to mount up and ride out, tracking that bastard Dooley Kling so he could catch him and rip him limb from limb. But if he was to save the woman he loved, he had to think, plan, listen to his head, not his heart. The man would not have left the message and the bag had he not wanted Reed to follow. So the trapper would leave plenty of sign, and he would keep an eye on his back trail. Reed would have to go very carefully.

He squinted into the sky. Maybe four hours of daylight left. Pushing, he could cover a lot of trail before dark. He packed little food, keeping down the weight. Why hadn't he bought ammo at the general store this morning? He counted twenty-five rounds on hand. It would have to be enough. He didn't plan on getting in a shootout with Kling, not with Tressie in the way. All he needed now was water, a bedroll, and a mackinaw. Those tied to the saddle, Reed mounted up.

He didn't think of the letter in his shirt pocket again until dark caught up with him and he could no longer track his prey. By then he had followed them off the main trail. And he'd been right about the old bastard. Kling was making sure to leave plenty of sign to follow.

As Reed dismounted, he scowled into the western sky, where the purpling peaks jagged against the silvering sky. Along the crest, lingering daylight sparkled on ice and snow, then faded. Reed shivered.

She was up there somewhere, and if Kling hurt her, he'd kill him. Slow and easy. The thought surprised Reed,

for he'd never deliberately considered killing anyone before, not even during the war when he was firing at the
unseen enemy. Shooting off a gun at someone because he
threatened you was not the same as setting out to kill
Dooley Kling. But dammit, the man had Tressie, and God
only knew what hell she was going through. Reed tried
not to think of that, or of the possibility of losing her. It
might drive him crazy.

Boldly Reed built a campfire for the night. Let the son
of a bitch know he was coming. Besides, he needed light
so he could read the letter.

Rose Langue wrote how only recently it had reached
her ears that Evan Majors had been killed in a mining ac-
cident several months ago. She told in great detail about
how she had learned of Evan's death from the prospector
who tried to use Tressie's tintype as an ante for a poker
game at the Busted Mule.

Rose apologized for the delay in getting the word to
Reed and Tressie and hoped they were faring well. And
then she added some stuff about Lincolnshire that Reed
scarcely scanned. He hadn't taken to the lanky Englishman and didn't care about what the man was up to.

Rose ended her letter with a request to stop by and see
her the next time they were in Virginia City. The letter
was dated August 7, a full month previously.

Reed held the two wispy sheets of paper between his
fingers and stared into the fire, for a moment emptied of
all feeling. Orange flame darted in a burst of wind that riffled the letter's pages. Slowly he creased the paper and inserted it with great care back into the envelope he had slit
open with his knife. Then he dragged over his saddlebags

and placed the letter inside. He wanted to keep it safe so he could show it to Tressie.

Head in one hand, Reed massaged both temples with thumb and fingers. Tears pooled in his eyes and ran down his cheeks like trails of fire, and he wiped them ferociously away. Now that they were free, he and Tressie, to build a life, this bastard Kling had come along. And somehow it was all tied up with Race Brannigan, the father he had always despised for abandoning him. What a hell of a legacy the old man had left.

Before dawn erased the glittering stars, Reed was on the trail, following tracks left by the two horses he knew carried Kling and Tressie.

A streak of sunlight burned across Tressie's cheek, awakening her from an exhausted sleep. For a tense moment she lay very still. Where was he, and what was he doing? She heard only joyful bird song. Straightening her stiff legs, she cocked an ear and listened harder. Despite the sun, she still felt cold and numb from spending the chilly night on the ground. Struggling to sit, she cried out with pain. He'd left her tied, arms behind her back, and the thongs cut into her tender skin. Still, there was no sign he was in camp. Maybe the man had changed his mind and simply ridden away, leaving her there for Reed to find.

She rocked forward, backward, and was finally able to move to a position where she could see their camp. Her gaze drifted over Kling's saddle, the pile of blankets where he'd slept, the coffeepot steaming in the coals of last night's fire. So he was still around somewhere. But where?

And what did he have in mind for her today? Was Reed this very moment on their trail?

The aroma from the simmering pot was nearly unbearable. Her throat was so dry she could scarcely swallow and her empty stomach roiled with the harsh pangs of hunger. Her entire body ached and itched, her eyes burned, and her bladder was about to burst.

Other than that, I'm okay, Tressie thought, and chuckled bitterly. At least she hadn't lost her sense of humor.

Licking at cracked lips, she scooted around until she had a full view of the meadow. Bitterroot bloomed among the daisies, each plant's singular roselike flower opening its lovely face to the sun. She thought of digging the fleshy root and cooking it up, smelling the pleasing fragrance not unlike sweet tobacco. The idea flooded her mouth with saliva.

"Well, I see you're awake," boomed Kling, and she jerked to rigid attention. The man was as quiet on his feet as Reed.

"I need to go to the toilet," she said.

"Is that all you do, girl, is pee?"

She shrugged and he loosened the rawhide around her ankles, half dragging her away from their camp. Pinpricks of pain darted up and down her numb legs, and she swayed to and fro. "I can't till you untie my arms." If he wanted to humiliate her, he was doing a good job of it.

He yanked the lashing off, and the pain was so intense she saw stars.

"And don't you run, either," he spat. "I'm a-fixing coffee, and if you run that'll mean I'll have to leave it to haul you back. That'll plumb rile me." Kling stomped away, sparing her no further glances.

Before returning willingly to Kling's custody, Tressie briefly considered her chances if she made a run for it. She could hide out in the woods; he might not find her. But of course he would. There was very little undergrowth and the man was as cunning and single-minded as an animal. Besides, Reed would catch them before the day was out, she was sure. And if she ran off into the wilderness, he might never find her, nor she him.

Back at the campsite, Kling seemed inclined to talk, bragging about how clever he'd been following them all these months. "Ever since you lit out from Virginia City," he crowed. "Seen everthing you did, too." His eyes glittered at her over a steaming tin cup of coffee. "Maybe you'll give me some of what you give him."

"Shut your filthy mouth!"

"Makes me no never mind. I get ready, I'll just take it. Appears to me like you like it just fine."

Tressie wanted to crawl out of hearing of the dirty sneering words. It didn't matter what he thought of her; just the same, the judgment embarrassed her. To think of this pig actually watching her and Reed make love sickened her. "You're lying. You didn't see anything."

"Well, how else would I know?" Hoarse laughter spurted from his mouth, startling the horses. They whinnied and tossed their heads, their hooves clinking in the rocky soil.

"Why are you doing this?" she asked.

"Ask your high-and-mighty fella. That is, if you get a chance."

"Oh, I'll get a chance, all right. He'll kill you."

Kling regarded her steadily until she began to fidget. Then he tossed the dregs of coffee into the fire and rose, stretching trunklike arms high into the sky. "Time we was on our way."

He hadn't given her any coffee, but he did offer her the water canteen before breaking camp. She drank slowly and deeply, noticing with interest that he made no effort to cover the campfire or remove signs they had been there.

She prayed he wouldn't tie her on the horse again, but he did. Then he stood for a long time gazing down their back trail before mounting up and leading her mare across a tranquil meadow.

Far into the morning Kling startled Tressie by beginning to talk. At first she paid little attention to what he said, for her thoughts were with Reed, wherever he might be.

". . . if I'd a known he was Race Brannigan's boy when we met in Wyoming . . . but I didn't . . . not till later when I went through his stuff and found that deerskin bag. Had Brannigan's mark on it, like ever other thing a his. Wonder he didn't mark my woman. Your man's mama, you know. Bright Fox."

Tressie finally realized Kling was talking about Reed.

"Bright Fox? Wasn't that Reed's mama's name? The Sioux squaw?"

"What I said, wasn't it? So he did tell you. She was my woman first, though, before Race Brannigan and his charming ways come along." His chuckle was diabolical. "For a while I thought there might actually be a chance I was the boy's father, you understand? But later I figured out that she had been gone from me a tad too long. So Race and his whelp killed my Bright Fox. And dear God, she was a purty little thing."

Tressie felt disoriented. Memories of Bitter Leaf and Caleb somehow got all tangled up with the tale Kling told. What was he saying? That Reed's mama had been wife to Dooley Kling? How could that be? And who was this Race Brannigan? Didn't Reed carry his own daddy's name?

The giant man rode in silence for so long Tressie decided he wasn't going to finish his story, but he finally took it up again, after their horses had worked their way slowly and carefully along the narrow lip of a canyon.

As they continued their slow crawl up the face of the mountain, Tressie craned her neck to see behind and below. Surely if she looked hard enough she would see the lone rider that would be Reed Bannon. But the growth of pine and aspen and jagged outcropping of rock prevented seeing much of anything but deep and impassable gorges.

Kling's harsh voice brought her back. "Bitter Leaf did remind me a little of Bright Fox, but she was dumb as dirt, that girl. And Bright Fox, well, she fit her name to a tee. Bright and smart and quick. Didn't speak a word of English; still, I never had to say a thing twice to her, she caught on that quick. Tanned me a dozen buffalo hides our first year. Do you know what that's worth to a man like me? A trader?" Kling snorted. "Hell, 'course you don't, with your lily-white hands and puny body."

"If I'm so worthless, why don't you just let me go?" Tressie asked. A brutal hate eating at her insides made Tressie sick. This was real hate, not what she felt for Papa. Then what was that emotion, and how could she deal with it?

"You ain't worthless," he said. "I need you for bait. I just wanted you to know what that woman meant to me, so you could see I'm within my rights to pay back the son for him and his father's sins."

Her mind skittered around, trying to follow. "Reed never even knew his father," she finally argued.

"Don't make any difference. He's still the son of Race Brannigan, and his birthing killed my woman."

"And that's why you're doing . . . this?" It was difficult to believe that a man could spend months, maybe years, for all she knew, getting back at a man for stealing his wife.

"Don't make light of this, you little slut," Kling shouted, and jerked on the mare's reins, causing her to toss her head and kick out backward.

Tressie slipped sideways. Frantically she hugged the mare's heaving sides with both knees and shuddered. On her right a sheer precipice plunged into rugged oblivion; on her left the mountain pierced the sky. At any moment she and the mare could plunge to their deaths. She bit her lip bloody to keep from crying out and giving this monster satisfaction.

Why didn't Reed come? He surely couldn't be far behind. This madman was liable to kill her, maybe even himself, if something didn't happen soon.

In early afternoon, with the hot sun beating down mercilessly, the two riders reached an escarpment about twenty feet wide. Underfoot the sienna bedrock flared around the face of the mountain for about two dozen yards. Scrubby brush and grasses grew through narrow cracks in the smooth stone. Otherwise it was as clean as if it had been swept.

Tressie breathed a tremendous sigh of relief when Kling

dismounted and freed her to do the same. The climb ha
been exhausting for both riders and animals. Perhaps h
would camp here for the night.

To her great relief Kling did not retie her ankles an
wrists, but went to stand on the rimrock, gazing down th
way they had come. Maybe he would fall and break hi
dirty neck. Tressie rubbed miserably at her numb legs. Af
ter riding tightly bound for so long, she couldn't stand
and so remained sprawled where he'd dragged her off th
horse.

She again eyed the mammoth back of her captor. On
hefty push and he'd go over, trembling end over end
maybe for miles before what was left of his scroungy body
bounced to a stop. Tressie crabbed awkwardly towar
him, crawling, scooting, moving on hands and bare feet
When she was near enough to smell him, she paused fo
an instant to slow down her rapid breathing, the patterin
of her heart he was sure to hear. Around them fell a grea
stillness broken only by the screee of a hawk high above
and the whistle of wind.

Just as she raised from the half crouch, both hands
reaching for a spot between his shoulder blades, Kling
roared and half turned.

"He's down there, I saw the—" At that precise instant
he caught sight of Tressie, all ready to shove him over the
edge, and backhanded her. She tumbled some ten or fifteen feet.

Knocked half silly, Tressie shook her head and tried to
rise . . . to run. He was upon her too quickly. Dragging her
up with one hairy paw, he belted her across the mouth
and tossed her away like a huge cat playing with a mouse.

Tressie bounced and rolled, vision cut by sharp bright flashes of light followed by total darkness. She sank into the abyss, sure she was dying. When she came to, rawhide strips cut her ankles and wrists, tied so tightly the knots were gummy with her blood. More blood ran over her forehead and into one eye. She hurt all over as if her body were one huge wound. And all she could think of, past the racking pain and fear, was that she was still alive and Kling had seen Reed coming. No matter what kind of effort it took, she couldn't let the brutal Dooley Kling kill the man she loved.

Reed came upon the leavings of Kling and Tressie's brief stay on the escarpment just at dark. And there he would spend the night. All along it had been impossible to travel at night because the fingernail of a moon set not long after sundown. On the desert one could travel by starshine, but not up here in the mountains. He tried not to think of traveling by starshine; that brought back too many memories of nights on the prairie with Tressie.

He didn't find the blood until the next morning. Touching fingertips to the dried smear across the smooth rock, he felt for a moment her pain, the fear that must be riding with her. A deep hatred sickened him, assaulted his senses. He spread his palm over the place where she had lain, closed his eyes, and groaned.

"Tressie, darlin'. I'm coming," he whispered. "Be safe, I'm coming." The bright white realization that this time he wouldn't run away filled him with a sharp-edged purpose.

There was only one way off the escarpment besides the

way he had come: a tenuous almost invisible path skirting the back side of the mountain. He took it, riding slowly and carefully. Kling had made sure there would be no mistaking the route he had taken, for a strip of cloth from Tressie's faded flannel shirt hung like a flag on a dried shrub clinging to the lower edge of the trail. The scrap of fabric had a smear of blood on it, as if the son of a bitch were mocking him, saying, if he had so chosen she could be at the bottom of this ravine littered with tumbled boulders the size of houses.

At midday Reed rode up on two horses, one of them Tressie's, calmly grazing in a patch of scrubby grass. And far above he spotted two figures moving like tiny ants along a narrow ledge, heading precariously toward the snowy cap of the great mountain. His heart nearly stopped. At least she was alive, but where in God's name was Kling taking her? And why?

If he had wanted to kill Reed, or for that matter the both of them, he could have done so easily. There was most surely only a mad reasoning behind this wild flight to the top of the world.

On impulse Reed cupped his hands around his mouth and shouted a war cry from his childhood. The shrill tones ululated across the wilderness chasms, bounced back and forth from cliffs to bluffs to mountaintops. Tressie's mare screamed, her head tilted upward and lips curled back as if she understood precisely what was going on.

Reed unsaddled his gelding, worked off the bridle, and rubbed at the velvety nose. "See ya later, pal."

For a moment he considered his options. He had a

pocketful of jerky and he hooked the canteen over his head and under one arm. The mackinaw and bedroll he fastened on like a backpack. When he found her, she would be cold, so he had to take them. Last, he studied the rifle. It represented extra weight, and regretfully he left it behind, choosing instead the long-bladed knife, which he inserted in the backpack.

Tressie and Kling reached the cave when it was almost too dark to see anything. For the last few hours, ever since hearing Reed's shrill yodel, she had moved as if in a trance. She thought of nothing, felt nothing. Just kept moving. She must stay alive, she had to. Not for hate but for love.

Kling climbed behind her and when she faltered he'd shove her upward. At times she yearned to let go and take him with her. But there was Reed down below and on his way. She imagined him holding her safe in his arms, and continued to crawl across the windswept face of the mountain.

Above the shelf onto which Kling had shoved Tressie, snow blanketed the rocks. No longer intent on climbing, she began to shiver from the cold.

Kling bumped her forward. "In there. Get inside."

Tressie stumbled on stone-bruised and battered feet, into the pitch-blackness of the cave. The cold hard floor sloped sharply downward and she fell, fetching up finally when the rock flattened out. The air was dank and remarkably warmer than outside. She kept very still, listening for Kling. Maybe the bastard would fall and break his neck.

But when he did come, he trod easily down the incline. He carried a small armload of wood he'd obviously gathered around the cave's entrance. It didn't take him long to build a small fire.

Seeking the welcome warmth and light, Tressie asked in a faint voice, "Where are we?"

"Where we belong," Kling replied. "A final resting place, of sorts. He'll be here come morning. And then it'll all be over but his suffering. And that will go on as long as he remembers how you died. And he'll remember, I'll see to that."

The fire's warmth washed over her and she felt herself drifting off to sleep. That frightened her and she shook her head, rubbing at both eyes. She was having trouble concentrating on the meaning of his words. Kill her and not Reed? She didn't comprehend. "What are you going to do?"

"You struck color down yonder, you and him, didn't you?" The question was a snarl of contempt.

"You were watching. Surely you know."

"Don't get smart with me, girl. Yes or no will do."

Tressie didn't answer, but moved even farther away from his threatening bulk. From there she could see his fearful face reflected in the glow of the flames.

He roared, "*I said, yes or no.*"

Tressie flinched and hugged herself, her teeth chattering madly. She didn't even remember what he had asked, but replied anyway. "Yes." She supported herself with both arms, propping them behind her, and disturbed something that rolled on the stone floor, setting up a noisy clatter.

"What was that?" Kling shouted, and Tressie realized

that he was nervous, perhaps even a little scared of what was yet to come.

Looking around at the walls of the cavern, Tressie said, "I don't know. It came from in there." She pointed deeper into the cave and scooted back out of the firelight so that she disappeared from his view. Something cool and smooth lay against her leg and she explored it with the fingers of one hand. It was round with two deep-set cavities on one side . . . like eyes! She clutched the thing, came up with it, and knew immediately what she had. It took every ounce of courage she could muster to hang on to the human skull.

"Dooley, is this sacred ground? Indian burial ground?" she asked.

He grunted, muttered, "Where you at, girl? There ain't no place you can go. Better git yourself back here where I can see you."

She sighed and inched forward into the firelight. "Is it true that the Indian spirits guard their sacred ground? I heard they can even kill anyone who strays where they don't belong."

"Bull. That's pure bull. No such thing as spirits."

"Would you like to sleep in a graveyard?" Tressie asked after a moment's pause.

"Well, 'course not, but that's different."

"Is it?" Tressie had been almost ready to show him the skull when a thought occurred to her. The man was already on edge. If she could get him nervous and overwrought before Reed arrived, then maybe she could distract him with the skull at the proper time. Frightened, he might make a mistake that would give Reed the advantage. Kling was a huge man, strong and vicious, and Reed would be no match for him physically.

She cradled the fearful object in her lap and asked sotto voce, "Do you ever dream of Bright Fox or Bitter Leaf?"

"Dream? Woman, grown men don't dream. I'm gonna fix some coffee. Git yourself on over here by the fire where I can see you."

She didn't move, but persisted, "Surely you think about them. Where their spirits are. Their people place a lot of faith in the spirit world, I hear. Suppose Bitter Leaf knew what you did to Caleb. What do you think she would do?"

"Do?" Kling coughed out a laugh. "What could she do? Dumb little slut."

Tressie said very softly, "A mother's love is fierce. I wouldn't be surprised but what her spirit might skin you alive. I wouldn't want to fall asleep and wake up to find a fearsome Indian spirit skinning me like game."

"It ain't spirits that bother me, it's gals like you who go on and on. Besides, if I was to worry any about haints, it'd be that Bright Fox would fault me not stealing her back from that filth Race Brannigan."

"Why did you desert your son, leave him with strangers?"

"I said *shut up*! What'd you do with the boy, anyway? You ain't so high and mighty or you would have took care of him."

"Caleb . . . Caleb died. I tried to save him. I loved him like he was my own, but I couldn't stop him from dying." She choked down a sob.

Kling banged the coffeepot down near the fire. "*Enough,*

woman. Enough. I don't want to hear no more about the little half-breed brat."

Tressie felt a burning in her throat. She didn't want to start crying, for fear she would never stop. "He was your son. How can you be so callous?"

"He killed his mama."

"That wasn't his fault."

"Shut up, girl. What do you know? Of course it was his fault. Whose, then, if not his?"

She supposed men like this had to find someone else to blame for all their troubles, no matter what. "Is that why you want to hurt Reed? Because you think it was his fault that Bright Fox died?"

"His daddy took my life." The huge man actually sounded as if he were about to cry.

"But you had Bitter Leaf."

"Not the woman only—women only ain't worth this. He shouldn't a took everything that was mine. I had my wagon, my trade, folks looked up to me. Even the Indians would trade with Dooley Kling. Until Brannigan come along with his oily ways. Lying and cheating, selling them whiskey."

Tressie wondered briefly what had happened to Race, decided it didn't really matter. "But that's still no reason to—"

Kling launched himself at her, grabbing her shoulders and shaking, pounding her about the head.

She cried out and struggled with him.

He threw her backward, tired of the game. "I told you to shut up."

Tressie curled up where she fell, eyes filling with tears.

This monster was beyond remorse. Out there somewhere was the man she would always love. Her need to seek revenge on Papa faded and was gone. She'd beheld the ugliness of such desire in the face of a beast. Tressie knew that never again would she long to see Papa's expression when he learned of Mama's death. At last she could let him go to meet his fate, whatever it might be. Her own destiny lay with the man coming for her. Slowly and very quietly she crawled along the cave floor until she found the skull. She fell asleep with it clutched in her arms.

Kling awoke her, hovering inches from her face, his own features pulled tight in anger. Through hot tears of fright she tried to read the maniacal expression there. What she saw made her whimper. He had most surely gone mad, and she feared she, too, was headed in the same direction.

"I heard him," Kling hissed. "It must be daybreak. He's coming. Git up." Kling kicked at her and Tressie tried to scramble to her feet, but the skull came up between them.

The flickering firelight cast eerie shadows across the empty eye sockets and in the ghastly hole where a nose had once been. The mouth filled with teeth grinned, all the more terrifying because of the missing lower jaw.

Kling's eyes rolled wildly. "Bitch," he screamed, and fell back away from her. "I saw you walking. *You did this to me!*" He pointed a trembling finger at Tressie.

He had gone mad. Tressie dropped the skull and scrabbled up the incline, heading for the cave opening.

Kling lunged, grabbed her by the back of her shirt, and flung her down into the unholy darkness below the fire.

She screamed and flailed along the smooth floor for a handhold. It seemed as if she fell forever.

Kling roared and stumbled after her. "*No,* I need you here for when he comes. He has to pay with your pain. *Come back! Come baaaaack.*"

Tressie tumbled up against something hard and unforgiving that bruised and battered her but stopped her descent. The harsh rasp of her own heavy breathing echoed from below. She realized that she rested in a curve of the cave's wall on the edge of a precipice. Rocks clattered around her and then dropped away into nothing. She never heard them hit bottom.

The darkness was so complete she could almost see more with her eyes closed. Quieting the harsh breathing, she listened for the sound of Dooley Kling coming after her, but heard nothing.

Was he going to leave her here? How would she get out? Even if he left, she would be afraid to turn loose and start up. And what about Reed? He would surely be here soon. Had Kling gone back up there to lay in wait for him?

Reed began to climb as soon as the sky was light enough to reveal the shape of the mountain. The snow above gleamed and shimmered like a beacon. He reached the entrance to the cave to hear Dooley Kling shouting accusations in the voice of a madman. With extreme care he crept into the cave, closing his eyes to accustom them to the blackness as he went. A fire burned ahead somewhat below the entrance, and it looked like the flickering eye of some kind of strange animal.

Kling continued to rave from down there somewhere. A huge shadow, thrown from the fire's glow, danced across the wall and roof of the cavern, then disappeared. Reed hugged the stone and moved cautiously past the fire, testing each step so he'd make no noise. Then he heard Tressie scream, a scream that grew fainter and fainter, like she was falling away from him.

"Tressie," he shouted, his heart thudding hard enough to break free from his rib cage.

From the darkness, Kling bellowed and Reed turned to face that sound, knife held at the ready just below his waist. He shifted one foot and kicked something that rolled along the stone floor. At that moment, Kling arose from the blackness like an apparition. Firelight painted his huge figure in red and black. The thing bobbling noisily across the smooth floor met up with him. He stumbled, clawed the air, scrabbled with both feet. The skull bounced upward and at the last moment he grabbed at it, catching it in both arms before he fell backward.

Reed heard his scream for a long, long time, and when the echoes ceased there was only the sound of a woman sobbing.

"Tressie?" he called, almost afraid to speak above a whisper. What he had seen had nearly driven him speechless.

The sobs quieted. Then, "Reed? Reed, is that you?"

His breath caught in his throat. Dear God, she was alive. "Where are you?"

Tressie could scarcely answer. She was caught up in the splendor of her imaginings. Reed was safe, she was safe. Together they could do anything, but mostly they could be together, always.

"Down here," she cried. "But be careful, it's steep."

"You wait right there," he shouted, and she wanted to laugh. Where would she go?

"I'm going to get a light from the fire so I can see you. I'll get you out, darlin', I'll get you out."

She snuggled back into her niche. "I know you will, Reed. I know you will," she whispered.

Twenty-one

Through Tressie's tightly squinted eyelids, light from the torch wavered dimly. Even knowing Reed was nearby, she couldn't muster the courage to open her eyes and take in the danger of her situation. All she could do was cling to the rough outcropping that had halted her tumble into the hell that had claimed Dooley Kling.

Dragging in a deep, cleansing breath, Tressie smelled the wood smoke and the dank surroundings of the cave, tasted the crisp mountain air, and experienced a release of fear. Not so much from the danger Kling represented. It was more like her own bitter emotions and the intense need to avenge her mother's death had simply slipped away.

"Tressie? Darlin', you still okay?"

Reed heard a response that was no word, but only a quivery sound. Surely it had to come from her. In his veins Indian blood pounded furiously to a drumbeat all its own, for this cave was sacred and forbidden. He could sense the spirits hovering in protest at being disturbed. He had no intention of bothering them any longer than was absolutely necessary, and he chanted a few consoling Sioux words remembered from his childhood to quiet their ire. All he wanted was the woman he loved wrapped in his arms far from this haunted place.

Flame from the torch threw grotesque dancing shadows around her hunkered figure. The cave's ceiling sloped inward so that he had to bend lower and lower as he moved toward her. By the time he could make out her wide eyes and trembling lips, he squatted on his haunches.

Holding the torch to one side, he extended his hand, palm up. "Honey, take my hand."

"I c-c-can't turn loose."

"Oh, sure you can. Look in my eyes and just let go. Put your hand here, darlin', where it belongs. Easy as can be."

She sobbed thickly, then dragged in a heavy breath and slowly unfolded one arm toward him. "Reed? Oh, Reed."

"I know, I know." His fingers closed around hers and he shuffled backward, putting gentle pressure on her to follow.

The rasp of their breathing and the crackling of the torch filled the cavern as they inched their way carefully up the sloping rock floor to the small fire. He felt her trembling and dropped the burning pieces of wood to hug her close.

Tressie locked both arms around him so tightly he grunted. "It was Dooley, Dooley Kling. Why, Reed? Who's Race?"

"My pa. Let's not talk about it. We've got to get you warm." Reed shrugged from the bedroll and mackinaw strapped to his back and spent several minutes bundling her near the fire.

Though she allowed him to wrap her securely, she protested when he sat her down. "Oh, I don't want to stay here. No, we can't stay in here, Reed. We've got to get out of here. I can't—"

Touching lips to the opening he'd left so she could breathe, he gentled her. "Hush, shhh, darlin', everything's okay. You need to rest, get your strength. Going back down the mountain will be harder than coming up."

"Nu-huh, it won't," she declared. "I'll be with you going down. Oh, God, Reed, he was going to kill me. Torture me in front of you and kill me. He said you and your pa killed his wife."

Reed flinched, sank down beside her and hugged her padded shoulders awkwardly. "It's a long story I'll tell you sometime. Or at least what I know of it. But he wasn't going to do anything. He just said that to scare you. I would never have let him do something like that to you. Don't you know by now? You are my life, my only life."

She felt the love flowing from him, as if it were a living, breathing thing. "Oh, I'm so stupid sometimes."

"Only sometimes?" He smiled, teasing.

"You know what I mean. So set on hating my father and paying him back that I couldn't see the gift you were offering me. I could have lost it all. And you know something? I don't even really hate Papa. Or if I did, I don't anymore. All the way here, seeing the way hate had turned Dooley Kling into such a terrible human being, I truly realized what you meant when you said my desire for vengeance would eat me alive."

Reed patted at her clumsily. Her words filled him with a joy he almost couldn't comprehend. Despite her ordeal, he wanted to shout with pure relief that they were both alive and together.

Dear God, to feel her body pressed to his. He resisted

a desire to strip her down and check out every inch to make sure that monster hadn't left his mark on her. But she was shaking so hard he was afraid to unwrap her.

He had to get her down off this icy precipice in one piece. That wouldn't be easy, with her bare feet and scant clothing.

"Reed?" The voice was weak but he could already hear the old Tressie coming through.

"What, darlin'?"

"Do you think we could go now?"

If only they could. "Honey, there's not enough daylight left to see us down off this mountain. I'm afraid we're going to have to spend the night right here, snug and warm."

"And surrounded by ghosts." She shoved the drape of the mackinaw back off her head and peered out at him. Leeping fingers of flame danced shadows high on the walls. The bronze of his cheekbones gleamed and when he turned his full gaze on her; little flickers of light were reflected in the dark eyes.

How she loved him, and how close she had come to losing that love. The thought made her shudder. If she had to stay in this cave overnight, at least he was with her, and that was a far better choice than she had had a scant hour ago.

"Reed, I'm sorry I've been such a baby."

He took her face between his hands and kissed her lightly on the tip of her nose. "You were very brave. You stayed alive." He lowered his aim and their lips met. The explosive sweetness of being together tinged the gentle kiss with ecstasy. The bedroll and mackinaw ended in a pile around them.

He'd thought to only hold her, keep her secure, because

of all she'd been through, but she pressed against him with a fierce longing, whether for succor or from desire he couldn't tell, and so he turned loose all his pent-up emotions. There in that sacred cave, with the spirits of his ancestors looking down on them, Tressie and Reed at last came together with hope for the future, with no reservations from the past.

The next morning, while he fashioned wrappings for her battered feet from the tail of the mackinaw, he finally remembered the letter from Rose that he had carried so carefully. After he tied the last strip of fabric around the clumsy but effective shoes, he sat beside her and, with dread for her sorrow, tried to tell her about her father.

"Yesterday . . . last night, I couldn't think of anything but that you were alive, that I hadn't lost you. But now it's time . . . I mean I think we'd better talk about your papa."

"Papa?" she whispered. "What about him?" She almost couldn't ask the question for fear of the answer. All these months searching, she'd never once considered she might not want to know if the news was bad.

"He's . . . I mean, there was this man . . . Oh, just let me read you Rose's letter. It explains it better than I can."

She listened without comment through Rose's tale of Cray and how he'd showed up in Virginia City with the tintype of Tressie and her mama, and how Rose had pried the story out of the miner with the help of a few gold nuggets. But when Reed came to the part where Cray told Rose about Evan Majors dying in the cave-in, Tressie began to cry. The huge tears that had shimmered along the bottom of her lids spilled over and poured down both cheeks. At first she made no sound, just sat there with her little fists balled in her lap, those torn strips of cloth wrapped around her extended feet, and cried silent grieving tears. But then she hiccuped and swallowed hard and stopped crying.

After a moment's silence, she asked, "What else does she say?"

Reed caressed her gleaming cheek with the back of his hand, then produced a bandanna from one of his pockets and wiped her face.

"Just to make sure and not forget her and come see her if we're ever in Virginia City."

She nodded. She was filled with a great sadness over her father's death. Yet that sorrow paled somewhat when she realized that he had died sometime back while she was still searching for him with a heart filled with hate, or maybe even before that.

"It's odd, feeling this way," she told Reed. "It's like I can at last see the possibility of a life besides that old one. And at the same time I know I'll cry more tears. When we're safe and down off this mountain. I cried over so many things after Mama died because I was so sad over losing her.

"Oh, Reed, I'm so glad I forgave Papa. That makes it easier somehow. But the worst thing, the very worst is that I didn't get to tell him, I didn't get to say 'I love you' to him. I didn't get to say good-bye."

She choked a bit over the words, and Reed laid a hand on her arm, just to let her know he was there. It was best to stay quiet, let her talk it all out, and so he said nothing.

After a sniffle or two, she went on, "He could have been dying while I tended Mama at birth, or while I was burying her and the poor babe. Isn't it strange how things can run beside each other like that, and us not even know it? How you were down South fighting at the same time I was trying to survive in that soddy, and how we came together anyway?"

"It's been hard, Tressie. But it's over." He paused, gazed at her with awe. How strong she was, how determined. And she loved him. They were going to have a wonderful life together. If not for the sadness of the occasion, he would whoop with joy.

He gestured toward the cave's opening where the morning sun blazed. "It's time to be happy, darlin', we've done it, we've come through."

A reluctant little chuckle broke from her throat, as if she were practicing feeling good again. The sound echoed through the dark chambers, setting off the spirits, who tossed the joyful noise back and out into the world.

Together they stood at the mouth of the cave. She clutched at Reed's hand and gazed into the distance, seeing the promises, seeing their life together. In the brilliant sunlight the precipice fell away into a lush green valley broken by gleaming trails of icy snowmelt.

After a silent moment, they started down.

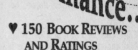